HAVEN SENT

Book 7
The Guard Trilogy Extended Series
The Guards of Haven

N. L. Westaway

Original Cover Photo by Averie Woodard
Cover designed by Beach House Press

N. L. Westaway
Visit my website at www.NLWestaway.com
ISBN: 979-8-9907502-4-1
Printed in the United States of America

First Publication: December 2025 Beach House Press

Haven Sent

To the reader,

This novel, like the other books in succession, is not a standalone story. Book 7, *Haven Sent*, is the next in series and carries the reader forward through The Guard Trilogy Extended Series, *The Guards of Haven*.

The Guard Trilogy
The Guard – Book 1
The Unseen – Book 2
The Believer – Book 3

The Guard Trilogy Extended Series/The Guards of Haven
The Haven – Book 4
Haven Lost — Book 5
Haven Found — Book 6
Haven Sent — Book 7
TBD - Book 8 — Next Book in Series
TBD – Book 9 — Last Book in Series

This book is dedicated to the women who support other women, those who lift other women up and celebrate their successes, and to the men who not only stand beside them but who stand *with* them, and all who support the fundamental rights and freedoms inherent to all humans.

"It has been said, 'time heals all wounds.' I do not agree. The wounds remain. In time, the mind, protecting its sanity, covers them with scar tissue and the pain lessens. But it is never gone." ~ Rose Fitzgerald Kennedy

"Has it ever struck you that life is all memory, except for the one present moment that goes by you so quick you hardly catch it going?"
~ Tennessee Williams,
The Milk Train Doesn't Stop Here Anymore

Acknowledgements

This *thank you* goes out to you, the reader, without whom these books would be merely undiscovered stories.

The following is a list of characters introduced in The Guard Trilogy Extended Series ~ The Guards of Haven, Books 4 - 6. This list will continue to grow through Books 7 - 9.
At the back of this book there is also a list of the main characters and their roles from the original trilogy, should you need it.

Hayley – *Twin to Ryley, daughter of Lynn and Redmond*
Ryley – *Twin of Hayley, daughter of Lynn and Redmond*
Nainsead/Nana (Pronounced *Naincey*) – *Redmond's mother, and the twins' grandmother*
Enzo/Pop/Poppy – *Redmond's father, and the twins' grandfather*
Max Sinclair – *Husband to Julian, Friends & Keepers of North Haven, and father of Lane*
Julian Sinclair – *Husband to Max, Friends & Keepers of North Haven, and father of Lane*
Lane Sinclair – *Daughter to Max & Julian, love interest of Lyndon*
Kristjana Stephansson (Jana) – *Baker from Iceland, Love interest of Kris*
Geir Sigurdsson (Pronounced *Gear*) – *Vet, friend of Jana's from Iceland*
Dr. Grier Stone (Pronounced *Grear*) – *Psychiatrist, friend of Lynn, love interest of Zuriel*
Tina Barone (Teeny) – *Bartender, best friend of Natalie*
Kelly & Kerry — *Students, Roommates to Natalie, twin brothers*

The Guards of Haven
Leonardo Winter (Leo) – *1st Son of Haven/Architect*
Kristopher Snow (Kris) – *2nd Son of Haven/Chef & Restauranter, love interest of Jana*
Bennet Frost (Ben) – *3rd Son of Haven/Professor of Human Kinetics*
Marquis Malouel (Marq) (Pronounced *Mark*) – *4th Son of Haven/Gallery Owner*
Zachery Glacier (Zach) (Pronounced *Zack*) – *5th Son of Haven/Firefighter*
Nicolas North (Nic) – *6th Son of Haven/Oncology Nurse*
Hayden Polar (Den) – *7th Son of Haven/Bodyguard*

The Seraphim from Pleiades (The Seven Sisters)
Purah (Pronounced *Pur-ah*) – *The Steward from Celaeno - the 7th Star of the Pleiades*

The Earthbound (From the 198 forced down to Earth by Thaddeus & the Insurgents)
Anael – *Creator of The Guards of Haven, Mate to Thanael, birth mother of Natalie*
Thanael – *Co-creator of The Guards of Haven, Mate to Anael*
Professor Julianna Forest (Jules) – *Friend to The Guards, mother of Mason*
Francesca (Frank) – *General Manager at SNOW, friend to The Guards of Haven*
Inanna (Ina) – *Mate to Francesca, friend to The Guards of Haven*

The Insurgents (From the 14 Insurgents now Earthbound)
Thaddeus Smyth III – *Leader of the Insurgents*
Lyndon – *Tracker at the Celaeno building, Ottawa, love interest of Lane*
Amahle (Pronounced Amah-lay) – *Facilities Manager at the Celaeno building, Ottawa*
Marcus – *Facilities Manager at the Merope building, NYC*
Kendrick – *Facilities Manager at the Sterope building, Norway*
Zuriel (Pronounced Zuri-el) – *Tracker at the Merope building, Brazil*
Addison – *Tracker at the Sterope building, Norway*

Halflings (The offspring of Earthbound Seraph & Human matings)
Taylor – *Son of Lyndon, group home resident*
Mason Forest – *Student, friend of Lane and Natalie, son of Julianna*
Natalie Harwood – *Biological daughter of Anael and Reider Stephansson (Jana's father)*

The Archangels
Diniel — *Female Archangel, Protector of infants*

Prolog

August 2025

TIME.

It was *Nathaniel Hawthorne's* philosophy that, 'Time flies over us, but leaves its shadow behind', noting the passing of time and its impact, even when we are not openly aware of it, suggesting that the experiences and memories of our past remain with us, although the moments themselves have passed, and the *shadow* representing the lingering effects, our memories, and the imprint of time on our lives. 'Time heals all wounds' is a common idiom that suggests time can help us to heal from emotional and physical pain and overcome difficult experiences. 'Time is a gift' emphasizes the limited and precious nature of time while encouraging the thoughtful and meaningful use of it.

Time itself is officially marked by dividing the day into units: 24 hours, each hour containing 60 minutes, and each minute containing 60 seconds. The most accurate timekeeping is based on atomic clocks, which measure time based on the vibrations of atoms, allowing for extremely precise measurements. In TV crime shows and documentaries depicting abductions, the police always emphasize when someone goes missing that *time* is of the utmost importance, and that the first 24 hours are considered the most crucial for locating a missing person.

Thaddeus has been missing… more like *absent* for over two years now. Before this lengthy absence, Den had returned to his regular facility watch in Amsterdam. Leo had taken to being at South Haven on and off, and when the Norway facility had finally closed its doors, Zach had relocated to South Haven. And with the Norway location having been shut down, Thaddeus's facility manager, Kendrick, had temporarily relocated to New York City to cover for Marcus while he was in Brazil. They'd only learned of this because Marcus had been the manager on site at the time when Nic had gone there posing as the local *conservationist* interested in a facility tour while covertly searching for Thaddeus. However, Marcus had returned to his post in New York fairly soon after, and if Thaddeus had been at the Brazil facility at all, the assumption was it had only been to shut the place down. The building itself has since been sold, several of the staff having been relocated to other locations, but still, no one had reported seeing Thaddeus there. As for the whereabouts of Kendrick now, no one knew. The thought was that he had returned to Norway to take care of any final business, but it was unclear where he was currently.

As per Lyndon, communication with Thaddeus had basically been cut off, other than a few business-as-usual email correspondence to the facility managers. After torturing Zuriel, the only one who had actually spoken with Thaddeus since his departure from the Celaeno Building had been Lyndon. And during that brief phone conversation with Thaddeus, Lyndon assumed he had still been in Brazil. Thaddeus had been furious with Lyndon for disturbing him, but Lyndon had been curious to know what, if anything, Zuriel had told Thaddeus about that lead in Japan. When Lyndon had questioned whether Lazarus had tracked down the lead, Thaddeus had begrudgingly shared what the other tracker had found. The target's ex-husband had been there, but that *Westlake* woman had not been with him. "*Another dead end,*" Thaddeus had said, but Lyndon had already known the target wouldn't be in Japan, because he'd spotted her at the hospital in Florida where he'd taken Zuriel. When Thaddeus had asked Lyndon if *he* had any leads, he had opted to say nothing about what he'd discovered about the target, Ms. Westlake, Lane's *aunt*. He wasn't going to tell Thaddeus because he would never do anything to hurt Lane, *ever*. Lyndon's focus on getting free from Thaddeus and his malevolent ways hadn't changed, especially now that he was working *with* The Guards of Haven to take Thaddeus down.

Yeah, about that....

It has been 2 years, 5 months, 2 weeks, 4 days and 14 hours since Natalie had been brought to North Haven and thrust into her new reality when wings had burst from her back. Jana too had been confronted with a new reality, one that abruptly introduced her to her half-sister the halfling, coupled with the absolute truth about Kris, the man she had been falling in love with, who apparently was one of several quite literal, *Supermen*.

It's been the same length of time, give or take a few hours, since Zuriel woke up in the hospital under the watchful eyes of Dr. Grier Stone. And about the same time since Lynn was caught at the hospital in her failed disguise. But who's counting?

Does time really *fly* when you're having fun?

What about when you're *not* having fun? Because the almost 2-minute wait since Leo's last text to the group had felt more like 2 hours. Texts from all parties had been coming in steadily since everyone had gone into search-and-rescue mode 3 hours and 47 minutes ago, when any and all communication from Lane had simply stopped.

As a person gets older, time is often measured when noticing how much a child has grown, or how long it has been since a loved one died. And time often speeds up in the presence of angels, but in that moment, when we had learned that Lane had vanished, *time* had come to a screeching halt.

But let me back up… waaaay back.

* * *

Chapter 1

Cleveland Hospital, morning *after* Valentine's Day, 2023, South Florida

THEN.

On my call with Lane the morning of Valentine's Day, she had told me she would be heading over to the group home to see Lyndon, but not until after making an appearance at the party Natalie and her roommates were hosting. Her intention in meeting up with Lyndon was to get things back on track with him, since he'd been so busy of late. His *busy* had involved him traveling to Florida and being at the hospital where I worked.

Following my call with Lane, I had another call. This one was with Mac to update her on how Lyndon had been at the hospital again, and that I felt it was *Zuriel* he'd been there to see, not me. Although we'd both agreed, it didn't explain why he had brought him to *my* hospital. In an attempt to lighten our conversation, I'd shared that Redmond and I were doing a Valentine's date night at home, while Zach babysat the girls at South Haven, the three of them having a movie night and sleepover. But I'd known better than to tell her about my chatting with Zach and Leo on a plan to get me into the psych ward.

Later in the afternoon, when I'd dropped by South Haven, I'd learned that Thaddeus was still unaccounted for, and that Den, Marq, and Ben had been back to watching their target locations more closely. On a high note, Zach had already gotten my disguise done and ready for use. It had been perfect except for one minor detail on the ID badge that had needed adjusting, which he'd fixed by the time I'd dropped the girls back off for their sleepover. And though my Valentine's date night with Redmond had gone exceptionally well, I hadn't anticipated that by the early morning after, I'd be using that disguise Zach had created so soon.

I'd woken in the wee hours from another extremely vivid dream where I'd once again found myself in Thaddeus's private lab in the Celaeno building. This time in the dream, there hadn't been any medical staff or equipment, nor a massive angel hanging from straps attached to the ceiling. Instead, above the door on the wall hung a massive set of white, black-tipped feathered wings affixed with huge silver nails to a panel similar to that of a butterfly presentation board. Unlike butterflies on display, these wings had been cut flush from the owner's body with traces of flesh and dried blood still visible on the white feathers nearest to the attachment ends of the wings. The dream images of the lab had shifted then to a hospital room, and in it I'd found Zuriel resting in the bed, hooked up to several monitors. When I gazed down at his handsome face, his eyes had abruptly opened and he'd mouthed the words, '*Help me*'. I'd woken up then, noticing the clock on my nightstand read 4 a.m. Redmond had still been asleep, but I had known what I needed to do. I had to get into the psych ward.

At the hospital, I'd gotten into my disguise next to my car in the parking lot. Once through the staff entrance, I'd followed Zuriel's distinct signature up the stairway to the entrance just around the corner from the Behavioral Health Center. Filled with overconfidence, I had stepped from the stairwell only to be assaulted by what I had assumed was the hangover I had previously thought I'd dodged.

But it wasn't a hangover. It had been much worse. Abrupt tingling on the back of my neck had been followed by a wave of nausea so overwhelming I hadn't believed I could make it to the bathroom before throwing up. Mid-sway in my attempt, I'd froze as static electricity prickled down both my arms. At the sound of the entry latch for the door to the stairwell clicking behind me, while still struggling not to vomit, I'd turned slowly around only to find myself face to chest with an enormous figure filling up the opening of the entry's doorframe. I had tilted my head back to look up and found stunning eyes glowering down at me, scrutinizing me from the top of my head down to my ID badge then back up to my face. When his eyes narrowed and his brows furrowed into a menacing scowl, I'd known he had endeavored to see beyond my façade. *"You,"* he'd said in a deep, questioning voice, further examining me. Then he'd said, *"It's you,"* as though to make his first declaration clearer. When I'd gone to step back, he'd wrapped a hand around my forearm so fast it had blurred. It was then, as his massive fingers had tightened around my tiny forearm, that I'd realized I had forgotten the purple wine stain facial prosthetic in my car. It hadn't been the only thing I had forgotten. All the self-defense moves I'd mastered had deserted my memory. I'd known the jig was up when his eyebrows rose with an expression of understanding topped with his roaring my last name, "WESTLAKE!"

Lyndon, in all his fierceness, loomed up before me, his dark green eyes steely and questioning. Then, before I could protest, he backed up and pushed through the door to the stairwell, yanking me through it with him.

"I don't know who you think I am, but you better unhand me before I call security." I made a pathetic attempt to pull my arm free of his grip.

"I know who you are, Ms. Westlake. You won't call security. Would be hard to explain this." He waved his free hand up and down, alluding to my getup. "Why are you in this ridiculous disguise?"

He was right. I couldn't call security. "Let go of me," I demanded. His expression softened, as did the crease between his brows, and then, to my utter surprise, he let go of my arm. "What are you doing here?" But I knew why. *Zuriel.*

"The bigger question is why are *you* here?" he shot back, crossing his big arms over his muscular chest. He wore dark, loose-fitting jeans and a snug forest green long-sleeved t-shirt that hugged his muscles and complemented his dark green eyes.

"I… work here." I mirrored his crossed arms, widening my stance as if it made a difference. All it did was uncomfortably bunch up my lab coat.

He gave me a smirk, then swiftly released his arms to grab the ID badge that hung below my crossed arms. "I know you're Lane's aunt," he said, letting the badge drop back down. He returned to crossing his arms. "She told me she had an aunt living in Florida…," he began to explain.

"And you just jumped to the conclusion I was this person's aunt?" I interjected with a poor rebuttal.

He gave me an expression that told me he knew I was full of shit. "I've been looking for you for some time, Ms. Westlake," he said then. "And I know you know who I am. Who my… *boss* is."

I opened my mouth to cast doubt on his declaration, but then thought better of it. "How do you know I'm Lane's aunt?" I gave him a scrutinizing glare.

"She told me." Letting his crossed arms free again, he leaned back against the wall to face the stairs leading up to the next floor.

"When?" I questioned, his statement throwing me off. Had Lane really told him about me? Did she trust him that much?

"A few hours ago, when she was at my place." He pulled a cellphone from the back pocket of his jeans as though to check something, then slid it back in again.

I already had a long list of questions for him, but only one that had nagged me. "Why, if you knew who I was—where I was, haven't you…."

"Taken you to Thaddeus?" he finished for me. Recrossing his arms, he said, "I didn't know where you were, not until recently when I recognized you the last time I was here. I overheard you on the phone with Lane… and, well, I still hadn't been sure then. Trust me, in all the time while getting to know Lane, I had no idea my target—you, that *you* and this aunt of Lane's were one and the same.

But it was clear when I put two and two together, you were the aunt she'd previously told me about. I hadn't known what to make of it then, but Lane cleared most of it up for me tonight."

"Quite the conundrum," I said, letting my arms fall. I stepped to the side and then slumped down to sit on the ascending stairs to face Lyndon. This wasn't exactly how I thought my plan would go, not even close. I gave a sigh and pushed the fake glasses further up on the bridge of my nose.

"Indeed." Lyndon once again uncrossed his arms, this time placing his hands behind him to lean against the wall.

I wasn't sure if the movement was a gesture to show he was of no threat to me, but I gave him the benefit of the doubt. "I'm going to make a tiny leap here," I said before pausing, noting the heavy emotional concern that showed on his face. "The challenge here is the fact that you have feelings for Lane, right?"

"Yes." He readjusted his posture and stared down at his feet. "I would never do anything to upset Lane. I've struggled at great length on how I might explain to her about who… what I am. I never fathomed she was cognizant of my existence, of… my kind, *everything*, all of it. And you…." He glanced up at me.

"Me?" I bent my right knee and placed my foot on a higher step to lean my elbow on it.

"You can… sense us—my kind," he clarified, watching cautiously.

It wasn't a question, but I said nothing to sanction the statement.

"Thaddeus had long suspected as much, but it wasn't until I'd heard you say it to Lane on that phone call that I let myself believe it possible." He blew out an audible breath.

"And I'm guessing Lane told you that, too?" I asked before removing the fake eyeglasses I'd been wearing.

"She didn't come out and say it, no. But when I questioned her about what I'd heard, that's when she confirmed things."

I let out a heavy sigh. "What else did she tell you?" I slid the glasses into the breast pocket of my lab coat.

"Everything." Lyndon raised his hand to his neck, rubbing the palm of it over the back of his neck several times.

"What *everything*?" I frowned up at him. I wasn't ready to reveal my hand just yet.

He gave me that knowing look again, but I was hesitant about what he truly knew.

"I know Lane trusts you," I said, still unsure what *everything* Lane would have shared. "Tell me why you are here."

"I think you know why." He shot a glance at the closed stairwell door.

I did know. "Then tell me why you brought him here, of all places?"

Lyndon straightened away from the wall and slid his hands into his jeans pockets, the fabric straining across the back of his massive hands. "Believe it or not, for no other reason than it was the last place he'd been before…."

"Before he'd been beaten," I blurted, pushing up from my seat on the stairs. Then I put my hands on my hips in an attempt to gain some of my slightly shaky ground back. When his mouth gaped and he said nothing, I wondered if I had revealed too much? "Why was Zuriel in Florida?"

"I sent him looking for you—the target. Got a lead you might be in Miami—with your husband, William."

"Ex-husband," I corrected, hands still on my hips.

"Whatever, ex-husband," he said, shaking his head. "But Zuriel said the address I'd given him was no good."

"How did you even find out I was in Florida?"

"Let's just say I got lucky. But it was Zuriel who found out you'd moved out of the condo in Miami." He bent a knee, placing the sole of his boot against the wall behind him.

"How did he locate where I was?" I raised my hands in question.

Lyndon dropped his foot to the floor. "He didn't—not exactly."

"Just where I worked?"

"That's the funny thing," he said, pulling one hand free of the jean pocket to rub the back of his neck again. "I don't think he was here for you—at least I didn't think so at the time."

"What do you mean?" Feeling uneasy, I slid my hands into the lab coat pockets.

He let out a deep sigh of his own. "He told me he had a *lead*, one that brought him here. When I came here to tell him Thaddeus wanted to speak to him...."

"I'm guessing now you wish you had just left him here?"

He nodded. "I get it—I do." He returned his hand to his pocket, both hands straining in their tight confinement now.

"Get what?" Confused, I shook my head and shrugged.

"I believe… he was watching someone else at this hospital." Lyndon returned to staring down at his feet.

"Who?" I extended my arms, hands still in the pockets, causing the lab coat to flap open.

"Some doctor," he said, rocking his weight slightly from one foot to the other, eyes still down. "He was seriously infatuated with the female. She's the reason I brought him back here—was hoping she could help him—even gave her name to the ER doctor when I brought him in," he said, racing the words out. "It was a long shot, but there wasn't more I could do to aid him—he needed real medical help."

I dropped my arms. "What did Thaddeus do to him anyway? Why did he need a hospital? I thought you Earthbound had speedy healing."

Lyndon's head shot up at what I assumed was my use of the word *Earthbound*. "He took his wings." Lyndon lowered his head again.

"What?!" I said, horrified. I had known about the wounds on his back, but that was all the information I'd gotten.

"Cut them from his body," he added, raising his head to look at me.

"What did that monster do with them?" I asked reluctantly, recalling the awful images from my dream of wings stabbed through into the wall.

"I have them now—they are safe," Lyndon clarified, his expression mournful.

"Didn't you think leaving someone like *Zuriel* here was a tad risky?" I said, a hint of cynicism in my tone.

"I know it was, but I couldn't chance Thaddeus finding him—but couldn't let him die either—he's my friend." He glared at me. "Now he's in a coma."

Did he think Zuriel being in a coma was somehow my fault? I drew my hand from the coat pocket to scratch behind my ear under the wig. "It was probably the drugs."

"Drugs?" He tilted his head like a confused dog.

"Benzodiazepine—it's a drug used for sedation," I said, scratching under my wig at the back of my neck.

"I know what *benzos* are—why did they put him in a coma?" Lyndon straightened, leaning his back against the wall.

"The *benzos*, as you called them, is a medication that contains sulfur, and your kind does *not* fare well against sulfonamide drugs."

Lyndon pulled a hand free of his pocket again, then ran the palm of his hand over the scarred side of his face.

"Sulfur burns, yes?" I asked with a chin raise.

He dropped his hand from his face. "How did you know?"

"Yer not the only one who knows things." I tapped my nose with my index finger before stepping forward to the entry door.

Lyndon pushed away from the wall as though he were going to block my way. "How did you know Zuriel was at this hospital?"

I reached for the door handle. "I work here, remember? I was working the day you brought him in." Though the sensation I'd felt that day hadn't been just him and Zuriel. There had been a third Earthbound, one I couldn't see, but who had been near enough that I'd felt them. That unfamiliar signature had heightened the impact of Lyndon and Zuriel's presence further. Since then I'd sensed the other twice more at other locations.

"If you work here—why the disguise?" Lyndon flicked one of the curls on my wig.

"Crap," I said then, letting go of the door handle, remembering I needed to return to my car for the missing piece to my disguise. "Because that ward is one of the few places I don't have access to. Hence the get-up. But I forgot the matching facial prosthetic in my car." I lifted the ID badge to show him. "I'll be right back—wait here," I said before turning to the descending stairs.

"Fine," Lyndon said, his voice echoing in the stairwell as I raced down to the first level.

I was to my car and back in less than 10 minutes, glasses back on, purple wine stain birthmark in place, and found Lyndon exactly where I'd left him. "He's awake, by the way," I stated, pulling the stairwell door open and returning through to where I'd stood before our confrontation.

When Lyndon followed behind me, I turned back to him, placing my index finger to my lips in a gesture to keep quiet.

Lyndon rolled his eyes. "How do you know he's awake?" he questioned in a hushed voice.

It was my turn to give him a knowing look. "I have more questions for you too, but right now I need to get in and check on your friend," I said in an equally hushed tone. "Stay here—you can't come with me."

Lyndon remained near the stairwell door as I went off around the corner to the secure ward.

However, as fate would have it, I was too late.

When I told the ward nurse at the main desk I was here to see the coma patient, she had informed me he'd already been checked out by his doctor. And when I'd asked *who* his doctor was, she'd said, *"Dr. Stone."*

"I'm going with you," Lyndon announced immediately after my account of the situation *and* explanation of how Zuriel's doctor just happened to be a friend of mine.

"I know this is a lot for both of us, but…," I began to say before stopping on the stairs to look up at him. "Do you trust me?"

"If Lane trusts you, I trust you," he said without hesitation.

"Good," I said. I wanted to trust him too, but the jury was still out on that. "Then let me deal with this—let me speak to Grier." I pushed open the door to the side exit, then swiftly traveled the walkway that led to the far guest parking lot.

"This doctor friend of yours is the reason I brought him here," he said, easily keeping pace with me as I rushed to my car.

"Didn't you say he was stalking her?" I pressed the unlock button on my car key fob.

Lyndon rounded to the other side of my car. "Yes—no, not really."

I glanced across at him over the top of the car. "Should I be worried—is she in danger?"

"No—Zuriel is not like that," he said, leaning a thick forearm against the roof of my car.

"Look, you can explain all the intricacies of tracking down targets later, but if they are together—I need to figure out how to explain to Grier about Zuriel—navigate this information so she understands who—what he is," I rushed out, opening the driver's side door to get in.

He pounded a fist on the car's roof. "Zuriel is *my* friend—he is from *my* world, and I need to protect him."

"Like you protected him from Thaddeus?" I threw at him before climbing into the driver's seat. I knew the remark was cold, but I wasn't going to pull any punches, not if *my* friend was in any kind of danger. I hit the button to unlock the passenger-side door, and Lyndon got in. "Just let me do the talking." I ripped off the wig, glasses and the facial piece of my disguise, then reached behind my seat, placing them back into the bag on the floor.

"Fine," he said, tugging the seatbelt across his burly chest.

"Fine," I shot back, turning forward, having nothing better in response.

Lyndon remained unexpectedly quiet on the drive until I tossed out another question that had been troubling me for months now. "Who else was with you when you brought Zuriel to the hospital?" I stole a glance his way.

Lyndon was looking at me, brows furrowed. "With me—what are you talking about?"

"I know there was another with you—another of your kind," I clarified, focusing back on the road.

"You sensed another?" he said, his question genuine.

"Yes." I nodded as though my *yes* wasn't clear enough.

"No one was with me," he said resolutely.

I glanced at him again. "Oh, there was someone there—outside," I reaffirmed, nodding a few more times.

"I swear to you, I was alone in my endeavor to bring Zuriel to the hospital." The passenger seat creaked as Lyndon adjusted it back for more legroom.

"Where is Thaddeus now?" A shiver ran down my back, and I checked the rearview mirror, reassuring myself no one was following us, but the road was typically quiet for this time of morning.

"I don't know," he responded, his voice a tad sheepish.

I frowned. "How can you *not* know?"

"Like I said—I don't know," he said a little firmer. "But he took everything with him."

"What do you mean by everything?" I glanced at him again as I came to a stop at a red light.

He stared at me stone faced as though not wanting to elaborate.

"Seriously—I know about all his labs, what he really does." I gave him back a fierce look that screamed, *tell me*. "I've even been in his private lab in Ottawa."

"Right—that was you, I remember." He nodded. "Both his condo and private lab were emptied."

The light turned green. "And?" I asked, hitting the gas and continuing onward to our destination.

"And he's never done that before. He has a residence at every facility, but the one in Ottawa functions like his home-base, you could say. He's left abruptly on occasion, but he's *never* taken all his personal belongings with him."

"Did he say anything to you before he left?" I asked, turning onto the road that led to Grier's cottage.

"All he said was that he was returning to Brazil."

I already knew the part about his going to Brazil. "So you have nothing helpful to add then," I stated, pulling into Grier's driveway. I noted the time on the car's clock showed it was approaching 6 a.m.. The pink in the sky was hinting that the sun was just beginning its rise. "Wait here," I said, popping my seatbelt and opening the driver's side door. I got out of the car, shrugging off the white lab coat. Then I tossed it and the ID badge on the front seat before shutting things up.

"I'm coming with you," Lyndon said, rushing out of his seatbelt to get out of the car.

"Just wait here—you're just going to freak her out," I said, attempting to block his way up the stairs.

"Move," he said, easily holding me off as he gripped the railing and proceeded up the stairs to the front deck.

I scurried up behind him, darting under his outstretched arm as he worked his way up the stairs. "Let me at least greet her first, okay?" I requested, reaching the door first. I gave the front door a swift knock.

Lyndon stopped behind me where I stood, and a moment later the door cracked open just enough to reveal Grier's sweet face.

"Lynn, what are you doing here?" she whispered through the crack in the door.

"Everything alright?" a deep male voice questioned from behind her. Then a beautifully handsome face with sparkling pale grey eyes, which I'd only ever seen in my dreams, appeared above Grier's head. "Lyndon—my friend, what are *you* doing here?" Zuriel asked, his voice joyful.

Lyndon's arm moved by my head to press a hand to the door, shifting it further open to reveal Grier dressed in her hospital attire. The movement shuffled her back several steps as Lyndon gently pushed past her to embrace his friend in a bear hug. The door opening wider was followed up by the delicious and familiar aroma of what I had come to know as Grier's fresh-baked lemon cranberry muffins. My stomach growled as I took in the glorious scent, and my head spun as I watched the Seraph, whose job it was to find me, embrace the Seraph who had haunted my dreams.

"Grier," Zuriel forced out in an air-restricted breath, the strain due to Lyndon's tight embrace. "This is Lyndon… the friend I was telling you about."

"Lyndon, it's a pleasure to meet you," Grier responded as Lyndon reluctantly released Zuriel. "He tells me you brought him to the ER when he was injured, that you saved his life," she added in an appreciative voice.

"Lovely to meet you, Doctor." Lyndon gave her a slight bow.

"Please call me Grier," she said, smiling up at Lyndon.

"Do I know you?" Zuriel directed at me as I stood in the doorway. His short, jet-black hair was wet as though he'd recently showered, and he was in similar scrubs to what both Grier and I were currently wearing.

"Oh, Zuriel, this is my good friend, Lynn." Grier extended a welcoming arm my way. "Lynn—get in here." She rolled her hand, gesturing for me to come in.

"*Lynn*?" Zuriel questioned. Confusion coupled with recognition flashed in Zuriel's expression, but still he asked, "How do the two of you know each other?" He pointed a finger back and forth between Lyndon and me, the question for us and not Grier and me.

"We have a lot of catching up to do, my friend," Lyndon stated. "Let's talk." Lyndon put an arm around Zuriel's shoulders, turning and leading him towards the far side of the open living room.

"Grier… why is Zuriel here? And how is it that you're his doctor?" I asked, stepping up to her as she watched the two massive males stroll into her kitchen. Taking her by the shoulders, I turned her my way. "Grier," I said again, raising my eyebrows.

Grier blushed. "Why are you wearing scrubs?" she asked, as though avoiding my questions. "And how do you know Zuriel and Lyndon?"

"Let's sit down—I have a few… *bizarre* things to share with you," I said, turning her towards the adjacent living room sitting area, all the while attempting to corral my scrambling brain and all the pertinent information it possessed.

"Bizarre stuff about what?" Grier plopped down at the far end of the soft, cozy couch, tucking her feet under her to sit sideways.

"There are some… *unusual* things you need to know about Zuriel… and Lyndon… and…," I said first, before I led into the long list of unusual things building in my brain.

"Zuriel already told me everything," Grier cut in before I could even take a seat.

There was that *everything* word again. I stared back at her as I lowered myself onto the couch, continuing to face her. Then I shot an inquisitive look over to Lyndon and Zuriel, who now stood in the kitchen engrossed in heavy discussion. "What do you know?" I asked, turning back to her. I kicked off my shoes, then bent my right leg to tuck it in under me, leaning my shoulder against the back of the couch and resting my hands in my lap.

"That he's… an angel—that Lyndon is, too," she said, her words coming out calmer than I would have expected. She glanced over at the two Earthbound in her kitchen. "And I know they are stranded here… that there are more of them trapped here on Earth. And I know about Thaddeus *and* what he did to him." Her focus lingered on Zuriel before shifting back to me. "What I don't know is how you're involved. But I suspect our talk about your dreams and waking premonitions may have something to do with all this, yes?" She took up one of my hands and gave it a light squeeze, then just held it.

She was a therapist, I reminded myself, oddly comforted by the fact. "You could say that." I squeezed her hand back. Normally, I was the one who had to explain things, reassuring the other person who was receiving the information that all was well. Apparently, Zuriel had explained things already, just not *everything*. "It's a long story—right now I just need to know that you're okay."

"Of course, I'm okay." Grier turned her attention back to the kitchen, a shy smile turning the corners of her lips. "I'm more than okay."

Chapter 2

"I know you sent me to Miami, but I mean, what are the chances you bring me back to the same town our target lives in, let alone the hospital she works at," Zuriel stated, running a hand through his damp hair, his expression filled with bewilderment.

"That's what you find baffling in all this?" Lyndon questioned him back. "How did you end up here?" Lyndon made a forceful gesture of pointing down to the floor.

"Don't worry, brother—all is well. I am well." Zuriel placed his hands firmly on Lyndon's shoulders.

"Care to explain what's going on here—with the doctor?" Lyndon knew Zuriel had not trailed their target, *Lynn*, to this city. In truth, he had followed *Grier*, this other female instead.

Zuriel dropped his hands to his sides. "I told her—she knows everything...," Zuriel said, attempting to explain.

"How could you…?"

"Lyndon, you don't understand." Zuriel ran his hands through his damp hair.

Oh, but he did, Lyndon mused. He was fully aware of the delicate nature of curiosity and the desire to know more about a female you were drawn to. His interest in Lane had started in a similar way, but Lane hadn't just been someone who had simply caught his eye, not in the beginning anyway, and she was much more now. She was a dream come true in his normally nightmare-filled world, and he had told her everything as well. "Start from the beginning," Lyndon said. "The truth this time."

Zuriel glanced over to where Grier and Lynn sat in the living room. He ran a hand through his hair again, then said, "I was following up with a lead in Miami—at the real estate office with the agent who handled the sale of the home the target and her husband owned."

"Ex-husband," Lyndon corrected. "And I know about the other lead in Japan—Sebastian and Lazarus already looked into it. A dead end, obviously."

Zuriel's eyebrows bunched. "He wasn't there—the ex-husband, I mean?"

Lyndon exhaled a frustrated breath. "He was there—obviously *she* was not," he said, raising his eyebrows, eyes darting in the direction of the women in the other room.

"True—true." Zuriel nodded his head. "So, yeah, I went to speak to the realtors, and they said they didn't keep records from that far back at the office."

"Obviously, we don't need to follow up on any leads—considering we know the whereabouts of the target—the exact location." Lyndon's lips pressed into a thin line, his impatience growing as he turned his head to look at the women again.

"Right—right, sorry—it's been quite the morning for me already," Zuriel said apologetically. "The Grove Realty is where I first saw Grier. And since the agent had stated he would have to check their home office for the file, I realized I would have some time to kill."

"So you decided to what—stalk a pretty girl?" Lyndon leaned his hip against the side counter, glancing down at the freshly baked muffins resting on a cooling tray.

"Yes and no," Zuriel said, running both hands through his hair. "Lyndon, I have never been drawn to any human female before."

"I understand—truly I do. But how did you end up here?" Lyndon tapped the counter with his index finger.

"Grier told me I had a severe allergic reaction to a drug I was given in the ER—put me in a coma. She said I've been in a coma for six months."

"I'm aware of all that—and the drug must have been sulfur based," Lyndon said, passing a hand over the scarred side of his jaw. "Why did the doctor bring you here?"

"I… I'm not sure how it was possible… but while in the coma, I somehow managed to visit her." Zuriel ran a hand down his face. "Grier called it astral projection."

"I'm sorry?" Lyndon questioned, squinting at Zuriel.

"It's also known as astral travel, and it occurs in multiple cultures—it's an out-of-body experience," Zuriel tried to explain.

"I know what it is—but how did you manage it?" Lyndon leaned his hands back against the edge of the island.

"My guess is that my desire to see her again—be with her, is what allowed my physical body to free my *astral* body to travel through the astral plane to find her. I know it sounds crazy," Zuriel said, rubbing a hand across his forehead, "but it really happened. I was here in her home office, pretending to be a patient in need of therapy…."

"You might be in need of therapy," Lyndon cut in. "Go on."

"I was here—every week, in her office," Zuriel continued.

"And?" Lyndon shrugged a shoulder.

"And… I also visited her in her dreams. Those visits were much more… *intimate*." The corners of Zuriel's mouth hinted at a smile.

Lyndon's eyebrows rose in surprise.

Zuriel glanced away out the back patio door before his focus returned to Lyndon. "We have spent 6 months getting to know each other. She just didn't know that I was actually trapped in the hospital—in a coma."

"How is it that you are awake now?" Lyndon raised his hands in question. "Don't get me wrong—I'm grateful you are out and back to your steady self, but…." Lyndon lowered his hands and shrugged, shaking his head, still bewildered.

"I knew Grier was only *on call* at the hospital, so I took a little astral trip to visit another patient in the ward—planted a suggestion in his feeble mind, one that would have the good doctor called in. Once I knew she was at the hospital—I set off the alarms to monitors connected to my physical body to draw her to my room. Her coming into the room, coming up next to my body in the hospital bed—it's what woke me."

"So she just checked you out and brought you here?" Lyndon shrugged again.

"Pretty much." Zuriel grabbed up one of the muffins from the cooling tray on the kitchen counter, bringing it to his nose for a sniff. "I love lemon and cranberry. Try one—they're amazing," he added before taking a bite.

"And you told her what you are?" Lyndon questioned, watching as Zuriel took another bite of the fresh treat.

"Yup," he said, chewing. "She seemed pretty open to the reality of it, considering she'd already spent 6 months *with* me here, all the while I was literally comatose." Zuriel popped the last bit of muffin into his mouth.

"So now what?" Lyndon stared down at the warm muffins, the lemony aroma wafting up his nostrils while the red cranberries glistened up at him. He ran a hand across his stomach.

"Now it's your turn," Zuriel said, pulling Lyndon from his hunger pains.

"My turn?" He shot a glance at the women before focusing back on Zuriel.

"Tell me how I ended up in the hospital, what's been happening during my slumber, and how it is you are here with *her*—our intended target?" Zuriel tapped the counter next to the rack of muffins, then extended his hand in the direction of the living room. "All I remember was Thaddeus trying to beat more out of me than I had to tell him."

Lyndon ran a hand over his scar. The explanation he had was not going to be a pleasant one. "He's gone. Thaddeus—went to Brazil—took all his belongings with him." Lyndon stared back down at the pleasant smelling muffins.

"Good riddance," Zuriel said. "But that's not like him."

"Strange, I know." Lyndon went on to explain how he'd found Zuriel in the lab, unconscious and beaten to a pulp. He told him how Thaddeus had said to get rid of him, that he never wanted to see Zuriel again. And how he had taken him from the lab, patched him up, dressed him in some of Thaddeus's discarded clothes. Then he had brought Zuriel to the only place he thought might be able to help him. He'd given the ET doctor Grier's name, stating she was *his* doctor in hopes she would help him. Lyndon explained that he had no idea she was a psychiatrist, nor that she was only on call at the hospital. His hope had been for Zuriel to be given something to ease the pain, help heal his wounds. Instead, they'd unknowingly given him something that had harmed him. "I've been beside myself with worry, unable to get into the ward, unable to free you." Lyndon lowered his head.

"I'm fine—fully healed." Zuriel reached out and patted the side of Lyndon's arm. "You saved my life, brother."

Lyndon raised his head and placed a hand on Zuriel's shoulder, pulling him forward and into another embrace. *"Your wings,"* Lyndon whispered in a sorrow-filled voice.

"I know," Zuriel confessed, pressing his cheek against Lyndon's shoulder.

"But I have them wrapped up and stored in a safe place," Lyndon breathed out, still holding his friend in a strong embrace.

"Thank you, brother," Zuriel said, giving Lyndon several pats on the back. "I have all I need right here."

Lyndon released his friend, hurriedly swiping a rogue tear from his face before glancing over to where Zuriel's lady-love sat chatting with *her* friend. Glancing back and giving Zuriel's hospital scrubs the once over, he said, "Looks like we need to get you some new clothes." Then, in a low voice, Lyndon went on to share the details about his blossoming relationship with Lane, about their time at the group home with Taylor, at the birthday party, in his apartment, their first kiss, and about their revealing conversation from last night when he'd learned she was fully aware of the existence of Seraphim. Lyndon explained further how her parents worked for some group of specially trained operatives who were aware of their kind, and that they devoted their time to saving halflings. Then he explained about how he saw Lynn, and lastly about the connection between Lane and her.

"She—*Lynn*, our target, is your girlfriend's aunt?" Zuriel gave his head a rattle.

"And she's friends with *your*—Grier, whatever she is," Lyndon tossed out, a smile spreading across his face.

"And now they all know about our kind." The corner of Zuriel's mouth quirked up in a half-smile.

Lyndon just nodded.

"You've already met Lane's parents and two of her *uncles*. But you say there are more?" Zuriel leaned back against the counter.

"Yes… and Shayne," Lyndon began, rubbing a hand across his jaw.

"What about Shayne? Other than he would be more than hostile if he ever got ahold of either of us." Zuriel stole another muffin from the rack.

"He works for her uncles—at a restaurant they own," Lyndon shared, stealing up one of the muffins for himself finally.

"Oh, boy. What's going to happen now, Lyndon?" Zuriel took a generous bite of the soft muffin.

Lyndon sniffed the muffin in his hand, taking in the lush scent of cranberry mingling with lemon. "Well, I'm supposed to meet the rest of these uncles of hers, today."

Chapter 3 

"Grier, how the heck did you become Zuriel's doctor?" I asked, leading with a straight question, hoping for a straight answer, even though I knew she wanted more clarity on my association with him and Lyndon.

"I'm not sure how to explain it, but do you remember the patient I told you about—the one I was treating here in my home office?" Grier gathered her long red hair into a side ponytail, holding it firmly in her fist.

"The *handsome* one—yes," I said, my brain unscrambling, my skin tingling with having two Earthbound so near me.

"I'd been treating him for months…." Grier paused and let out a little giggle before shaking her head. "To tell you the truth—I thought I had lost my mind at first."

She wasn't the only one. "What does this have to do with Zuriel?"

"He's the one I've been treating—he's my in-person patient," she said, letting her hair drop free from her grip.

"But how? Grier, he's been in a coma for months." I felt like I should be whispering, but what was the point?

"Trust me—I know." Grier ran her fingers through her long hair as it draped over her shoulder and down her chest. "Apparently, he saw me before that—not here—but in Miami. He explained to me he had been doing some work for Lyndon."

"Wait—Lyndon told me Zuriel had been watching you, but I thought he just meant at the hospital," I stated, still confused. "How could he have been here *with* you… yet still unconscious in the hospital at the same time?" My eyebrows pinched together.

Grier's face and neck flushed. "I'm not certain, exactly, but I… I suspect it has something to do with his fascination with me—the connection, that gave him the ability to come to me, manifest here—in my office, during waking moments and…." Grier swallowed. "…during my sleep." She blushed again, rocking her head back and forth as though she too still struggled with what she was saying.

I gave my own head a shake despite the fact it was already spinning from my unforeseen encounter and subsequent car ride over here with Lyndon. I drew in a long breath hoping to calm my nerve endings.

"Remember us talking about astral projection?" Grier asked then.

"You mean the dream-walker stuff," I said with a shrug.

"Yes, it's a real thing, Lynn." Grier turned to look back towards the kitchen, wrapping a strand of hair around her fingers.

I glanced over as well to see that the two large Earthbound angels were still in deep discussion. "Go on," I prompted, shifting my attention back to Grier.

Grier turned back. "It allows a person's consciousness to function separately from their physical body, to travel outside the body." She moved her hands in a manner much like a magician would, as though what she was telling me was mystical.

"And this is how you believe he was able to come here?" I dragged my hands through my hair, realizing I must look a fright after having that horrible wig on my head.

"Yes, I believe so." Grier fiddled with her hair, nervously twisting it into a long spiral, the ends reaching to her waistline.

"I've seen—experienced, a lot of unusual—not easily explained things, so I would never negate what you think you witnessed." After this, her believing in such things, it wouldn't be so difficult for me to explain to her my otherworldly involvement, I realized.

"Lynn, Zuriel has been visiting me once a week for 6 months, *and* he's been in my lucid dreams." Her neck and face bloomed bright pink. "These dreams I've been having about Zuriel…." She paused. "… I was dreaming about him last night, when my pager woke me. It was the hospital needing me to come in to help with a patient."

"Zuriel?"

"No—someone else. I hadn't even known Zuriel was at the hospital. Not until monitors started going off in a patient's room down the hall from where I was. When I approached the patient's bed—I recognized him immediately." Grier twisted her hair, eyes widening. "When I asked the nurse whose patient he was, she showed me that the chart had *my* name on it. Then she told me how he had been brought to the ward after a reaction to a sedative they'd given him, and that he'd been there for 6 months, Lynn." Grier released her hair, letting her hands drop to her lap.

"Well, speaking of dreaming. Last night I dreamed that Zuriel woke up, and this morning I went to the hospital to try to get in to see him, but he was gone, signed out by you?" I said, sharing my side of this irrational story.

"Well, he did wake up," she laughed out. "That explains the scrubs and why you came here?" She slapped my knee and laughed again.

"And obviously he was willing and well enough to leave," I said. "The drug must have fully left his system—or maybe you were the real medicine he needed." I gave her a few eyebrow raises. "How do you feel about that?" I asked. Clearly, she wasn't afraid of him. And boy, could redheads blush, I mused.

Rosy-faced, she said, "I'm… I'm a little—a lot overcome, knowing that angels are real, but my connection to him—although unconventional, is a strong one, a loving one, and I feel good with him—safe with him." Her voice softened as she spoke those last words.

I nodded my understanding in spite of how illogical the story may have seemed. I'd never witnessed this phenomenon myself, though I'd had many of my own bizarre lucid dreams and unusual waking moments. It was what it was. I didn't have all the answers to the universe either, but here we were.

"Lynn, you seem awfully calm about this," Grier said, leaning the side of her head against the back of the sofa.

"Me?" I pointed at myself. "You think I'm calm?" I chuckled out. "I'd say you are shockingly relaxed after all you've been through and learned."

She nodded. "I always knew something wasn't quite *normal* during my sessions with Zuriel. It always felt so… *dreamlike*, but I never imagined." She closed her eyes briefly and shook her head again.

Saying nothing, I reached for her hands and held them in mine, letting her continue to verbalize her thoughts.

"Lynn, am I crazy to think it's possible to have a normal relationship with someone like Zuriel?"

"Crazy? No. Normal? Definitely not," I said with an amused laugh, giving her hands a gentle squeeze. "I'd be lying if I didn't admit that I'd lost my shit too when I learned about their kind." I gave Grier a reassuring smile. "And… there's a lot more to explain," I added, then paused. I was fairly confident Redmond was as another person who would be losing their shit when he woke and couldn't find me. Regrettably, I'd left my cellphone at home beside the bed. "But first, can I borrow your phone, *and* can I get one of those muffins I smell?"

Chapter 4 

The Beach House, same morning *after* Valentine's Day, South Florida

I'd sent a quick text to Redmond, letting him know that I was at Grier's, and how I had to use her cellphone because I had left mind by the bed charging. I told him that I would explain *why* later and not to worry. I hadn't known at the time what the others had been through, and it hadn't been until later that morning after Valentine's Day when we'd all fully understand how much *everything* had changed.

When I arrived home a few hours later, I found Redmond and Zach sitting in the living room with our faithful woolly white mammoths, Summer and Snow, passed out on the floor in front of them.

"Zach—good, you're here. I was going to call you once I got home—I have some interesting news." I took a seat on the opposite couch across from them, noting how nicely Zach was dressed. He wore a dress shirt in a colour that matched his pale blue eyes, paired with well-worn blue jeans and tan loafers. "Where are the girls?" I directed at Redmond.

"At school," he said, his expression impassive.

"I dropped them off this morning," Zach added.

"Right," I said, turning in my seat, checking the clock on the wall. My brain was a bit scrambled. It *was* a school day, but they'd slept over at South Haven last night.

"Lynn, I needed to talk to both of you," Zach said, redirecting my attention.

"Why are you in scrubs?" Redmond asked me, a crease forming between his brows. He, too, was in jeans—black ones, but he wore a Harley Davidson t-shirt, one he reserved only for wearing when he rode his motorcycle.

"I'll explain later. What's up Zach?" I said, a little too dismissively I realized when Redmond's face turned stoney.

Zach went on to fill us in. Apparently, while I was out doing '*whatever*,' as Redmond had put it, some pretty wild stuff had been happening up north. The first of which being that Natalie had gone through her transition. "Mason brought her to North Haven. They put her in my room there," Zach said. "She was supposed to be hosting a party at her home—but when Mason arrived to help with the decorations, she'd told him she hadn't been feeling well. Then shortly after she said her upper back was paining her." Zach flexed and contracted his back, the fabric of his tailored shirt pulling against his chest with the movement.

"How do you help a person through something like that?" Redmond asked, grimacing.

"Nic was there, and Julianna came over to assist as well. It was a good thing too because Natalie's wings had come out fully on display for all to see within minutes of her arrival." He contracted his back muscles again.

"Oh-my-god—is she okay?" I asked, more as a demand than a question, arching my spine, my back suddenly having sympathy pains.

"She was still unconscious when I got off the phone with Nic, but both Julianna and Mason are with her now, should she wake. Nic is monitoring her vitals, and Rachel—Olivia's daughter, was called to come assist Nic." Zach leaned forward in his seat, resting his elbows on his knees.

"When she wakes, how are you going to explain to her what happened?" Redmond questioned, hints of his worried father voice coming through. "What about her friends—won't they be worried about her—it was her party that she left?" Redmond rested his forearm on the arm of the couch.

"Mason contacted her best friend, Tina, and told her that Natalie had had a severe allergic reaction to something during the party setup and that he had taken her to the hospital." Zach returned to leaning back against the couch.

"But she's not at the hospital—what's going to happen when the friends go there to find her?" I questioned. I knew all too well how tricky hospitals could be.

"It's covered. Mason explained that she is in isolation—that she can't have any visitors. But he also gave her the number of the nurse attending to her—Nic's number. Mason asked Tina to update Natalie's roommates on her condition. He also told her that he had contacted his mother, who is a professor at the university—as you both know, and that she would inform the university of the situation on Natalie's behalf." Zach gave me a stiff smile.

"Sounds complicated," Redmond expressed, rubbing his thigh as though he were restless.

"What's even more complicated is that Jana witnessed the whole thing," Zach added, leaning forward, elbows on his knees again.

"Her relationship with Kris was already difficult enough," I said, remembering my conversation with him about his feelings for Jana. I glanced Redmond's way, but he was staring down at the floor.

Zach brushed a thumb across his jaw. "Well, the thing is, apparently Jana had some difficult questions for Kris just before everything with Natalie went down."

"Like what?" I asked, knowing she would have a growing list at this point. I looked at Redmond again. This time him was staring at Zach.

"She asked why the photo in Kris's room of he and Frank showed a date on it, that in her reality, was not *logically* possible. Meaning how could they look the same despite the date on the photo being 23 years ago?" Zach gave a slow tilt of his head.

"Yikes," I said, trying to fathom how to explain something like that.

Zach gave me a smile, but his expression was grave. "Kris tried to explain, but then they'd been drawn into the commotion with overhearing Natalie's screams."

"I'm in the *knowing*—and I can't imagine witnessing that." Redmond said, his expression now sympathetic.

"She passed out right after seeing Natalie's wing emerge." Zach ran the fingertips of both hands along his jaw to meet in a kind of prayer formation, his chin resting on the tips.

"Where is Jana now?" I asked, worried she may have bolted after coming to.

Zach dropped his hands to his thighs. "Kris set her to sleep in her room. She's resting," he said with a relieved sigh.

"Where's Lane?" I asked, curious about what she did after her talk with Lyndon last night.

"Lane told Leo she had some big news to share," Zach said, tugging the cuffs of his sleeves as though the length had shortened somehow.

I rolled the hem of my hospital shirt through my fingers. "About?" I asked, even though I had comparable news to share.

"Lane was over at Lyndon's and she pressed him about the question he'd posed to her—about believing in the supernatural, and before she knew it, things were all out on the table." Zach cracked his neck as if he was displeased at what Lane had done.

"What things?" Redmond asked.

"Well, first, when she questioned why he worked for such a horrible person, he confessed that Taylor was *his* son."

"Thaddeus, is Taylor's biological father?" Redmond questioned, his concerned father's voice returning.

I went to correct Redmond, but then held my words as Zach spoke again. "No—Lyndon is Taylor's father. Said he feared what Thaddeus would do to Taylor if he didn't comply with his orders—and why he stayed working for him was all to protect Taylor."

"That makes a lot of sense," Redmond said, nodding.

"Leo was furious with Lane." Zach blew out a whistle and tilted his head as if he concurred.

At the sound of Zach's whistle, both Summer and Snow let out tired *"groans"*.

Zach bent forward, reaching out to ruffle the fur of our now-awake eavesdroppers. "Shhhh, sorry lasses," he said, brushing the palms of his hands over their plush ears.

"Why?" I asked, despite knowing how difficult it was navigating these things, what to share and what not to share. I shot a look at Redmond to see he was slowly shaking his head in disapproval.

"Because she told Lyndon that she knew everything—about his kind. However, Leo was much more understanding after she gave him the details about why Lyndon was really staying at the group home, how much he hated Thaddeus, and how he has been making plans to break free from him."

"So, did she tell him everything-everything?" I asked, the word *everything* ringing in my ears. I knew what I knew—what Lyndon had told me, but I still didn't know the full extent of what Lane had shared.

"Not exactly," Zach said, rubbing his hands together. "She said her parents worked for a group of people, a team of specially trained *men* who were aware of his kind and the celestial world—and that they search out and help halflings like Taylor."

"Interesting that she held so much back," I said, my turn to nod. At least I knew now what information Lyndon actually had.

"She said she felt the rest wasn't her information to share." Zach raised his eyebrows like he agreed.

"True." I nodded again. But she had shared my sensing ability with Lyndon. I'll have to ask her myself what more she told him.

"Lyndon asked Lane if that was why Shayne knew her—knew her parents, and she told him *yes*," Zach added.

"Did Lyndon tell her anything more?" Redmond asked.

"The last thing Lyndon told her was about what Thaddeus had done to Zuriel. That he had hidden Zuriel from Thaddeus—taken him to a hospital, *and* that he would be leaving to go check on him." Zach glanced at me. "Before he left, Lane told him she would arrange for him to meet *the team*. I'm heading there now—but wanted to give you both the heads up."

I nodded my head once more but remained silent, pondering how things might be going over at Grier's house, now that she had not one but *two* Earthbound in her home.

"Lynn?" Zach said, pulling me from my thoughts. "How are you feeling about what Lane shared with Lyndon?"

"Well…," I began, glancing from Zach to Redmond. He was already glowering at me. "I have more to add to that."

Chapter 5 

Despite my best efforts to explain why I went to the hospital and what had happened with Lyndon, plus numerous variations in apologies, Redmond remained furious with me for not telling him about my plans to get into the psych ward. Mainly he was distraught over me putting myself in potential danger. It didn't matter to him that things had worked out in our favor, or even that Darius hadn't sensed me in any danger, and he'd left immediately after Zach had, saying he had *work* to do at the studio. I knew it was a lie and hoped he just needed to blow off some steam.

In the interim, I changed out of the scrubs I'd been wearing and into black track pants and a long-sleeved heather grey tunic, and then I reached out to Lane, telling her I wanted to get the *real deal* on what had happened between her and Lyndon. I was fairly sure Lyndon would have already told Lane all about our escapades by now, but I was dying to hear how things had gone down between the two of them *before* Lyndon and I had collided. I knew how much Lane believed in Lyndon, that she trusted him. We'd even laughed over it on our call yesterday because she had asked me, *"Haven't you ever had a gut feeling about someone?"* then said, *"Ha—look who I'm asking,"* realizing what a silly question that had been. I couldn't ignore the way she had expressed her feelings about how Lyndon treated Taylor, though. We knew *why* now, and it would have only heightened how she felt about him. She had been developing feelings for him, I'd known it. I knew she grasped how delicate that was, because her emotions had been a mess then. I could only guess how she must be feeling now. She had hated lying to him, but at least now she wouldn't have to play dumb anymore. We had agreed that she needed to get Lyndon to tell her something that would convince the others *they* could trust him. And she had. It was clear his loyalty was to Taylor and did not reside with Thaddeus. Lane had expressed there was a *protective* nature to Lyndon, and that she felt safe with him. I too had felt this—not immediately, but when he'd released my arm and stepped back, it was there. He had given up control, trusting me, and I knew then he wouldn't hurt me, nor would he deliver me to Thaddeus. Knowing what I know now, he probably hated the evil bastard more than any of us. And he'd cared for Zuriel enough to tend to his wounds and take him somewhere he thought he would be safe. Zuriel was safe and in good hands now with my friend Grier.

Sitting on my bed, I watched as the video call window swirled and then connected.

"Emma Peel strikes again," Lane shot out, grinning wildly as her image came into view. She was on her bed with her laptop like I was. Even through the so-so quality of the video feed, her lovely clear complexion appeared radiant next to the black turtleneck she wore, the shiny dark waves of her hair framing her face and tumbling over her shoulders.

"Emma Peel wouldn't have messed up her disguise like I did," I said sardonically.

"Good thing you hadn't been confronted by the *evil Z. Z. Von Schnerk*," Lane added using a sinister voice, expanding on the reference to the 1967 Avengers TV show.

"No, just a big scary—albeit attractive tracker Seraph who has been searching for me for several years now," I countered.

Lane just grinned bigger.

"Okay, I'm sure you've heard aaaall about my unexpected meet-up with Lyndon, but I want to know what went down at his place before all that." I moved my laptop from the bed to my lap, leaning back against the headboard of my bed.

"Tell me what you thought of Lyndon first," Lane said, fiddling with her ear.

"Besides the fact that he has a steel grip?" I gave her a bulgy-eyed expression.

"Aunt Lyyynn." Lane faked a pout.

"Well, clearly he is much different from the persona he projects to the world. And I'm pretty sure the only reason I didn't totally freak out when I saw him was because you had praised him *and* you trusted him."

"And?" She gave me a tightlipped grin.

"And he proved himself worthy of my trust. He could have very easily stolen me away and presented me to Thaddeus." I tilted my head. "He's a lot more patient than I had anticipated he would be—I'm not easy to deal with," I added, laughing the last part out. "Now tell me—how did things go down at your end? Zach only gave us the highlights."

She yawned then, causing me to yawn. "Well, you know I was finding it challenging to keep secrets from him. And during our previous time together, I could feel that he wanted to tell me things too," Lane began. Then she went on to give me the play-by-play of the night's events. "When I got to the group home, I texted him from my car, and he'd responded saying he would send up the elevator for me. When I got off the elevator to the lower level, I half expected him to be waiting for me in the doorway of his apartment like usual, but when I came up to the door, it was actually locked.

"Locked?" I said, scrunching up my face.

She smirked and shrugged one of her shoulders. "It wasn't like him to not greet me at the door."

"What did you do?"

"I knocked and then waited." She shrugged again. "I heard the lock disengage. Then the door opened a crack, and I pushed it the rest of the way open."

"Did he greet you at the door?"

"No, he was across the room, sitting on one of the armchairs."

"Did he say hello at least?"

"Actually, he told me to come have a seat, and patted the armchair next to him, the one I had come to accept as *mine*."

"Then what did you do?"

"I took off my boots and hung my jacket, then went over and stood in front of him."

"Did he say anything, then?"

"Nope, but I smiled at him and said, *'Happy Valentine's'*. But, he didn't smile back."

"Oh Lane, that must have been maddening *and* confusing."

"I felt so stupid standing there holding out the gift I brought him," she said, her tone filled with frustration.

"Did he have something for you? What did you bring him?" I shot a quick glance at the nightstand on Redmond's side of the bed. The massage oil that had been there last night was now gone.

"He questioned my bringing him a gift—stating he hadn't gotten me anything. I got him a framed photo I had taken of him and Taylor," Lane said, pulling my attention back. "I watched him unwrap the gift, and his face seemed to brighten. Then he even smiled." Lane's voice lilted. "I told him I thought it would be nice to have a photo of the two of them in his home."

"How did he respond to that?" I asked, pondering what Redmond may have done with the oil, knowing how annoyed he was.

"Said that he'd never done Valentine's day and apologized for not getting me anything. I told him it didn't matter—that I was more interested in just time with him, anyway."

"I didn't get Redmond anything," I admitted, not exactly proud of myself for that. I'd make it up to him, though. "Then what?"

"He told me to sit again, then said, *'Thank you for the thoughtful gift'*. I sat down and just smiled at him, unsure of what to say. Something felt different with him, but I couldn't put my finger on it. Then I asked, *'How have you been?'*" Lane rolled her eyes. "All he said was, *'Busy,'* and continued to stare at me. I asked if everything was alright, saying that he seemed *distant*."

"What did he have to say about that?"

"Just that he had a lot on his mind. I hated that we weren't talking like we usually did, so I reached out for his hand and gave it a squeeze. Then when he placed his hand over mine, I said, *'I missed you'*."

I smiled at Lane, waiting for the next step in what was turning out to be a romantic moment.

"Then I said, remember when you asked me if I had ever witnessed something otherworldly?"

Okay, maybe not so romantic, I mused. "And?"

"He brushed it off, but I wanted to give him another opening to share more. Obviously, I know everything, but I needed him to *want* to tell me." Lane gave me a haughty expression, tilting her head side to side. "I couldn't go first. I was afraid if he knew the truth—that I'd known about him all along, he might kick me out, and it would be the end of things. I couldn't risk that." She shook her head *no*.

I mirrored her head shake. "But you've already fallen for him, haven't you?" I switched my head shake to a nod.

"Yes, and I wasn't willing to lose him," she said, her voice softening. "So I said, *'If I tell you a secret—would you tell me one of yours?'*"

"That was kind of a long shot—don't you think?" I gave her a skeptical side-eye.

"I know, but I felt like I was running out of options."

"Did he take the bait?"

She raised an eyebrow. "It wasn't *what* he said, it was more about *how* he said it. He said, *'What secrets could you possibly have, Lane?'* in almost a sarcastic tone," Lane emphasized.

"And you said what?" I asked, my eyebrows stretching up my forehead.

Lane grinned. "That I wanted to kiss him."

My mouth rounded as I drew in a breath. "Wowsers—not what I expected."

"I know—neither did he. I was instantly embarrassed. It had been waaay too forward, I felt."

"What was his response?"

"He closed his eyes, and I thought I had mistaken his feelings for me, but when I went to pull my hand free of his—instead of letting me go, he held my hand tighter."

"Lane," I breathed out.

"Aunt Lynn, when he opened his eyes, he had tears in them. He said my name then, as though he were in pain," Lane said, her words breathy.

"Oh-my-gawd-wadjado?" I rushed out, my heart pounding.

"I leaned forward and pressed my lips against his," Lane said before covering her mouth with her hand.

I gasped. "I'm guessing you didn't share that tidbit with Leo."

"Ya—right! Nope. Of course, my phone rang right then and Lyndon broke the kiss, suggesting I pick up the call." She made a sour face.

"Who was calling?" I was pissed, and it wasn't even my moment.

"At the time, I figured it was just Mason wondering where I was—I hadn't gone to the party—went to see Lyndon instead first."

"I'm guessing you didn't pick up?"

"No way—I've been waiting a long time to kiss Lyndon." She laughed a little.

"Did you kiss him again?" This conversation felt like we were a couple of teenage girls sharing secrets.

"No," she said with a pout, "but he did say he'd been thinking about kissing me as well. But then he changed the subject to wanting to make me dinner as his Valentine's day gift."

"Boooooo," I said, shaking my head.

"Hey, I was thrilled over the shift in his mood. And get this, when *his* cellphone rang, for the first time—he didn't pick it up," she said in mock surprise. "Not only didn't he pick up the call—he shut off his phone. When I questioned it he said he didn't want to be bothered this evening. I asked if he could do that, and he said, *'I just did.'*" She made another joking expression of surprise, her mouth agape.

"Okay—no booo this time," I said with a grin.

Lane laughed. "We joked and flirted while he prepared our meal. He could be a professional chef—you know. After dinner, I asked him if he ever considered it. But he said, *'no'.*" She gave me a weak smile. "I was feeling better now that his dark mood had left, and asked if it was about the money—his working with Thaddeus."

"Quite the leap."

"I know. I took a chance. I wanted to get at the heart of why he stayed with Thaddeus, but he told me he had *'plenty of money'*."

"Why stay?"

"I couldn't understand either and said if it's not the money, why do you stay here—in this tiny apartment?"

"To be close to Taylor, obviously," I answered like a genius.

"Yes, but not just for that. He said he was afraid of what would happen to Taylor and the group home if he left. He added that it was his home just as much as it was Taylor's."

"I can see that," I said, agreeing. "We know how Taylor ended up there. Why didn't Lyndon just take him out of there?" We knew he'd been given back to Children's Services. Thaddeus had originally adopted Taylor, then surrendered him like an unwanted pet when he couldn't manage his special needs, but clearly there was more to the story.

"That was my question, too. I asked why he didn't just make a new home somewhere else—just the two of them."

"What did he say?" Seemed like the obvious option to me.

"What he usually says, *'It's complicated'*. But I made him tell me why."

"Why?" I asked impatiently.

Lane pulled at the collar of her black turtleneck sweater. "He explained that he had other duties that often take him away and he couldn't always watch over Taylor. Said that he was in good hands there, *'that the staff adore him, and he loves them'*. And that he couldn't provide the type of care he needed like the trained professionals could, particularly with the special physical requirements and conditions that would change as he grows up."

"Was that when he told you Taylor was his son?"

"Zach told you," she said as though disappointed, like he'd stolen the plot twist.

"Ya—but I wanted to hear your version."

"Actually, that wasn't when he told me," she said smugly. "My suggestion to him was to have a private home and a dedicated person to stay with Taylor, but he disagreed. He made it seem as though he had to atone for something, and I asked if his protecting Taylor was his penance?"

"What do you think he's done—did he tell you?"

"No, all he said was, *'I just don't trust him'*, meaning Thaddeus. And that Thaddeus was a despicable person."

"That's old news," I said with a sneer.

"Exactly. Then I said, stop working for him. It's like an albatross hanging over you, robbing you of your peace, but then he said, *'I can't—not yet'*."

"Not yet?" What was this guy's deal, I wondered.

"He thinks that if he stops working for Thaddeus—he'll do something to Taylor."

"But why?"

"He said to punish him. That's when he told me Taylor was his son."

"Oh, boy," I huffed out.

"Oh boy, is right. I asked him why he didn't tell me about Taylor. It was clear he loved him. But he said that Thaddeus was the only one who knew. That once Thaddeus had learned about the Earthbound having offspring, he'd demanded 'seed' from the males of his group to be used for his experiments. Thaddeus artificially inseminated several women, Lyndon told me."

"How does he know Taylor is his?"

"Taylor was the only offspring Thaddeus was able to keep alive."

"Lane, holy shit." My heart ached in my chest.

"Devastating, I know. Either the mothers died during pregnancy or the babies died due to genetic complications," Lane shared. Not that I needed those details.

"All but Taylor," I said, thinking about his sweet little face. "Leo had told us about the mothers and the offspring they had encountered."

"Me too," Lane said. "Thaddeus informed Lyndon that the baby would survive, but it was clear by the scans he had several genetic abnormalities. The worst part…." Lane paused. "…Lyndon was instructed to drop the woman off at the hospital, that even if she survived—which she did not, the child would more than likely die like the others."

"What a sadistic fuuaack!" I pounded my fist into Redmond's pillows beside me.

"Lyndon did as he was told," Lane continued, "and the woman did die. Lyndon told Thaddeus the child had lived. Said he second guessed telling Thaddeus the minute he did it though, because it was soon after that Thaddeus set in motion Taylor's adoption, acting as if he were some hero unaffected by the baby's physical issues. In truth, all he wanted was to do experiments on him." Lane drew in a shaky breath through her nose, letting it slowly out through her mouth. "Then, when Taylor showed to be autistic, Thaddeus was furious. That's when Lyndon found out Taylor was his. Thaddeus had said, *'Figures, this one turned out to be stupid—it was your sample that made him, after all.'*"

"Oh my gaaawd, Lane," I said, disgusted.

"I know. Thaddeus didn't want him anymore—said he was too difficult to handle. That he had to continuously sedate him, and doing so only screwed up his test results."

I threw up my hands. "How the hell did Lyndon not kill him right then and there?"

"He'd wanted to rip his head off, but instead he went another route, suggesting the group home. Told Thaddeus it would make him look good—that he was going to look bad if anything happened to the child or if he died in Thaddeus's care. Thaddeus had hated the idea but had hated the potential of looking bad more, but he's held it over Lyndon as an unspoken threat ever since."

"I knew Taylor's story was horrible. But that's worse than I ever imagined." I took in a steadying breath. "How did you eventually get to the part where you told him you knew about his kind?"

"Uhm… the topic shifted to you."

"Me?"

Lane huffed out a breath. "He caught me off guard—said he knew about my aunt. I tried to sidestep, saying that you're not my real aunt—biological that is, but that I really needed—longed to have a female in my life, someone to talk about stuff like relationships, etc..

I tried to explain again how I had grown up surrounded by uncles—my dads' close friends, but then he cut me off, saying, '*I know you know more, more than you're letting on.*'"

"I know Lyndon knows about me—he said as much," I said, cutting her off.

"Yeah—I know. I tried to explain, but he said there was no need and that he was actually relieved, and happy not having to lie to me now."

"He must have had a million questions—since you'd only been playing at not knowing."

"The first question he had was how I knew about his kind, and about Taylor? I told him I hated lying to him, too. Then I told him how I had come to be at the group home. And that after you had visited here, I was asked to keep an eye on Taylor—keep him safe. And I knew Taylor was safe with him."

"And you told Lyndon he was the reason you stayed," I said, eager to bring us back to the romantic part.

"I did. Then when I said, *I never intended to fall for…*, he filled in the *him* part with '*A beast like him*,'. And I said, '*no—for an angel*'. That's when he kissed me again."

"Ooooohh," I let out, my heart swelling in my chest. "Lyndon told me he would never do anything to hurt you, Lane. And I believe him."

"I do too. Although I wasn't sure what else I should reveal to him. I trust Lyndon—I really do, but I knew I couldn't just share the truth about my uncles, so I gave him a half-truth, explaining that my parents worked for—took care of a facility, that was basically the home—her home, for an elite team who were, *in the knowing*, using the term you'd coined for those in on things. I stated that my Uncle Leo and my Uncle Kris—whom he had met, were one of seven uncles who were also on this team."

"I'm guessing he bought it?" We had previously agreed she couldn't tell Lyndon about The Guards of Haven, not yet anyway.

"Hook, line and sinker," Lane said. "He realized it explained Shayne being friends with my parents. That obviously I knew about him, too. And Julianna—though I explained that she really was my professor." Lane tucked a section of her hair behind her ear, then fiddled with the lobe.

"What else did you tell him—he said you told him *everything*, but I didn't know what that meant exactly." I ran my hand across the top of Redmond's pillow, wondering when he would be back from the studio.

"I told him that the team knows how he feels about Thaddeus, that he didn't want to work for him—that he hated him. That it would be a good idea for him to talk with them about what he knows about Thaddeus. *And* that they might be able to help him escape Thaddeus's hold on him."

"Good idea to let Leo and the gang tell Lyndon the full truth when the time comes."

"My thoughts exactly. I felt the same way when he asked how you—*my aunt*, fit into all this. I said you could explain."

"Really—he didn't pressure you for more?"

"He was fine with it, but shared that he knew you could sense him—them. Told me about overhearing our phone call. Said it explained a lot as to why Thaddeus was so adamant on finding you."

"What else?" I asked, pondering how I would explain myself to Lyndon.

"We talked more, but I was careful not to say too much where you were concerned, focusing more on how I had learned things growing up, etc.. It was late by then and I'd had to get going or my parents would have blown a gasket. That's when he said he needed to see about Zuriel, anyway—needed to make sure *he* was safe."

"And that's when he ran into me," I said in a sing-song voice, before elaborating quickly on our collision, ending the adventure at where I'd left him at Grier's place.

"He told me much the same," Lane confirmed. "He's supposed to meet me here in an hour. I need to meet up with Jules to discuss my internship, but he'll be staying here with...."

"Your *Uncles*?" I finished for her. It was crucial that Thaddeus's people didn't find out about them. Knowing could put everyone in danger. But clearly things were about to change, at least where Lyndon was concerned.

"You got it," Lane said, "So I better get a move on." She shifted off her bed, taking her laptop with her.

"I need to hear more about this internship of yours—and you still need to catch me up on Jana and Natalie."

"I will—I promise," she said, setting the laptop down on her desk, tilting the screen up so her face was still in view. "I'm sure there will be plenty more to share after this gathering."

"Which reminds me, I need to circle back with Grier—get the what's-what on Zuriel and how she's navigating this whole thing.

"One more *in the knowing*," Lane said with a wink. "Later, Aunt Lynn—love you."

"Love you, too," I said before logging off the video call.

Chapter 6 

North Haven, the afternoon of February 15th, Ottawa, Canada

Lane's discussion with her parents and the other males in her life regarding her views and feelings about Lyndon had gone better and been more favorable this time around. This was due to the fact that Lane had shared further details of how Lyndon was Taylor's father and about his intentions to leave his service under Thaddeus. Those details coupled with the unexpected run-in between Lynn and Lyndon, their conversation and the joint actions that followed, had been the clinchers that finally swayed all of them into believing what Lane had been begging for them to see. Lyndon could be trusted. He had proven himself trustworthy because he could have easily taken Lynn to Thaddeus right then, but he hadn't. In fact, he had trusted her to take the lead concerning his fellow tracker, his *friend*, Zuriel. Lyndon had told Lane his truth. And today he would have the opportunity to tell the other the rest.

When the chime for someone's arrival sounded, Lane strode from the kitchen to the front door. Both Leo and Kris were on her heels, but before opening the door, she turned back to them. "Seriously, I'm not a teenage girl—back it up," she said, the palms of her hands raised as if she were literally going to push them back.

Like scolded puppies, the two retreated several paces back and into the living room area across from the entrance. Her fathers, Max and Julian, were already seated on the long couch, endeavoring to appear calm.

Lane swiveled back to the front door to grab the doorknob, turning it and drawing the door open. "Well hello there," she said in greeting to the well-dressed male at her door.

Lyndon stood on the front step, his hands unthreateningly behind his back. His lush black hair was bravely pushed back away from his face, his fabulous masculine features on full display, his scar no longer a concern. He wore a long pale grey overcoat, the front of it open over navy slacks and a dress shirt in the same colour. The clothes were dressier than he usually wore and looked new, the dark blue colour enhancing his already beautiful deep green eyes. When he just stood there looking nervous, Lane reached for him, taking hold of his arm, and gently guided him through the entryway. "Let's get this party started, shall we?" Lane said, shutting the front door, feeling the weight of the moment.

"Yes, let's," Lyndon responded, giving her a tender smile.

"Here—I'll hang up your coat," she offered, helping him slide out of his overcoat. Stepping to the side, she then pressed her hand against the wall. A door to a concealed closet opened, and then she swapped out her coat for his before shutting the closet door. "You look strikingly handsome today, by the way." She gave him a quick wink.

"Thank you," Lyndon said, before turning to survey the others in the room.

"You've already met my Uncle Leo and Uncle Kris," Lane announced, shrugging into her coat.

"Lyndon—welcome," Leo said, nodding and taking a stride forward.

"We are pleased you are here," Kris added, remaining where he stood.

"Hello again," Lyndon responded, his face stoic.

Both Max and Julian stood from where they'd been seated on the couch. They were both dressed in casual black slacks and sweaters,

Julian's a heather grey that matched his long hair, and Max in black mirroring the colour of his hair. Observing the two men now, Lyndon could see where Lane got her colouring and gorgeous wavy black hair.

"Lyndon, you remember my fathers, Max and Julian," Lane said, continuing the reintroductions. Then she adjusted the strap of her purse over her shoulder, resting it across the front of her coat.

"Yes, thank you for welcoming me into your home," Lyndon said, giving a courteous bow of his head.

"We trust our daughter," Max said. "Please don't disappoint her."

"I would never," Lyndon said, raising his big hands, placing the palms of them over his heart.

"If you continue to guard our daughter, you are welcome in my home," Julian offered, his tone softer than that of his husband.

"Lyndon," Lane said, drawing his attention. "I have to go see Professor Forest about my internship—but I'll be back soon." Lane turned to the others. "Can I trust you all to play nice while I'm gone?"

"Scouts honor," Kris tossed out, making the three-finger salute.

"Like you were ever a scout," Lane tossed back, chuckling as she zipped up her coat.

Facing Lyndon, she said, "I'm sorry I can't stay—but it will be fine—trust me."

"Always," Lyndon said, giving her a nod of his head and a sincere smile.

Lane reached for his hand and squeezed it. Then she reached up, leaning in to plant a kiss on his cheek. "I'll see you soon."

Before Lyndon could respond, Lane opened the front door and was on her way. "Bye, all," she called as the door shut behind her.

"Lyndon, come have a seat," Leo said, leading the way to the large seating area where Julian and Max currently stood. Lyndon liked Leo's manner and the timber of his voice, and how it made him feel at ease. Even with Leo's thick muscularity, the way he dressed in casual khakis and a loose dress shirt gave way to an easygoing style. Kris, in his faded jeans and black t-shirt, seemed even more relaxed. As they approached, Max and Julian relaxed back down in their previous spots on the couch. Across from them, Leo and Kris took up residence in the two light blue fabric-covered chairs.

Lyndon glanced around the open space, smiling when he saw the amazing kitchen. To the right there was a billiard space with a pool table and snooker table, a bar, and a huge TV with a large multi-seat sectional couch. "Thank you again for having me here," Lyndon said, turning his focus back and taking the open spot next to Lane's parents. Lyndon shifted his focus to Leo, watching as the large man leaned forward in his chair.

"Where is your boss?" Leo asked, his earlier easygoingness now razor sharp intent.

Lyndon shrugged a shoulder. "I told Lane that Thaddeus had informed me he was heading to Brazil—for what, I don't know— don't care. Any day he's away—is a good day." He interlaced his fingers, resting them on his lap, surveying the men around him.

"You told her he took all his personal belongs with him, like it meant something," Leo stated, his attention firmly on Lyndon.

"Yes." Lyndon nodded. "He took his clothes with him—not that it means anything. It's the fact that he took what he calls his *most prized possessions* with him on this trip."

"Dare I ask?" Leo said, leaning back in his chair.

"Thaddeus is as sick as they come," Lyndon stated. "Only he— and maybe a handful of serial killers would have things such as these for keepsakes." He cleared his throat. "He takes the vertebrae, the sacrum and coccyx, and the scapulae of the halflings he performs experiments on." He dropped his gaze briefly to his hands in his lap, then returned to look at Leo. "He has them bleached to an unnatural white, then stores them in a special cabinet in his private lab—but I noticed they were gone when I was there last." Lyndon followed Leo's gaze as it shifted to Kris.

"Lane told us your feelings about working with him. How about *you* tell us in your own words?" Kris stated, getting right to it.

Lyndon blew a slow breath out through his nostrils. "You already know I loathe the sick bastard. I detest being beholden to one such as him, but I… I feel you need to understand *why*, in the beginning, we made the choices that we did—not that it excuses what happened after." Lyndon shifted his focus back and forth between Kris and Leo.

"That would be a good start," Leo said, leaning forward again in his chair.

"We hadn't been privy to Thaddeus's plans prior to us—all the Earthbound, ending up on Earth. Thaddeus and I…." Lyndon paused. "…We had been partnered on the Celaeno star for quite some time. It had been our time together that had allowed for discussions over the grievances concerning our roles." Lyndon tightened his laced fingers, the knuckles cracking. "My apologies. It's something I do when I'm stressed," he said, turning to Lane's parents. "It's an impolite habit." He raised his clasped hands.

"We are all feeling the stress, Lyndon," Max responded.

"Please go on," Julian prompted him.

Lyndon turned back to Leo and Kris. "Of course, Thaddeus's complaints had been monumental, while mine had been more about a lack of recognition for my contributions. All we had wanted was more freedom to come and go from Pleiades to Earth as we pleased. None of us knew of his plot to cast down the others on Celaeno to Earth."

"I understand your role had been to oversee the biology of regeneration, the morphogenic processes as they relate to changes in an organism's behavior, morphology, and physiology in response to unique environments."

"You are correct." Lyndon was surprised at their knowledge and had expected to be berated for his words, but instead Leo had shown interest in his skills. Relieved, Lyndon relaxed his finger. "Being that regeneration was basically regulated by asexual cellular processes, Thaddeus originally thought my skills were useful for his plan of populating the Earth with pureblood Seraphim."

"What about his other followers?" Kris asked, displaying no judgment.

"Thaddeus had made sure we all had money, but just enough to survive. He has some of them running his facilities."

"We know all about the facility managers: Amahle, Kendrick, Marcus, and the other three," Leo stated, his tone still without judgment.

"The others—like me, he treats like his personal tracker dogs." Lyndon tightened his grip, then quickly loosened it again to avoid the rude cracking of his knuckles.

"We're familiar," Kris said. "However, we've lost track of the one called Ariadne."

Lyndon drew in a ragged breath. "Us too," he shared. "She deserted our modest faction within days of our being cast down."

"Why only two females in your group?" Kris queried, leaning an elbow on the arm of the chair.

"Thaddeus considered us all equal on Pleiades, but here on Earth, females—human or Seraph, are inferior in his mind. But he's a fool."

"I'm not sure I understand why you were so reliant on Thaddeus," Kris said, rubbing the back of his fingers along his jaw.

"We felt indebted to him. Like I said, he was the only one prepared to be on Earth. We all had to rely on him for protection and shelter in the beginning. He'd constructed an identity and background for himself, but none of us had any records to show who we were. Getting any kind of real jobs back then was almost impossible—that's how we got stuck serving the monster."

"Lane also told us why you stayed," Kris added. "I'm sure there is more to it, though. Why did you choose to live at the group home?"

"It was my idea to be stationed at the group home, even though Thaddeus treats it like he's doing me a favor." Lyndon rolled his eyes.

"A favor?" Leo questioned.

"After he discovered that my *specialty* was more about tissue loss and not the independent creation of complete organisms, he had considered me mostly useless. That's when he set his focus on learning about creation, by testing on the halflings." Lyndon felt a hand on his arm and turned to see Julian's sympathetic expression. "All I cared about was making sure my son was safe and no one ever hurt him again." Lyndon held Julian's gaze. No one said anything in response, though indifferent expressions from the others shifted swiftly to that of empathy. "Besides, it provides me with the solitude and privacy I prefer, and I'm grateful not to be under his thumb. Before all this… exchange of information, I was working to come up with a plan for Taylor's safety and our freedom."

"That's very brave of you," Julian said, patting his arm.

"What do you know about Thadeus's interest in reproductive endocrinology?" Leo asked then.

"I… I don't know…anything, actually," Lyndon said, frowning. "This is new information to me."

"We obtained a list—one we assumed were patient names, those in Thaddeus's study of childhood diseases," Leo elaborated. "When we ran the names through our many databases, it turned out to be a list of doctors, reproductive endocrinologists—top physicians in their fields, to be more accurate. The first doctor on the list is located in Brazil—he works for a group who are leaders in assisted human reproduction—is that why Thaddeus was there?"

"Why would Thaddeus go to Brazil when there's one of the top fertility clinics closer in New York City, or the one in Los Angeles rated the highest for IVF success?" Kris asked, scrutinizing Thaddeus's choices.

"Honestly, I have no knowledge of these doctors." Lyndon shook his head several times, his worry and anger rising. "I swear to you— on my son's life, I know nothing of these places or these specialists.

Leo glanced at Kris as though skeptical. "Were you originally assigned to track down Lynn?" Leo asked, changing topics.

Lyndon breathed a sigh of relief at the shift in subject. "Marcus had seen her before—then he saw her again, this time talking to a Watcher. I'm guessing she can sense them too, like she can my kind." Lyndon paused but got no confirmation. Continuing, he said, "Marcus spotted her, but I'm the one who figured out it was her in the recording of Thaddeus's private lab—I recognized her from when she visited the group home."

Kris looked at Leo this time, then back at Lyndon. "How did you track her to Florida?" he asked, moving the topic of Lynn along.

"He seemed more and more desperate to find her—I couldn't have cared less, but I'd found out she was married to some guy who lives in Florida—correction, *lived* in Florida. They're divorced, yes?" No one answered. "Anyway—I wanted to stay close to home—keep watch on Taylor *and* spend more time getting to know Lane, so I sent Zuriel."

"How did he find her?" Kris asked, stealing another glance at Leo.

"He didn't, really." Lyndon relaxed his hands again, flexing his fingers. "Zuriel spent time following several leads but hadn't found anything major," he began again. "Thaddeus had wanted to speak with Zuriel, but I had a bad feeling about it. I knew it wasn't going to go well, but I hadn't anticipated the outcome. I'd told him that Zuriel had taken a chance on a lead. However, it had been the wrong woman. When I left him, Zuriel was in good spirits, focused on his return to South Florida, but when I went to retrieve him…." Lyndon paused to take a breath. "…Thaddeus had him… suspended off the ground with straps around his shoulders and waist, beaten to unconsciousness. He was so gaunt. It was clear he had been given little to no fluids or nourishment." Lyndon shook his head slowly, staring down at the floor. "He told me he threatened to take Zuriel's wings if he didn't tell him everything. Zuriel told him what he knew, but still… he took his wings."

"What did he do with them?" Leo asked.

Lyndon glanced up at Leo to see the crease between his brows deepening.

"His magnificent wings were jabbed through and speared to the wall over the door," Lyndon breathed out. "There were still remnants of his flesh clinging to where they'd been severed from his back." Lyndon brought his hand up to cover his face. When he felt Julian's hand on his arm again, he lowered his hand, then said, "Thaddeus called him a liability, said he never followed orders—he always followed orders—just not this time. Then he blamed me—said it was my error in judgment for sending him in my place. Told me to take Zuriel away—said he never wanted to see him again. The last thing he said was that he was returning to Brazil and would be gone for some time."

"What did you do?" Kris asked, leaning forward in his chair like Leo was.

"After he left, I got Zuriel down and tended to his wounds as best I could. There were barely any medical supplies left in the lab, for whatever reason. I carried him up to Thaddeus's condo and bandaged him up using the few supplies I'd found. I checked on him several times, making sure his breathing was steady and his heartbeat remained strong. Then I dressed him in some of the abandoned clothes I found—couldn't find anything for his feet, though. When he seemed a bit more stable, I took him to the place where I'd last found him."

"That's why you brought him to the hospital Lynn volunteers at," Leo added in conclusion.

"Yes. But I didn't know that then. When I originally came to find Zuriel, he'd been outside the hospital observing a doctor, a female of *personal* interest. And apparently a friend of Lynn's, Grier." He went on to explain their unusual association. "I told Zuriel about Lane and her relationship to Lynn."

"Clearly you care about him," Julian said, reaching out and touching Lyndon's arm again.

"He's not like the others—and he's my friend." Lyndon panned the faces of the men before him.

"Can we trust him not to tell Thaddeus where Lynn is?" Leo questioned him.

"Seriously? How can you even ask me that after what I just told you?" Lyndon asked, glancing at each of them.

"Please understand, Lyndon. We are just being cautious. Knowing Thaddeus as you do, I'm sure you get where I'm coming from," Leo said, leaning forward once again in his chair.

"You can trust Zuriel." Lyndon panned their faces again.

"We know why you stayed with Thaddeus," Kris stated. "But why did he?"

"Zuriel hadn't wanted to do this role—none of it, but he didn't have any other options. He had considered taking off like Ariadne had, but like me, he believed he was too ingrained in this life to find another way out now." Lyndon stared down at his hands. "He understood the difficult choices I'd made regarding Taylor. And I respected the positive attitude he embraced in spite of what had happened to us." Raising his eyes, he said, "I know he misses his life among the stars of Pleiades, his role of watching over Earth's mammals, specifically the ocean's gentle giants and even the tiny sea creatures." Lyndon shook his head. "I don't know how he does it, but he can communicate with them even over long distances." He smiled then. "His sole purpose was to make sure a balance was kept in the ocean between the largest and a variety of species throughout the entire food chain, down to the tiny zooplankton." His smile widened as he thought about his kind friend. Continuing, he said, "Zuriel and Marcus had originally been assigned to work out of the Brazil location, but then when it closed, they were reassigned to New York City."

"So when you borrowed Zuriel to track down Lynn, that's when Addison was assigned to New York?" Kris questioned.

"Correct." He nodded, understanding that these men had intel on all of them.

"What's your take on Marcus?" Leo asked then.

"He's an asshole. He's not a monster like Thaddeus, and I'm sure he hates being beholden to him, like I do. Still, he enjoys his indulgences." Lyndon huffed and shook his head.

"Are you *friends* with any of the others?" Max asked, no longer keeping his thoughts to himself.

"No." He shook his head again. "Did you know Julianna before she was Lane's professor?"

"Yes," Max said with a nod.

"How is it that you know Shayne?" Lyndon asked, having his own list of questions.

"Let's just say we go way back," Kris offered with a wry smile.

"Who was with you at the hospital when you brought Zuriel there?" Leo asked, tossing out another shift in topic.

"Like I told Lynn, no one was with me." Lyndon glanced at each of them, shaking his head leisurely back and forth.

"Could it have been Thaddeus?" Julian asked, his voice shaky.

"He wouldn't waste his time," Lyndon assured him.

Kris leaned back in his chair. "What about Addison?"

"If Lynn sensed someone—if it *was* Addison, he wasn't *with* me."

"Why was Addison hanging around outside Frank's restaurant?" Kris asked, continuing his inquiry about Lyndon's fellow tracker.

"Frank? Wait, you mean Francesca? You know her, too," Lyndon confirmed. He could tell by their expressions that there was more to the question, but he let it go. "With one of the Earthbound close by, Marcus probably sent him to check out the place. Addison is an ass— a miscreant. He was working out of the Norway facility—but it's closed down now, as you probably know already." He was no fan of Addison, that was for sure.

"Why close it down?" Leo questioned this time.

"No idea."

"Where is Kendrick now?" Leo asked, dealing out more inquiries.

"Again, no idea. But I could probably find out—if you needed. I should warn you, though, Kendrick is waiting to hear back from some woman regarding her sons who, based on the photos she showed him, are halflings."

"We know about that too," Leo stated.

"How? Wait—no—the woman, that was Lynn in disguise again, wasn't it? And I'm guessing the photos of the sons were fakes?"

"You got it." Kris gave him a smug grin.

"Hold on, she had two bodyguards with her. Were they the same guys who were with her in the lab?" Lyndon asked, catching onto things. "Kendrick said they were huge." He glanced back and forth between Leo and Kris, wondering if they were in fact, said bodyguards. "Lane said you two belonged to some *covert* organization."

Max and Julian remained quiet while Leo and Kris exchanged glances. Then Leo said, "We know the organization works under the guise that they are helping kids—sick kids, but we know he's experimenting *on* these children, and the halflings he locates. We are also trying to locate these halflings, but for the purpose of keeping them safe. We also keep watch over the labs."

"What are you—some secret branch of the government?"

"Think of us as more of a covert special ops team," Leo said, clearly not wanting to give him more.

"Look, I came here alone. I answered all your questions," Lyndon said, needing some interchange.

"I have a question," Julian said, speaking up. All eyes turned to him. "What are your intentions with our daughter?"

Lyndon turned in his seat to face Julian and Max. "Respectfully," he began, then literally took a knee in front of both of them. "…I would die for her."

"Let's hope it doesn't come to that," Max said, motioning for Lyndon to stand.

"If that is the case, then we have something to show you," Leo stated, pushing up from his chair.

Lyndon stood next to Kris as Leo placed his thumb on a scan pad and then punched in a code next to what looked to be a very solid door. The heavy door made a loud click and then swooshed into a space in the wall like a pocket door, revealing stairs that descended to a lower level.

At the bottom of the stairs he was led through a series of designated underground spaces utilized for the team's top-secret ventures, including a spacious room with a full facility gym and training area, along with a tactical room loaded with all kinds of weapons.

Upon returning through the door to the main level, Kris asked, "Do you have any questions for us now that you've seen our facility?"

"Not at the moment—but I do feel better knowing that Lane has a safe home, and people watching over her." He pictured Lane's beautiful face and smiled.

"Then now would be a good time for you to meet the others," Leo said, turning to continue up the hall to the open living space they'd been in earlier.

As they emerged near the kitchen, Lyndon saw five massive men standing in front of the long kitchen island, each as tall as Leo and Kris, with thick muscular builds easily seen through the variation in clothing they each wore.

"Lyndon, this is Professor Bennet Frost. He works at the university Lane attends, *and* he's our martial arts master." Leo pointed to the first man in the lineup.

"Call me *Ben*," he said, extending an arm, his hand out for a shake.

"Hello," Lyndon said, shaking his hand, noting the man had long hair that he kept back in a braid.

"This is Marquis Malouel, our security expert," Leo continued, introducing the next man.

"*Marq*," the dark-skinned giant said, stepping up and clasping Lyndon's hand in both of his. His long white dreadlocks spilled forward over his shoulder as he gave Lyndon a nod with his full-grip handshake.

"Marq, it is," Lyndon said. "Greetings."

"Next we have Zachery Glacier," Leo said, extending a hand towards another giant, this one's hair a pale blond brush cut.

"Everyone calls me *Zach*," he said, "and my talent is with pyrotechnics and explosives." He mouthed a silent *boom*, emphasizing it with a spread of fingers on both his hands.

"You still have all your fingers—you must be good," Lyndon said, glancing down at the man's hands before exchanging another shake.

Zach laughed before taking over Leo's role, introducing the man next to him. "This big fella in the scrubs is Nicolas North. He's our medical specialist." Zach slapped Nic on the back.

"I'm going to guess, *Nic*—yes?" Lyndon offered, feeling more relaxed, extending a hand to the man with the long midnight-coloured hair.

"Excellent guess," Nic said with a gracious smile before shaking Lyndon's hand.

At the end of the line stood the largest man in the group, his resemblance so similar to that of Leo's they could be brothers, though his hair and eyes were much darker than Leo's.

"Last but not least, we have Hayden Polar, our maestro of hand-to-hand combat," Zach said, bringing his hands up as though to protect himself.

Haydon chuckled and tossed out a few fake punches.

"I'm sure I could learn quite a lot from you, Hayden," Lyndon said, going in for the last handshake.

"I go by *Den*—I know, not so on trend like the other names," he said, grinning, giving Lyndon's hand a firm grip and shake.

"Neither of you shared your specialties," Lyndon said, turning to Leo and Kris.

"He's an architect—has a photographic memory for anything relating to buildings," Kris answered for Leo.

"And what about you, Kris?"

"Weapons of all kinds," Leo said on Kris's behalf. "His forte is knives."

"And I'm a brilliant chef," Kris added. "Is anyone hungry?"

A resounding "Yes" was shared by all, followed by several "Whoops".

"You're all… *big* guys, a few of you are even bigger than me, and your varying expertise makes you quite a powerful force… and I say this with no disrespect." Lyndon put up his hand in surrender. "But I'm doubtful any of you are a match for my fellow Earthbound."

Leo smiled at him and then took a step back from the group. "Here's the thing, Lyndon," Leo said, right before an expansive set of white, grey-tipped wings burst through the back of his tailored shirt.

Chapter 7 

The Beach House, late afternoon, February 15th, South Florida

Redmond still wasn't back from his *work* at the studio, and I wasn't sure when he'd be home, since he hadn't responded to any of my texts. I'd also texted Zach to see if he was upset with me too, but all he'd texted in his response was that he hadn't anticipated I'd have gone to the hospital on my own without telling someone. I didn't bother to write back, but my reasoning on the situation was that my gut had said to *go*. However, I suppose I could have left a note for Redmond. He'd still be mad that I went on my own, but at least he would have known where I had gone.

What's done is done, I thought. And right now, I needed to see if I could get in a call with Grier before I had to go pick up the twins from school. I sent Grier a quick text to see if she wanted to circle back,

Hey, are you feeling up for a chat?

Grier wrote back,

Zuriel is resting. Did you want to come by?

As much as I would prefer to talk with her in person, with Redmond already mad at me, not being here when he got home was the last thing I should do. I texted her another suggestion,

I need to stick around home. How about a video chat?

A video call would be better than our texting back and forth about the current state of things.

She seemed to agree and wrote back with,

Sounds good. Give me a few minutes to get on my laptop.

Grier had shared with me a secure reusable link for video chatting about a month ago, a method that she normally reserved for her online clients. I would have been okay with a regular phone call, but being able to see someone's face when exchanging sensitive information always felt better to me, and I texted back with a simple, 'Perfect'.

I adjusted the pillows behind my back, getting comfortable on my bed again for my second video call of the day. Then, I clicked on the link to open the virtual waiting room for the call.

A few moments after I entered what Grier had called the 'safe space' room, her smiley face appeared on the screen. "Hey, neighbor," she greeted me.

"Hey, back," I said, noticing she had changed out of her scrubs too, and currently donned her yellow hoodie pullover. "Where are you?" I didn't recognize the background decor.

"Oh, right, I'm in my office. Didn't want to wake Zuriel." She turned in her chair, arms out as though introducing me to the space. Behind her was a large bookcase. The center shelf contained a row of small, framed photographs of beach dunes done in grey-scale, giving the backdrop a soft, relaxing feel to the space.

"I'm guessing you've had quite an interesting day."

"*Unexpected* is the word I'd use." She rolled her eyes. "How are things at your end?"

"Buh! Other than Redmond being pissed at me, I'd say things are relatively okay. But it seems you and I weren't the only ones having an eye-opening time."

"Really? Do tell." She leaned in closer to her laptop, like I was the one that had all the juicy details to tell.

"How much did Zuriel tell you about Thaddeus?" I asked, directing the conversation. I did have some interesting stuff I'd learned about Jana and Natalie, but I wasn't ready to go into all that just yet. I was more interested in how my happy doctor friend was faring with her new reality.

Grier leaned back in her office chair. "He told me about the whole fake organization helping sick kids thing. About testing on those special kids with the gene mutation." She made a disgusted face and shook her head.

"And you said he told you about what Thaddeus did to him." There were probably more than just physical scars to deal with.

"He told me he doesn't remember much, but Lyndon filled him in on what happened. After he left, Zuriel explained what he'd learned from Lyndon." Her expression was filled with sorrow. "He can't fly anymore."

"Ah, so you know about the whole wing-thing," I said, sad for Zuriel but grateful I didn't have to deliver that news.

She frowned and nodded. "Thaddeus told Lyndon it was his fault Zuriel lost his wings."

"It's not Lyndon's fault Thaddeus is such a bastard," I stated.

"I can tell he is guilt-ridden, though," she said, pouting. "Lyndon shared that he had a son named Taylor. Thaddeus was the only other person who knew until now."

"There are more out there like Taylor… but I can explain that later."

"Zuriel told me about the different groups of angels, including the halflings."

"So you got the scoop on… regular angels, archangels, the Fallen, the Horsemen, the Watchers, and his kind, the Seraphim?"

"Yeah." Grier picked up a light green ball from the corner of her desk and squeezed it several times.

Stress ball, I figured. "I know it's a loaded question, but how are you feeling about all this new information?"

She squeezed the ball twice, then said, "I'm a doctor, a fact person, and celestial beings weren't part of my medical curriculum, so it's… a lot." She gave the ball another squeeze before setting it down.

"I'm with you on that. I'm ingrained in the supernatural, and it's a lot, even for me." I took a breath and then blew out a sigh.

"Oh, right. Zuriel has shared so much with me, but he didn't really know how to explain… *you*. All he said was that Thaddeus had been trying to find you, that you have an ability to sense different types of angels, including their kind. When I asked Lyndon, he said he thought it best he left it for you to clarify." She gave me a sweet smile.

I nodded my head, thinking about where to begin. All this sharing ahead of time from Zuriel and Lyndon had made my job of bringing Grier into the *knowing* much simpler. But I understood her need to know how I was involved.

"Lynn, can you tell me?" She leaned into the screen.

"Think you're ready?" Was I ready?

"Logical brain be damned. Go ahead, lay it on me." She picked up the stress ball again as though in preparation for what I had to share.

"Okay… here goes," I said, then led in with how I'd been having premonitions since I was a young child and how they'd gotten more intense as I'd gotten older. Then, I brought her through the journey of me finding my mother's journal, and my abilities heightening as the gathering got closer. I told her about my friends being descendants of certain key angels, their abilities, where they were now, about what had happened and what I'd discovered at the gathering. The kicker being that I was the daughter of the archangel Gabriel, *and* whose biological mother was a descendant of an angel who is both one of the Leaders of the 200 Fallen Angels and one of the Four Horsemen. "Thaddeus found out about my abilities and has been searching for me, using Lyndon first and then Zuriel to find me, but neither knew where I was and they'd directed Thaddeus to a dead end. So I should be safe for now."

"Wow!" she said, bringing up and resting her elbow on the desk. "I'm guessing Redmond knows." Grier smushed the stress ball in her hand.

"Oh ya. He's fully immersed." I gave her a quick grin.

"How did he find out… and adjust to all of this?" She placed the ball somewhere off-screen.

"He was part of the gathering, actually. Kind of the missing piece to things you could say—but that's a story for another time."

Returning her elbow to the desk again, she made a fist, resting her cheek against it. "Do your daughters know any of this?"

"They do." I nodded.

"How did you help them to comprehend all this?" Grier opened her fist and leaned her chin against the palm of her hand as though the weight of the topic was exhausting.

"It was easier than you'd think," I said, adding, "Gabriel still visits. Redmond's family has met him and thinks he's a long-lost cousin, but the twins know he's my biological father. They call him Gup, their version of Gabriel and Grandpa. They know who my biological mother was… and they know about my adoptive mother, Sally, who they call Grandma Sal. Though they've never met since she passed away long before they were born."

"That must have been hard—not having your mom with you for the birth of your babies."

"It was excruciatingly hard. Was even harder that I couldn't ask her questions about what I'd found in her journal. Redmond and she never got to meet either. But then you're all too familiar with what it's like to miss your parents."

"That I do. Though I can't imagine having to explain Zuriel to my parents," she laughed out, swiftly lightening the mood. "Just the fact that I have you as a close friend—someone I can talk to about all this unearthly stuff, makes it feel less heavy."

"I'm grateful you feel that way. I wasn't sure how I was ever going to be able to broach the topic with you. I hate secrets between close friends." I gave her a grateful smile. "Now tell me… how are things developing between you and Mr. Z?" I leaned my head back against the headboard, feeling more relaxed now that the proverbial *angel* was out of the bag.

She laughed, straightening from leaning on her hand. "Funny you call him that—he prefers I call him 'Z'. Even pushed for it during our therapy sessions, but I felt it was too familiar—too unprofessional then." She gave me a smirk.

"But now?" I raised my eyebrows, holding back a smile.

She laughed again. "Now it feels so natural to call him Z."

"And?" This time I smiled.

"And if we hadn't gotten to know each other like we had… been so… *intimate* with each other, the way we had." She paused, her face flushing. "If I didn't know what I know now—I would never have entertained the idea of dating a man like Zuriel ever in my life—and most definitely not one of my clients, but…."

"But?" I raised my eyebrows again and cocked my head to one side.

"I've never felt like this about anyone before." Grier shook her head lazily. "I admit it—I was drawn to him from the first moment I saw him." She continued shaking her head as though she was in disbelief of her own words.

"Grier, you told me about your struggles with those sessions—but he isn't one of your patients—not really," I pointed out, lifting my shoulders in question.

"He was, though. It's what kept me on task to stay professional all these months."

"And now you know he was just reaching out to you… from a coma." I tightened my lips trying not to laugh at the absurdity of it all.

"Right, totally normal," she said, leaning her chin back on her hand again.

"Totally," I said with a wry smile. "It is what it is—welcome to my world."

"Don't get me wrong—I'm thrilled to have him in my life, but…." She paused, straightening again in her seat.

"Buuut?"

"But now what?" she questioned, blowing out a breath.

"Well, now I'm guessing you'll figure things out together. And he'll have to build a new identity for himself. I've got friends who can help him with that, so don't worry." I gave her an exaggerated wink.

"He's already been making plans for us." She put the palms of her hands to the sides of her face, resting both elbows on the desk.

"Like?"

"Like for my birthday next week." She let her hands fall away from her face, then pointed both of her index fingers at me. "I told him I wanted to celebrate with him and my friends this year."

"Ah yes, if I recall it's the 1st anniversary of your 40th birthday—which I missed last year. You can count us in."

Grier clapped her hands, then paused her excitement to check her watch. "I should check on Z—see if he's awake," she said, grinning. "Need to figure out something for dinner—he has quite the appetite."

"I would too if I'd been in a coma for 6 months," I agreed. Just then both Summer and Snow, who had been asleep on the floor next to my bed, let out woeful "*groans,*" indicating that it was *their* mealtime. "Speaking of famished. Sounds like my furry children are ready for their meal." I shifted my laptop onto the bed before standing. "I'll let you go. But text me if you need me—or even if you don't."

"Thanks, Lynn. I'll check back with you later."

"Later." I gave her the peace sign, then logged off.

As Summer and Snow chomped on their afternoon meal, I stood staring out the patio doors to the ocean beyond, recalling the changes and happenings of the last 24 hours. A familiar shiver ran the length of my spine, and not a second later, Gabriel appeared beside me.

"Looks like you really did it this time," he said, arms crossed as he gazed out at the view.

"What?" I said, staring up at him. He was wearing a light grey suit I'd never seen before. It wasn't like him to visit in such formal attire, and it had me wondering where he had been before coming here.

"Don't I have enough to deal with?" he said in response, still staring out the patio doors.

My cellphone chimed then from where I'd left it on the kitchen counter. I strode over and picked it up to read a text message from Lily that said,

> *Hey girlfriend. Redmond said he forgot to tell you the twins were doing a sleepover here tonight. He had an errand to run and asked me to text you, let you know he packed their PJs and school clothes this morning for easy drop-off at school tomorrow. I promise not to*

keep them up late, but I can't promise Darius won't feed them junk. Have a great evening ;)

I was cool with the girls staying over at Lily's, but, "What the hell, Redmond?" I said aloud, glancing up from my cellphone only to find that Gabriel was gone.

Chapter 8 

"Natalie!" Jana cried out, her vision clearing as she took in the unexpected surroundings of her bedroom. *She'd been in Kris's room, hadn't she? Wait, no.* "Natalie—where's… my sister?" she questioned aloud, panicked, grasping then that she wasn't alone.

Kris's gorgeous ethereal face stared down at her, his brows pinched. He was kneeling next to the side of her bed, she realized, and he had her right hand wrapped in both of his. "Jana, Natalie is fine," he said in a soothing voice. "You're both safe."

"What happened?" she asked, trying to make sense of the images streaming through her memory. *Had it been a dream? Were they safe? Safe from what, exactly?*

"You passed out," Kris answered, leaning back from hovering. "You've been in and out of consciousness since then."

"I was on the couch in your suite… no—we were in your bedroom… the photo… oh my god the screams." She fumbled out the words, ending with a gasp.

"Natalie is resting—she'll be okay," Kris said reassuringly. "Nic is with her."

Jana hadn't seen the girl's face, but she'd known *who* it was. She pulled her hand free of Kris's grip, raising up on her elbows to glance over to the tiny rosebuds that still thrived in the small pot adorned with a pink ribbon. Kris had given it to her for her birthday in December. "Was it real?" she asked, shifting her attention from the flowers to Kris, observing the anxious expression on his face.

"Real?" Kris's brows knitted tighter.

Jana pushed herself up into a sitting position, bringing her knees up to her chest and resting her back against the headboard. "Tell me," she said, encircling her bent knees with both arms, pulling them in tighter.

Kris let out a weighted sigh and sat back on his heels. "What do you want to know?"

Questions raced through Jana's now-sharpening mind. "What did I witness in that room?"

"What do you remember?" Kris moved to sit on the edge of the bed as though stalling for time.

Jana removed her arms from around her shins, raising her hands to cover her eyes and face. "Her back," she muffled through her hands, "Her skin went from red, to purple… then to black…." She swallowed back the queasiness that was swirling. "Then her back… the flesh… it ripped open… and something that looked like long white bones pressed out through the wounds." Jana began to sob into her hands, unable to hold back. The bed shifted, and Jana felt the weight of Kris moving closer to her. Ever so softly, the warmth of Kris's fingers rested against her hands. Then with a gentle lift, Kris removed her hands from over face, drawing both of them up to his lips.

"Jana," he said softly against her fingers. "Natalie is well… she is not injured… she is not in pain… she is resting, and she will be awake soon." He opened her hands and placed the palms of them against the sides of his face.

"What… what was it… what came out of her back?" she asked, afraid to find out yet still needing to know the truth of it.

Kris held her hands tight to his face, then closed his eyes before releasing a breath and uttering one whispered word, "*Wings*."

Jana's mind raced, recalling Kris's earlier words about Superman and kryptonite… how he had a genetic variance, extremely slow hair growth and a sensitivity to sulfur, an anomaly similar to Natalie and her unique genes. *"A superior gene mutation,"* Ben had told her. The number of people who had it was unknown, although Kris had it too. Then she remembered the photo from Kris's bedroom, the one that appeared to have been taken 23 years ago. "How old are you?" she asked him again. "And don't say, *It's not polite to ask a person their age,*" she added, recalling his mocking answer from before.

Kris opened his eyes at her question and removed her hands from his face, letting them rest down atop her knees. Then he rose, taking a step back from where he'd knelt next to the bed.

"The truth," Jana demanded.

"Too many lies—I know," Kris said, stepping back further and settling down into the small chair next to the side table, its size only made smaller by his massive frame. "But not all of what I told you was a lie." Kris leaned forward, resting his elbows on his thick thighs. "Truth. We did live up north in Nunavut, aiding the communities in need there, and we do refer to it as First Haven, but it wasn't a group home."

"We can't have a relationship based on half-truths," Jana said, wrapping her arms around her shins again.

Kris nodded. "Funny, Lynn said the exact same thing to me."

"I take it she's *not* your executor?"

"No." Kris shook his head.

"What about you being Lane's uncle?"

"That's true, what I told you about her parents giving us that label, and not just to explain us all living together. We *are* a family. She calls me uncle, but like I said, she is more like a kid sister to all of us."

Jana liked the *family* comment, and she understood that you didn't have to be blood related to be considered family. "What about your birth records?"

"That's also true. There are no official records, just the ones that Marq created for us."

"Why did you need to have new records created—because of this special ops team you say you're involved with?"

"That's part of it." Kris stared down at the floor.

"Is there really an extremist group out there experimenting on kids?"

"Yes," he said. "It's true. I am—we are… we are trying to locate these kids—keep them safe and out of the hands of this horrible collective."

"This collective… the one you told me disguises itself as a well-known medical foundation, lying about its research and treatments," she said, recalling the details she'd first learned.

"Yes!" Kris said again, this time more firmly.

"I'll ask you once more," Jana began, moving off the bed to stand in front of where he sat. "How old are you?" *Was she truly ready for the answer*, she wondered?

Kris stood abruptly to stare down at her, his dark blue eyes sparkling as tears formed at the edges. "My truth," Kris took in a long breath. "I was created in the year 1901," he said, voice steady, his expression unwavering. "And I'm in love with you."

For the next 2 hours, Jana sat on her bed with Kris, patiently listening to *his* truth. His story began with how long it had been since the first Seraphim from Pleiades were cast down, 122 years ago, and how they had not been built for the challenges presented once trapped on Earth. Anael and Thanael, who Kris had originally referred to as his foster parents, had used the power of creation held within the rings they had in their possession, normally used to create living things, new species needed to help balance Earth's ecosystem, to create seven warriors. The cast down angels, now recognized as the Earthbound, had had to learn to live among humans. Anael and Thanael had remained near the location they had originally been sent to, Nunavut, because they hadn't wanted others of their kind to suffer as they had, unprepared for the harsh climate and desolate location. As time passed and with help from the Inuit people of the area, they created a safe place for themselves, though the exact location of this Haven remains on a strict, need-to-know basis.

"Anael and Thanael are an actual couple?" Jana questioned, knowing now they were not foster parents.

"They had been paired at the time for several centuries—one of the longest pairings since that of the essential land and water pairing before living organisms were created," he said, his voice filled with reverence. His words were so profound they made Jana's heart ache. Kris continued by sharing that there were several other pairings at the time of the takeover who remained together, and others who eventually paired off for companionship and survival. "As time went on, most of the Earthbound went out among humans to learn languages and skills they hadn't needed for life on the stars, like cooking, reading, and writing. And as humans evolved, they did too, learning to drive cars and educating themselves in the ways of the economy. They learned different ways to survive, some choosing to stay hidden, while others elected to live among humans. They also learned that they were no longer immortal." Kris took both of her hands in his.

He paused, but Jana felt there was more. "Immortal?" she asked, frowning.

Kris briefly looked away, then refocused back on Jana. "Angels are immortal. Earthbound angels are not."

Jana squeezed his hands. "What does that mean?"

"Now they can be killed like humans… despite their exceptional healing abilities." Kris stared down at their joined hands.

"You say *they*, but what you mean is *we*—you and your brothers, I take it?"

"Yes." Kris glanced up, gazing deep into her eyes. "There was never a need to create warriors, because there had never been a threat of war amongst the Seraphim. We were originally created to help the Earthbound survive, but like the others, we have our weaknesses, as you know. But still, we are not susceptible to human diseases."

"And you live longer than we do," Jana said, filling in what he wasn't saying.

"We age—just slower, and like the Earthbound we also feel hunger and thirst. Kris licked his lips as if he were thirsty now.

"I'm guessing that comes with some challenges?"

Kris nodded. "Free will was part of our evolution. And corruption. Some took advantage of the slow aging process to obtain power and wealth, and some participated in the ruin of both humans and Seraph. None of us was immune to the pull, the need… the curiosity. Some reveled in their findings, drinking, drugs, and sex, while others swiftly returned to their original observer ways. Some… like me, weren't so lucky," he said, changing from holding both her hands to just one of them now covered in both of his. "Until now." He kissed the back of her hand, his focus never leaving her eyes.

Jana stared into the depths of his deep blue eyes. "You've changed your ways."

"I have—please believe me, Jana." Kris moved her hand to his chest, placing the palm of it over his heart.

"I believe you, I do," she shared, feeling the beat of his heart against her hand. Still, a difficult question lingered in her mind. But instead of asking what weighed on her, she asked, "So are there other humans out there that know about the Earthbound?"

"Some." Kris pressed the palm of her hand firmer to his chest. "As time went on, those who didn't stay in hiding found human companions."

"And some… had offspring," she said, her focus going to her hand on his chest.

"They are known as *Nephilim*, though we use the term *halflings*," Kris clarified, pulling her attention back to his face.

"Like my *sister*, Natalie. And these are the children Thaddeus has been after." Now she understood.

"Yes," Kris confirmed. Then he enlightened her on the nuance with halflings and their 20th birthday, the proper development of their wings. "But once we understood what Thaddeus had been doing, all eyes were on him. It's been 22 years since Thaddeus betrayed Purah," Kris stated, before he continued on with the story of the special bracelets and a traveler staff, and how the other Stewards from each star, along with Purah had sent Thaddeus and his supporters to earth.

"Why does he feel the need to experiment on these halflings?"

"He thought the Seraph and human couplings were abominations. Since angels together can't conceive offspring, he wanted to know how it was possible they even existed. In the beginning, he just wanted to kill them all."

"Who made him gaaw," she started to ask angrily. Pausing and shaking her head, she swiftly switched her question to, "Who gave you your names?"

Kris caressed her hand that he held to his chest as if understanding her anger. "Anael and Thanael provided us with our given names. All the original Earthbound—including us, had initially gone by formal names using *of Haven*, like Kristopher of Haven, or Kristopher, Second Son of Haven. That was until the need for last names became a requirement. We chose our own surnames."

"Not that any of this makes logical sense, but I'm confused as to why Thaddeus needed Purah."

Kris released Jana's hand from his chest, transferring it to rest on his knee. "Seraphim can't travel like other angels," he said, tracing each of her fingers with his fingertips.

"Travel—you mean use wings?" Jana held his hand still, then laced her fingers through his.

"Yes and no," he said. "All Seraphim have wings, but it is the Steward who sends them down to Earth, to the location of their choosing to do whatever work was needed. Once they are there, they use their wings to get around."

Jana already knew the answer, but she said anyway, needing to make it really real. "And you have wings," she breathed out. "Is there anything more I should know?"

"There's more." Kris drew their intertwined hands to rest against his chest.

"Like?"

"Well, there are several types of angels that exist… but when you get to meet Lynn, she'll explain that *and* her role in all this."

"Her role?"

"Let's call it celestial ancestry, for now." Kris squeezed her hand before bringing her hand to his lips for a quick kiss. "Oh, and Earthbound can't veil themselves. That's the reason we are so good with disguises." Kris smiled at her, his tears from earlier now a distant memory.

"And we've come full circle." Jana smiled warmly back at him.

In the time she'd been here in Ottawa leading up to Valentine's Day, her relationship with Kris had grown, and still she had wanted more. Kris had continually reminded her that what mattered was *now*, not the past, and she had done her best to keep her curiosity from affecting their time together. Now she understood why he had held back, and though she was still digesting these latest *truths* about who and what he was, she appreciated he had put her feelings first. With *his* truth, he'd not wanted to venture further with their relationship, not until she knew everything. And now she did. Even with all Kris had shared, there was still more she wanted to know about him. And *her* truth… she was in love with him, too.

Chapter 9 

I'd texted Redmond several times after the message from Lily, but he'd not responded to any. When he'd finally gotten home last night, it was well after midnight. This morning when I woke, I noticed he hadn't come to bed and had probably slept on the lower level on the couch in the music room. Then, when I'd come into the kitchen to make coffee, I realized he had already left for the day. *And* he hadn't left a note.

"Payback is a bitch," I said to myself as I spooned coffee grounds into the coffeemaker. Pushing my disappointment aside, I set my focus on circling back with Lane to get the emotional side of things since, like Grier, she too was also involved with an angel.

Before settling down on the couch to drink my coffee, I retrieved my laptop from the bedroom and set it up on the coffee table in the living room. Then I sent a text to Lane,

> *Morning sunshine. Feeling up for some girl time?*

Her response was immediate,

> *Already set up in my bedroom with the door shut. Ping me when you're ready.*

"In her room with the door shut?" I said to myself, figuring she must have major updates for me. I opened the video chat app on my laptop, then sent a quick message to Lane saying I was ready.

"Morning," I said in greeting when Lane's sleepy face came into view. She was still in her pajamas, but then so was I.

"Hey," Lane said in response, her energy mirroring her tired face.

I reached for my coffee and brought it to my lips. "Late night?" I asked before taking a sip.

A *Kiss the Ground* labeled coffee cup came into view as Lane took a drink of her own morning brew. "You could say that," she said, followed by a gulp of her coffee. "There's lots going on around here." She took a second sip.

"I figured as much, but I want to hear about your internship meeting with Jules first."

"It's in Italy," she shared, taking another swig from her mug.

"Woooow, niiiiiiiice," I swooned. "That's a good start."

Lane gave me a sleeping grin. "I'll be covering two avenues. One is in dolphin research, and the other is in Environmental Science & Policy."

"Hooraaay and booooo," I said, expressing my joy for dolphins and boredom for policy.

Lane let out a tired laugh. "The dolphin one is the Environmental Research and Conservation Internship Program, and the booooo one is all about environmental preservation and sustainable living, which are policies and practices at the forefront of national priorities. Both are great, actually, and obviously I couldn't resist working with dolphins, so I applied for both."

I brought my legs up on the couch to sit cross - legged, holding my coffee cup with both hands. "So now what—you wait to hear if you get accepted?"

"Nope—I just submitted for both and got both. They're in the same region, just not at the same time, but they're back to back, so I'll be gone twice as long." Lane held her mug briefly in front of her mouth before taking a long sip.

"There are worse places to spend your time." I took a sip of my coffee.

"Yeah. I figured for a first go at using my training, I'd pick somewhere beautiful."

"Have you told Lyndon yet?"

"Yes, we talked last night about it." She grinned behind her coffee mug. "He had reservations about my being gone and on my own, but said he was thrilled I was going to have such a great opportunity."

"He could visit you, no?"

"He could," she said, setting her mug down. Then she reached out of view to retrieve a well-worn dark grey sweatshirt. She pulled it over her head, her dark wavy hair spilling out around the frayed neckline as she slid her arms into the sleeves. "But I'll be sharing a communal space with other researchers, and won't have much privacy. But I should be able to see him in my off time."

"Eewww privacy," I teased.

"Aunt Lyyynn," she giggled out.

"When do you have to leave?" I took a sip of my coffee, enjoying how the heat of the mug warmed my hands.

"At the end of the month," she said, fiddling with her ear.

"Wow, that's fast." I felt a tad anxious at hearing this.

"Lots of intern spots elsewhere have already started, and these were filling up, so I'm lucky I got in when I did. It helped that Jules had some pull." Lane's mug came into view again as she tipped back the last of her coffee.

"I thought you said Jules had a connection for you from her time in Brazil?"

"It was—he is. They worked together, but now he's working in Italy." Lane yawned.

"Frankly, I'm thankful you aren't going to Brazil. I know it's a big country, but I hated the idea of you being anywhere near where Thaddeus could be."

"Lyndon had the same thoughts." Lane quirked an eyebrow.

"How is *your* angel?"

"He's gooood," she said, rubbing her eyes and letting out another yawn. "Sorry—I was up late."

Yawns were contagious, and I let out my own, then said, "Tell me how you two are getting on first, before you tell me how it went with your uncles."

"We're good—great, really. Our conversation the other night changed him. I think he needed to have someone to talk to—to get the heaviness out, you know?" Lane tucked her hand in her sleeve, then slowly ran the soft cuff of it over her mouth and chin.

"I can see that for sure." I nodded. "He carries a heavy burden—I don't mean Taylor. I mean, tolerating his role with Thaddeus."

"Oh, yeah, exactly," she agreed. "Him telling me—having a person he could confide in, seriously lightened the weight of the secret. We both hated lying to each other, but it wasn't like either of us were hiding something simple."

"True. And I'm guessing he is less reserved now that he can speak freely."

"Yes, in a way. He says what's on his mind now—doesn't hold back. I think he understands that he's safe with me. He remains a gentleman, though. Which is something I have always liked about him. It's sweet, and kind of shows this innocent side of him." She grinned. "And man can he kiss," she added with an exaggerated gasp, causing me to almost spill my coffee.

"Well, thank goodness for that," I said, laughing, lifting my mug in a toast. "No need to kick him to the curb now."

"It's been a long time since I've been kissed, Aunt Lynn. And never like that before. You know—where your body tingles and your head spins." She tucked her other hand in the opposite sleeve.

"Lane, you've got it bad," I laughed out.

"Oh—I know!" She placed her tucked hands against her cheeks.

I took the last sip of my coffee and set the mug on the coffee table. "Now tell me how things went with Lyndon's visit with your uncles."

"Believe it or not, it went remarkably well." Lane's dark eyebrows raised up her forehead.

I let out a relieved sigh. "Good."

Lane's eyebrows relaxed, and then she said, "Kris told me Lyndon shared everything—came clean with whatever he had of value. Answered all their questions, making it clear where he stood with his feelings on Thaddeus and his position in the organization."

"Excellent." This was better than I had anticipated.

"He has no love for any of them other than Zuriel. And well, Zuriel won't be going back to work with Thaddeus, of course. And Lyndon's time rarely overlaps with anyone else, he told them. And he doesn't often even see the others unless he's asked to—or he needs information."

"Does Lyndon know everything now—the full deal on who your uncles really are?"

"Yup. They showed Lyndon the lower level here once they felt they could trust him." Lane pushed her hands free of the sleeves. "You'll love this part. After meeting everyone, Lyndon asked them if they thought they could *take* on one of his kind."

"Ha!" I shot out in a laugh. "What did they say?"

Lane laughed too, then said, "Instead of telling him *what* they were, Leo just busted out his wings right then and there."

I slapped my thigh, amused, imagining the moment. "I'm guessing that was a pretty good convincer."

"Right?" Lane smiled. "Lyndon said he was shocked, of course, but once they shared how they had come into being, he was beyond fueled to take on Thaddeus with them. Having a group of humans on your side that you could trust was one thing, but having a crew of warriors at your back was another."

"One hundred percent," I said in complete agreement.

"When we met up last night, he was genuinely happy. He finally saw the potential of freedom, I think." Lane's smile widened.

"And he isn't alone anymore," I added.

"I said as much to him."

"The two of you still have a lot to navigate."

"We do." Her smile softened.

I smiled too, yet I still felt the weight of the situation. "I think it's good that you have your own things to focus on while he gets familiar with Leo and the others."

"I agree." She gave a quick nod. "I want him to focus on working with them. There'll be plenty of time for things to grow between us. And he's not putting any pressure on me, either."

"It's all very exciting, Lane. Enjoy it—the newness—the romance of it all. Don't let the thought of his boss get in the way of your joy."

"I won't. Plus, I'll be plenty busy myself come the end of the month."

"Big time. So what's next?"

"Lyndon plans to travel back down to Florida to introduce Zuriel to Zach, and a few of the others who frequent South Haven."

"That's a great idea." I pondered whether Redmond would be interested in meeting him too.

"Lyndon said that Zuriel is going to need their aid for things like creating a new identity, etc., and that it would be good for him to have a safe community to turn to if needed."

I frowned, recalling something Leo had told me. "I might be remembering this wrong, but I thought Seraphim could die if their wings were removed."

"So did I." Lane shrugged. "But it seems Thaddeus figured out a way."

"Not sure if that's a bad thing or a good thing." I curled my upper lip in a sneer. "Working through no longer having wings will be Zuriel's biggest hurdle, I imagine. The physical and psychological aspects of that healing are going to be tough."

Lane tucked her hands back in her sleeves. "I guess it's a bonus that his new lady friend is a shrink."

"Ya, but they're gonna need each other, especially with Grier adjusting to her new reality as well."

"She's got you there to help—but it can't hurt having a big strong male at your side," Lane said, her smile brightening again.

"You know, you should come down with Lyndon when he returns to see Zuriel. That way you can meet both him and Grier—you're both kind of in the same boat, *boyfriend-wise*. And you could finally meet Redmond and the twins. That's if Redmond is talking to me by then," I huffed out.

"That's a great idea. I will totally talk to Lyndon about coming down," she said elated, then she grimaced. "Redmond is still angry, eh?"

"Well, he's not talking to me, so, ya." I sighed. "I'm almost afraid to ask, but how is Natalie doing?" I didn't want to talk about Redmond.

"She's fine, still unconscious, though."

"Is that typical?"

"It was expected." Lane shrugged one shoulder. "When she wakes up, she won't remember anything. It'll feel like a bad dream. She did have an allergic reaction, which may have triggered her transition. She *was* overdue. It was a good thing Mason was with her." Lane popped a hand free of her sleeve, then ran the hand through her wavy hair, stopping to fiddle with her earlobe again.

"How are they going to explain all of this to her?" I chose *not* to use the word *everything* again to encompass things in the *knowing*.

"I'm guessing they'll start with the rare gene thing, explain how Mason has it too, etc." She shrugged her shoulder again. "Let her know that she's at a special clinic that does research on people like her and Mason. After all this time, they still don't know why the twentieth year is the trigger." Lane scrunched up her face as though frustrated at the lack of clarity.

"Leo said they believe it was some kind of latent hormonal trigger linked to the slow aging that comes from the Seraph parent." It was my turn to shrug. "Although halflings—at least the ones they have encountered, age at the same rate as we do."

"Yeah, I heard that too. Natalie will need to be told about her wings, and learn about the function and how to use them. That won't be easy." Lane shook her head. "And she will need to be taught how to fly."

"Can you imagine? Wings? Talk about a sublime gift. Would be awe-inspiring and frightening at the same time," I said, attempting to fathom how you would tell a person such things.

"I hate to admit it—but I'm envious. The flying part—not the mental anguish that comes from learning you have wings," Lane said.

"Having the ability to fly would be cool." I nodded. Lane had been around winged people all her life, I realized. "Couldn't Shea maybe come and help? I mean, I don't know the woman, or even where she might be, but…." I tried picturing her in my mind from how she'd been described to me. "…Zach said she was 30 years old. And resembled Cleopatra with the dark eyeliner she wears, and he said her mother, Shrina, resembled an Egyptian Sophia Loren. Both sound gorgeous." The unfortunate thing about Shea was that she'd been born missing both her legs from below the knee.

"That's spot-on accurate. Shea is a drop-dead beauty," Lane said.

"Zach had told me her mother had died in childbirth and that she'd been raised by her grandparents." I grabbed my mug, then remembered I'd finished it already. "Do you think she'd come help a fellow halfling?" I set the mug back on the coffee table.

"Maybe. I haven't seen her in years. She's in touch with Leo and Den, but she has her own life. Den trained her—got her a gig with an underground bodyguard organization. One used by the uber-rich and pretentiously protected."

"Like Madonna pretentious?" I asked with a little vogue hand gesture.

"More like United Arab Emirates, Qatar, and Bahrain sheikhs and daughters of royalty pretentious," Lane corrected, giving me another eyebrow raise.

"Wowsers!"

"Yeah—she's *lethal*, Den told me." Lane put her hand up like she was doing karate.

"How could she fight—protect someone agility wise, if she is missing half her legs? I assume she wears prosthetics, but still?"

"She uses high performance lower leg prosthetics. If you get to meet her, she'll tell you all about them. They're beyond cool."

"How often does Den see her?"

"They get together between gigs to talk shop. She has some juicy stories, I tell ya." Lane grinned wide-eyed and nodded.

"I bet she and Den both have some wild tales. I'll need to hit him up for some next time I see him—for entertainment purposes, of course." I gave Lane a cheeky grin.

"Of course," she said, giving me the side-eye.

"On the not-so-entertaining front, how's Jana? Zach told us she witnessed Natalie's transition." I gritted my teeth.

"She passed out," Lane said, her expression sympathetic. "Finally roused yesterday afternoon. Kris was with her. They talked through everything. She knows it all now. The whole *wing* thing too."

"Oh man. That had to be hard."

Lane nodded. "He said it explained how he ended up on her father's property. Meaning he must have fallen out of the sky due to the sulfur exposure, landed in the water, and then tried to fly again only to land at her father's place. He remembered it had been the only house he'd seen from the air."

"Yaaah, I always wondered about that, too."

"Oh, and he told her that you're *not* the executor of his estate." She covered her mouth with the end of her sleeve again.

"I see. And does she know about Thaddeus?" The real truth was much more difficult to digest, especially knowing what he had been doing, and that Natalie, her long-lost sister, was exactly what he was looking for.

"He gave her all the gruesome details," Lane said, grimacing.

"What about the whole aging thing?"

"He explained how long he's been alive and about their extraordinary healing abilities."

"Should I presume they haven't talked about the challenges surrounding those facts?" I had wondered about Kris and Jana, Grier and Zuriel, and now Lane and Lyndon, each couple navigating a future together.

"That's a delicate topic," she said, her expression turning melancholy.

We were both fully aware of the issues with the slow aging, not to mention the inevitable heartbreak. "Have you had a chance to speak with her?"

"Briefly, yes. She's been in the kitchen baking nonstop since her talk with Kris. She said it helped to calm her nerves."

"I can see that—she's a baker by trade, after all. Comfort is comfort."

"True, and I'm happy to have her chocolate Icelandic cinnamon rolls or the *Skyr* cake any day."

"Cheers to that," I said, my stomach suddenly feeling hollow.

"I asked her, 'Is the truth so bad?'"

"What did she say?"

"She countered, asking me how you keep something like this a secret?"

"A reasonable question. What did you tell her?"

"I told her we have allies, like you, Aunt Lynn," she said, smiling.

Her smile was sweet. "The ally thing is mutual—you know that." I squinted playfully and pointed at her.

"I know," she said, her smile turning mischievous. "Jana said that Kris shared his feelings and why he had been holding back, too."

"Was she understanding?"

"She said clearly he had his reasons, and that she was freaked out at first, but isn't afraid now. And that she is strangely relieved to know the full truth."

"Well, that's promising."

"It is. Still kind of sad, though."

"How so?"

"She told me she wished her dad were still alive. He never knew he had another daughter. She asked if this was something she could share with her friend Geir back in Iceland. Kris told her, we would have to figure that one out. She trusts Geir, but *knowing* can be hard for some, as we know. He explained that we like to keep those in *the knowing*, to a tight-knit group."

"We do—but it's still hard."

"I asked her whether she feels he needs to know. I mean, it's not like she's harboring a criminal."

"What did she say about that?"

"That all Geir really wants is for her to be happy. And she is happy, she said."

"I'd say that's good, wouldn't you?"

"I do."

"What did Kris tell her about Natalie?"

"He explained the halfling thing, that it's people like Natalie they are trying to save from Thaddeus. Natalie's road would be challenging, but they would ease her into things a bit at a time. Start with why she's here first. Then move on from there, gauging her understanding and acceptance."

"That sounds like the best way. What about Anael—Natalie's birth mother? Could she help her to acclimate?"

"Not sure they would ask her. She was grateful when she heard they had found Natalie, but she had no intention of coming to see her. She did, however, make monetary provisions for Natalie, and now that she is an adult, she's financially set."

I nodded. "Secure finance would be a bonus." I remembered being told that Anael did not have any desire to be a parent. Her only goal was understanding the human experience of pregnancy and childbirth, nothing beyond that. I touched my neck, feeling for my necklace.

"You could always come up, Aunt Lynn—help with Natalie's absorption of things."

"Ha! Me come up there? Right now I'd be astonished if Redmond let me go off-island to get groceries by myself at this rate."

"Really?"

"He hasn't spoken to me since yesterday morning. He and Zach were here when I got home. He left right after Zach. I was asleep when he got home, *and* he was gone before I got up this morning. Seems he's still majorly pissed at me." I flipped through the charms on my necklace.

A rumbling sounded from up the drive and then travelled under the house. "I hear Redmond's motorcycle—he must be home. I've gotta go."

"Behave and be a good listener," Lane said, shaking a finger at me.

"Yes, Mom," I rolled my eyes. "Text me if Natalie wakes up," I said with a wave.

She waved back and logged us off the video call.

As I closed my laptop, I heard the slam of the door from the carport into the lower level. A minute later, the door at the top of the stairs opened. I turned and glanced over the back of the couch to see Redmond standing in the kitchen. "Where have you been?" I dared to ask.

Just then, Summer and Snow came sauntering down the hall and into the kitchen from where they'd been sleeping in the twins' rooms.

Redmond bent to pat each of them, then returned to standing. Stone-faced, he shoved his hands in the pockets of his jeans. "At North Haven, talking with Zach."

"About?" I pinched the charms on my necklace between my fingertips.

"You." His expression remained impassive.

"Me?" I questioned, running the charms on my necklace back and forth.

"About your going up to Ottawa."

Chapter 10 

"She's awake," Kris had told Jana first thing this morning when he'd come by with breakfast for her on a tray. He'd explained that Nic had already spoken with Natalie, clarifying for her what had happened and why she was here. They'd set her up in Zach's room, equipping it to look like a hospital room. Natalie had been quite confused by her surroundings until she'd seen that Mason was with her. He told her that his Uncle Nic worked here. When Natalie met Nic, he told her she'd had an allergic reaction to sulfur, that Mason brought here to this 'special clinic' because he also suffered from the same affliction. Nic had told her she had a rare condition, a very rare genetic one that only a few people had. Apparently, she had been mortified by the idea that she and Mason could be related, but Nic assured her that was not the case, only that their ancestors could have been of similar lines waaaay back and not to worry. He had further explained that due to their research on this genetic anomaly, not only did she have the gene herself, but they were also able to identify who her biological parents were. They'd stated that it was very lucky Mason had brought her to their aid when he did, because things could have gone very badly for

her. *And* because of their genetic research, they had also discovered that she was related to a girlfriend of one of the researchers.

It had been a lot for Natalie to process, Kris had told Jana, but the idea that she had a biological relative, a half-sister in fact, one who was currently here at this facility, had helped to lessen her worry about what had happened to her. The last thing Kris shared with Jana was that Lynn would soon be on her way from Florida and would enlighten both her and Natalie on how she was connected to all this.

Jana's friend Geir had texted her, 'Gleðilegan Valentínusardag!', the Icelandic greeting for happy Valentine's day, three days ago, but she hadn't responded to him until last night. She'd given herself the excuse that it wasn't a traditional part of Icelandic culture, but the truth was that her life was a bit of a whirlwind at the moment, with the whole angel-boyfriend-sister-wing thing, and she'd only really gotten her legs firmly under her last night. Although today she was a bundle of nerves, knowing she was about to meet her sister.

The sound of soft knocking on the door to Jana's room reached her in the bathroom as she leaned against the counter. Staring at the floor-length mirror, she took a quick survey of her outfit. She'd chosen to wear a casual pair of jeans and a pale pink thermal pullover. Exiting the bathroom, she found Nic standing in the doorway to her room. She had half expected to see Kris, but then recalled he was making a stop at the restaurant with Mason.

"Are you ready to meet Natalie?" Nic asked, leaning a shoulder against the doorframe. He was in his official medical attire of light blue hospital scrubs, with a stethoscope draped loosely around his neck.

"Ready as I'll ever be," she said, smoothing back a strand of hair too short to be secured snugly into her ponytail. Before leaving, she slipped her socked feet into a pair of soft canvas loafers.

Nic led the way through the open living space to the inner door that led up to the suite normally used by Zach when he visited. Zach, having relocated from Norway to South Haven, wasn't currently in need of his space.

"Natalie," Nic called out when they entered the suite. "Are you ready for us to come up?" Nic waited for a response, leaning a hand on the railing that led up the stairs.

"Ready-ready," Natalie's elated, youthful voice called back.

Relieved by her response, Jana followed Nic up the stairs to the bedroom where Natalie was set up.

"Good morning," Nic said, stepping into the room.

Jana crossed the threshold and came to stand beside Nic.

"Natalie, this is Jana—Jana, meet Natalie," he said in introduction.

Jana gave an anxious wave to the young woman, smiling back at her, before clasping her hands together nervously at her waist.

Natalie gave Jana an enthusiastic "Hi" and a wave in response.

"I'll be back to relieve you later, Rachel," Nic directed at the woman standing next to the large hospital-style bed. Then he backed out of the room and disappeared down the stairs.

Jana knew Rachel. Knew she was a friend of the family, daughter of one of Lynn's close friends, and that Rachel also worked as a nurse with Nic at the hospital.

"Nice to see you again, Jana," Rachel said, before latching a bag of some kind of clear fluid onto a tall pole. The bag's IV line ran down and attached to Natalie's wrist. Natalie was sitting upright in the huge bed, dressed in hospital scrubs similar to the light blue ones Rachel was wearing.

"Same," Jana said, "and thank you—you know—for all this." She pointed back and forth from Natalie to the equipment in the room, indicating what she was trying to convey.

Rachel gave her an encouraging smile. "I'll leave you two ladies alone to chat," she said as she circled around the bed. She patted Jana's arm reassuringly before heading out of the room.

"Thanks, Rachel!" Natalie called after her. Then she took the control box for the bed and pressed the option to lower it down to about chair height. "Come sit—please." She tapped the open space in front of her on the spacious bed.

Jana strode to the bed and sat near the end of it. "So... what did Nic tell you about this place, their research—about the people here?"

Jana asked. She was aware Natalie had been informed about what had happened to her, but Jana hadn't asked what Natalie knew about where she was.

"Just that I have a rare gene—that there's some radical group hunting people like me down because of it. I'm told this is the best and safest place for me right now." She picked at the medical tape that held her IV in place. "Oh, and that one of my professors is associated with this group—the good guys. As is another professor at my school—she's my friend's mom. And of course, that you and I are sisters." Her smile was so big her cheeks bunched.

"Yes. And you are very safe here," Jana said, smiling. Feeling more relaxed now, Jana kicked off her loafers and adjusted her legs to sit cross - legged facing Natalie.

"But you don't have this gene?" Natalie mirrored Jana's sitting position.

"No." She shook her head. "It comes from your birthmother's side."

"Nic said my biological mother was a client of theirs. That they tracked down my name based on the records she provided them."

"That's what I was told as well."

"It's your boyfriend who's one of the researchers here, right?"

"Kris, yes." It wasn't exactly true. "He told me that you lost your parents when you were young."

"Car crash." Natalie's smile dropped as she nodded. "I was only 10 years old when they died."

"I'm so sorry, Natalie." Jana swallowed, unsure what to say next. She understood what it meant to lose a parent, but she'd been an adult when her father had died. Her mother had died when she was young, but she hadn't known her and it hadn't felt the same. "He also told me you went to live with your aunt—and I understand she was *not* a good person."

Natalie turned away and blew out a breath. "That's a nice way to put it. She wasn't very happy about having to take care of her dead sister's kid. There was some bullshit with money—but I don't have to worry about that now." Natalie turned back to face Jana. "So we have different mothers, but the same father, right?"

"Right." Jana gave her a weak smile. "My father is your biological father. His name was on your birth certificate, and that's how they linked us." Having been made aware of the horrible upbringing Natalie experienced with her aunt, Jana wished so much that her father were here to meet her.

"What's his name?" Natalie's face seemed to brighten with asking the question.

"Reider. Reider Stephansson," Jana said, feeling her heart filling with pride at speaking his name aloud.

"Cool name," Natalie said, nodding.

"I think so too."

"We look alike," Natalie said, her eyes exploring Jana's face. "Same shaped faces. Hair colour… and our eyes are similar."

"We have our father's eyes," Jana shared. "Yours are much darker, probably like *your* mother's. I'm told my mother and yours look a lot alike."

"How did they meet—your father and my mother, do you know?"

"I do, but I didn't know about her until recently. My—our father traveled to New York City briefly to deal with some paperwork regarding my deceased mother."

"You lost your mother too?" Natalie's eyes turned glassy.

"She left us when I was a baby—so I didn't know her. I was only 11 years old when I found out my mother had died. But her death was the reason my father went to New York City, and that's where he met Anael, your birthmother." Jana paused, then said, "He only told me about meeting someone when I was much older, though not the details. And he would have told me if Anael had ever reached out to him, *and* had he known, he would never have kept the pregnancy a secret from me." A sudden rush of emotion caused Jana's chest to ache. "He would have loved to have had more children, and I always wanted to have siblings growing up."

"Me too. I miss my parents—I bet you miss your dad too, eh?"

"I do," Jana said, placing a hand over her heart.

"How did you come to be here—find out about all this? Are you part of the team—researching for people like me?"

"No. The fact that they found you—that we're related, is quite an unusual coincidence, actually. Kris has the same unique gene you do." Jana glanced up at the bag of liquid hanging from the pole next to the bed.

"Nic said I had an extreme reaction to a cream I'd used. Something about an allergy to anything sulfur based—that it's linked to the rare genes." Natalie tapped the IV on her wrist. "That's what the medicine is for."

"You were very lucky. Kris actually suffered amnesia from his exposure to the compound. He hadn't known how severe his sensitivity was until then."

"Wow, I'm guessing he's better now, right?"

"All better," Jana assured her.

"My friend Mason has the gene, too. He's the one who brought me here. Do you know him?"

"Oh yes," Jana said. "Are you familiar with the restaurant Après Snow, downtown?"

"Yeah, Mason works there. I actually applied there, but they didn't have any openings." She laughed nervously, then picked at the medical tape on her wrist again.

"Well, Kris owns it. That's partly how I know Mason—from his working there," Jana explained, joy filling her at the idea of spending time with Natalie there.

"And I guess you know him from this place, too."

"That's right," Jana said before glancing around at the other equipment in the room.

Natalie reached for Jana's hand. "I'm glad you are here, Jana… to help me understand all this."

"Honestly, I'm still navigating it all myself," she said, accepting Natalie's hand with a gentle squeeze. "And we'll get through this together."

"Hello-hello, came Kris's cheery voice from the doorway, causing both Jana and Natalie to turn his way.

"Kris, we were just talking about you," Jana said, waving him in.

"Me?" he asked, resting his fingers against his chest in question.

Jana laughed. "Yes—about how Mason works for you at the restaurant."

"And how we share the same weird genes," Natalie added with a chuckle. "Nice sweatshirt, by the way." She pointed at the restaurant logo for Après SNOW.

"Thanks—I know a guy; I can get you one," he said with a cheeky grin. "And we do have the same weird genes. You're going to meet a few others like us soon. Right now, I'm just here to tell you about a special visitor that's coming to talk with you both." Kris turned his attention to Jana. "Lynn will be here this afternoon."

Chapter 11 

It was Leo's request to have me at North Haven when Natalie woke up, though the shocking part hadn't been Redmond's endorsement of the idea that I get to Ottawa *as soon as possible*, it had been the fact that he had recommended I go *alone* while he watched over things at home. Mind you, it had felt more like he had *let* me go on my own, and not that he trusted me to. He'd made it crystal clear that I was to go from the airport to North Haven and nowhere else, then return home after speaking with Natalie. I was pretty confident he'd expressed the same to Leo when they'd spoken. I'd had to call my volunteering supervisor at the hospital to let them know I had to call out due to a family emergency that needed my attention up in Ottawa. They had been understanding, but the twins hadn't been thrilled about me going without them, but had understood how important it was to help Leo with this new halfling.

Last night after tucking the girls in, I'd packed *just the minimum I'd need for my short stay* as per Redmond's recommendation, so I wouldn't be bringing much with me, just a few warm winter clothes and only the essentials that filled a carry-on suitcase and knapsack. Leo had booked me on a flight for an early charter this morning, and

I'd opted for wearing a comfortable pair of dark green yoga pants and a long matching tunic, along with lightweight running shoe/hiking boot crossovers for the transition from South Florida in February to the weather up north. And based on the captain's *prepare for landing* announcement, we were on schedule to land in Ottawa just short of 11:00 a.m.

When I strode out of the security screening from the charter section of the airport, Leo was there waiting for me. He wore a navy jacket over a grey thermal pullover and casual loose-fitting jeans. Several women in the area were staring at him and smiling, possibly in hopes he would look their way. "How was your flight?" he asked, taking my suitcase and giving me a one-arm hug. "Here," he said, taking off his coat and draping it over my shoulders.

"Unexpected." I raised my eyebrows. "And thanks," I said, sliding my arms into the sleeves of the too-big coat. I swung my knapsack over my shoulder and glanced over at the women to find they were no longer smiling. Instead, they directed stern, disappointed, dagger-sharp stares my way. I smiled, holding back a laugh. "Hey, have you spoken with Gabriel lately?" This morning before leaving for the airport, I had called out for Gabriel but had got no response again from him.

"No, why?" Leo's brows pinched.

"He's been kind of MIA lately, but he popped in the other day saying something to me like, '*You really did it this time*, and complaining about having '*enough to deal with*'. I called out for him before leaving to come here, but he was a no-show."

"Any idea what he's talking about?" Leo led the way to the exit.

"Not sure. Thought maybe he was mad at me for something." As the sliding door to the outside swooshed open, I was assaulted by the familiar cold air of Ottawa in February and stopped. I shivered, exhilarated, then drew in the recognizable scent of snow.

Leo glanced back over his shoulder when he noticed I'd paused in my following. "For trying to get in to see Zuriel—not telling anyone where you were going, maybe?" He smirked.

"Not you too," I groaned, continuing in his direction. "I get it—I made a mistake, but things turned out, wouldn't you say?"

He extended an arm to halt me as he checked for oncoming vehicles before striding onward across the crosswalk to the parking garage opposite the airport exit. "I'd say you got bloody lucky."

"New topic," I said, shifting gears, moving forward when he did. "What have you told Natalie so far?"

Leo paused when we reached the entrance to the parking area, then drew in a long breath. "She was confused when she woke up, obviously, but she calmed quickly when she saw Mason was with her," Leo said on an exhale, continuing forward as he explained what Nic had told her about what happened to her and why she was there at the *special* clinic. As we approached a huge, dark, window-tinted SUV, Leo drew a car fob from his coat pocket and pressed the button to unlock it and pop the back hatch door.

"I would have been confused too. What does she know about the people running this clinic?" I pushed up the sleeves of the coat and did finger quotes for the word *people.*

"Similar to what we told Jana at first. Covert team—searching for people like her." Leo slid my carry-on suitcase into the back cargo area of the SUV. "She knows about Ben—her professors, and Jules both being a part of things. Both sent word assuring her not to worry about school."

"Did Nic tell her about Jana?" I asked, circling to the passenger side of the vehicle.

"Yes," he said before unlocking the doors. "And how we'd stumbled upon the connection as part of our research."

I climbed up and into the SUV and shut the door, settling into the cushy leather seat. "So she understands why she's being kept at North Haven and not in a hospital?"

"She does." Leo drew the seatbelt across his chest and down to secure the buckle. Then he tapped the seatbelt latch at my hip as though I needed a reminder to *buckle up.*

"Thanks," I said, reflecting on how Redmond must have told him to keep me safe or at least remind me to keep safe. "Where's Jules now?"

Leo started the car and then backed out of the spot. "She and Lane are meeting again to go over Lane's paperwork for her upcoming internship."

"Gotcha." I nodded, watching as we pulled out of the parking area and onto the road that led away from the airport property. *How many times had I driven this road*, I wondered.

"Jana spoke with Natalie earlier," Leo shared, drawing me from my musings. "She met Kris too, and he explained that there was more they both needed to know. More about Natalie's ancestry. And she was told that we had someone coming to talk to her about all that."

"Me—you're leaving it all up to me? Great." I groaned again.

A short 20 minutes later, we pulled into the drive at North Haven.

"We're here for backup, Lynn," Leo smiled over at me.

I gave him a tight smile, not quite confident with the backup just yet.

Out of the SUV, Leo retrieved my carry-on suitcase. Setting it in front of me, he yanked up the handle for my use.

"So, Jana and Natalie already met?" I asked, hefting my knapsack up onto my shoulder. Taking the handle of my suitcase, I dragged it towards the main doors.

"They did," Leo said, opening the door and crossing the threshold into North Haven.

"Did Jana tell her about…," I attempted to say before a familiar voice called out from the kitchen.

"Angels," Jana finished for me.

"Jana—hey!" I said in surprised greeting as the tall blonde strode our way. She was in socked feet, comfortably dressed in faded blue jeans and an oversized navy sweatshirt that was more than likely Kris's.

"Not yet," Leo said. "That's where you come in. We thought it was best you explain *your* journey first, then ease her into the facts of her own celestial roots after." He gave me an encouraging grin.

"And then *you* can tell her about the wing thing," I added, sarcasm clear in my tone.

Leo chuckled. "Right—if needed."

If needed? Was he serious? I couldn't imagine it *not* being needed.

Just then, Nic came through one of the seven doors along the far side of the open living space. "Lynn, I'm so grateful you're here," he said, dashing over to where the three of us stood.

"Glad I can help—at least, I hope I can." I rested my hand on the extended handle of my suitcase.

"Your story will make all the difference." Nic gave me one of his charming smiles. He was in a pair of dark blue scrubs, and his long midnight hair was smoothed back in a tight braid.

"Come, Natalie is waiting to meet you. Told her I had someone special coming to see her."

"Special—I like that," I joked, attempting to lighten the weight of the situation. "What does she know about me?"

Nic and Leo both grinned.

"What?" I dropped my knapsack from my shoulder, holding it just above my feet.

"That you're... like her, *adopted*," Nic said, his smile tightening. "That you didn't have your birth parents there to explain the nuances to you. *And* that you're here to tell her what it's like."

"That's it?" I rested my knapsack on the floor and shrugged off Leo's coat.

"Well... also that you have experienced some interesting things with *your* genetic makeup, like heightened intuition," Leo added, taking the coat from me.

"I basically told her about your spidey sense—and she's super stoked to hear more," Nic elaborated, a cheeky grin spreading across his handsome bronze face.

I knelt to undo and remove my hiking shoes. "*Right*," I huffed out, standing and grabbing up my knapsack. I rolled my carry-on to the nearest sofa, then dropped my knapsack on it. Then, I unzipped the front pouch to remove what I needed. "Okay, let's do this." I turned back, waving my mother's journal.

Chapter 12 

Nic and Leo stayed put while Jana led the way to the suite Natalie was staying in. At the top of the stairs to the bedroom, we found the door wide open, and an eager Natalie propped up in bed.

"Natalie, this is Lynn," Jana announced as I entered the room after her.

"Hey Natalie," I said, raising my free hand in greeting.

"Welcome." She waved an arm for us to come over. "I hear you're going to help me make sense of all this," she tossed out, wasting no time at all.

"Ha—no pressure," I said, trying to hide the slight edge in my voice. I surveyed the room and spotted an armchair near a full wall of books, but before I could retrieve it, Jana, having read my mind, was already grabbing it and rolling it over to the side of the hospital bed next to Natalie.

"Here, sit," Jana said, patting the back of the chair, before circling around to the other side of the bed. Then she climbed in, scooching up next to Natalie, who I noticed was just as tall as Jana.

"How are things going with the two of you?" I asked, curious about their time together.

"Really great," Natalie said, turning to look at Jana.

Jana smiled back, nodding at her, then took Natalie's hand in hers. "We are anxious to hear what you have to tell us."

"So much for small talk." I chuckled. And apparently, the two had gotten quite comfortable with each other since meeting this morning. *All good,* I thought before plunking myself down into the armchair to begin my story. "Okay, soooo, my mother had this journal—I gave it to her as a gift, actually. Hoping she would write down family stories etc." I held it up in the air for them to see. "And at first, I thought she hadn't written much in it, just a few lines on the first page." I opened the journal to show them the first page. "But booooy, was I wrong." I flipped to near the end of the journal. "There's about an inch thick of her writing in it here near the back that I'd never noticed before." I paused, but neither Natalie nor Jana said a word. They just stared back at me, waiting for more. I grinned and continued. "You're not going to believe this—I didn't at first, but after everything that came after, there was no denying what my mother had written. This journal…." I closed the journal and patted the front cover. "…its content, is what sent me and four of my girlfriends along with a few of my *guy* friends down a mysterious rabbit hole."

"Like *Alice in Wonderland*?" Natalie suggested.

"Kinda—we didn't need to leave this realm. But here's the thing: I'd been looking for more information on *my* biological parents—like you, I'm adopted."

"Nic told me we had that in common." Natalie smiled.

I glanced back and forth between the two women. Jana was extremely pretty, and though they did look alike, Natalie, even in her recovery state, her unique beauty was obvious. "Right," I said, getting myself back on track. "You see, the records I'd got from the adoption agency only had my birthmother's name. The space for my birthfather's name was blank, but that didn't stop me. I enlisted the help of a P.I. to track down more information on both of them for me."

"Did he?" Natalie asked, shifting her body slightly to turn my way.

"He did. Even managed to find my birthmother's best friend from high school, of all people, and it was she who told him how my birthmother had gone to see my adoptive mother. And I found mentions of their meeting in the journal." I opened the journal again to the specific spot. "In this grouping of pages here, on the first page she'd written on, it mentions some woman—my birthmother, had come to see my mom, telling her something about how…." I paused. "…Bear with me, this is going to sound batshit crazy, but…." I paused again. "…she wrote about how exposing *the secret* could cause illness or affect my mother's life expectancy—how if you told someone they would now share in the burden of keeping the secret. The closer a person was to the source of the secret, the deadlier the results would be. That even writing any of it down would be the same as telling someone."

"I'm sorry—what?" Jana questioned, glancing at Natalie and then back at me.

"I know—I know, I thought it sounded ridiculous, too." I raised my hand in the air as if it would help. "Even my mother thought the woman was nuts. Look here." I pointed out the specific passage before reading it aloud,

> *She was convincing, but I didn't know what to think. A coincidence maybe? I'm not the type to believe this kind of mumbo-jumbo, but she'd seemed like a normal, educated, and sane woman. It had been a shock when she'd arrived at my door. I'd had no idea she even knew where I lived, but she had known our names from the adoption. I hadn't recognized her. It had been 27 years since we'd first met, and she'd only been 19 at the time.*

"So this woman—your birthmother—went to see your mom and what, said she had a secret that could make anyone who knew sick?" Jana raced out in question, her expression skeptical.

"Yes, but knowing didn't make you sick. The *telling* of the secret did," I clarified, even though I knew it still sounded foolish.

"She told your mom even though she knew it would make her sick?" Natalie questioned, her expression equally skeptical.

"Yes." I paused and stared down at the passage in the journal. I knew how it all sounded. Knew it would be hard to explain and hard to convince them of the truth. I closed the journal. "It was something we all had questioned, my friends and I, but we know now it was the sacrifice my birth mother was willing to make." I glanced back up at them, running my hand over the tan leather cover.

"Uhm, okay, but I'm still lost here," Jana said, her eyes so wide they showed most of the whites.

"I'm sorry. I wish there were an easier way to explain all of this, but for it to make sense—for you to believe what I'm going to tell you — you have to hear it from the beginning, all the way through." I stared at them, pausing for some kind of recognition or acceptance that they understood that I was not bullshitting here.

"Well, I'm not going anywhere anytime soon," Natalie said, raising her wrist, the one attached with an IV. "So lay it on us."

"After everything I've witnessed and been told, I'm open to just about anything," Jana added, her wide eyes relaxing some. "Please go on, Lynn."

For the next 2 hours, while Jana and Natalie leaned together at the head of the bed like young girls listening to a bedtime fairytale, I sat in my seat next to the hospital bed, presenting my tale to them. I began with my birthmother, the part about how she had shared the story from when she was 18 years old, about her encounter with Gabriel and how she was now part of something *big*, something that would change fate, change humanity. Her role had been to have a child, *me*, and place me with the right family, keep me on her path, place me where *the line of sons was strong*, keep me hidden, keep me safe. I continued from there with the dream she had had about four women: a witch, a healer, a linguist, and a scribe, and how they stood together, and behind them stood four angels. Then I described how my mother told my Aunt Kay about what my birthmother told her, how my aunt had in turn told a friend, and how it resulted in both my mother's and my aunt's cancer diagnoses and their eventual deaths. I explained that my mom had never believed in any of this stuff. That she was a nurse—a fact person, not someone into fantasy on any level. I showed them in the journal how my mother had written numerous times that she had wanted to tell me all this herself, but that she never did, and I'd had to read about it in here. What followed the journal entries were the letters. Letters for each of my girlfriends from their mothers that told similar stories about a witch, a healer, a linguist, and a scribe, how these roles were now passed down to each of my friends. "I'll show you," I said, flipping to the very back of the journal to where I had copies of the letters. Sliding the copies of the letters across the bed for them to read, I said, "From there it was clue after clue, like pieces to a bizarre puzzle that led us to locating the codex, the book of balance, which eventually led us all to the gathering." I paused when Natalie leaned forward to take the top letter from the pile.

Natalie stared down at the letter in her hand, her mouth twitching from side to side. "Well… uhm… okay, but you mentioned something about your *guy* friends—where do they come in?" she asked, letting go of Jana's hand to unfold the letter she'd chosen.

I smiled, thinking about my wonderful friends. At this point in my tale, I was surprised that was all she had asked. At least she wasn't freaking out, I thought. "Like with my girlfriends having roles in this, three of my guy friends also ended up having parts, too. A cipher, a guardian, and a theologian, oh, and a believer."

"A believer?" Natalie leaned back in the bed, resting the unread letter on her lap.

"That makes four," Jana said, pointing out the obvious.

"I'll get to that," I said, nodding before going on. I continued by elaborating on how my girlfriends were all descendants of Archangels, and my guy friends, including my husband, who was the *fourth*, were descendants of Fallen Angels, leaders in fact of the two hundred Fallen, the Four Horsemen of the apocalypse, to be more precise. I paused, but when they said nothing and only gawked at me. Then I threw out a few of my otherworldly skills, like with my premonitions and how I can and have sensed celestial beings like Armaros, who was also a Fallen Angel.

"Ooohkaaay, so let me get this straight," Jana said, eyes wide again. "Your friends are all descendants of angels?"

"Yes," I said, nodding several times. Her question was surprising considering what she knew now about Kris and his crew.

"And you can sense these angels?" Natalie said, more as a statement than a question.

"Correct. I know—you're wondering where this is all going." I rested the journal at the end of the bed.

"I'm not even going to attempt to guess where this is going," Jana said, eyebrows raised.

Natalie only nodded this time.

"I'm getting there—trust me," I said, leaning over and placing my arm on the bed. "And just so you know, what I'm giving you is the short version." I grinned, then continued into the story about the 200 Fallen Angels, the 70 generations, what the Archangels had done, about their Charges, what Gabriel had eventually done to help keep the balance, and all the nuances surrounding that. "My birthmother was a descendant, and Gabriel—the angel she had her encounter with, is my actual *birthfather*."

"You're telling us that you are a descendant as well, but of *two* angels?" Natalie stated.

I tilted my head from side to side. This always felt so weird to explain. My friends and I had learned about things a bit at a time, which gave us some breathing room to absorb it all, understand the possibilities and implications of it all. I grasped how much I was asking of them, but I didn't know how else to say these things they needed to hear. Clarifying, I said, "My birthfather is an Archangel, and my birthmother is a descendant of one of the Fallen—one of the four horsemen, Zaqiel."

"Cool," Natalie tossed out this time, her belief in it all possibly expanding.

"How many kinds of angels are there?" Jana asked, only slightly more relaxed now.

"There are several groups of angels," I began, understanding now that perhaps Jana was only familiar with Kris's kind and the Seraphim from Pleiades. "Standard angels… the Archangels… the Seraphim from Pleiades, and The Watchers, which comprised two subgroups, the original Fallen and the Sanctuary Angels," I presented, counting them off. Then I added the part about Watchers residing in Sanctuary and that they were advocates of The Fallen Watchers, aided by Archangel Zadkiel. I didn't bother to share the fact that they were gifted with the ability to have offspring, mainly because they all resided in Sanctuary—not on this plane. I did, however, tell them how the human records were wrong, that there were no *baby* angels like cherubs, and only those who resembled the male and female likenesses of human beings. "And there you have it," I ended, grateful neither had asked me about the taboo topic of the afterlife. I didn't have any answers to that.

"What about…," Jana began to say.

I put up my hand again to halt her. "And there is another group known as the Earthbound," I finished for her. "But it wasn't until ten years after the gathering when we met and learned more about these Earth-stranded celestials," I clarified. "Did Kris tell you about what happened?" I asked, directing my question to Jana.

"Mostly." Jana shrugged her shoulders. "But please share what you know."

"I'll do my best," I said, tapping my index finger several times on my chin and doing some math in my head. "Let me see… 122 years ago, 198 Seraphim from Pleiades were cast down by a rogue group composed of two Seraphim from each star. Together, those fourteen devised a plan such that they could come and go to and from Earth whenever they wanted."

"The Pleiades—the Seven Sisters," Natalie said, shocking me by sharing her own bit of knowledge.

"You've heard of it?" I asked, taking my turn at a question.

"I used to go to the roof of the apartment I lived in with my aunt, to get away from her smoking, but found I liked stargazing, so I read up on it." She shrugged a shoulder. "The Pleiades—it's visible to the naked eye, and it's a popular target for stargazers."

"I did not know that," I said, curious.

"It's a bright open star cluster located in the constellation Taurus. Looks like a misty patch of light with individual stars—you can see them easily with binoculars or a telescope," she shared, smiling, evidently pleased at being able to contribute and tell us about her love of stars.

"Well, I'll have to take a look myself—next clear night," I said, impressed.

"Sorry, go on," Natalie said, shrugging again.

"Don't say sorry—that was excellent, really," I said, patting her outstretched legs.

She gave me an innocent smile and leaned into Jana.

My heart warmed at seeing the bond that was already blooming between the reunited sisters. "Where was I?" I hesitated, searching my memory banks. "Oh ya! In truth it was the leader of this group who had concocted this plan, which included casting down those from the Celaeno star—the others hadn't known of it," I said, leading into the story of how these first cast down Earthbound had to learn to live among humans, and how they needed to protect themselves now that they were more vulnerable than before. I explained about Anael and Thanael, the pairings, and how they had used the rings to create warriors to help them survive. "They'd never needed to create ones like them before—there'd never been a war amongst their kind," I explained. Then I went on to describe how most of the Earthbound went out among humans to learn languages and skills. As man evolved, so did they. Some chose to stay hidden, while others elected to live among humans. I ran through the part about Thaddeus and his crew later being cast down by Purah and the Stewards, *and* the disturbing shit Thaddeus had been doing ever since. "Unfortunately, being so long on Earth, the Earthbound began to feel the effects of it, hunger and thirst, along with changes in appearance—aging, and a host of other human-defined weaknesses. *And* they were no longer immortal."

"Do they age?" Natalie asked.

"Yes," I said. That would have been my question too, though I had expected more of an interrogation of all I'd just shared. I shifted my focus from Natalie to Jana. "As time went on, those who stopped hiding found human companions." Shifting my attention to the medical equipment next to the bed, I pondered for a moment on how to share the next part. Choosing my words, I said, "This choice proved to be heartbreaking for both, due to the fact that the Earthbound age at a rate of one year for every ten human years. And they have to continue to cover up this fact, burdened with reinventing themselves in order to continue to exist in the human world." I glanced at Natalie, then stole a look Jana's way to see her expression was now sorrowful.

"What happened to these warriors?" Natalie asked, pulling my attention back to her.

"Collectively, they are known as *The Guards of Haven*. They all have special abilities, *aaaand* they are the ones who belong to this covert team you were told about. They were originally created to help the rest of the Earthbound survive, but now they watch over Thaddeus and his cronies." I looked at Jana. Her expression was less mournful, but still it was clear her thoughts were heavy.

"This is the same guy who runs this fake medical group—am I right?" Natalie responded.

"Yup." I nodded, astonished at how well she was handling everything being thrown at her thus far.

Natalie took up the letter from her lap, refolded it and then returned it to the other unread ones in the pile. "And these Guards of Haven, they're here, at this facility?" She stared at me, and I noticed a line forming between her brows.

"Yup." I glanced at Jana briefly; she too had her brows squeezed.

"Have I met any?" Natalie asked then.

"Yup," I said for the third time. "Nicolas North."

Natalie's eyebrows rose. "You mean Nic—the one who's been taking care of me?"

"And your professor, Bennet Frost—*Ben*," I said, grateful to be close to the end of this lengthy story.

"Professor Frost? They told me he was involved, but I had no idea. Who else?" Natalie urged, her voice filled with enthusiasm now.

"You'll meet them all eventually. There are seven in total," Jana shared, emerging now from what I could only assume were her internal reflections.

"Did she meet Leo yet?" I asked Jana.

"Yes," Natalie answered for her. "He runs this place."

"Leonardo Winter—*Leo*, is another one of the Guards," I said, the heft of it all suddenly feeling lighter.

"And Kris," Jana said, smiley, though I could see the shimmer of building tears in her eyes.

"Your boyfriend?" Natalie took Jana's hand in hers.

Jana grinned again as she held back tears.

"And why can't the seraphim just return to the stars?" Natalie questioned, her focus flipping from me to Jana and back again.

"Seraphim can't travel like the other angels."

"What do you mean, travel?"

"They can't just dematerialize and reappear in another location." Natalie nodded her head slowly.

"That's where the Stewards come in. Unfortunately, the Earthbound were sent down without proper preparation—but that's another story."

"And that's why they're called *Earthbound*." Natalie rolled her eyes like she felt stupid for not grasping the name sooner.

"Exactly." I patted her leg again. "Once a Steward sends a Seraph down to Earth—to the requested location, then their… *wings* are used to get them from place to place."

"Wings?" Natalie hollered. This time it was her eyes that widened, showing their whites.

I had foreseen as much, but keeping my voice calm, I said, "They are the only angels who have wings. And Earthbound Seraphim can't veil themselves," I added, aiming to halt a speeding barrage of questions.

"So these Guards of Haven are like the Earthbound, only they were created here on Earth," Natalie said, affirming what I'd told them, leaving the word *wings* hanging in the air.

"Yes." I gave a firm nod.

Natalie turned to look at Jana, mouth agape. "So Mason's mom—Professor Frost, is one of the Earthbound?"

"Correct," Jana said, looking at Natalie and then back my way.

"That makes him a descendant like you," Natalie said, focusing back on me, assembling all the bits and pieces of info together.

"Kind of." I tipped my head from side to side again, confirming neither yes nor no. "He's what they call a *halfling*."

"So, am I a descendant too, like you?" Natalie questioned.

I smiled and blew out a breath. "Yes and no. You're like Mason. Your birthmother is one of the Earthbound."

"Who is she?" Natalie glanced at Jana again.

"Remember the Seraph I mentioned who created the Guards of Haven, *Anael*? She's your biological mother."

"Are you a descendant?" she asked, turning to Jana, brows pinched.

"No, both my parents were human." Jana gave Natalie a sad smile, as though disappointed at the fact.

Natalie sat up in the bed, leaning towards me. "How do they know for sure I'm one of these halflings—genetic testing?"

"Partly," I said, noticing then a young man in blue jeans and a white long-sleeved Après SNOW logo shirt standing in the doorway to the bedroom. "Hi—come on in," I said, directing the greeting at the dark-haired, extremely good-looking male I knew to be the elusive *Mason*. I had met him and his mother, Jules, via the North Haven video feed during the Christmas gathering at South Haven this past December, but this was my first time meeting him in person. I hadn't sensed his arrival, nor had I sensed Natalie's presence here before meeting her, and I hadn't sensed Taylor at the group home either when I'd visited way back. It was abundantly clear now that I most definitely could *not* sense halflings.

Mason strode casually over to where I sat and mouthed the words, "*Hi Lynn*." Then he turned to face the ladies in the bed.

Natalie's face beamed with excitement at seeing Mason. "You are not going to believe what Lynn just told us," she said, grinning at Mason. "Wait." She laughed then. "You probably already know all of this."

Mason gave her an absolutely dazzling smile, then sighed and mouthed the word, "*Yes*."

Be still, my beating heart. *What a doll*, I mused, grasping what all the young women's bluster was about. I cleared my throat. "Mason, we were just telling Natalie about how they determined she was a halfling like you. She knows about the genetic testing, but did you want to explain the birthmarks?" I suggested, well aware he had a dialog app he often used for people who didn't understand sign language.

He mouthed and signed *"Yes"* again, then took out his cellphone from his jeans pocket. A few moments later, after he'd typed into the app, a pleasant male voice began speaking from the phone. "Each of the Earthbound has snowflake-shaped marks on each shoulder blades representing the spots where wings emerge. And although the marks are not identical, no two pairs are alike." Mason paused the app.

As Mason's app had interpreted the details, I'd observed Natalie's expression change from the clear understanding she had earlier to one of confusion. "Mason, can you turn, pull up your shirt—show Natalie your markings?"

Mason nodded, then turned his back to us. Reaching over his shoulders, he yanked up the back of his white shirt. The skin of his back was bronze and smooth, the only markings being the pale snowflake-shaped designs on each of his shoulder blades.

"I have birthmarks just like that," Natalie exclaimed, pointing, shifting from her position beside Jana to kneel at the edge of the bed. "My mother always said they looked like those paper snowflakes you make in preschool, only smaller and more delicate."

Mason let his shirt drop before turning back to face us.

"Mason and I both have that rare gene," Natalie said, her brows scrunching tighter as though she *almost* had things figured out.

Then Mason hit the play button on his app again. "Most don't survive to their 20th birthday," the voice app stated then.

"I guess I should count myself lucky," Natalie said as though relieved, swinging her legs over to sit on the edge of the bed.

Mason knelt down next to my chair and in front of where Natalie now sat.

"You are," I said gently, knowing everyone had felt the same anguish over her having suffered the transition.

"Are there many like us?" Natalie directed at me. "Halflings?"

"I'm the only one like *me* in existence, but there are very few like you, *halflings*. Although the Earthbound and the Guards of Haven have your same unique genes as well," I said, hoping that was good news to her. I took Natalie's hand. "Jana, can you hold Natalie's other hand?"

Saying nothing, Jana came to the edge of the bed, taking up the same position as Natalie, before clasping her other hand.

"What—wait—what's going on?" Natalie questioned, but she didn't pull away. In fact, she gripped our hands tighter. "What do the markings mean?" Her expression was pleading as she glanced at each of us.

"Remember how I explained that Seraphim were the only angels who had wings?"

"Yeaaaah." Natalie's mouth gaped.

Mason hit the app's play button again. "The wings are composed of all white, but the tip colour of the primary feathers varies," the app stated for us. "Those from the Pleiades stars are black tipped to match the markings on their backs. The Guards of Haven are in shades of grey, as are their markings. Their wings lay dormant in the shoulder blades and only come out when needed. They are connected to their cardiac and respiratory systems, which allows them to adapt to any atmosphere." Mason paused the app and glanced over at me.

"Halflings…," I began to say.

"Are you saying I could grow wings?" Natalie interrupted.

I took in a breath to speak, but then Mason's app continued for me.

"Halflings who survive proper development of their wings will have the full capacity of them, but they lack the instinct of their use. It must be taught," the voice explained.

"WHAT?" Natalie screamed, trying to break free this time of my and Jana's grip.

"Natalie, it's okay," I said, seeking to calm her worries. "Your biggest challenge is learning to accept what you are. You weren't raised with a Seraph parent like Mason was, but we're all here to help you." I turned to Mason. "Please show her." I held tight to Natalie. "Halflings have grey, white-tipped wings," I stated, turning my attention to Mason.

Mason stood, stepping back, and a second later his immaculate grey, white-tipped wings bloomed out from the back of his shirt.

"Holy shit!" Natalie shouted, her voice turning panicky. "I'm twenty-one. Maybe that won't happen to me."

"That's the thing, Natalie—it's already happened," I said, lightly rubbing my free hand over her back.

"The pa-pa pain in my ba-ba back," she sputtered out, as the reality crashed into her.

"Yes," I said, turning then to Mason as he knelt again, his wings retracting out of sight. I took his hand and transferred Natalie's hand from mine into his.

Natalie stared down at Mason's hand around hers. "What about my roommates—do they know where I am?" she asked, glancing up at him.

"Mason contacted Tina already—she knows you had a pretty bad allergic reaction, and that Mason took you to the hospital," I answered for him. "She was told that you can't have visitors right now. And she's updated your roommates on the situation. They have Nic's phone number if they have questions." She already knew all this, but I stated it anyway.

"What am I going to tell them?" Natalie breathed out, slouching in her spot on the bed, still holding Mason and Jana's hands.

"You can't tell them." I knew how hard it would be. "The fewer people who know, the safer you are, the safer they—we all are." I placed both my hands over the one that clasped hers.

"I can't tell Teeny? But she's my best friend." Natalie looked at me and then shook her head slowly several times back and forth in disbelief. "What about school?" Natalie asked, looking at Mason again.

"Jules—Professor Forest, Mason's mom," I rushed out, "contacted the university on your behalf, remember?" Her memory was undoubtedly scrambled from trying to digest all this bizarre news.

"But I have to attend school—the financial support I'm getting depends on my being in school," she said, still panicked.

I didn't know the answer to that and looked Mason's way. "Do you know?"

He gave me the thumbs-up as if to say it was covered.

"There—see—nothing to worry about," I interpreted, trying to be reassuring.

"I know it's a lot. But we'll work it all out, okay," Jana said then as though to give her more hope.

Natalie turned her attention back to Mason. "How am I going to do this?"

Mason tapped something on his phone with his free hand and then the voice app said, "I'm going to help you." Mason set down his phone and overlapped the hand I had overtop his and Natalie's.

Jana copied Mason's action. "We are all going to help you," she added, placing her free hand over ours.

Chapter 13 

The Merope Building, Saturday, February 18th, New York City, USA

Lyndon tapped his boots together, knocking the snow off them that he'd picked up from landing on the roof. Then he proceeded down the inner roof access stairs to the level for Marcus's office, intent on getting some intel for Leo on the whereabouts of Kendrick.

"What are you doing here?" Marcus asked, spinning his chair to face forward and address Lyndon as he stood in the doorway. He was in his typical seasonal turtleneck and matching dress pants, the colour of today's outfit a similar shade to his shoulder-length auburn hair. He only ever wore brown, black, or grey, and rarely was there any variety in the pieces of clothing.

"I had a local errand to run," Lyndon said. "Question for you." The cold leather of Lyndon's jacket creaked as he leaned a shoulder against the frame of the door.

"What's on your mind?" Marcus spun back to retrieve a folder from the shelf behind him.

"Kendrick… he was here in New York City in your stead when you went to Brazil, yes?"

"Yeah, he wasn't here long—a week at best." Marcus turned back to the computer, a manila file folder in his hand.

"When was the last time you heard from him?" Lyndon crossed his arms, his leather jacket releasing another creak.

"Personally," Marcus said, setting the folder down. He leaned his elbows on top of his desk, steepling his fingers. "I try to avoid talking to him at all costs, if I can. Maybe he's with Thaddeus." He dropped his hands and leaned back in his chair. "Why so inquisitive?"

"I was just wondering about what happened with his lead on those twin halflings in Norway, now that the facility has closed." Lyndon released his crossed arms and straightened.

"I'm guessing it was a bust, and I probably wouldn't bring it up if I were you."

Lyndon nodded. "True," he said before turning and heading out.

"Thanks for stopping by," Marcus called out in a sarcastic tone as Lyndon strode up the hall to the elevators.

He wasn't interested in sticking around chatting with Marcus; he just wanted the intel. It wasn't like him to chitchat, and he preferred not to bring any unnecessary attention his way. Besides, he actually did have an errand to run in the city.

Lyndon left through the main doors of the building, heading in the direction of the Grand Bazaar. The indoor market featured selected members of the New York Handmade Collective of local artists and crafters who sold a variety of handcrafted jewelry, art, pottery, stationery, vintage items, and artisan foods. His interest had been specifically in the upcycled wood products and handmade jewelry, and he had ordered something custom for Lane that he needed to pick up today. He wanted to give her an early gift for her 26th birthday before she left for her internship at the end of the month. Her birthday was a ways away on the 20th of March, but he'd wanted her to have something to take with her. He'd found the perfect pair of earrings for her when he'd visited the shops on an earlier visit to New York City, but the second part of the gift was ready now.

Lyndon stopped at the edge of the marketplace, admiring the fine engraving work on the top of the box that now contained the earrings he'd purchased prior.

"So, tell me about Anael's daughter," came the inquisitive voice of the New York facility's newest tracker, *Addison*.

Lyndon slid the tiny box into the inside pocket of his leather jacket, then glanced up, wishing he'd not lingered here after completing his errand. "What are you talking about?"

"*Natalie*, I believe, is her name," Addison said. "But I may have heard wrong."

"Heard from whom?" Lyndon scrutinized Addison from head to toe much like Thaddeus had often done to him. The Seraph had a menacing appearance with his blond hair cut so tight you could see his scalp, and his clothing a contrast in all black. Even his overcoat was black.

"I overheard *someone* talking, saying something about Anael having a daughter." Addison shoved his hands into the pockets of his coat.

Lyndon squinted. "Why would I know anything about that?" *What was this bastard playing*, Lyndon wondered.

"I heard your name mentioned in the same conversation." Addison took a step closer to Lyndon, staring at the scarred side of his face.

"Who was talking about me?" Lyndon demanded, fighting the urge to cover his scar.

"Oh, I can't say." Addison rocked on his heels. "But I'm sure Thaddeus will find this bit of information interesting."

Keeping his expression impassive, Lyndon said, "If it's true—if Anael does have a daughter, why would she be here?"

"I didn't say she was here, but I had wondered the same thing." Addison's eyebrows bunched as he continued to stare at the scarred side of Lyndon's face.

"Whatever," Lyndon said dismissively, taking a step to leave.

"You have somewhere urgent to be, do you?" Addison asked then, his tone patronizing.

"As a matter of fact, I do." Lyndon paused. "And before you ask, DON'T!" Lyndon pointed a finger at him and then pushed past him to continue up the street.

Addison spun from the push. "Hmmm, so quick to hurry off. Maybe you know more than you're sharing."

"I'm done talking with you," Lyndon tossed over his shoulder.

"Wait," Addison called after him. "Anael's offspring wouldn't by any chance be that female you've been spending so much time with, now could it?"

Lyndon halted in his steps, fists clenching as he turned back to the infuriating Seraph. "She. Is. NOT. Anael's daughter."

"Right," Addison mocked. "Now what's that human saying? *Methinks thou dost protest too much.*" Addison tilted his head as though he thought himself clever.

Lyndon strode back over to where Addison stood on the curb, then calmly said, "The line is from Shakespeare's Hamlet. '*The lady doth protest too much, methinks*' spoken by Queen Gertrude. If you're going to quote something, at least endeavor to get it right."

"Well, look at you. That female's smarts must be rubbing off on you." Addison took a leisurely step back from Lyndon.

"She's not Anael's daughter," he repeated more calmly this time. "Besides, she has two fathers—they used a surrogate, and she looks nothing like Anael." *Don't let this asshole get under your skin,* Lyndon told himself.

"Seems you know quite a lot about this young female? Anything else you'd care to share?" Addison stepped to the side this time and out of the way of pedestrians.

Lyndon held his tongue, mentally chiding himself for sharing far too much already. He needed to keep his mouth shut and halt further engaging with this idiot.

"Still…," Addison said, when Lyndon endeavored to leave again.

Lyndon shook his head and closed his eyes. Opening them, he said, "You must be insane if you think for one minute Anael would involve herself with humans, let alone be host to and carry a young for them."

A ringing cellphone emanated from somewhere on Addison's person. Pulling a hand from his coat pocket, Addison held up his finger as if in command for Lyndon not to speak. Then he retrieved his phone from the inside pocket of his trench coat. Checking the screen, he said, "Duty calls." Grinning haughtily, he turned on his heels and briskly strode off in the opposite direction.

Lyndon arrived at the group home, setting down on the far side of the backyard out of view. From his vantage point, he could see Lane through the large window sitting with Taylor at one of the round tables in the playroom. Today was Lane's last day volunteering here at the group home. Since she was going to be away for a while in Italy for her internship, it would be awhile before she got to spend time with Taylor again. Calmer now at seeing Lane, Lyndon circled around to the entrance, then stomped the snow once again off his boots before proceeding inside.

At the opening to the large playroom, Lyndon hesitated, his heart swelling with emotion as he watched the exchange between Lane and Taylor conversing with the use of ASL. Lane was wearing black jeans and a deep plum coloured sweater that complemented her glossy black wavy hair. *Beautiful as always*, Lyndon thought.

When Lane noticed him in the doorway, she waved, then used the casual salute ASL sign for "hello."

He signed back the same and then crossed the room to the table where the two of them were seated.

"I wasn't sure if I would see you today," Lane said to Lyndon before handing over one of the educational sensory toys to Taylor. "You said you had to go to New York for something—an errand?"

"I did," Lyndon said, smiling at her. He once felt nervous in her presence; but now, he only felt comfort.

"We're both happy you are back," Lane added, turning her attention back to Taylor.

Lyndon knelt down in front of his son, the boy's focus changing promptly from the toy to Lyndon. "I missed you," Lyndon said while signing the words, extending his index finger to tap his chin before pointing at Taylor.

In place of echoing Lyndon's signing, Taylor used the sign for *"Me too,"* making the 'Y' handshape with both of his hands. Then he went back to playing.

"He's learned so much from you," Lyndon said to Lane, standing again.

"He's very smart." Lane followed with the double hand sign for *"Genius."*

"So are you." Lyndon reached out a hand to caress Lane's chin with his thumb.

Lane took his hand in hers and kissed his palm. "Can you stay?"

"Absolutely." Lyndon bowed, bringing Lane's hand to his mouth to kiss her knuckles. "I have a little surprise for you." He winked then, releasing her hand. "Let's go downstairs."

"Okay." Lane's cheeks flushed. "Carley should be over in a few minutes to work with Taylor," Lane added, getting up from her chair, grabbing her coat and purse off the back of it.

"He'll be fine on his own until then," Lyndon assured her. Then he bent and placed a gentle kiss on the top of Taylor's head.

In Lyndon's apartment on the lower level, Lane made herself comfortable in *her* leather armchair, while Lyndon hung up their coats. "How did your errand go?" Lane asked, dropping her purse next to the chair. After removing her shoes and setting them to the side, she crossed her socked feet atop the ottoman.

Lyndon retrieved Lane's gift from his coat pocket before crossing the room. "The errand part went well," he said, lowering himself down into the adjacent armchair, gift hidden in his big hand.

"And?" Lane said as though sensing there was more.

He was still angry about his encounter with Addison but was hesitant to mention it for fear of ruining their time together. Instead, he said, "I spoke with Marcus about Kendrick's whereabouts."

"I take it he had nothing on the topic." Lane made a pout.

"Yup." Lyndon nodded. "But I don't want to talk about them," he said, extending his closed fist out to her. "Happy early birthday, my beauty."

Lane's face beamed with excitement as she quickly removed her feet from atop the ottoman to place them back on the ground. She shifted in her seat to face him, then reached out and flipped his hand upright. "Com'on, open that big hand of yours," she pleaded, attempting to pry open each of his fingers.

When she gave up, he gave in, opening his hand, releasing one finger at a time to reveal what had been hidden within. "Take it," he surrendered. He and Taylor had given Lane a joint gift this past Christmas, but this was the first gift he'd ever given her just from him.

Lane drew his hand closer as if to see the item better. "Are those… constellations?" Lane questioned, staring at him wide-eyed.

"They are." Lyndon moved out of his chair to sit on the ottoman, facing her. "I had it specially made. This one is for Pisces and this one is Aries." Lyndon pointed to the engraved constellations on the lid of the small wooden box.

"I'm not familiar—tell me about them," Lane requested, her expression filled with enthusiasm.

"Okay," he said, a pleased smile stretching across his face. "Well, the Pisces constellation is in the northern sky—known as one of the 12 zodiac constellations. It's represented by two fish swimming in opposite directions connected by a cord." He pointed at the tiny carving for Pisces again. "In Latin, *Pisces* means 'the fishes'. The constellation is quite large, but it contains faint stars." He glanced up from the box to see Lane was still focused on him, listening intently. *This was going very well*, he mused. Continuing, he said, "Aries is also located in the Northern celestial hemisphere, and in Latin it means 'ram' and it is known for its association with the Golden Fleece in Greek mythology. It's one of the forty-eight constellations described by Ptolemy. He was a Greek mathematician, astronomer, geographer, astrologer, and music theorist who lived in Alexandria, Egypt, during the Roman Empire. I met him once." Lyndon paused when Lane's eyebrows raised up her forehead. "Anyway," he said, shaking his head, realizing he had veered off topic. "Aries remains one of the eighty-eight modern constellations."

"Why both?" Lane tenderly lifted the little box from his hand.

"Because you are what they call a 'cusp' baby."

"I'm a what?" Lane laughed out.

Lyndon smiled again, enjoying the sound of Lane's laughter. "A person can't be a Pisces *and* an Aries at the same time in terms of their sun sign, but they can be a *cusp* baby, meaning they're born on the cusp between the two signs. Born between March seventeenth and March twenty-third, like you—your birthday being on the twentieth. Do you know much about your sun signs?"

Lane shook her head. "No, not really."

Lyndon took the box from her. "Cusp people can exhibit traits of both signs. Aries is a fire sign, known for its assertiveness, impulsiveness, and directness."

"Sounds familiar." Lane grinned knowingly at him.

"Thought it might." Lyndon gave a little chuckle. "Pisces is a water sign, characterized by its sensitivity, emotional depth, and dreamy nature." Lyndon gave her a playful smile. "The sun transitions between these signs during this period, and individuals born during this time are said to be born on the 'Cusp of Rebirth'." Lyndon handed her back the box.

"Wow, you know a lot about this stuff," Lane said, accepting the small box and holding it in her right hand. "I love it—it's so beautiful and the constellations are expertly crafted." She lifted her free hand and wrapped her fingers around the back of Lyndon's neck. Then she leaned in and planted a firm kiss on his lips.

"I've been around," he said when she released his mouth. He stole a quick kiss, then tapped a finger on the lid of the box. "Open it."

"What?" Lane questioned, lifting the tiny, engraved lid. "Oh my goodness," she squealed, drawing in a long breath as she realized there was more to the gift than the tiny wooden box.

Inside, Lyndon had placed the delicate gold earrings he'd had custom made for her. "I hope they're to your liking."

"They're… *exquisite*," Lane breathed out, giving him an approving smile. She reached her free hand up to touch one of her earlobes. "Can I put them on?"

"Of course—they're yours."

Lane tipped the earrings out onto the palm of her hand.

"I noticed you don't often wear jewelry—gold studs on occasion, so I didn't want to get you anything too extravagant, just in case it wasn't your taste." He shrugged a shoulder.

"These are perfect." Lane turned both earring tops to face him. "What are the markings on them?"

"This one here—the one that looks kind of like a capital H is the glyph symbol for Pisces, and the other—the V-shaped one, is the glyph symbol for Aries." He grinned, watching as she adorned each of her earlobes with the dainty earrings.

"How do they look?" Lane asked, resting her fingertips on the sides of her slender neck.

"Sensitive and imaginative, like Pisces." He lightly caressed the lobe donning that symbol. "And impulsive and fiery like Aries," he added teasingly, tickling the soft skin behind her ear.

Lane giggled, grabbing for his hands. "That sounds like me—but don't tell anyone I said so." She pulled him in for another kiss, this one lingering longer than the first. Breaking the kiss, Lane said, "You know—you're really great at the whole gift-giving thing." She leaned in for a second kiss. Then she knelt between his legs, wrapping both her arms around his shoulders, pressing her chest against his, and nuzzling his neck. *But you're even better at the kissing,*" she said in a soft whisper against his ear.

Chapter 14 

The Beach House, Sunday, February 26th, South Florida

It was Benjamin Franklin who said, *'Lost time is never found again'*, serving as a reminder to utilize our time wisely, that every moment should be valued and used purposefully, since wasted moments cannot be recovered.

Over the week that followed Valentine's Day and my 24-hour visit to Ottawa, I'd spoken with Mac and Alison, bringing them up to speed on what had transpired, the reason for my quick trip up north, and why I hadn't been able to see them. They'd not been impressed with my escapades of wearing another disguise and going to the hospital on my own, but they were sympathetic to my current distressing situation with Redmond.

On a more positive note, Leo and his fellow Guards had brought Lyndon firmer into their fold, explaining further how they had been educated by Anael and Thanael about Pleiades, Thaddeus and his minions, and about the fall of the Seraphim from the Celaeno star. They had tried to keep track of all the Earthbound, but they had later lost contact with several of them, and currently only knew the whereabouts of 75 percent of the originals. Together with Lyndon, Leo and the others took huge leaps of faith forward with several more meetings and exchanges of intel, learning more about the ins and outs of Thaddeus's organization, while Lyndon learned more about their team, their skills, where they had been set up originally and where they were currently. They'd each taken turns sparring and training with Lyndon, learning what fighting and weapons skills he possessed, and even teaching him a thing—or ten. Lyndon had also gone to South Haven to see the accommodation and meet up with Zach and Leo there.

During this time, I hadn't sensed any other celestials, not even Gabriel. I'd called out to him several times, but he'd been a no-show, and I wondered now if he, like Redmond, was mad at me for my most recent solo escapade. I had, however, finally provided Grier with all of *my* details when we'd attended her birthday dinner celebration/beach bonfire get-together last week that Zuriel had organized. She'd already met Zach and Leo on New Year's, but now that she understood the particulars of their existence, it had helped to explain their *bigness*. Grier had inquired about Darius as well, asking if he was one of these Earthbound, but I'd explained he wasn't, though he still had his role. Then I'd enlightened her about my girlfriends and the series of events leading up to the gathering and where they all were now. The birthday gathering had been fun and a welcome break from the enormity of all that had transpired.

Then, to emphasize the magnitude of things to Lyndon even further, laying things out on the line as to how immense this new secret alliance was, Zach, Leo, and I, along with Redmond, who was still barely speaking to me, arranged to meet with Lyndon at South Haven yesterday, where we explained to *him* how it was that I fit into all this. During the discussion, we *hadn't* shared much about Redmond's role or his ancestors in hopes of avoiding any dialog about the twins, steering clear of questions about our combined lineages or if we'd produced extraordinary offspring. Although the avoidance was largely to keep things hush-hush about what abilities the twins actually had.

The high note of the visit was the fact that Lane too had decided to come down to visit. It would be a short visit, mind you, because she had to fly out at the end of the week for her new internship in

Italy. She and Lyndon had spent the morning over at Grier's house, as Lane had been eager to meet both Zuriel and Grier, and she had also wanted to speak with Zuriel about their shared interest in ocean conservation. Lyndon's update for Zuriel had been an emotional one, mainly because Lyndon had returned something extremely precious that had belonged to Zuriel, his severed wings. This afternoon, Lane and Lyndon were coming over to the Beach House for the first time, to have lunch with us *and* to formally meet the twins.

At 11:45 a.m. there was a *"knock"* on our front door, but I was already heading in that direction, having sensed Lyndon's unique signature. "I got it," I called out before quickly opening the door. "Welcome!" I said in greeting to Lane and Lyndon as they stood holding hands at the front entrance. "Come in—come in!"

"Aunt Lyyyynn," Lane said cheerily, letting go of Lyndon's hand to step forward and embrace me in a hug. "What a view!" she exclaimed, releasing me to stare across the open living room. Then she strode forward to the brilliant view out the wall of floor to ceiling windows that revealed the seagrape trees and the beach and ocean beyond.

"We tolerate it," I joked. "Good to see you, too, Lane."

Lyndon stepped forward to shake my hand, and I pulled him in for a hug instead. I knew it might be uncomfortable for him, but I still wanted him to know we cared about him. "Good to see you again," I said mid-hug. There was a brief hesitation in Lyndon with my boldness as I squeezed him, but it vanished quickly, and he gently squeezed me back.

"Thank you for inviting us to your home," he said upon the release of our hug.

I patted his arm. "Of course—you're always welcome."

He nodded in response, giving me an innocent smile before moving forward to where Lane now stood gazing out at the view.

"Wonderful to see you both again," Redmond said, pulling their attention as he crossed from where he'd been in the kitchen to the living room. He extended his hand to Lyndon for a handshake.

"Redmond—thank you so much for having us," Lyndon said, shaking his hand. "Beautiful kitchen you have there," he added, admiring the room beyond the dining area.

"Thanks, it came with the view," Redmond quipped, reaching past Lyndon to take Lane in a hug. "Always good to see you, Lane."

"You too," she said, giving him an extra squeeze.

It was then that the twins made their entrance, racing up the hall from their bedrooms to great our guests.

"Heeeey, Lane," Ryley said, announcing her arrival and pulling everyone's attention from the view out the windows. Redmond had dressed them in similar clothes to what I'd chosen to wear, jeans and long-sleeved t-shirts. Although the shirts they were wearing were yellow for Hayley and green for Ryley, donning the same *Fender* guitar label he had on his shirt.

Ryley's greeting was quickly followed up by Hayley's "Hiii, Lane."

Lane hurried over and embraced them both. "I'm soooo happy to see you two again." Lane had met the twins over the video feed from North Haven last Christmas when we'd celebrated at South Haven, but this was the first time they'd met in person.

"Us too," the girls said back, hugging her again. Letting go of Lane, the twins came to stand next to Redmond.

"Lyndon, these are our daughters, Hayley and Ryley." He placed a hand on each of the girls' heads as he said their names. "Girls, this is our new friend Lyndon."

Ryley stepped up right away, hand out for a shake. "Nice to meet you."

Lyndon stared down at Ryley's tiny hand. Bowing low, he said, "It is my pleasure to make your acquaintance." Then he took her little hand in his massive one and gave it a gentle shake.

Ryley stepped back and then gave her sister a supportive bump with her shoulder to indicate it was her turn.

"Hello," Hayley said, tilting her head back to stare up at Lyndon.

"Hello," he said in response, dropping slowly to one knee to rest at Hayley's level and lifting his hand.

Hayley's eyebrows pinched as she studied Lyndon's face, then she dropped her focus to examine his massive hand.

"May I shake your hand?" he asked politely.

"You may," she said with a cheeky smile, placing her hand in his and adding a playful curtsey.

"Thank you. It's wonderful to meet you," Lyndon added before returning to his feet.

Hayley took a step back to stand beside her sister again.

"Who are these lovelies?" Lyndon asked as our fur-babies casually ambled up the hall into the dining area.

"Those are our other girls, Summer and Snow," Redmond replied.

Lyndon bent down to give each of them a pat on the head and a ruffle of their ears. "Lovely to meet you, ladies."

"Mum, can we go outside and play?" Ryley asked, running a hand down Summer's back, repeating the gesture next on Snow.

"Just until lunch is ready," Hayley added, linking her arm through her sister's.

"Yes," I said, glancing at Redmond, suddenly feeling the need for his approval. He hadn't let me make any decisions today other than what I chose to wear. He'd chosen to wear cargo pants and a black Fender logo t-shirt, but even after I'd put on my favorite jeans and a periwinkle long-sleeved t-shirt, *his* favorite, he hadn't indicated his approval one way or the other, and I was still feeling unsure whether I'd made the right selection.

He nodded at me. "Just don't tire the dogs out, okay?" he directed at the twins.

"We won't," the girls answered in unison as they proceeded to the sliding glass door.

"Come on," Ryley said, waving the dogs over as she slid open the door to the back deck.

"Can I offer anyone a drink?" Redmond asked when the sliding door shut.

"We have wine," I suggested, moving to the kitchen to pull out wineglasses.

"I'll take *red* if you have it?" Lane said, coming to stand at the kitchen island.

"Wine, Lyndon?" Redmond asked, holding up a bottle of red in his right hand and a bottle of white in his left.

"Yes, please—whatever Lane is having," he said in response, following Lane to the island.

I set out four stemmed wineglasses in front of us on the kitchen island as Redmond opened the bottle of red wine. "That's a great colour on you," I directed at Lyndon, complementing the light heather green t-shirt he was wearing.

"Lane picked it out for me," he said, running a hand down the front of it before glancing over at Lane.

"Brings out the colour of his beautiful eyes," Lane said, taking up his hand to hold it again.

"Okay, lovebirds," Redmond cut in, pouring wine into the last glass. "Let's make a toast."

"What should we toast?" I smiled at Redmond, but he didn't smile back.

Instead, he lifted his wineglass to the visiting couple and declared, "Here's to family and new friends."

Pushing past my disappointment at Redmond's lack of reply, I raised my glass and winked at Lane before smiling at Lyndon. "To family and friends," I said, clinking my glass to the others. Then I took a long sip of my wine.

"Lyndon, I hear you like to cook," Redmond said, setting his wineglass on the counter next to the ingredients he'd set aside for making our lunch.

"I do." Lyndon nodded and then glanced at Lane.

"He's an amazing cook," Lane said, running her hand down Lyndon's arm.

"Redmond is making our lunch today—he loves to cook too," I interjected. "And I love to eat, so we make a great match."

Redmond gave me a thin smile as though he didn't fully agree with the *match* comment.

"What are you creating?" Lyndon took a hesitant step towards the kitchen counter that held the food ready to be prepped.

"*Pasta al limone*," Remond said, adding a chef's kiss hand gesture.

"Lemon pasta?" Lyndon questioned with delight. "May I watch?"

"You can help if you like." Redmond pulled out an additional cutting board from a lower cupboard.

Lyndon's face beamed with delight as he grinned at Redmond. "I would enjoy that very much—thank you."

"It's one of those dishes that's so simple, yet so delicious." Redmond placed the second cutting board on the counter. "I'd had it once at my favorite Italian restaurant in New York, and I wanted to make a version of it at home. *And* I wanted it to be just as lemony and creamy as the restaurant version. This lemon pasta version is just that and super easy to make."

"Where do we start?" Lyndon took up the space open in front of the extra cutting board Redmond had set out.

"All we need are a few simple ingredients: pasta, garlic, lemon and Parmesan." Redmond pointed at the recipe in his cooking notebook laid out next to the pile of ingredients.

"How can I help?"

"I'll take care of the pasta and lemon prep. How about you take care of the garlic and parsley?" Redmond slid the items next to Lyndon's cutting board.

"Those are fresh lemons from our lemon tree out front," I cut in. "Redmond planted it last year. He grows his own herbs too," I added, pointing at the kitchen window displaying a tidy garden along the inside window frame.

"That is fabulous," Lyndon replied, looking my way.

Redmond did not look my way.

Focusing back on Redmond, Lyndon said, "I prefer to use fresh ingredients as well. Even a simple dish has the best flavors when you use fresh elements."

"We'll watch from the sidelines," I tossed out, pointing a thumb over at the dining table. Lyndon smiled back at Lane and me, but Redmond once again ignored my comment.

"Everything okay?" Lane asked in a hushed voice, sitting down at the dining table.

I took the seat adjacent to Lane at the far end of the table. "Nope. It's been a week, and he's still pissed at me." I sneered in his direction before taking a sip of my wine. "Whatever. You're here," I said, patting Lane's hand. "That's all that matters right now." Then I squinted, leaning in to examine her earring. "Those are the ones Lyndon got you, eh?" Lane had shown both the earrings and the box to me on our video chat the day after Lyndon had given them to her.

Lane pushed her hair back and leaned closer, turning her head to show me both of her ears. "Aren't they perfect?"

"They really are." I smiled, then chin-nodded over at Lyndon. "And so is he," I whispered.

Lane's cheeks flushed, and she let out a giggle.

Her laughter had Redmond halting briefly to glance our way before he continued with reciting his recipe instructions to Lyndon. "We need the following:

2 pounds spaghetti cooked (with ½ cup pasta water reserved)
2 tablespoon lemon zest
6 tablespoons lemon juice
6 garlic cloves minced
6 tablespoons fresh parsley plus more for serving
0.5 teaspoon crushed red pepper
0.5 cup olive oil
0.5 teaspoon salt plus more for salting pasta water
0.67 cup freshly grated Parmesan cheese plus more for serving

"And black pepper for serving. We can leave out the crushed red peppers if you are sensitive to spice," he ended, looking our way.

"I like all those ingredients," Lane said with appreciation, grinning at the two *men* in the kitchen. "Lyndon knows I love pasta."

"Oh, she does," Lyndon teased, smiling at Lane before returning his attention to Redmond.

"Well, you've come to the right place." Redmond raised the box of dried pasta in the air and then turned back to Lyndon. "I like to make this dish with a long pasta, like spaghetti. I'm using linguini today, but you can make it with a shorter pasta if that's what you like."

Lyndon nodded several times. "I'm guessing you cook the pasta *al dente*, yes?"

"Yes, it's best for this dish."

"Lane, when is it best to cook pasta al dente?" Lyndon asked.

Lane smirked as if pleased at being included. "When you're tossing it with the sauce for a couple of minutes so it continues to cook. And if you overcook it, it can become too soft." She frowned and shook her head, and then she laughed. "No one likes mushy pasta."

"You're a good student," Redmond acknowledged. "Do the two of you cook together often?"

"I mostly watch," Lane confessed. "But sometimes I help chop stuff." She laughed again.

"I'm the same." I said, hoping to make Redmond smile. But he didn't. Not at me anyway.

"Every cook needs a good assistant." Redmond tapped Lyndon's arm with his elbow and smiled at him. Then he continued with the lunch prep, adding water and then salt to a huge pot before setting it on the closest burner. Handing Lyndon a large skillet, he said, "Heat the oil over medium heat."

"What oil do you use? Lyndon turned his head as though searching.

"I prefer the flavor of olive oil, but you can use any high-heat cooking oil for this." Redmond pointed to the variety of cooking oils lined up on the far side of the stove.

Lyndon grabbed the extra-virgin olive oil bottle from the lineup. "Half a cup you said, correct?"

"Correct." Redmond slid the measuring cup across the counter Lyndon's way.

Lyndon pulled a knife from the block containing the prep knives. "Six garlic cloves, minced," Lyndon said, snatching up a head of garlic from the decorative glass dish near the stove. "And six tablespoons of fresh parsley. Plus more for serving," he added, reciting from memory the items on Redmond's recipe list.

"You got it, Chef," Redmond cheered. "Add the garlic, parsley and crushed red peppers to the oil and cook until fragrant, about a minute."

"Thank you, chef," Lyndon responded, continuing with the task of chopping and mincing.

"I hope everyone likes garlic?" I tossed out. I loved the aroma of garlic heating up in olive oil almost as much as I loved eating it.

Lyndon and Lane exchanged flirtatious glances at the mention of garlic.

"What?" I questioned, poking Lane in the arm.

Lane smiled at Lyndon again. "If you are going to be kissing after dinner, it's best you *both* eat the garlic," Lane stated matter-of-factly.

Both Lane and I laughed, and so did Lyndon, but Redmond just continued on with his meal prep.

For the next 15 minutes, Lane and I sat quietly watching as the men did their thing.

"What's next?" Lyndon asked, breaking the awkward silence.

Redmond smiled appreciatively at Lyndon. "We reserve some of the pasta water," Redmond said, straining the al dente pasta. "Then we add the lemon zest, lemon juice, salt, reserved liquid *and* pasta." Redmond added the items to Lyndon's now-ready oil and garlic. "Cook until the pasta is heated through, also about a minute."

Lyndon stirred the pasta mixture gently, allowing everything to heat through for a few more seconds, and then he turned off the heat. "Parmesan cheese," he requested, grinning, hand out like a surgeon requesting a scalpel.

Redmond laughed then, and the moment reminded me of when we would cook together. I was always the helpful nurse during his meal operations. He glanced my way as if reminded as well. I smiled at him, but he glanced away.

"I find if you add two to three tablespoons of butter at the end it makes it a much richer sauce," Lyndon said, sharing some of his own cooking expertise.

"I do the same," Redmond said. "Even better, I stir in a half cup of heavy cream." Redmond moved to the fridge and pulled out a small carton of cream. Then he measured out the amount needed and added it to the mixture. "Salt and pepper, and we're all done."

"I bet this would be great with sauteed broccoli or spinach." Lyndon stirred the last ingredients into the aromatic sauce.

"I've done it with peas and roasted zucchini," Redmond said, popping open another bottle of red wine. "If you want to include some protein, you could add some lemon shrimp, grilled chicken, chicken sausage or even pan-seared scallops. They are all delicious with this." Redmond strode over to the dining table with the wine bottle.

"The twins don't eat fish though, so Redmond only does that version for us," I said as he proceeded to top up our glasses.

Redmond paused to look at me then.

Considering how much fun he seemed to be having cooking with Lyndon, I was hopeful my comment might spark a memory from the *night* of Valentine's Day, maybe even prompt a smile and perhaps steer him away from thoughts of my *faux pas* from the next morning. But it didn't.

Instead, he only smiled at Lane and then turned back to Lyndon. "I already prepared a caprese salad starter," he said, pulling the oval serving dish from the fridge drawer. "The girls and I got fresh bread from the bakery this morning, and I made some homemade honey butter."

"How lucky we are to have two great chefs catering to us today," I said, tapping Lane's wineglass with mine, attempting to keep my own spirits up.

"I'm guessing you'll have plenty of authentic Italian meals while you're in Italy," Redmond said, addressing Lane.

"I'd love to go to Italy someday." I gave Redmond a wistful smile, but again he ignored me, continuing to focus strictly on Lane.

"That's the plan," Lane said with a chuckle. "But the only reason my fathers were accepting of the destination for my internship was because my Uncle Marq would be relatively close by with keeping watch on the facility in Rome." Lane turned to me, giving me an eye-roll.

"Don't worry about that—just enjoy your time there," Redmond said, setting the open wine bottle on the dining table. "Lynn, can you get the sparkling white grape juice for the girls?" He directed at me.

"On it!" Surprised Redmond had addressed me, I got up quickly and went to the fridge to retrieve the fancy juice for the twins, as he went to the patio door.

Opening it, he stuck his head out through the opening and then bellowed, "Giiiirls! Lunch is readyyyyy!"

Just as I set the bottle of grape juice on the table, a rumble of footfalls and pitter-patters soon sounded as the twins followed by Summer and Snow bounded up the back steps to the deck.

"We're hungry," Ryley said, speaking for them both as they came through the open door.

"Go wash your hands first," Redmond said before they could plunk themselves at the dining table. "Hurry before you starve to death," he added before closing the door.

"Oooookaaaaaaaaay," they called out as they hustled up the hall to their bathroom.

Unconcerned, both Summer and Snow sauntered into the living room away from the commotion, and then they proceeded to flop down on the cool bamboo floor like they always did after playing with the girls in the backyard. They were getting up in age but were always up for a run-around and a ball toss as long as they got a long, uninterrupted nap after.

Padding up the hall back into the dining area, Ryley said, "Can we sit beside Lyndon?"

"Pleeeese," Hayley added, practically begging as she came to stand beside her sister.

Lyndon stood silently, holding the large serving dish filled with the lemon pasta in his hands, glancing back and forth between me and Redmond.

"That's up to Lyndon," Remond said firmly, despite evidence of his tight lips holding back a smile. "Go take your seats."

The girls scurried around to the far side of the table with the long bench seat. Plunking their little butts down, they slid to the ends, Ryley on the left side of the bench and Hayley on the right, making just enough room between them for Lyndon to sit. Ryley patted the open seat between her and her sister.

"It would be my pleasure," Lyndon said then, smiling sweetly at them. He shrugged his shoulders, glancing at Lane before he continued bringing the pasta over to the dining table. He returned to the kitchen briefly to grab his wineglass before granting the twins' wish by settling down on the bench seat between them.

Redmond rounded things up by placing the platter of caprese salad on the table next to the pasta dish. Then, he added the bread and honey butter to complete the meal presentation before pulling out the chair at the opposite end of the table from me.

As we chatted lightheartedly about our favorite things to eat, Redmond filled Ryley's plate and poured some sparkling white grape juice for her. I did the same at my end for Hayley's, and then I handed off the serving tongs to Lane for her to plate her food next.

Once everyone had their meals dished out, I raised my wineglass. "Here's to family and friends," I toasted again.

"I second that," Lane said, clinking my glass.

"Cheers," Redmond replied, clinking Lyndon's now raised glass.

Lyndon clinked Lane's glass and then mine. "Salute," Lyndon said, adding to the Italian-themed meal.

Hayley raised her plastic cup and tapped it against my wineglass. "Salute, Mum," she said, copying Lyndon.

Ryley did the same at her end with her father, and then the girls each took turns clinking theirs with Lyndon's wineglass.

"Salute," Ryley cheered, clearly enjoying the gathering.

"Saluted," Lyndon responded, tapping Ryley's cup before taking a sip of his wine.

"How did you get that scar?" Ryley brazenly asked then.

"Ryley, that's none of your beeswax," I said, shaking my head at her.

"It's okay," Lyndon said, unperturbed. "I had a bad reaction to a chalcogen, and it left me with this burn scar."

"What's a… *chalcogen*?" Ryley frowned.

Remaining focused on her, he said, "Chalcogens are a group of chemical elements."

Ryley scrunched up her face. "And one got on your face?"

Lyndon chuckled. "It did. You have to be very careful with chemicals."

I cut a glance at Lane. She was staring lovingly at Lyndon, a sweet smile lifting the corners of her mouth. I dared a look at Redmond to see he was smiling warmly at Lyndon.

"Can I touch it?" Ryley boldly requested.

"*Ryley*," Redmond said, his tone stern.

"It's fine, really," Lyndon assured him. Then he leaned to the side in Ryley's direction so she could reach it.

"It feels soft," Ryley said, satisfying her curiosity. Her mouth was agape as if she had expected it would be rough. "I have a scar on my knee." She pulled her right pant leg up, bending her knee to show Lyndon the barely there scar.

"Can I touch it?" he asked lightheartedly.

"Yup," Ryley said, letting him run his big finger over the scar. Then she moved on to show him another scar, this one on the pad of her thumb.

Lyndon pouted in concern. "How did you get those?"

"Surfing," she bragged, letting the pant leg drop as she set her foot back on the floor.

"She cut her knee and thumb on an outcropping of coral while surfing," Redmond clarified with a nod.

"Can I see your scar too?" Came Hayley's soft voice in request.

"Of course," Lyndon said, turning and lowering his head so his left cheek faced her.

"It looks like a *Wood White* butterfly," she said, eyes bright and wonder filled.

"A Leptidea sinapis," Lyndon said in response.

"Huh—you know it?" Hayley squinted suspiciously, like she'd caught him at something.

"I do." Lyndon grinned at Hayley, his expression jovial. "That butterfly is from the Pieridae family." Keeping his attention just on Hayley, he added, "They have white wings with grey markings near the center or tip of the wings."

Hayley's eyes widened. "And a system of delicate pale veins that run along the wings, making a branching pattern," Hayley declared excitedly as she softly traced the white lines of his scar with her tiny finger.

"That's right." Lyndon gave Hayley an appraising smile.

Her face beamed. "I think it's beautiful," she said, smiling proudly back up at him.

Lane reached across the table and gave Hayley's little shoulder a gentle squeeze. "So do I, Hayley. So. Do. I."

Chapter 15 

Into March, in spite of the evolving alliance happening between Lyndon and The Guards, to my dismay, the conflict between Redmond and me still remained.

Redmond had insisted on taking the girls for school drop-off and pickup, and that he would be the one helping them with their homework. On the days when I volunteered at the hospital, he stayed home but was usually down in his music room. On days I was home, the only time he spoke to me was when the twins were around, and that was usually only during mealtimes. When he wasn't with the girls, he was either at South Haven training with Zach or at the music studio pretending to work with Lily.

Luc had come down and stayed with us for a few weeks during Redmond's second month of stepping back, claiming he was here to do some jamming/recording with Redmond and a new client at the studio. When I'd found a moment to talk to Luc alone about Redmond, he told me that Redmond hadn't said anything on the topic of what I'd done, and when I asked his opinion on how to make things right again, Luc suggested that I just give Redmond time.

My nightly routine with Redmond of us getting ready for bed and talking while we did, had changed to me getting ready on my own and *waiting* for him to come to bed. On nights he was up late spending his time in the music room, which was most evenings, I had taken to reading in bed while waiting for him. I had already worked through three of the spy novels from author Michele Packard in this time and was on to a fourth. But still, each night, when Redmond eventually came to bed, he didn't bother to speak to me, not a word, not even after I'd said our usual *'goodnight'*. And because of our waning communication, I'd prodded Grier for any tools or techniques that could help to restore our relationship, but like Luc, she felt that giving Redmond time and *not* giving him any cause to worry, *trust building* she'd called it, would go a long way in healing the damage I'd inadvertently caused in my marriage. I was anxious for things to go back to the way they'd been, but as time went by, I realized things might never be the same.

I wasn't the only person whose relationship had drastically changed. Grier had lost her only in-person client, Zuriel, but had gained a love connection she never dreamed she'd find. She was, however, helping him cope with his grief over not being able to fly and the pieces of memory related to the cruelty he suffered at the hands of Thaddeus. Grier remained busy with her online clients as well, but luckily she hadn't been called to the hospital again during her on-call hours. This freedom had provided her with the time needed to explore her budding relationship with Zuriel. And while she was busy with work, Zuriel continued to meet with Zach and Leo at South Haven, building that relationship.

Leo and the others aided in acclimating Zuriel into their covert world, which in turn provided him with the tools required to stay off the grid. Along with securing his finances, having his banking funds transferred to a protected account, they had provided him with a new identity. He would still go by *Zuriel,* but they'd established for him a *human* identity with the surname Rian, believed to be an old Irish name meaning water or ocean, which suited him well, considering his affinity was for the ocean and its creatures. They'd also created him a history and background that related to Oceanic Environmental work. Marq had made his new driver's license, passport, forged his education and certifications, citing various companies from around the globe where he had supposedly worked, most of whom were either absorbed by larger companies, contracts that had been completed, or were owned by fellow Earthbound. Should he need any references, they'd likewise created a short list of fake professors and supervisors that potential employers could contact and leave a message, upon which Zach, Marq or Leo, *and* Jules would respond with glowing praise for him. Jules had written a letter of recommendation for his *fake* job with her during her time in Brazil. And like Lyndon, Zuriel had also taken to training at South Haven to improve his skills in self-defense. With Redmond's approval, I had continued with my training at South Haven with Zach while Den was away at his post in Amsterdam. Periodically, Redmond and I met with Leo and Zach at South Haven to discuss the evolution of both Natalie and Jana's integration with all things otherworldly. When I'd spoken with Lane on her birthday, she'd been so happy sharing about her internship in Italy and telling me how great things were with Lyndon, that I'd felt the need to lie when she'd asked how things were with Redmond and me. I'd told her that things were better, but in reality, Redmond had continued with his need for time and space, all the while I agonized over the possible outcome of losing him should it not be enough.

Then, when April arrived and crept closer to the end of the month, during what I had begun to refer to as the *healing time*, we'd received the most heart-wrenching news. It had been Alison who called to tell us that Mac's mother, Monica, had passed away, and that during the planning of her funeral service, just three days following her death, Mac's father had succumbed to his grief, dying of what we believed to be a broken heart. Alison and I had previously talked with Mac about watching her parents' health decline, stating how we always think we have time, when in reality, every moment is precious. Mac had felt so helpless at the time, and Alison had offered assistance with finding resources and services to help both of Mac's parents. We had reminded Mac that she wasn't alone in this, and that even though I couldn't be right there by her side, I was only a text, phone, or video call away. The four of us, Alison, Olivia, Vick and myself, had already been through the loss of our own moms, Monica being the last of our mothers to leave us. This past year we'd had several talks with our whole group about the Ottawa crew coming down for a get-together, but with everything that had gone on with

Iceland and finding Kris etc., a friends gathering had been put on the back-burner. Instead of the joyous visit we had all hoped for, in turn we had assembled in Ottawa at a funeral for both of Mac's parents.

Olivia and Alison had been with Mac almost every day leading up to the funeral, and I had been very appreciative of that since I wasn't local like they were. Darius had flown up with Redmond and me two days before, while Lily had remained behind to take care of the twins, the dogs, and the house for us. Luc and Dunya had arrived the day before and had spent time with Derek, who had already been in Ottawa visiting with Jules. Vicki and Eric had been in the middle of their travels to the Galapagos and had sent their love and condolences to Mac and her family, along with a beautiful flower arrangement with their regrets for not being able to make it back in time for the funeral. The rest of our crew, Olivia and Mike, along with Alison and Ken, had all been in attendance. I'm not sure why I hadn't expected it, but Uriel, Vretil, Raphael, and even Michael, who I thought would've been watching over Vicki on her adventure, had all been at the funeral. Although strange enough, there had been no sign of Gabriel.

Redmond had been his unwavering, *wonderful* self throughout the time in Ottawa with Mac and her family and our friends. He even sang and played guitar as part of the service, doing a rendition of *You'll Never Walk Alone* by Gerry and the Pacemakers. It had been hearing him sing the song that had finally broke me, and I'd surrendered a torrent of tears made from both the grief I felt over the loss of Mac's parents and the months of waiting for my husband to return to me. Still, I treasured Redmond for performing the song, and I loved the comfort he always managed to provide others during difficult times. Nonetheless, when we'd returned home after our time in Ottawa, he'd gone right back to being his *distant* self.

Uncertain of what was going to happen with us, I did my best not to let the girls see that anything was wrong, but they had asked several times what was up with their Da and me. I'd made excuses, but had still worried they knew there was more to it. Eventually, I'd had to tell them that I had made a big, bad mistake and that their Da was furious with me, which was the truth. I'd made sure to let them know we still loved each other and that things would be fine. That part I wasn't sure was true, but I said it because I was the one who needed to believe it was.

Was Redmond's love strong enough to survive this? I didn't know. I loved him, but I understood that I might have stretched his love beyond its limits. I'd pushed him too far, and now I feared that he would not be able to get past it. I'd never seen him like this before. Every time I reached for him, tried to hug him, or even just touch him, he pulled away. It was as though he'd taken this enormous step back, not from our life in general or from the girls, just me, from us as a couple. I urged him to talk things out, but he would simply say, *"I'm not ready—I need space to process everything,"* and then he would quite literally walk away. It was a blow to my heart, to my very soul each time he spoke the words of his obvious disappointment in me. It was clear that the only way Remond and I were going to get through this was for me to give him what he asked for, what he needed. *Time.*

Gabriel's words still echoed often in my head, *"You really did it this time"*, though I hadn't seen him since he'd spoken them. To my astonishment, when my birthday arrived near the beginning of May, Gabriel, my overly aloof birthfather, made a quick appearance to wish his only child a *happy birthday.* The twins had been thrilled to see him, though I hadn't been in the mood to celebrate. For the girls' sake, I had told them I wanted a day on the beach watching them and Redmond surf the waves. Gabriel had sat with me exchanging pleasantries while we watched the girls fearlessly endeavor to keep up with their father. It wasn't like Gabriel to be so *unavailable,* but I'd not interrogated him on his *absence* during our time together, and instead had mentioned the extensive integration of Lyndon and Zuriel into our ever-expanding *in-the - know* group. Then, when I'd mustered the strength to share my concerns over my injured relationship with Redmond, Gabriel had chosen that precise moment to disappear.

Later, after devouring homemade pizza made for my birthday dinner, the twins' request, and mint chip ice cream for dessert instead of cake, Redmond's favorite and *my* request, everyone's bellies were finally full. And after a day of sun and surfing, the twins' little bodies were exhausted, making them as pliable as you could get when needing to tuck them into their beds, and they had drifted off to sleep after an exchange of drowsy *"Goodnights"*. Redmond, it seemed, was exhausted too. I could tell, because he'd gone to get ready for bed ahead of me instead of heading down to the music room, like usual.

After brushing my teeth in silence, our new normal, I left the bathroom to get changed into my pajamas and ready myself for bed. But, instead of finding Redmond already in bed asleep, I found him seated on the end of the bed, holding the latest spy novel I'd been reading, along with a large manila envelope.

Handing it to me, he said, "Don't open it yet."

"Oookaaay," I said, taking it and standing in front of him, wondering if I should be pleased or worried he was actually talking to me.

He stared at the envelope in my hand. "You know how we had to obtain a marriage license to get married and then after the ceremony we had to sign it to make it official, but it wasn't fully official until we received the certificate?"

"Yes?" I glanced from Redmond to the envelope as the turbulence of his words scrambled my brain.

"Did you know that to renew your vows, there are no legal requirements, so you don't need a license or an officiant, that it's only symbolic?" He continued to focus on the envelope.

"I did know that," I said, glancing back at him a little more hopeful. Was he going to suggest we renew our vows?

He glanced up at me. "And you know how you had to file a Dissolution of Marriage to end your first marriage, and then sign a Petition for Dissolution of Marriage to make it official? But it's not completely official until the court signs the final order, the divorce decree?"

At that not-so-fun reminder, all I could do was nod. Is that what this envelope contained? Divorce papers? My stomach did a flip as dread seeped in.

Redmond's expression remained stoic and then he said, "To make an agreement between two people legally binding, it needs to include an offer, an acceptance, consideration—something of value exchanged, and a clear intention, with all parties having the legal capacity to enter the agreement."

"That all sounds very *official*, but I'm pretty confused right now," I said, intent on opening the god-damn envelope now.

But Redmond grabbed it back and said, "I want to make a legal agreement with you."

I swallowed hard. "What kind of agreement?"

He examined the envelope and then looked back at me. "Are you satisfied with being a wife and mother?"

"Yes, how could you even ask me that?" I frowned. "I love being your wife and mother to the twins," I added, trying to soften my tone.

"Is the volunteering not enough to keep you busy?"

I closed my eyes and drew in a breath. Opening my eyes, I said, "Please understand that I went from being a full-time computer engineer to volunteering in the NICU watching over critically ill babies, all while trying to solve the mystery of the gathering and my role in it, and now…," I blew out the breath. "…I chase down wheelchairs." I paused and glanced at the novel in his hand. "I just want to feel like I make a difference."

"But you did—you do, Lynn." Redmond sighed audibly, shaking his head. "You found Kris, and he and the others are forever grateful to you for that."

"I didn't find Kris." He was wrong. "Jana's friend Geir was the one who reached out to Den—that's how we found him."

"But it's not your job to save everyone—protect everyone." He shook his head again. "Look, I know we've both been trained by some of the best—The Guards. And I know if we had to, either of us could hold our own."

He was wrong again. I hadn't been able to hold my own. When Lyndon had grabbed hold of my forearm, I'd forgotten everything I'd learned. All those months of training were lost to me, and if I hadn't been so *lucky*, it being Lyndon who had found me, things could have been much worse. Lyndon wasn't a threat, but he could have been, and I would have been at his mercy.

"Lynn," Redmond said, pulling me from my doom musings. "But you're not a covert agent like *Matti Baker* from one of these novels."

He held the book up. "We are not trained in counterterrorism, and you are not a contract operative." Redmond tossed the book behind him onto the bed.

I knew better than anyone that I was no covert agent. Not even close. "But she does have a secret identity as a wife and mother though," I said, having no defense. Redmond was right. I'd been playing at being a spy but had forgotten the key factor, that you are only as good as your team. And I hadn't been a team player with going out on my own.

"I've updated the terms of our marriage," he said, pulling papers from the envelope. "We can't change the license, so instead, I want to add a new agreement. I've drawn up the papers for your review." He turned the paperwork around so I could see the first page.

"To create a legally binding agreement between two people, you need a written contract that includes clear terms, signatures from all parties. In some cases, you need notarization or filing with a relevant authority, but a notary or witness is optional in this case. And while verbal agreements can be binding, a written contract provides a clear record of the terms and is easier to enforce," he stated, handing me a pen.

I took the papers and read the terms.

It was clear, and the details were outlined in plain English. The agreement stated it was between me, Lynn Westlake, and Redmond Credente. The offer basically said, starting now, verbal communication must be made for and prior to circumstances meeting any or all of the following: investigating a hunch, found information, or curiosity. Going anywhere after nightfall or before sunrise. Meeting a friend, an acquaintance, or a stranger. Driving anywhere not previously scheduled. Or aiding any celestial beings. All weather considered dangerous or not. It also stated that text messages, voice messages, or third-party contact were not acceptable forms of communication, and that if my actions involved any level of inconvenience, risk, or danger, discussion over said action *must* be approved by Redmond. It wasn't that he had to approve everything I did, just the things that fell under that list, *and* he was dead serious about it. He'd signed his signature under the final statement in the agreement section that read,

> *I, Redmond Credente, promise to continue our marriage, nurture, and invest in said marriage as long as the above offer is met. Should the above agreement not be met, dissolution of marriage will be forthcoming.*

For the statement above where I was to sign, all it said was,

> *I, Lynn Westlake, agree to the terms outlined above.*

Without looking him in the face, I took the pen, and then signed the papers.

And for the first time in months, since that night on Valentine's Day, as we got into bed, Redmond said, *"Goodnight."*

Happy Birthday to me.

* * *

In the week that followed, we'd had a wonderful time celebrating the girls' 10th birthday at South Haven, with Den making a special visit just for them. Gabriel, too, had dropped in for cake and hugs, but when I asked why he hadn't answered my calls, he'd hurried off to deal with some 'celestial business', he'd called it. The Sunday after the twin's birthday was Mother's Day, and Redmond had helped the girls fix a delicious lunch in honor of their *mum*. I'd managed to keep it together through the rest of Mother's Day for the girls' sake, but my heart had been heavy knowing Mac would be without her mother on Mother's Day for the first time. Losing your mother, that kind of pain never goes away, but somehow, you find ways to live with the grief and their absence. Redmond had done a marvelous job of indulging the girls, though I could tell his heart hadn't been into it. How could I blame him? I'd put myself, the mother of his children, in danger without telling him what I'd planned. Things had worked out, but it didn't matter. Still, I had agreed to his *terms* and signed the papers. All I felt I could do now was hope for the best.

For Redmond's birthday in June, I'd helped the twins plan a barbecue with Grier and Zuriel and a few of the others who were at South Haven, but things between Redmond and me still remained rocky throughout the summer. But, by the time the girls went back to school in August to start 5th grade, I could feel the weight of things slowly beginning to lighten between us. However, it wasn't until November that I'd felt the big shift arrive.

The major turning point in healing our relationship had occurred at the wedding of Dunya's daughter Aleah. Darius, Lily, Redmond, the twins and I had all driven up to Orlando for the wedding together. Luc was there, of course, and he'd walked the bride down the aisle. Dunya's ex-husband had *not* been invited, and Aleah had wanted it that way, for both her and her mother. He hadn't been a part of Aleah's life for many reasons, but mainly due to the way he had treated her mother, and how he had always expressed his disappointment over having a daughter and not the *son* he'd wanted. He had stated that any university education would be a waste of time and money for a daughter, his opinion of women made perfectly clear, making the choice to step away from any contact with him that much easier. Luc, on the other hand, had been honored to take his place. He had always made it clear to Aleah how much he cared for her mother, and how proud he was that Aleah had chosen to further her education and do the things that made *her* happy. The theme of the day had definitely been *happiness*, and not just for the bride and groom, or Dunya and stepdad Luc. The happiness had also been granted to Redmond and me, and I'd known it right then during the ceremony that we'd reached a restorative moment. Redmond had turned to me, taken my hand, and said, *"No hesitations. I would do it again for sure—marry you all over again."* Then he kissed me. Our first kiss in 9 months.

This past December, we'd finally made good on our promise to take the girls on a ski trip, and had spent Christmas at the Calabogie ski lodge near my brother's place just a few hours outside of Ottawa. We'd met up with the North Haven crew at Après SNOW the morning of the 23rd for a special brunch where we finally got to meet Jules in person. Shayne had also been in attendance, and he too was a stunner, like the rest of the Earthbound males. It had been glorious to see everyone together for the holidays. As our gifts from them, we'd each been given the opportunity to pick two items from the restaurant merchandise shelf near the hostess stand. The twins and I had chosen grey hoodies for the cooler months in Florida and white short-sleeved t-shirts for the warmer because we thought it was funny to wear something in the hot weather that had the word 'snow' and a snowflake on it. Redmond had chosen a long-sleeved t-shirt and a short-sleeved t-shirt, both in black, stating either would be perfect for riding his motorcycle.

We'd also participated in Mac's family tree cutting tradition along with Alison and her family that afternoon of the 23rd. We spent Christmas Eve and Christmas Day with James and his doggies Radar and Night, who wasn't such a *nightmare* anymore. I'd felt Gabriel's presence on Christmas Eve, and the next morning the twins had told us he had made a special visit to see them. Though I wasn't sure why he hadn't come to see Redmond and me. The rest of the holiday week had been devoted to getting our skiing fix in before having to head home the following weekend.

As January flew by and into February marking it the 1 year revisit of Valentine's Day, it coupled with the lingering effects of the wedding and the Christmas holidays, the continued focus on love and family showed to have had a therapeutic effect on my emotionally distant husband, and added to my peace of mind, further mending the unintentional, yet cavernous wound I had caused him. Healing, soothed by *time*, had altogether transported Redmond *and* me back from the place where we'd gotten lost.

Chapter 16 

As one more blissful no-sign-of-Thaddeus year whizzed by, we found ourselves on the tail end of another wonderful Christmas, which was followed up on the 27th of the month with Redmond and me celebrating our 13th wedding anniversary. We'd finally taken that long-awaited weekend away together, venturing out on the motorcycle for a romantic getaway to Melbourne, Florida, just a short ride north of us.

It had been on a Friday the 13th in the Fall of 2010, during the very first video chat between Redmond and me, before we had even started dating, that Redmond had educated me on the nuances surrounding the number 13, the good and the bad. He had explained why some people consider Friday the 13th unlucky, how there were scientific names for the fear of that day, *paraskevidekatriaphobia*, and *triskaidekophobia* for the fear of the number 13. It's estimated that over 20 million people in the United States alone are impacted by a fear of Friday the 13th, making it the most feared date in history. Some people are so paralyzed by it they change their regular routines for work, avoid taking planes, and some don't even get out of bed. He told me that the fear went back as far as *The Last Supper*, and may have originated from that day. It had something to do with the combination of there being 13 people present; it being the *13th of Nasan Maudy*—preparation for Passover, and the night before *Good Friday*. He'd named several historical novels that mentioned its reference, as well as a more modern one by Dan Brown, *The Da Vinci Code*. I'd never read the book, but I had loved the movie version. A movie I hadn't loved was the actual 1980s film *Friday the 13th*, which at the time had scared the crap out of me. These days, other than disappointing Redmond, not much scared me.

For this number 13 reference, in typical Redmond research fashion, he had discovered that this many years of marriage was *not* considered unlucky. Not that anything out of the ordinary had occurred; it was just the fact that the 13th anniversary was all about the *finery of life*. For the tradition of this anniversary, it states the gift should be made of dainty lace, lovely and delicate, like '*the balance of a steady marriage*' or gemstones of warm citrine in an expression of a jovial, vibrant ray of sunshine to '*embrace all the joys of life*'. And even though things with us had remained *steady* and *balanced*, Redmond had chosen the sentiment of *embrace all the joys of life* and had gifted me a tiny citrine stone charm for my necklace. When he'd asked my girlfriends about his choice of gift, Alison had said she liked the honey colour of the gem, Mac had told him the stone represented happiness, and Olivia had added that it was associated with the Solar Plexus Chakra, and believed to help with balancing chakras and promoting emotional resilience. *Hear, hear*! I was all for that. In exchange, I'd gifted him with my support in having a garage built under the house in the carport space, which Redmond had informed me was to protect our vehicles from further ocean-side salt spray damage.

As the new year entered, and the next month passed without drama, exchanges between Lyndon, the Guards of Haven, and the rest of us slowed down and became routine, the topics becoming less complicated, and the interactions more leisurely. Everyone had had plenty to keep themselves engaged with the new alliances and the introductions of Grier, Jana and Natalie into *the knowing*. It had provided us all with an abundance of frequent dialog on how much had transpired over the last 2 years.

Speaking of *time passing*, when May came along, I had decided I was done with getting older, and would no longer be celebrating my birthday. I'd informed Redmond that as an alternative, I would now only be celebrating the *anniversary* of my 30th birthday, making this past one in May, the 27ᵗʰ anniversary. The twins thought it was silly, but what did they know, they'd only celebrated 12 of their birthdays so far. Redmond, on the other hand, had marked his birthday in June with a new tattoo. An intricate black and gold Celtic knot representing *family* that he'd had done in a combination of blackwork and geometric styling on his left pectoral muscle over his heart. It had been done so beautifully that I was now considering getting something similar done for myself as a first tattoo. With regard to the construction of Redmond's garage, the construction of which had begun in January, had unfortunately suffered numerous delays. But now with summer break almost at an end, I am happy to say the garage was finally completed last week, and just in time for the twins to head back to school.

The girls had repeatedly expressed how excited they were about going back to school, but I was sure their enthusiasm had more to do with the fact that in a few weeks they would be going into junior high, the location of the school being only a few blocks from our home. That last part I was thrilled about, especially after having driven them to the primary school at the south end of the island for the past 6 years. I know to an adult, going into grade 7 may sound like no *big deal*, but the tricky part, the part I hadn't been thrilled about, was the fact that the building that housed the grade 7 and 8 classes, was also attached to the high school. Double doors at the end of the main hall were all that divided the two buildings.

Hayley was more excited about school than Ryley, especially the language studies class. They had both taken Spanish the year prior, and had done well, but due to Hayley's enthusiasm in that class, she had been granted the opportunity to partake in the enhanced program, and would be learning French this year. They were both exceptionally bright and had participated in advanced-level classes. But during the state testing performed in the last month of grade 6, Ryley's results had shown her to be above average and right on target, while Hayley's test scores had shown an elevated aptitude in both mathematics and science, as well as in languages. Her results had been followed up with the recommendation that she be enrolled in the Grade 8 level classes for those disciplines. She'd still be following the grade 7 program for other subjects, but for the other three subjects she'd be with the upper grade students. The fallout of this meant that, for the first time, they would be separated in their schooling. Redmond and I weren't sure if it was going to be a good thing or a bad thing.

The next stage of departure from their twinness had been in respect to their hair. I'd had their hair cut into matching bobs several years back as it was easier to keep tidy, but they'd only agreed at the time because one of their surfer idols had had her hair cut that way. However, this summer for the very first time, they'd opted for different hairstyles. Hayley had kept hers in a similar bob, one long enough she could pull it back into a ponytail if needed. Whereas Ryley had let her wavy bob grow out, *free and wild*, as she had put it, echoing that of a talented longboard surfer, Ginger Caimi, who was making waves in the sport. I wasn't against *different*, but they'd already suffered some twin departure in their physicality with Ryley sprouting up to 5 foot 5 inches, an inch taller than me, clearly taking after their dad, while Hayley remained behind in her growth at 4 feet 11 inches. Nevertheless, to my disbelief, Hayley had been the one who had begun to show signs she might surpass her sister in *other* physiological ways.

According to the National Sexuality Education Standards, we as parents of tweens, had been sent a report by the district school board, stating students were to have a clear understanding of the following subjects: *Anatomy and Physiology, Puberty and Adolescent development, Healthy Relationships*, and *Personal Safety*. This meant they should be able to describe male and female reproductive systems, including body parts and their functions, explain the physical, social, and emotional changes that occur during puberty and adolescence, and describe how peers, media, family, society and culture influence ideas about body image, all by the end of the 5th and 6th grades. All of which we fully supported.

As part of the standards, they'd also been taught about the characteristics of healthy relationships, i.e. family, friends, and peers, and how to compare positive and negative ways friends and peers can influence relationships. They had learned positive ways to communicate differences of opinion while maintaining relationships. They'd also been instructed on the subject of *identity*, and sexual orientation as it pertained to romantic attraction to an individual of the same gender or different gender, plus how to treat others with dignity and respect. And it was a subject that had come in handy when Hayley's little-girl feelings for Den had clashed with her big-adolescent emotions.

The girls' teacher, Mr. McCray, *Gavin*, who we had become good friends with, had also become *special* friends with Den. Gavin had asked Den to come volunteer at the girls' school with activities and such, and on this particular occasion, the week following their 12th birthday, Hayley had spied the two of them holding hands near Den's SUV in the parking lot. We'd known she'd had a crush on Den, but Hayley had seen Gavin and Den together numerous times, so we'd never suspected she would have such a sensitive response to evidence of their more-than-friends relationship. After school that day, I'd found her on her bed in her room, hugging her pillow with tears in her eyes.

When I'd asked, "What has you so upset?"

Instead of getting an answer from Hayley, her sister had yelled from her adjacent room in response, *"She saw Mr. McCray and Den holding hands."*

Then I'd asked, "How did that make you feel?"

Hayley had answered for herself, and said, *"Good, happy."*

I'd been surprised by her reply, and questioned, *"You weren't sad to see them holding hands?*

"Yes… and no," she had said then. "You can like girls or boys or both, Mum."

"And you have special feelings for Den, I know…," I had begun to say, but then she'd cut in.

"But Mr. McCray looks at Den the same way Da looks at you — when you don't think we notice. And that makes me happy." Her lip had quivered some when she'd said it, but she didn't need me to explain Den and Gavin's relationship to her. It was clear to me she understood.

Instead, I'd said, "I'm very proud of you. It couldn't have been easy to see Den holding another person's hand, considering the close bond between the two of you."

She'd nodded and then said, "I'll be okay… but I bet a couple of Da's chocolate chip cookies would make me feel even better."

Hayley had gotten her first period the very next day, which explained the heightened reactions she'd been having. It had been serendipitous for us that the twins had already learned about how the timing of puberty and adolescent development can vary considerably but can still be healthy. They'd also been taught ways to manage the physical and emotional changes associated with puberty and personal hygiene, which can be awkward for young people. Some of the more difficult topics they'd been educated on covered pregnancy and reproduction, how puberty prepares human bodies for the potential to reproduce, sexually transmitted diseases and HIV, which had been followed up with explanations of some *age-appropriate* modes of transmission, as well as ways to prevent transmission, which were all part of the guidance about keeping yourself safe. Included in the safety class were also harassment and bullying, why it's wrong, and why people tease, harass or bully others. They'd learned ways to communicate about how one is being treated, plus effective ways students can respond when they or someone else is being teased, harassed or bullied, and how to persuade others to take action in these situations, because too often people stand by and do nothing. They had even learned about sexual harassment and sexual abuse, as well as *refusal skills* like a clear 'no' statement, walking away, and/or repeating the refusal. For each of these new and potentially difficult topics, they had likewise been educated on how to identify parents *or* other trusted adults to whom they could ask questions about any of these areas. And again, Redmond and I were all for it.

Things sure have changed. Back in my day, you were lucky if you could score a copy of the Judy Blume book *Are You There God It's me Margaret*, which you read with a friend in secrecy, like the topic of getting your period was taboo or something.

With change being the theme that month, for their 12th birthday, the twins had requested a roller-skating party with their friends from school, but with the request had come the caveat that Redmond and I were *not* to hover. Apparently, I hadn't been the only one who had wanted to change how they celebrated their birthday this year. The day following their birthday, Ryley had asked me when I thought she would be getting her period. I had already given her and Hayley a copy of the Judy Blume book and a more modern, detailed book on puberty for girls to help ease the transition. But it hadn't been until I'd read the stats on *twins and puberty* that I'd learned it's often the less slender twin, surprisingly enough, who started puberty *first*, which meant that Ryley, despite her growth spurt, having the more athletic build, would more than likely be *last*.

As is often the case with big emotions, big reactions soon follow. Such had been the event when Hayley had gotten her period *first*. Ryley had acted out, and in fact, she had gotten her *first* detention when she'd rebelled by riding somebody's skateboard in the schoolyard at recess, and as a result she'd been tasked to write an essay on all the dangers that could occur from her doing so. When Ryley had gotten over being angry with her sister, Hayley had offered to help her write the essay. Then, by the end of June, Ryley's first experience with periods had arrived, and unsurprisingly, she had not been thrilled about it. Although I think it had more to do with the inconvenience of not being able to go to the Oceanic Center with Zuriel and Grier. Ryley had talked about wanting to become a marine biologist ever since summer camp there, and when she'd learned about Zuriel's forte with marine life, she'd been stoked at the invite for her and her sister to tag along with them for the *Friends of the Ocean* fundraiser. Sadly, she'd had to pass due to crippling cramps. Welcome to the girls' club.

I'd taken both of them to get their *first* bras the following weekend, not that they needed them yet. It was mainly to give Redmond a break from the ever-budding estrogen in the house. Obviously, Redmond had been privy to the period events, but the bra buying had been *his* first of many occasions to come that he would *not* be permitted to partake in. However, as for the other daughter challenges, I had left several of them in Redmond's capable hands.

First had been with the chores, meaning increasing them in difficulty, including taking Summer and Snow down for their potty breaks and picking up after them. Next had been the proper use of their tablets, which included granting access to age-appropriate music and books. Ryley wasn't as big a reader as Hayley, but she did love having her sister read to her. They had already read through all the *Babysitter Club books* by Ann M. Martin and were now venturing into the *Scarlet and Ivy* book series by Sophie Cleverly. The first in the series was titled *The Lost Twin*. Interesting enough though, Ryley was the one who loved to write. Her interest was poetry, and she always chose to buy colourful writing notebooks with her birthday money from Nana and Poppy. Ryley's writing style usually conveyed things in a mostly animated way, while Hayley's writing had always been very precise in description. This year, both of them had asked to buy special notebooks with the money they had received from their grandparents at Christmas. Hayley had asked hers to be in a journal format, and she had taken to writing in it daily.

Redmond's parents were doing well, though with age creeping in as it does, last year they'd opted for selling their fancy New York City condo and had joined Nainseadh's five siblings and their spouses, moving into the same affluent senior living community outside the city where they all lived now. Their children and spouses, *and* grandchildren, were also all doing great, thank goodness.

Even with the ever-changing atmosphere around us, including hormonal tweens in the house, I'd like to think that Redmond's and my healthy balance and well-earned happiness had come from our ongoing open conversations, continued trust building, and some shared healing. Though it definitely helped that I hadn't been presented with any clandestine opportunities over the past two years to rock the marital boat.

With regard to my girlfriends up north and the rest of our motley crew, they, too, have been through their own list of changes.

Chapter 17 

My girlfriends and I still do our video chats, though the frequency with Vicki and Olivia has gone down to once every couple of months. Vicki and Olivia have both been brought up to speed on the relevant changes and though they remain adamant about *not* being involved, they were content in the knowledge there had still been no sign of Thaddeus, *and* been put at ease with knowing we had Lyndon, our inside man, on the job as it were. Alison, Mac, and I still continued to chat every two weeks, sometimes more, even if we only had 15 minutes to touch base. As a descendant of Archangel Vretil, Alison's eidetic memory was a gift for recalling in high-precision things that she had seen once, or had only been told about and hadn't been present for, recording details as though she could see it in her mind, and she always had her notebook and pen at the ready should there be anything otherworldly to discuss.

At the beginning of this year, Alison had changed her role with the division of Children's Services, to working with the Indigenous Child and Family Service Agencies as an Indigenous Child, Youth, and Family Advocate, ensuring child safety and well-being, which was often within a culturally sensitive framework. Ken had changed his creative focus from that of a 3D animator to designing high-quality custom t-shirts and selling them online. Last April, their son Kevin turned 14 and was at the age when most teens stop spending time with their parents, but like most kids and young adults who went through COVID at home with their parents, he still had a very close relationship with his.

The year following the passing of Mac's parents had been an exceptionally arduous and emotional one for Mac, and I was grateful my girlfriends had rallied around her, helping her get through the worst of it by finding joy in conversation over memories of all the time they'd been able to spend with Monica and Fred. Vicki called in when she could, and Alison and Olivia were local to support Mac as she navigated what all of us had already experienced with the loss of our own parents. No one wants to be on the *I lost my parents* team, but you don't truly know what that loss feels like until you experience it yourself. When Mac had posted on social media about the loss, her first words had been, *'I'm not even sure how to put this out there.'* Her mother was her rock, her shoulder, her cheerleader, her confidante and one of her very best friends. Her dad had been kind, funny, generous, and one of the best storytellers, but watching her dad try to navigate his world without his soul mate had been exceptionally difficult for her to witness. Mac had also written in her post, *'If my mom taught me deep love and patience, my dad taught me how to not take life too seriously, to laugh often, to stand up for myself, and that when life knocks you down, it may kick you in the head while you're down there, but tomorrow is a new day.'* They would have been married 67 years that August. The loss had also been tough for Mac's sons. Her youngest son, Declan, turned 19 this past July, and has since moved out of the house and into a rental with a few of his buddies, which had Mac in tears over her baby leaving home too soon. Her eldest son, Carter, turned 22 this past March, but to her glee he had opted to stay home while finishing his university degree. Her husband, Don, was still booking fishing charters for the warmer months, and Mac had begun packaging and selling her maternity skincare products online. And though she wasn't working at the hospital with Olivia anymore, she still provided Olivia's clinic with the products she made and at reduced prices.

Vicki was happily settled in her new home with Eric in Greece, stating that they'd chosen it because the weather agreed with them, as did the food. To assist them with the transition of locations, making it much easier for them, I'd had a real estate friend of mine, the same realtor who had helped me sell Mom's house and get my brother his home in the country, help sell Vicki's home in Ottawa. Each time we chatted with Vicki, she reminded us that there was lots of room for visitors in their new home, and we were all more than open to meeting up there in the future.

Olivia had found her calling with the Childbirth Program at the hospital, and her two daughters had continued to move forward in their careers. Kate, now 30 years old, is now in charge of the Training and Development team at the University of Ottawa, and is still living in the garden home she bought after COVID. Rachel turned 28 this year and currently rents a house with two of her nurse coworkers. Unlike her mother, Rachel has fully immersed herself in supporting the Earthbound, assisting Nic anywhere he needed her for backup. Plus she still had an interest in learning more about magic from Mac. Olivia knew she couldn't control what her daughter did and she respected Rachel's desire to help the Earthbound, but she had been most pleased to hear that she, at Lane's suggestion, would be attending St Lawrence College to complete her Bachelor of Science in Nursing Honors this fall.

As for my friends further south, starting with Derek, well, apparently, Julianna had been interested in more than his brain and really was sweet on him. The two continue to maintain a long distant relationship that seems to work for both their schedules, and we were all pleased to witness the happiness that had blossomed from that friendship. Derek continues to do research with Nic and discuss their findings with Leo, breaching topics such as genetic classifications and ancestral groupings within a population, tracking the migration of the Earthbound and their offspring, and analysis of mitochondrial DNA, the haplotypes, haplogroups, and zygosity, to name just a few topics. Then there was epigenetics, the study of how our behaviors and environment can change the way our genes work and how it all links back to the migration of the Earthbound and how the different environments they encountered may have impacted them, stuff that made my brain hurt when he'd explained it, as well as reproductive endocrinology, which seemed to have been Thaddeus's focus before he had disappeared, that and cellular regeneration. Not a scary combination at all, no. Along with all that, considering what had happened with Kris, Zuriel, and Natalie's exposure to sulfur, Derek and Nic continue to research a safe way to test the vulnerabilities that the Earthbound had to various compounds mentioned in Thaddeus's journals.

Further south, just north of us near Orlando, Luc and Dunya were still living their happy life absent of drama except for the occasional visit to our neck of Florida.

Even closer to home, Lily and Darius too were living their happiest lives together, Lily in the music studio and Darius in his fitness space. They still spend major holidays with us, though sadly their trips to Miami to visit Darius's mother had ended when she'd passed away last November, and it was a terribly sad day despite her having reached 90 years of age. She had said to Darius that she had *lived in her house since the day she'd married his father*, and despite his passing when Darius was 2 years old, had been determined to stay until her own life came to an end. And she had, passing in her sleep, the kindest way someone could leave this earth. And like with Redmond and me, Darius continued his training at South Haven with Zach and sometimes Den.

Den visited occasionally these past few years and sometimes volunteered at the girls' school, but his focus had been mainly on the Amsterdam facility. Redmond and Gavin still got together on occasion to surf, but with Den absent most of the time, there hadn't been much socializing with the two of them. With having very few local friends, and with the twins changing schools this year, we wouldn't have the same crossover of seeing Gavin at school drop-offs either. I hadn't asked Den where he saw that relationship going; it hadn't been any of my business, but I'd be lying if I didn't wonder about the possible heartbreak in their future.

We'd had the occasional visit from Purah at the beach house, mainly for follow-up from our end, because, like the others, she had not seen hide nor hair of Thaddeus. Though she had made several inquiries about Leo on her first visits. I had informed her that *he* would be more than pleased to see her too. Something had sparked between them, I'd known it, and at pursuing my suggestion to seek him out, which she had, plus with encouragement from the others, Leo and she had become closer, that spark growing into a flame, encircled by respect and friendship. Their occasional meetings had eventually turned into time together every 2 weeks or so. What was to become of *their* relationship was unknown. There were no precedents or guidelines for circumstances like this, but as we all knew, you need to hold tight to joy when you find it.

Akin to Den's watching of the facility in Amsterdam, Marq's focus too had been on watching the facility in Rome, with the occasional visit with Lane back when she'd been doing her internship in Italy. He was still contemplating the idea of opening another gallery in Ottawa like the one he had in Rome and had been considering a space down the way from Kris and Leo's restaurant Après SNOW. I had selfishly suggested opening one here in our downtown area, but I knew a bigger city like Ottawa was more conducive to having a fruitful gallery.

Kris and Leo were still at the helm, running the restaurant with the help of Jana and Mason. As Jana celebrated another of her birthdays with Kris this past December, she had decided that *his* birthday should and would be going forward, the day they had officially met, the day she had saved him/found him on January 8th. Their relationship had blissfully moved forward, and Jana had moved into Kris's suite. Jana's friend Geir, from back in Iceland, had remained blissfully ignorant of the true goings on in his friend's life, but he had been busy with his veterinary clinic and *his* new boyfriend. Both he and Jana were happy in their lives, and that was all that mattered to them. Jana's friendship with Lane had grown deeper too now that there was no need for any secrets, *and* the fact they were both involved in serious relationships with Earthbound males. Both Jana and Lane had taken the time to integrate my newest friend, Grier, into their little group of *women who date angels*, by creating a safe space for them to talk on a regular basis. Grier and I talk and visit often, and she still has her practice, helping patients remotely from her beach cottage. Zuriel secured a great job last year as a Marien

Educator just a few minutes north of us at Florida Atlantic University (FAU) Harbor Branch Oceanographic Institute.

As for our newest member of *the knowing*, Natalie, my feeling was that she'd had the most to adapt to. First, according to Nic, she was the "most flawless" halfling they had ever found, meaning she had no physical issues, though they suspected early on that she suffers from asthma, but they weren't sure if it was genetic or from all the smoke exposure living with her aunt. When Lyndon had been introduced to Natalie, it was then we learned that he already knew about Shea, mainly because Thaddeus had thought to capture her and use her for his experiments. Lazarus had been the tracker who had located her, but since she had been considered *damaged*, having no lower legs, *and* because she was a teenager at the time of her discovery, Thaddeus had chosen not to deal with the hormones of the *useless female*, as he had called her, and had continued his search for a more undamaged specimen. Lyndon said that Lazarus had lost track of her after and had assumed she was dead, like so many of the others. Lyndon had been grateful to hear Shea was in fact *not* dead, and that Den had discovered her around that same time period, taken her under his wing, guided, trained, and prepared her for life's challenges as a halfling, similar to what the others were now doing for Natalie.

Natalie's second challenge had been explaining to her friends what had happened to her. Mason had taken care of telling them all the initial story, and Nic, as her doctor, had explained that Natalie had been moved from the hospital quarantine to a facility that specializes in her rare condition. To convince Teeny and her roommates that she was truly okay, Natalie did video chats from her new room, playing it off as though she was in the new facility. The fake version of events had been that she had SCID, *severe combined immunodeficiency*, a rare genetic disorder that severely weakens the immune system. If any of them had looked it up, they would have found that individuals with SCID lack the ability to produce functional white blood cells, making them highly susceptible to infections that can be fatal. Teeny, being her best friend, had questioned the treatment options. Natalie had told her that they would have normally done a bone marrow transfer which involved transplanting healthy stem cells from a matched donor, usually a sibling, into the patient's bone marrow, but since Natalie did not have any siblings, they had needed to go with gene therapy, which was a newer treatment option that involved correcting the genetic defect that causes SCID.

Natalie had loathed having to lie, but it had been a necessary fib to keep her secret safe. Initially, Natalie had been worried about school and the financial tie to her attending, but Leo had assured her that her finances would not be an issue, and Ben and Jules had found a way for her to continue her school year remotely. Once she was *well enough,* she would be able to make up her clinical onsite hours during the summer semester. Since her funds would still be coming in, she was also able to pay rent to her roommates for the remainder of her lease. And with Jana moving into Kris's space, that left Jana's old room open for Natalie to take over. To keep with the story, Natalie had shared that Lane's parents had offered up the extra room at their place for her to use while she was still in school, and this had laid the foundation for her continuing to stay at North Haven. Natalie's roommates had all been in their final year at university at the time of her illness, and with them moving on that spring, Natalie would have had to find a new place to live, anyway. Brady had moved home to Vancouver after getting a job with a friend of his father's doing biotech research. Kerry and Kelly had both moved to California, Kerry obtaining a gig in his field of study, Exercise Science and Athletic Therapy, as Athletic Trainer for the Los Angeles Kings, while Kelly followed his dreams too becoming the NHL Entry Draft to play defensemen for the same team. And their relocating out of Ottawa had aided in keeping Natalie's secret from them that much easier.

Currently, Natalie was more than halfway through her program at the university, and with the help of Mason and Lane's extended family, she had fully adjusted to her new world. While dealing with the challenges of attending university and Natalie's new reality, Mason and she had grown closer as friends, and their friendship further developed into a loving relationship during the past 2 years. Romance aside, there was no one better for each to be friends with considering their shared genetic kinship. Mason had also helped her with how to use her wings, but I believe that Natalie's biggest challenge had been having to keep things from her best friend Teeny.

Meanwhile, Zach and the others still kept tight surveillance on all the remaining facilities to ensure there with no signs of Thaddeus. Frank and Ina were kept in the loop, of course, but slowly everyone had begun to get comfortable with the idea that perhaps Thaddeus would never be coming back. As for identifying the unknown Earthbound who had been lurking in my vicinity, we briefly discussed the possibility of it being one of the Watcher angels from Sanctuary. Apparently, they were well-known for their *observing*. But based on my ever-growing signature sensation and variation for different types of angels, I was fairly confident it was an Earthbound. However, I did wonder why I hadn't ever sensed or seen another Watcher angel in all these years. As an added windfall in our ever thought-provoking world, there had been no *mirror* incidents, no unwanted Archangel visitors, and no bad dreams with the twins.

Well… not until the night before Lane went missing.

Chapter 18 

The Group Home, Thursday A.M. August 7th, 2025, Ottawa, Canada

NOW.

During Thaddeus's absence, Lyndon had visited the other facilities and found that no other halflings were being tested on. Grants for their research had been halted with the shift in administration, so they'd had to switch gears to keep the money flowing in. In fact, the people working at the remaining facilities had taken it upon themselves to develop treatments for several childhood ailments. This subsidized in keeping up with the money-making and philanthropic ventures that kept Thaddeus in the good graces of the governing medical establishments for the countries they were practicing in. With the Brazil and Norway operations shut down, there was less capital and funding coming in; therefore, resources had needed to be redirected to more profitable locations, and only the most essential employees were kept on. Lyndon had no detailed view into the finances of Thaddeus's empire, but he suspected that some of the redirected funds were going to whatever venture Thaddeus was undertaking in Brazil.

Marq and Leo have been monitoring the Brazilian news outlets for the past few years in hopes of finding any evidence of what Thaddeus has been up to. In the medical field, they found that Brazil was positioning itself as a potential leader in gene therapy in Latin America, but had also faced a severe dengue epidemic as well as an Oropouche virus outbreak in 2024. In other news, the country was suffering its own political woes, inflation concerns and fiscal challenges, social issues and human rights, along with Amazon rainforest and environmental concerns with increased deforestation and violence against environmental defenders. And despite an overall decline in violent crime, it was mixed with persistent challenges with organized crime and drug trafficking.

Lyndon had also found that in Brazil, cybercrimes had increased significantly, as had the violence against women and girls, as revealed in the horrifying statistics from the Public Security Annual Report. Domestic violence cases rose in the first half of 2023, with that year having the highest rate of femicide, which remains a serious concern. Investigations into human trafficking and slave labor had increased in 2023, which led investigators to a lengthy, ever-growing list of serial murders of females involved in prostitution and the homeless community.

The descriptions of these particular murders were grossly similar to those of the 1888 Whitechapel murders, where five women had their throats slit, four of whom had their abdomens mutilated, and one of the four, Mary Jane Kelly, had the whole surface of her abdomen and thighs removed and the abdominal cavity emptied of its viscera. Her breasts were also cut off, the arms mutilated by several jagged wounds, her face had been hacked beyond recognition of its features, and the tissues of her neck were severed all around, right down to the bone. Many considered the sadistic butcher to be a copycat of the infamous 'Jack the Ripper', and, like the notorious killer, this modern masochist too remains at large.

Lyndon had reported back to Leo on all of his findings, adding that those still under Thaddeus's regime, appeared not to care where their unreachable leader had gone, and continued with enjoying the spoils of the successful ventures they were basically running now, and blissfully all while the cat was away. That was right up until the moment they had all received notice that the absent cat was now coming back to Ottawa.

Since Zuriel was no longer part of Thaddeus's crew, Lyndon had reached out to him personally and shared the latest news about Thaddeus's return. Zuriel had offered to help where he could, but clearly it was best that he stayed where he was and out from under Thaddeus's radar. The last thing any of them needed was for Thaddeus or one of his minions to get a whiff of where Zuriel was located. Prior to his phone call to Zuriel, Lyndon had called Leo with the news of Thaddeus's impending return. With Lane being away on her latest work trip, he'd asked Leo's permission to be the one to tell her about Thaddeus, and without hesitation, Leo had given him the okay on the task.

These past few years had been wonderful for him and Lane, with their having the freedom, albeit covert time together, to get to know each other fully. Lyndon had never had a relationship like this with a human female, or any female for that matter, and considered himself the luckiest male alive with having the honor of Lane's friendship and now her love in his life. They had confessed their love for each other soon after that first trip they'd taken together to visit with Lynn and her family, right before Lane's internship in Italy.

That internship had led Lane to a role in the technical and economic feasibility project for a floating offshore wind farm in Puglia, Italy. Since then, Lane has worked at various postings in locations around the world, starting with the opportunity to work with water conservation in the South African mining industry, and then building water resilience into refinery operations in Southern Europe. She has been involved in the exploration of deep-sea habitats using mapping sonars, ROV systems, and other exploration technologies in the Western Pacific around Guam, the Commonwealth of the Northern Mariana Islands one of the most tectonically and volcanically dynamic locations on the planet, along the Federated States of Micronesia, the Solomon Islands, and the waters offshore Howland & Baker Islands located roughly midway between Hawai'i and New Zealand in the Central Pacific Ocean. All of which are some of the most isolated landmasses on Earth. Through each of Lane's journeys, wherever he could be, Lyndon had been by her side, so to speak. Her prior posting, one with the Canadian Space

Agency *smartWhales* Initiative, which focuses on protecting the endangered North Atlantic *right whale*, had transitioned her to her most recent gig and one much closer to home. Currently, she was on the job in Dartmouth, Nova Scotia, on the eastern coast of Canada, and she had arrived a mere week ago for a short 7-day consulting engagement at the Ocean, Coastal and River Engineering Research Center.

Today, Lyndon and Taylor were scheduled to have their latest morning video call with Lane before she had to start her last day on the job. Lyndon had already texted her to say they were waiting in the playroom for when she was ready for them to dial.

Lyndon's phone pinged then with a text from Lane that read,

Good morning, boys! Ready-ready, dial away.

Before clicking the link to dial the video chat, Lyndon tilted the tablet in its stand to an angle where both he and Taylor could see the screen. Upon connecting, the video screen displayed Lane sitting at her tiny kitchen table, her beautiful face smiling back at them. She wore a navy blue, company-logoed long-sleeved pullover, and she had her now waist-length black wavy hair pulled back in a long braid that draped over her left shoulder.

"Good morning, my little prince?" Lane said to Taylor in greeting, touching her dominant hand to her chin to begin the sign for the words, "*Good morning.*"

In response, Taylor immediately extended his index finger and touched his chin before pointing directly at Lane, signing, "*I miss you.*"

Lyndon swept a flat hand from left to right in front of Taylor before saying, "*Weee* missed you."

Taylor then extended both his index fingers forward moving them in an arch towards himself, followed with the fingers and thumb together of one hand touching his cheek near his mouth, moving it towards his ear then back to his cheek to say, "*Come home.*"

"Tomorrow," Lane said, signing the word by creating an 'A' handshape, thumb extended, then touching her thumb to the side of her chin, moving her hand forward in a small arc as if pointing to the future.

Instead of signing back, Taylor clapped his hands together, his face beaming as a smile broadened his cheeks.

Lyndon clapped too, then said, "I wish you were coming home today."

"Time for your exercises," came the friendly voice of Taylor's therapist from over Lyndon's shoulder. "Hi Lane," she said then, seeing they were on a video chat with her.

"Hiiii," Lane responded, waving at her through the video feed. "Be good," she directed at Taylor, signing again, starting with a flat, open hand with her fingers together at her chin, moving her hand in a downward arc.

Taylor grinned again, then blew Lane a two-handed kiss before turning to the young woman.

Lyndon gave the therapist a quick smile. "Thank you," he said as she wheeled Taylor away. Focusing back on Lane, he drew in a long, weighty breath.

"I can tell from your now grim expression there is something troubling you," Lane tossed out, clearly seeing past what he had thought was a composed demeanor.

Lyndon sighed.

"Spill it," Lane demanded, worry showing on her normally cheery face.

"Well…." Lyndon drew a hand across the scarred side of his jaw. "My notorious boss has sent notice… stating he will be gracing us once again with his evil presence."

Lane slouched in her chair. "When?"

Lyndon shook his head. "Your guess is as good as mine—all that was stated was 'soon'."

"Promise me you'll text me if anything happens." Lane pointed a stern finger at him.

"I promise." Lyndon made an 'X' over his heart using his index finger, then placed his palm over the imaginary mark.

"Okay." Lane straightened in her seat, then shook her finger at him again. "I'd better get my final day started," she said with a *huff*.

"I'm heading over to North Haven to talk with Leo. I'll text you when I get back."

"You better," she said firmly, followed by an air-kiss. "Love you."

"Love you more." Lyndon repeated the 'X' mark over his heart, then blew her a kiss before shutting off the video call.

Outside the group home, on the happy wave of seeing Lane's lovely face, Lyndon playfully spun his car keys around his finger as he headed for his truck on the far side of the driveway.

"Where's that lovely *lady-friend* of yours?" an unexpected voice questioned, stopping Lyndon in his steps.

Lyndon's jaw clenched as he cut a sharp look in the direction of the inquisitor.

Addison stood at the rear of his vehicle dressed in ill-fitting dark grey trousers and a matching grey golf shirt. "On another one of her work trips perhaps, far, far away?" he suggested, expanding on his initial question.

"What are you doing here?" Lyndon sneered at the loathsome Seraph. He hadn't seen the piece-of-shit once during Thaddeus's absence. Not since that pivotal Valentine's Day several years back, when he'd been keeping an eye on Lane at the university. At the time, Lane hadn't been forthcoming with how much she knew about him or his kind. He'd been intrigued by her, but after that situation with his target—Lynn, being connected to Lane, he hadn't been sure whether he could trust his own judgement. Things were profoundly different now.

Addison stepped out from behind the car, casually sliding his hands into the pockets of his baggy pants. "I hear the boss-man is coming back to town."

"So it seems." Lyndon's grip tightened on his car keys.

Addison pulled a hand free of his pocket, tossing it up in query, and said, "I've tried to reach him several times while he's been away, but he never takes my calls. And he doesn't have voicemail, it seems."

"No one has talked to him." Lyndon clicked the unlock button on his keys and continued walking to his truck.

"What trouble have you been up to during Thaddeus's absence?" Addison strode towards him as if they were having a friendly conversation.

"I could ask you the same," he replied dryly.

"Work, work, work. You know me." Addison's tone was boisterous, as though he believed his own BS.

"Riiiight," Lyndon scrutinized as the Seraph continued his way. "What do you want, Addison?"

"Nothing, really—I was just wondering if you've heard any more on *when* he'll be back." Addison stopped within inches of the driver's side door of the vehicle.

Lyndon reached for the door handle. "I suggest you ask Amahle." Then he yanked open the door.

Addison stepped back promptly as if to avoid being hit by the door. "Where are you off to?"

Ignoring the question, Lyndon got into the truck and slammed the door shut. Sliding the keys home, he started up the engine and then put the truck in reverse. "Move!" Lyndon roared, wishing he could just run the asshole over.

"You really need to work on that anger of yours," Addison called out as Lyndon backed out of the driveway.

Lyndon pulled onto the long drive that led to North Haven, checking the rearview mirror again to make sure he hadn't been followed. He was already scheduled to meet with Leo today to talk about Thaddeus's impending return, but he'd called him on the drive over, informing him there was more to discuss, meaning the sudden reappearance of Addison at the group home, *and* his latest disconcerting inquiry about Lane.

Through the main doors into the home of his associates, Lyndon found his now friend and quasi leader of the covert group waiting for him in the spacious living room. "Any updates on Thaddeus's arrival?" Leo questioned, even before Lyndon had shut the door.

After a thorough discussion on the matter of Thaddeus and all it entailed, Lyndon swiftly shifted gears to the topic that had been plaguing him. "Addison was outside the group home."

"What—why? What did he want?" Leo's brows furrowed.

"Said he was curious if I had more info on Thaddeus's return."

"And that has you concerned?" Leo rubbed his jaw.

"No, but he asked about Lane."

"Why would he be interested in Lane?"

"This wasn't the first time he'd asked about her."

"What?" Leo frowned again.

"Back before I knew about all of you, I'd been watching Julianna, Lane, and several of her friends interacting at the university." Lyndon shook his head. "Seemingly, Thaddeus had felt the need to have Addison keep an eye on me, when he should have been in New York covering for Zuriel."

"Why didn't you tell us about this before?" Leo demanded.

"I just figured he was trying to push my buttons, and I thought he was more interested in Julianna being here because he asked me if I had notified Thaddeus of her being in Ottawa. I hadn't yet, but made sure later to inform Thaddeus before Addison could report back. But that hadn't been the problem. Addison realized my focus had actually been on Lane." Lyndon recalled Addison pointing out the fact, making some *Beauty and the Beast* reference but chose not to add that recollection in his explanation. "I told Addison to leave, but he'd kept his attention on Lane, making suggestive comments about how he was going to go check out the group home. I threatened to rip out his tongue if he even talked to her—kill him if he touched her." Lyndon rubbed the back of his neck. "Lynn told me she'd felt Addison outside Frank's restaurant, SNOW, but she'd not sensed him since. Clearly, Addison hadn't known Lynn and her family were even celebrating in the restaurant that night."

"Good thing. We figured curiosity had been the only motive for him being there because he'd heard that Francesca—Frank worked there."

"Back then, I never heard anything about it." Lyndon had learned during those first days in discussion with the Guards of Haven that Kris had been the original owner of SNOW.

"Was that the end of it?"

"No." Lyndon swallowed. "Not exactly."

"I'm not going to like this, am I?"

"Definitely not." Lyndon cracked his knuckles. "My focus had been on Lane—keeping Addison away from her, but the second unexpected encounter with him happened when I was in New York. It was just before Lane was scheduled to leave for her internship in Italy."

"And he confronted you again about Lane?"

"Yes, he did, but before that… he asked about Natalie." He hadn't known at the time that the young female student Lane had been speaking with had been Anael's biological daughter, Natalie, but something about her appearance had intrigued him, pulled at his memory banks. Obviously he knew why now; Natalie's look was so similar to Anael's.

"Natalie?" The furrow between Leo's brows deepened. "What did he say?"

"I'd gone to the New York City facility to talk to Marcus about Kendrick—do you remember?"

"Yes. You were digging into Kendrick's whereabouts for us."

"Right. Well, after my conversation with Marcus, I went to run an errand. I was picking up a birthday gift for Lane, actually, and there he was, on the street corner. Bastard must have been following me."

"And?" Leo bent forward in his chair, resting his forearms on his thighs.

Lyndon trolled his memory for how the conversation had gone down. "Without any preamble, Addison said, *'Tell me about Anael's daughter, Natalie'*, adding that he overheard someone talking about her. I questioned him as to why I would know anything about it, and he said that my name was mentioned in the same conversation—but I didn't know *anything* about Natalie then. Addison is *not* clever, obviously, but how could he know anything about her?"

Leo's gaze focused on the floor in front of him. "Jules was confronted by Addison at the university the same day you were. All I can think is that he must have stuck around, got lucky and overheard Jules talking to Ben about her that day. She'd called Ben right after the encounter."

Addison had left, but that hadn't been the end of it, Lyndon now realized. "Thing is, back then Addison implied he was going to tell

Thaddeus about it, about Natalie. And today he told me he had been trying to reach Thaddeus all this time but said he never got through to him. Must be why he asked if I knew more about his return."

"Why didn't he tell someone else what he overheard?"

"Like me, probably no one would believe him. Plus, he'd want to tell Thaddeus himself and not lose getting the credit for the intel."

Leo pulled his cellphone from his back pocket. "I need to text Shea—let her know to be on high alert where Natalie is concerned, not just the fact that Thaddeus is expected back." He typed out a message on his phone. "Was that the end of the conversation with Addison?" he inquired, sliding his cellphone back in his pocket.

"No. I said to him that even if it were true about Anael having a daughter, why would she be in Ottawa? And he said he didn't say she was—but that he had wondered the same. I was already over the debate at that point and went to leave."

"I'm guessing that's when he mentioned Lane again?" Leo leaned back in his chair.

"He questioned my urgency to leave, and I told him I was done talking with him. That's when he said, *'Anael's offspring wouldn't by any chance be that female you've been spending so much time with?'*"

"Dare I ask what happened next?" Leo's eyebrows rose up his forehead.

Lyndon shook his head, angry with himself. "I said too much. Told him she wasn't Anael's daughter—that her parents used a surrogate—that he was insane if he thought Anael would involve herself with humans, let alone carry a young for one," he rushed out. "Plus, I added that Lane looked nothing like Anael."

"What did he say?"

"Nothing, his cellphone rang, and he took the call."

"Did he believe you?"

"He took off before I could get more out of him." Lyndon cracked his knuckles again. "I should have killed him after the first time he noticed Lane."

Chapter 19 

Anticipating the need for privacy on my video chat with Lane, I tasked the twins with cleaning their rooms and joint bathroom before setting up my laptop in my bedroom. "Come get me if you need anything," I called up the hall to the girls before shutting the bedroom door.

I got comfy on my bed in front of my laptop as the video chat melody notified me that Lane's call was coming through. When her image came into view, I waved. "Hey girl!" I squinted at the screen. "What are you doing?"

"Hey, yourself," she responded. "Just some last-minute packing."

"Happy to be coming home?" I noticed she was wearing a well-worn oversized grey t-shirt, that was probably Lyndon's, and cut-off jean shorts that were frayed along the edges.

"I am," she said, but her enthusiasm was low.

"But?" I questioned, watching her fold a pair of dress pants and set them out of sight.

She chuckled, knowing I saw through her. "I wish I could pick up this little cottage and move it back to Ottawa. I just love it!"

There was the enthusiasm I'd foreseen. "Maybe you could get Leo to design you one—have it built near Ottawa." Lane had shown me pictures of the outside of the place and it had wood siding, cedar shingles, and stone accents that connected the home to its natural surroundings nestled among trees. It had a decent front porch and a garden space for enjoying the outdoors. The rental ad had described the private cottage on Lake William as a blend of the classic cozy feel of a small home with a distinct East Coast charm. It boasted a quiet neighborhood and just a short walk from a waterfront, a westerly exposure, and beautiful sunsets. It was only 12 minutes from Halifax International Airport and 10 minutes to the town of Bedford, and 20 minutes to Lane's office, she had told me.

"Let me take you on a tour, show you how cute the inside is." Lane grabbed up her laptop and strode from what I assumed was the bedroom. "Every room has large windows. The kitchen has a skylight—helps to make the small place feel more spacious and brighter." Lane walked from space to space. The open-concept home was cozy and charming and had exposed ceiling beams with mixed elements of new and repurposed materials, and even had a small wood-burning fireplace. "Whoever built this incorporated clever built-in storage everywhere to make the most of the limited square footage."

"It truly is adorable—I don't blame you for not wanting to leave."

The lights over Lane's head flickered several times. "Oh yeah, and there's that," Lane added, returning to the bedroom, setting the laptop back on the bed.

"What was that?" The lights flickered again.

"There's something wonky with the electrical." Lane angled the screen back, letting me see her better as she returned to packing. "The motion lights on the deck have gone off a few times too, but there's never anyone there." Lane paused. "Though...."

"Though what?" The tiny hairs on the back of my neck bristled.

"I don't know...." Lane placed another folded garment to the side of the laptop. "Have you ever had the feeling like someone was watching you?"

"Pffffff yaaa—hello!" I reached a hand to the neck of my shirt, feeling for the charms of my necklace under the collar.

Lane shrugged. "For most of my contract work, I've either shared a house or apartment, or stayed on a live-aboard boat with other people. This was the first time I was on my own." Lane pouted. "Wish I had a dog to keep me company."

"Did you tell Lyndon about the feeling of being watched?" I ran the charms back and forth on my necklace.

"No. You know how he gets?" She bundled a pair of socks, setting them with the other folded items. "Besides, it's my last night, so what's the point? I gave Lyndon your cell number, by the way."

"My number? What for?"

"You were my only family member he didn't have a number for."

I smiled at the words 'family member', but then asked, "Is it safe for him to have everyone's number in his phone?"

"Don't worry," she said, gathering up the stack of clothes she'd been assembling, moving them to what I could see now was a small carry-on suitcase. "He has them all under code names." She gave an amused chuckle.

"Like what?" I laughed with her in anticipation of her response.

"Let me see if I can remember them all." She paused. "Marq is under *painter*… Zach is *fire marshal*, Leo is *handyman*, Den is *elevator repair*, Ben is *OU surveillance*…."

"OU?" I interrupted.

"Ottawa University."

"Ah."

"Kris is *snow removal*."

"Good one."

"Right?" She chuckled again. "Nic is *Dr. Nicolas*—Taylor's doctor." She gave me a wink with that one. "And Zuriel is under *plumber*."

"Why plumber?"

"I asked him about that one too, and he said something like *'Zuriel has been through a lot of shit'*," she laughed out. "And he has my number under *home*."

"Aww, that's sweet. But Zuriel's is *too* perfect."

"I know!" She laughed again.

"What does he have me under?" I asked, curious now that I'd heard the others.

"Spam call," she said deadpan.

"What," said frowning. "But how will he know if it's me or a real spam call?"

Lane grinned. "He put an Asterix before the *S*."

"Clever," I said, nodding at Lyndon's craftiness.

"Other than yours, the code names cover services he would use for the group home," she said as she began removing her earring.

"Are you packing your earrings?" I leaned in as she removed the second earring.

"No-no, I take them off at night to avoid snagging them. Plus, I'd hate to lose them." She placed the earrings in the tiny wooden box that had been part of a birthday gift Lyndon had given her. "It wouldn't worry me so much if I were in my room back home. But here." She shrugged one shoulder. "If one ever came loose, it would probably end up rolling into a crack in the floor or something."

"Safer in the box," I agreed. "And probably why Lyndon got the box in the first place."

"He said the box was for my travels." She gave me a joyful smile.

"See." I smiled back at her. Lyndon's first gift to Lane had been a framed, handmade custom star map that had been created by both him and Taylor. Taylor's contribution had been a watercolour night sky background with the Pleiades constellation he'd drawn using his toy stylist tool. Lyndon had transferred the image Taylor created, the *Asterism*, Lane had called it, onto the watercolour background, and set it in a handmade frame he had made. He'd written under it the words Omnia Vincit Amor, meaning *Love Conquers All*, in elegant calligraphy. "Lyndon is superb at giving gifts with sentiment," I added.

"I love a gift with meaning—don't you?"

"I do. Redmond is excellent at it too—it's one of the things I love about him." I touched my necklace. "I remove my necklaces before bed as well."

"I take it he gave you that necklace?"

"On our first Christmas together, actually." I ran the charms back and forth. "What are you going to do when you get back?" I asked, trading topics.

"I'm not sure." Lane added a few more things to the carry-on suitcase before closing it. "I don't have another gig lined up yet. Thought maybe I'll finally get to working on my PhD now that I've earned more experience in my field these past few years and with traipsing across the globe." She slid the case off the bed and onto the floor, setting it back against the wall behind her.

"You're such an underachiever," I said sarcastically. "Remember when you said to me, *'I can't wait to finish school and get a job—have more independence'*?"

"Yes! I hated having to rely on my parents for money."

"I told you that it would be good for you to get out of dodge, out from under all those overprotective males."

"You did. And it's why I wish I could transport this cute little cottage with me. You know, have my own place."

"That will come. How did this job go, anyway?"

"It was good, but it wasn't as enjoyable as my previous contract."

"Ah yes, the project in the Bahamas," I swooned, leaning back against the pillows at my headboard.

"At least this one is closer to home. My flight from here to Ottawa is only two hours."

"The Bahamas is closer to me," I reminded her. "If you get another gig there, don't forget it only takes about an hour to fly *here* from there and vice versa." I gave her a toothy grin.

Lane smirked. "Well, they did offer to have me back if I was open to it." She waggled her eyebrows.

"But I know you hate being away from Lyndon and Taylor."

"I really do—I hate missing out on Taylor's progress and time with them both."

"Anyyy…. talk of marriage?" I asked warily. "Sorry—I don't mean to be *that* aunt, pushing for the next step in your life."

"You're not—I know you care about my relationship. And *no*. We talk more about having a place of our own in the future—once he's finally free from Thaddeus." Lane slid the laptop over and sat on the bed cross-legged.

"Are you sure you even want to come back—with Thaddeus expected anytime, I mean? And Lyndon won't be as freely available, I would imagine."

"I have mixed feelings about all that, but, like you said, I hate being away from my guys." She gave me a sad smile. "Leo notified Shea to keep an eye on Natalie, now that Addison has been sniffing around," Lane said as though in need of a topic change. "She's staying at North Haven for now."

"From what I hear, Shea is a badass."

"She is!" Lane said excitedly. "And she's almost as talented a fighter as Den." She mimicked a few fake punches. "How is your training going?"

"Meh." I scowled.

"What meh? You're in peak shape for someone your age—even for someone my age." She flexed her arm and tapped her bicep with her other hand.

"I guess." I *was* in pretty great shape, I had to admit. "But I'm still getting old—training is harder at my age. Same goes for Redmond." I adjusted the pillows behind me. "Trust me, there's a lot more moaning and groaning going on around here days after training—not just on the day of."

Lane laughed and gave me a skeptical look as though she didn't believe me. "Where is Redmond?"

"Over at South Haven."

"This late?" Lane slid the laptop closer to the head of her bed and then leaned over to rest on her side, propping the side of her head on her hand.

"Redmond and the others have been meeting regularly to talk security and surveillance ever since we got word that Thaddeus was heading back to town." The clock on my laptop displayed that it was already past 8:00 p.m..

"I just wish they could take Thaddeus down already—let us get on with our lives—have *normal* lives for once," she huffed out, surrendering her head down atop a pillow.

I nodded. "Ditto,"

"What are the girls up to?" She let out a yawn.

"Cleaning their rooms. Speaking of which, they've been awfully quiet while I've been on this call with you."

"*Barking*," from Summer and Snow resounded from beyond my closed bedroom door.

"Sounds like I'd better let you go." She yawned again.

"Yup, so it seems. And you seem ready for bed."

She rubbed her eyes. "It's been a short but busy week."

"Get some rest—and don't forget to text me tomorrow when you're finally safe and sound at home."

"I won't forget—goodnight, Aunt Lynn."

"Night-night—sleep tight." I blew Lane a kiss and then quickly logged off. As I climbed off the bed, a familiar flush of sensation I recognized as the one-and-only *Purah* suddenly rushed over me.

Out through the bedroom door, I spotted the dogs near the kitchen at the patio door. They were barking at something in the backyard. "Summer—Snow—stop that!" I yelled before calling out for the girls. When no response from them came, I jogged down the hall to their bedrooms but found their rooms empty.

Circling back around to the kitchen, I noticed the patio door had been left open, just not enough so that the dogs could get out. The dogs had stopped their barking now but were practically prancing in front of the door, anxious to get out. Before sliding the door fully open, I flicked the switch for the tiny twinkle lights that ran the length of the roof. When I slid open the door, a rush of humid August night air hit me, and the dogs pushed past me out onto the deck. When I peered over the railing, I found Purah and my missing children together in the backyard. "Hayley and Ryley—get up here right now!" I ordered.

All I got in return was a, "Heeey Muuum!" from Ryley and a wave from Hayley.

With Summer and Snow at my heels, I unhooked the latch to the gate at the end of the deck and rushed down the stairs to the backyard. "Girls—get back upstairs, please—and take the dogs with you."

"But Mum," Ryley whined.

"I'm not going to ask again," I said firmly, emphasizing the seriousness with the old hands-on-the-hips posture.

Without another word, the defiant twosome turned and retreated, taking the dogs back up the stairs with them.

I turned my attention to Purah. "To what do I owe the pleasure?" I asked with a tight smile. As usual, she was in her warrior regalia, staff in her right hand and her long white braided hair hanging forward over her left shoulder. Despite the heavy, humid night air, her skin appeared as fresh as a daisy. How could she not be sweating in that armor? Even in my summer tank top and shorts, I was too hot.

"I just returned from North Haven, where I provided Leo with my latest update," she began. I was aware she had been checking all the known locations for Thaddeus ever since Leo had informed her he would be returning. "And I wanted to come by and check on things here before heading back to the stars." Her iceberg-blue eyes twinkled. "It was so lovely speaking with the girls."

"Well, they're supposed to be cleaning up their rooms."

"How wonderful it must be to have offspring."

"Ha!" I couldn't help but laugh. "For the most part, yes. But at this age, they have a lot of mood swings and attitude changes with going through puberty."

"I would imagine there are social pressures and body image concerns too, yes?" She tilted her head inquisitively.

"Yes," I said, my eyebrows shooting up, surprised at her comment.

She tilted her head to the other side. "I've been reading a lot about human offspring. Leo gave me a book about human development. I read that young females their age often struggle with academic stress, experience sleep disturbances, or experiment with new behaviors, including those related to sex or social dynamics," she said as though reciting from a textbook.

"They start junior high next week, so I'm sure social dynamics will come into play." We'd had the sex talk, and that behavior didn't seem to be on their radar just yet, thankfully. "Right now, the behaviors they exhibit are more about rebellion and the desire for independence."

"Which can include verbal defiance, such as arguing, using disrespectful language, or constantly questioning rules," Purah, the would-be professor of teen girls added.

"Indeed, as you just witnessed." I gave her a tight smile.

"Hmmm." Her white brows furrowed. "Have either of them withdrawn from activities they previously enjoyed or shown a lack of interest in things that once brought them joy?"

"Not so far." I'd read a little myself about girls at this age, but having been one myself, I knew all about the shift that began with challenging authority figures. But it was the other forms of rebellion, like delaying tasks, pushing boundaries with curfews, or engaging in risky behaviors like sneaking out, that I was most concerned about. "How are things with you and Leo?" I asked, needing to get off the topic of my rebellious tweens.

Purah smiled brightly. "It is wonderful." Her words rang true, but her smile fell then.

"What is it?" I frowned up at her. "You can tell me," I said, placing my hand on her forearm.

"When I'm among the stars, all I think about is Leo," she said, leaning the top of her staff back against the space between the side of her neck and shoulder. "When I'm with Leo, all I think about is how being with him feels like I'm… *home*." Releasing her grip, she moved her hand to overlap mine that rested on her forearm. "I have had a joyous existence among the stars, and I miss my sister Stewards when I'm away." She squeezed my hand gently. "And I am grateful for my service to the Seraphim, but now…." She paused and closed her eyes. "Now, I no longer have a purpose on Pleiades."

"But you do," I said, overlapping my other hand over hers.

Opening her eyes again, she said, "I'm torn between my loyalties there and my longing to be here on earth, with Leo."

"What are the rules? I mean, is there someone you can talk with, find a way to leave—stay here on Earth?"

She shook her head.

"Is there any way we can help you?" I raised my free hand in question.

She smiled weakly and shook her head again.

I blew out a breath. My heart ached for her. "I'm *sooo* sorry, Purah." I didn't understand why love had to be so difficult for her, for Lane and Lyndon, for any of them.

"Thank you, Lynn," she said, promptly wrapping her arms around me in an unexpected hug. *"I like the hugging,"* she whispered.

Her words were spoken in a way that reminded me of when the girls were little. "Me too," I said, squeezing her back.

She released me and was gone in a flash before I could say another word. I wiped a stray tear from my cheek and gazed up at the night sky. As I dropped my focus back down, a rush of sensation swept over my body, the signature, I realized, was that of the veiled Earthbound. In response, I swiftly turned and rushed back up the stairs and through the patio door into the house seconds later, locking the door behind me. It had been over 2 years since I'd last felt this covert angel, not since that Christmas Music Event.

"Muuum!" the girls called as they rushed up the hall my way, Summer and Snow lumbering behind them.

"There's another angel outside," Ryley said, coming to stand at my side.

"I know." Just then, the noise of the door opening from the garage to the lower level sounded below us.

Hayley came and stood on my other side. *"Mum—someone's downstairs,"* she said in a hushed voice.

"Back up," I said calmly, even though I was anything but calm. Trying not to freak them out, I gently grabbed hold of each of their hands and began stepping away and into the kitchen. The *slam* of the door below sounded, and we all jumped, causing the dogs to bark and startle us further. Then the slam was followed by slow, heavy footsteps that echoed up the stairwell from the lower level. "Maybe it's your Da," I said, but I hadn't heard the outer garage door open. The girls let out harrowing *screams* as the upper door opened, and I yanked them back. "Shit!" I shouted when I saw who it was.

"What's going on—you nearly gave your old man a heart attack?" Redmond grumbled out, hand over his heart.

"We thought you were the angel," Ryley said, wrapping her arms around Redmond.

"What angel?" He turned to look at me.

"The one that's always *hiding*." I raised my eyebrows.

"Oh shit," Redmond muttered under his breath, eyes bulging. "Have either of you felt this angel lately?" He asked them.

They both shook their heads.

"We would've told you if we had," Hayley stated, giving Redmond a quick hug.

"Are you still feeling them?" Redmond asked me.

"No." I rubbed my arms and glanced at the girls.

"Nope," Ryley said, shaking her head again.

"Not anymore," Hayley added with a head-shake.

"Good," Redmond said, pulling out his phone.

"What are you doing?" I asked, stepping up to him for my own hug.

"Calling Zach," he whispered mid-hug, lowering his head to rest against mine.

Within minutes of Redmond's call, Zach was at our front door. Then, while the twins huddled next to me on the couch, I did my best to relay the evening's events to both Zach and Redmond, including my speaking to Lane. "I don't understand why this angel—I'm confident they're one of the Earthbound—continues to stalk me, yet takes no action." Who was it? What did they want? And what were they waiting for? Not that I wanted something to happen, but all this not knowing was giving my nervous system and brain matter a run for their money. I wasn't sure if it was fear I was feeling, or anger. I *was* angry with myself for letting my guard down. Thaddeus has been gone for several years, the same amount of time since I'd sensed this particular Earthbound. We'd been told that Thaddeus was coming back. Was he back already and just not in Ottawa? I couldn't let myself believe it had been him prowling around the hospital, at SNOW, or at the music event back then. If I did, it meant he'd just been outside our home. Lyndon had been adamant when he'd stated that it wouldn't be like Thaddeus to do his own legwork *or* lurk in the shadows. And Lyndon knew the bastard better than any of us. Either way, I despised being watched like this.

Redmond and Zach continued to speak in the living room, going over strategies for keeping us all safe while I got Hayley and Ryley back to their bedrooms and under the covers. To my surprise, the girls returned to their beds with very little persuasion *and* fell asleep just as easily. The dogs too were passed out on the floor next to each of their beds. Me, on the other hand, I was a wreck, and the idea of *sleep* was nowhere on my brain's agenda.

Returning to the living room, I found Redmond was the only one sitting on the couch now, yet I could still sense Zach nearby. "Where did he go?" I glanced towards the back deck.

"I think he's on the roof." Redmond pushed up from the couch and strode to the kitchen. "He'll be keeping watch on the house overnight, but said to let him know if you get even the tiniest of tingles that someone other than him is around."

I padded after him into the kitchen. "Great—I'm thankful, but my nerves are still a mess."

"How about I make you some *Sleepy-Time* tea?" Redmond opened the cupboard and retrieved the box of tea bags. Then he ran a comforting hand across my back several times. "It'll relax your nerves and calm your mind."

"Can't hurt," I agreed, watching as he got the kettle ready to boil the water.

Redmond placed a tea-bag in my favorite Canadian maple leaf mug, then poured the now-boiling water over the tea-bag. "I'll be right back—just going to check on them," he said, heading up the hall to the girls' bedrooms. ".

With the sooth-my-nerves tea in hand, I rested down on the couch while Redmond did his daddy-check on the twins. I plopped an ice cube into the mug to cool it a bit so I didn't have to wait to drink it.

"Sound asleep," Redmond announced, returning to the living room.

"Thanks, babe," I said before taking another generous sip of tea. "You go ahead to bed. I'll be there in a few minutes."

"You sure?"

"Yup," I assured him.

After finishing my tea and checking on the girls one last time, I finally climbed into bed and relinquished my need to stay awake. With Redmond next to me, the comforting tea in my belly, and the hum of Zach's protective signature emanating over me, the fog of sleep gently began to claim me…. *the fragrant scent of fresh flowers surrounded me as I stepped from the shadows into a long hall. At the end of the hallway were two large double glass doors, the surface of which was clouded over… I moved forward up the hall following the scent of flowers… halting in front of the doors, I glanced back over my shoulder to see only darkness and shadow. Turning back, I pushed open the doors and was instantly assaulted by a strong unpleasant odor of mold and mildew… I strode into an expansive once glamorous space with high ceilings, it's long since stunning architectural designs now a scene of decay marked by significant water damage and black mold growth on walls and surfaces… the large windows on the far side no longer offering a view to the gardens out back… the surrounding air was thick with humidity, the interior of the room lit only by the moonlight that found its way through broken glass of the windows… I glanced around the once-inviting space now filled with debris, fallen tiles, and remnants of lounge furniture that created a disturbing atmosphere and a testament to neglect and decay… the unsettling silence it held was broken only by the dripping of water. I stepped further into the room and peered out over an indoor pool… the surface of which was marked by stagnant, murky water, evoking a sense of unease and discomfort in what used to be an inviting atmosphere of ample natural light and architectural features… near the middle of the pool floated a large oblong-shaped object… slowly it began to drift my way… as the something drew closer a subtle sweet scent fragranced the air… it was then that I noticed there was a long dark shape in the center of it… almost to the edge of the pool the raft revealed the dark shape was the body of a woman, her silhouette adorned with dozens of white funnel-shaped blossoms clustered together amongst leathery, dark green leaves. I squinted, focusing my sight in the barely lit room struggling to make out the features of the woman's face… Lane's face… footfalls echoed and I glanced up to see a tall dark figure of a man standing on the far side of the pool… behind him appeared a second figure, the poor lighting marring my ability to see whether they were male or female… moonlight cut suddenly across the eye area of the second figure exposing no longer hidden soft pastel purple eyes, their pale violet colour glowing cool and misty, exuding tranquility and elegance… familiar voices call to me from the right pulling my attention, and I turned to find that a floor-length mirror now stood near the right side of the pool… in its reflection I saw my girls, Hayley and Ryley standing together holding hands… they stared out at me from the mirror mouthing the word 'Mum' over and over… then they stepped free of the mirror and out onto the end of the pool… as they teetered on the edge I called their names but no sound emanated from my lips… I tried again, reaching my arms out… just as they took one coordinated stride forward off the edge…* a bellowing, "Daaaaaaaaaaaaaa!" yanked me awake and into the here and now.

Pounding footfalls coupled with, "I'm coming!" from Redmond, echoed up the hall in the direction of the girls' bedrooms.

"Oh gaaawd!" I cried out, flipping the bedcovers off of me. Racing out of our bedroom, I ran up the hall and careened around the doorway into Hayley's bedroom. Redmond was on the bed with the twins, their small arms banded around each other, Redmond's huge arms enclosed around both of them.

"Dream, Mum," Ryley said before I could ask.

"Nightmare," Hayley followed up, peeking out from the mishmash of arms.

Redmond peered up at me, anguish marring his handsome face. Reluctantly, he loosened his hold from around the girls as I slummed down on the bed.

"About Lane?" I asked, but I already knew the answer.

They both nodded.

"Me too," I said, attempting to wrap my arms around all three of them. Redmond brushed his thumb over my cheek, and I stared into his eyes. "I need to call Lane."

Chapter 20 

A week had passed since Lyndon and the others in his circle had been notified of Thaddeus's return to Ottawa, ending the almost two and a half years since anyone in his organization had seen or spoken to him. 'Soon' was all they'd been told, not the precise date of his return, and in preparation the staff had been all a scramble to get his Ottawa condo and lab spaces ready should he show his face *sooner* rather than later. And while Amahle did her tenth pass-through of the lab spaces, Lyndon went to Thaddeus's condo to make a final review.

Lyndon ran a thorough inventory of the clothing that had been procured for Thaddeus's return. Each item was crafted from superior, natural fabrics, which offered a better feel, breathability, and durability. For his suits, fine, high-thread-count wool from established mills was all he would accept. Cashmere, a famously soft and expensive wool, was his preference for sweaters. Egyptian or Sea Island cotton was used for soft, luxurious, and durable shirts. He expected meticulous detail where garments featured tight, even, and straight stitching, often double-stitched or hand-finished for added durability. It was the quality evident in the small details that he demanded, which were often time-consuming to create, but he didn't care about that part. Even the buttons of his garments had to be made from premium materials like mother-of-pearl or real horn instead of cheap plastic. His tailored suits in particular had hand-finished edges and buttonholes, used layers of internal fabric called interlining to hold their shape allowing the suit to mold to the body, the artisanal touches indicating to the world their superior construction. A flawless fit, Lyndon had been told, is a hallmark of expensive clothing often achieved through made-to-measure or bespoke services. Most of the luxury brands Thaddeus preferred used minimalist designs and subtle details, such as discreet logos, focusing on the quality of the garment and not on overt branding, referred to as a 'Quiet Luxury'. Some of the high-end clothing items procured were produced in limited quantities, ensuring exclusivity and that the garments felt unique to Thaddeus. All of it was expensive clothing that could best be described as having high-quality materials, meticulous craftsmanship, a superior fit, and understated elegance. Unlike fast-fashion items, which may be flashier, Thaddeus preferred expensive pieces like these that could be defined by their subtle, lasting qualities that suggest taste and discernment rather than just wealth.

Even Thaddeus's bedding was high-end, it being a combination of linen and silk for its superior hand-feel, providing a soft, smooth, and supple touch, as opposed to inferior or synthetic fabrics that are often rough, stiff, or have an unnatural sheen.

Next to review was the contents of the efficient kitchen. The fridge had an ample supply of the *10 Thousand BC* bottles of exotic water he liked. He preferred it not because it was the most expensive, which it wasn't, but because he thought it was a highly sophisticated, stylish and world-class brand. It was sourced far from human contamination and pollutants off the coast of Canada, but Lyndon thought it pretentious, considering it took a three-day trip to reach the glacier where it was obtained. The refrigerator also held Serrano ham and prosciutto, along with high-quality artisanal cheeses; Harbison from Vermont, Humboldt Fog from California, Bri deMeaux from France, Colston Bassett Stilton from England, Manchego from Spain, and Pleasant Ridge Reserve a seasonal, alpine-style cheese from Wisconsin. For Thaddeus's sweet tooth, Marcus had flown in several mini icebox cakes from the Magnolia Bakery on the Upper West Side in New York City.

The upper cupboards next to the fridge contained *Berco's Billion Dollar Popcorn*, an extravagant caramel popcorn made with premium ingredients like rare Danish salt, bourbon vanilla, and dusted with 23-karat edible gold flakes, the going rate of which was priced at $250 a tin. Next to the popcorn, were St. Erik's Brewery potato chips, a Swedish brewery creation made in a limited edition of five potato chips, each with a unique, luxurious flavor profile, at approximately $56 a box, and ingredients that included rare almond potatoes, matsutake mushrooms, truffle seaweed, crown dill, and India Pale Ale wort. There were also packages of exotic dried fruits, including soft-dried dragon fruit and rare, soft-dried mango slices, as well as caviar-infused snacks from upscale brands for an extravagant treat.

Thaddeus's personal chef had been notified of his upcoming arrival and had gathered Thaddeus's favorite items for his prepared meals such as Wagyu beef known for its intense marbling and buttery texture, premium grade Bluefin tuna, fresh whole lobster, Alaskan king crab, diver scallops, and of course the world's most expensive delicacy, beluga caviar. Lyndon had never known a more overindulged, self-centered being in his whole existence, except maybe Nero or Marie Antoinette.

Last on Lyndon's list to review were items set up for Thaddeus's entertainment. Amahle had stated she had only been able to find one biography, his preferred non-fiction genre, that she felt might provide some amusement, a hardcover Pulitzer Prize Winner titled G-Man: J. Edgar Hoover and the Making of the American Century. In summary, it was about Hoover's life, exploring the evolution of American society throughout the 20th century, presenting a complex portrait of the man, detailing his achievements in modernizing the FBI as well as the abuses of power that marked his career. Apparently, Hoover was a more complicated figure than his later years suggested, and his story was crucial to understanding the expansion of federal power in America.

Whatever, Lyndon didn't care whether Thaddeus liked it or not.

Amahle had, however, found some of the most anticipated violent themed video games that she was confident Thaddeus would enjoy. The games she'd picked up were *Killing Floor 3*, a multiplayer game known for its brutal gameplay, *The Dark Pictures Anthology: Directive 8020*, a horror game with a distinct art style, and *The Sinking City 2* known to be brutal, blending Lovecraftian designs with survival horror and investigation. And just in case he wasn't happy with any of those, she'd added one more, *INDIKA*, which from Amahle's notes was a visceral game that was mostly a third-person narrative adventure set in an alternative 19th century Russia, and it features an ostracized nun who has the devil's voice in her head. Lyndon had further read online that from its foundation, the game offers *a flurry of whimsical absurdity, religious criticism and raw human suffering, always with a wink and a nod*. Several game reviewers stated that the entire game is *underpinned by a delirious tension between levity and agony, and the developers at Odd Meter got the balance just right*. He'd also read that the game character's reality was a frozen hellscape filled with pain and isolation, which he felt Thaddeus would like, but the character also encounters laugh-out-loud moments that make the experience feel more like a rom-com than a psychodrama about a sad nun, which he knew Thaddeus would hate, making it sound absolutely perfect in his mind, perfect in a way that would irritate the hell out of Thaddeus.

Lyndon chuckled as he stacked the games in a neat pile next to the game console that sat just below a brand new $10,000, 85 inch, Samsung Smart TV.

Despite his amusement over the rom-com infused video game, Lyndon's emotions were all over the place. He should have been thrilled at the fact that his sweet Lane was due home today, but for the first time he wished she was staying away longer. He hadn't been able to be with her on this trip due to Thaddeus's impending return and couldn't risk not being available should he arrive without further notice. Lyndon and the guards had all worked too hard over these past few years to jeopardize things now. Their hope had been that Thaddeus would *never* return, yet still they had prepared for it.

To calm his uneasiness, Lyndon took out his phone and video-dialed the one person he knew could always ease his worries.

"Where are you?" Lane answered, squinting at her phone's screen.

"In Thaddeus's condo." Lyndon did a slow spin, phone camera facing out, so she could see the space he was in. "Did I catch you at a bad time?" He noticed her hair was wet, as if she'd just gotten out of the shower.

"No—just getting ready. Why are you there?" she asked, propping her phone against something so she could brush her hair.

"Double checking that Thaddeus's *favorite* things are all here and ready for him." Lyndon rolled his eyes. "Who knows what frame of mind he will be in when he eventually shows up."

Lane swept her damp hair back into a ponytail. "When he does arrive, try to stay out of his way, if you can."

"I plan on it," Lyndon said, checking that there were ample towels in the ensuite bathroom.

Lyndon heard Lane's phone beep. "Do you have to go?"

"Nope. Lynn just texted me. She left me a voice message earlier while I was in the shower."

"What did she say?"

"Something about her being *overprotective* and to call her. I still need to pack my toiletries, so I'll ring her back on my way to the airport."

"Sounds good. I'll let you finish getting ready. But can you text me when you're on your way to the airport?"

"Of course—don't I always?" She gave him a bright smile.

He grinned in return. "And I love you for it—be safe."

"I love you too," she said, making a squeaky kissing noise before she hung up.

Finished with his assessment of Thaddeus's condo, Lyndon tucked his phone away and headed out back over to the group home.

Less than 30 minutes later, a text from his beloved popped up on his cellphone screen. It read,

> *My taxi is here. I'm all packed and on my way to the airport.*
> *See you soon. XO*

Lyndon typed back with,

At home now. Can't wait to see you. XOXO

Lyndon knew that once Lane was done with the 2-hour flight and was through security at the airport, she would be home and he would be able to breathe properly again. It didn't matter the destination, or the time it took for him to fly to her; every moment she was away from him made it arduous for him to breathe. In the meantime, to distract himself, Lyndon spent the rest of the morning getting things ready for Lane's return.

His apartment kitchen and living spaces were clean and tidy. He'd straightened up the bathroom, put away laundry, and put fresh linens on the bed. To create a pleasant atmosphere, he had purchased scented candles, *Summer Plum*, Lane's favorite scent. He knew she appreciated the small, thoughtful gestures like this for when she returned from her stints away. He'd made a trip to the grocery store too for supplies for her favorite meals, snacks, beverages, and a few bottles of wine. As a special welcome home to make her feel even more loved and appreciated, he'd picked up a bouquet of flowers, a dark blend of reds, purples, and bronze dahlias, and a card that on the front simply read, *'Home is wherever I'm with you.'* and inside where it was blank, he'd written,

> *Every day you were gone was a day too long.*
> *So happy you're home.*
> *Love Lyndon*

After placing the bouquet on the small dining table near the kitchen, Lyndon checked the time on his cellphone. Lane's plane would be landing soon, and he'd checked the flight tracker app he had on his phone ten times already. Yesterday, he had asked to pick her up from the airport, but her parents had beaten him to the request and would be doing the pickup this time. Lane had promised him that once she was unpacked and did a quick catch-up with her parents, she would be over to see him shortly after.

As Lyndon stared down at a photo of Lane on his cellphone, a text appeared on the screen. This one was from Zuriel,

>*Any sign of the asshole yet?*

Lyndon wrote back,

>*Nope. I don't give a shit where he is. Right now I'm waiting for Lane to get home, and that's all that matters to me.*

Lyndon's phone rang in his hand, displaying the contact name *Plumber*. "What's up, Z?" Lyndon answered.

"Thought I'd call so we could chat—keep your mind off things until your lady got home."

"I've just about run out of things here to keep me busy, so I appreciate it."

"This was a short contract for her this time, and I'm guessing that made you happy."

"Yeah, it did, but…." Lyndon sighed.

"But you can't stand to be away from her," Zuriel finished for him. "I feel the same way, and Grier and I only work thirty minutes apart. I don't know how you managed with Lane being almost nine hundred miles away, even if it was only a week-long trip."

"Hell, she was in South Africa for five months on one of her trips. That one just about killed me." Lyndon rubbed the back of his neck.

"Brother, you have it bad." Zuriel's laughter reverberated through Lyndon's cellphone.

"Don't laugh," Lyndon said, letting out a lighthearted chuckle. "Good thing I was able to go visit her then, see her during her off time. Otherwise, I don't think I would have survived."

"But you're worried about something—what is it?"

Lyndon wanted Lane home, but oh how he wished she wasn't going to be back so soon with Thaddeus's arrival looming. "I just don't want Lane on Thaddeus's radar or even for him to get wind of our relationship."

"That's understandable," Zuriel agreed. "But let's deal with one problem at a time."

Lyndon's phone beeped, indicating another call coming in. Checking, he saw that it was from *Handyman*. "Hey, Leo's calling me. I'll check back with you in a few. And thanks, Z."

"No problem," Zuriel said. "Later, brother."

"Later." Lyndon hit the button to take the other call. "I was just talking to Zuriel," he began.

"When did you last speak with Lane?" Leo asked, cutting him off.

"First thing this morning, why?" Lyndon did a quick check of his phone for any messages or texts he may have missed while on the phone with Zuriel. Returning his phone to his ear, he heard Leo draw an audible breath.

"Lane never got on the plane," Leo said on the exhale.

"Why—what the hell happened?" Lyndon's stomach lurched, and his heart pounded in his throat.

Leo took in another loud breath, the exhale of it echoing through the phone. "Lyndon, she's missing."

Chapter 21 

The Archangel Michael Monument, August 8th, Kyiv, Ukraine

Gabriel stood in front of the monument in the center of the historic Maidan Nezalezhnosti, or Independence Square. The area around the Archangel Michael Monument is centered in the majestic Byzantine and Ukrainian baroque architecture of St. Michael's Golden-Domed Monastery, a symbol of resilience and Ukrainian identity, and represents the *unconquered spiritual strength* of the Ukrainian people.

Tilting his head back, Gabriel gazed up at the 3.5-meter-tall statue in the likeness of his brethren Archangel Michael, adorned with a golden halo, sword, and shield, serving as a symbol of protection for Kyiv. *This is a place of both spiritual grandeur and historical depth, serving as a focal point for faith and culture, standing unbowed against conflict,* Gabriel mused. Dropping his head, he surveyed the area around where he stood, noting it was no longer lively with tourists and locals gathering, enjoying cafes and shops, entertained by the occasional street performer like it once had been. Despite the cultural backdrop, the presence of soldiers in camouflage fatigues, distributing Ukrainian flag bracelets, was a stark reminder of the current conflict and war-torn reality. The monument itself was meant to symbolize hope and resilience for the people, but the context of war and its impact on the people created a poignant and emotional contrast.

"Hello, Gabriel," Michael greeted him as he appeared next to the statue. He was dressed much like Gabriel was, in dark blue jeans and a loose-fitting grey pullover. Gabriel's was navy, but both were suitable for the pleasant climate. Michael still wore his hair long, where Gabriel had opted for a more current look.

"Thank you for meeting me here, brother," he said in response, then he glanced back up at the statue. "What was it that Archbishop Sviatoslav Shevchuk said about it?"

Michael placed his hand on the statue. "He said, *'We perceive today that the Archangel Michael, together with the whole Heavenly Host, is fighting for Ukraine.'* I only wish I could have influence or impact on the worldly turmoil here in Ukraine."

Gabriel was fully aware of the ongoing full-scale invasion of Ukraine by Russia, with its significant developments including battlefield maneuvers, diplomatic proposals, and continued long-range strikes. "Where do things stand now?" Gabriel asked.

Michael shook his head, then said, "I believe Russian forces continue their offensive operations in several directions in the Donetsk and Zaporizhia regions. Ukrainian forces, for their part, are engaged in fighting, including advancing near Kupyansk."

"Any chance of peace talks yet?"

"We'll see. There's to be a summit in Alaska on August fifteenth."

"I thought President Zelenskyy restated his stance that Ukraine would not give up land to the *occupier* in any peace deal?"

Michael shrugged. "Possibly."

"And you can't do anything to aid them?" Gabriel glowered.

"Isn't that why you wanted to meet with me? To talk about what we *can* and cannot do?" Michael scoffed, giving him a rueful smile. Then he turned and proceeded to one of the open benches in the vicinity of the square, and sat down. "Sit," he said, tapping the space next to him on the bench.

Gabriel did as requested and sat. He had appealed for Michael to meet him for a talk, after all, and *yes,* it was about the boundaries surrounding their involvement with humans.

"You said that you told Lynn that you are not permitted to help, yes?" Michael asked, getting straight to the point.

"Yes." Gabriel folded his hands in his lap, staring out at the humans walking by. "But what if I could? I mean, what if I could find the woman, this missing friend of hers?"

"No, Gabriel. You know the rules."

Gabriel turned to look at Michael. He was staring out at the people too. "What if I find out who has her?"

"The same applies." He looked at him with a side-eye. "You are only permitted to intervene if your Charge is in danger."

Gabriel remained looking at Michael. "But Lynn is involved."

"That is her choice to be involved," Michael grumbled.

"What if her being involved puts her in danger?" Gabriel turned fully in Michael's direction, leaning an arm over the top of the bench.

Michael gave him a quizzical look. "Is she in danger?"

"No." Gabriel looked away. "Not at the moment."

"You've already stuck your pristine nose where it doesn't belong."

"But…," Gabriel began, glancing at Michael again.

"Gabriel," Michael interrupted. "You know Archangel Diniel is watching your every move. It's also no coincidence that she's spoken with your granddaughters."

Gabriel sat up in his seat. "She needs to stay away from Hayley and Ryley."

"She's been told." Michael nodded. "But you've pushed the boundaries. And you're already on thin ice because of your behavior."

"My behavior?" Gabriel's brows pinched.

"You are far too close to your Charge. Too familiar with her family. Spending Christmas and birthdays together. Meeting her in-laws?" Michael challenged, shaking his head. "Seriously, Gabriel? You jeopardize so much."

"I know." Gabriel sighed in defeat, turning in his seat to face forward. "Lynn knows I'm avoiding her."

Michael groaned. "She must know you have other duties besides hanging around that beach house of hers."

"What am I supposed to tell her?"

Michael patted Gabriel's hand. "The truth."

"But I want to be with her and her family. I miss the twins so much when I'm away for too long." Gabriel's chest ached over how much he missed them.

"Then tell her… that the world is filled with menace and uncertainty that requires your attention." A laptop suddenly appeared on Michael's lap. "This AI technology, for example, is creating all kinds of havoc. Job displacement, algorithmic bias, privacy concerns, misinformation and deepfakes, cybersecurity threats, just to name a few. And don't get me started on the ethical dilemma and environmental impact."

"Environmental impact?" Gabriel felt as though they were suddenly off course.

"The energy consumption of AI infrastructure, particularly in data centers, is a growing concern. It contributes to carbon emissions and potentially hinders efforts to transition to clean energy. Not to mention the direct impact on humans."

"Like what?" Both Michael and Raphael had been fascinated with technology, but Gabriel had no interest.

"Like cognitive decline, for one. AI taking over tasks traditionally performed by humans can lead to a decline in cognitive abilities and a loss of critical thinking skills." Michael clacked away on the keyboard.

"I had no idea." He cared about humans; that was a fact.

"See, while you've been preoccupied with your human family, the world has been in global turmoil. Conflicts in Gaza and Sudan, ongoing fighting here in Ukraine. The humanitarian crisis in Gaza has escalated, with reports of famine affecting nearly a million people in and around Gaza City. Tomorrow, there is a *Global Day of Rage* rally being held in front of the UN in New York City in protest of the situation."

"If I used this as an excuse, Lynn might question my involvement on these fronts." They'd never talked about war before.

Michael typed again on the laptop. "Then tell her about the extreme global climate events."

"Like?" Lynn's beach house was under seasonal hurricane warnings.

"Like heatwaves gripping the western US. She must have heard about this. There're record temperatures recorded in Japan. Heavy rains caused flash floods in India, Pakistan, New Zealand, and parts of Spain. Wildfires in Europe, tropical storms, and volcanic activity. The list goes on." Michael opened a second window on his laptop.

"Things are pretty dire," Gabriel admitted, watching a CNN news page load.

"You think? What about the rest of the world's view of the United States? It's seen as complex and increasingly divided. There has been a notable decline in positive sentiment towards the U.S. with its closest neighbors, Canada and Mexico, adding to the growing complex geopolitical landscape." Michael closed his laptop.

"We have no impact or involvement in any of this; you know that." Gabriel grimaced, feeling even more helpless about what to do next.

"I do know that," Michael conceded. "But I also know what you *risk* if you keep up your superfluous involvement with Lynn and her family."

Chapter 22 

It's been 3 hours and 27 minutes now since Lane went missing.

Leo had explained to Lyndon that when the last passenger from Lane's flight departed the security area at the Ottawa airport, there had been no sign of Lane. Max and Julian had expressed their concerns about their daughter to the representative at the airline's information desk, but they'd been told that Lane never checked in for her flight and hadn't gotten on the plane. When Leo had also informed Lyndon that Nic was already on his way to Dartmouth to check the rental cottage Lane had been staying in, Lyndon in turn had texted Nic to let him know he would meet him there. Nic had been the one dispatched mainly because if Lane had been injured and the reason she hadn't made it to the airport, he would be the best one to aid her in that situation.

From the air, Lyndon surveyed the secluded property and the lake's edge and then set down out front on the small deck just as Nic exited through the front door. "Anything?" Lyndon demanded, his heart pounding in his chest.

"No sign of her." Nic ran a hand down his face as if he were unsure what to do next. His long, shiny black hair was secured back in a tight braid, and like Lyndon, Nic was dressed in training gear consisting of a pair of dark combat pants and a long-sleeved pullover.

"I'll double-check!" It wasn't that Lyndon didn't believe Nic, but he needed to see the inside for himself, and he strode past Nic into the tiny cottage.

The interior of the house presented that Lane had packed up all her belongings as she had mentioned to him in her text, and there were no signs that anything was amiss, no forced entry, no struggle or foul play of any kind inside. Exiting out the front of the home, Lyndon descended the steps from the deck in one stride, then stood on the short driveway searching back and forth up the quiet road. Somewhere between Lane's text to him about heading to the airport and getting there, she had vanished.

This contract had been short and fairly close to home, and Lane had travelled further for work than this town and never had any issues. Could her disappearance have something to do with *his* world, or was this just some random act, Lyndon wondered?

Nic came to stand beside Lyndon. "You said she was taking a taxi to the airport. Maybe her ride broke down," he suggested.

"Or someone took her?" Lyndon grumbled.

Nic put his hands on his hips, scanning up and down the road. "If so, who and why?"

Lyndon took out his cellphone and hit the contact *Home* to dial Lane's number. Instantly, music and then the words from Pharrel Williams' song *Happy* sang out from behind a cluster of bushes on the far side of the road. Lyndon cut off the call and stowed his phone, crossing over to the opposite side. Pushing the low branches back, he spotted a cellphone on the ground. Grabbing it up and flipping it over, he saw that the cracked screen displayed Gustav Klimt's painting, *The Kiss,* on the lock screen, and immediately recognized the phone was Lane's. Anguish blanketing him, Lyndon closed his eyes in an attempt to calm his growing rage. Lane had expressed to him that the painting was of *them*. She kept actual photos of the two of them on her phone but had chosen not to risk having any of them as her home or lock screen, should anyone unsavory notice. They weren't secretive about their relationship, but they were careful about who they were open about it with.

"What is it?" Nic questioned, meeting up with Lyndon.

"It's Lane's cellphone," Lyndon said, his eyes opening to meet Nic's tormented face.

Nic stared down at the cellphone in Lyndon's hand. "Lane told Lynn she felt like she was being watched."

"What?" Lyndon scowled. "She never told me that." Lyndon had offered to go with Lane on this short trip, but she'd cautioned him that he couldn't risk being away should Thaddeus arrive.

"They spoke last night," Nic clarified. "Lynn told Leo that despite the beautiful surroundings of the cottage, Lane had felt uneasy, like someone was watching her."

Lyndon scanned the perimeter of the property. "Are there any security cameras?"

"None that I found—but I think we should head to the airport and check with security there."

"Perhaps." Lyndon glowered down at Lane's cellphone, watching as the screen went dark.

Nick pushed the sleeves of his shirt up his forearms. "What are you thinking?"

Lyndon's thoughts had gone to the confrontations he'd had with Addison. "I'm thinking I need to locate a certain Seraph—and get some answers." Lyndon tucked Lane's phone into his back pocket. "You head to the airport. Call if you find anything."

"You got it." Nic took hold of Lyndon's arm. "We're going to find her, I promise."

Lyndon nodded, and Nic let go of his arm. Then Lyndon's wings unfolded, and he swiftly took flight.

Outside of Marcus's office, Lyndon gathered himself. He'd flown so fast to New York he was out of breath. It would do him no good to appear angry or distraught due to Lane's disappearance, so he schooled his expression, cautioning himself that he needed to get answers. He took a deep breath and then let it out on a smooth exhale before knocking twice on the office door.

"Come in," Marcus's voice barked from beyond the closed door.

Lyndon pushed open the door, but he didn't enter the office.

"What do I owe the pleasure of your visit?" Marcus said, his tone sardonic.

"Have you seen Addison?" Lyndon tried to keep his fists from clenching.

Marcus spun his chair to face Lyndon. "No, not for some time, actually. Not since we were in Brazil."

"When was that?" Lyndon focused on keeping his tone casual.

"Just before Thaddeus left."

"Is Addison still in Brazil?"

"Not sure." Marcus rested his elbows on the arms of the leather office chair. "He was only there to do surveillance of people and equipment coming and going. Who knows where Thaddeus sent him after."

"Wasn't he supposed to be here with you—now that the Norway facility is closed?"

"Taking over for Zuriel, you mean?" Marcus steepled his fingers.

Keeping a rein on his temper, Lyndon said nothing and only shrugged. Even though Marcus was an asshole, Lyndon knew he hated Thaddeus as well. But he also accepted that this was just how he was going to live his life now, under Thaddeus's thumb. He seemed to like his life and the perks. And like Lyndon, he just hated dealing with Thaddeus and his over the top depravities.

"I thought so too—but like I said, maybe Thaddeus had other plans for him. And *I'm* not going to question those plans."

"Do you find it strange that no one has heard from Kendrick, not since the sale of the Norway facility?"

"Guess you didn't get the memo—the sale fell through."

"No—guess I didn't." Lyndon could feel his composure fraying.

Marcus dropped his hands and leaned on one elbow. "The place has just been sitting empty all this time."

"Lots of absent resources considering Thaddeus just sent word he's coming back." But the empty facility would work as a great place for Addison to hide out, Lyndon mused.

"If I hear from Addison—want me to tell him you're looking for him?" Marcus's office chair creaked as he leaned back in it.

"No need." Lyndon shook his head, then turned and exited the office without looking back. He rode the elevator to the roof, but before taking flight, he sent a quick text to Leo that said,

> *Just heard the Norway facility was never sold and sits empty. We need to go check it out. Have Zach meet us at North Haven.*

Chapter 23

Following the terrifying news that Lane was missing, I'd made it clear to Redmond that I needed to go up to Ottawa. He understood completely, particularly with the dream the girls and I had shared last night. Leo had promptly booked me a charter and had insisted for safety's sake that I stay with them at North Haven. I'd called out for Gabriel this morning, and again before my flight, then a third time after the plane had landed, but he had remained strangely quiet.

"Where the hell are you?" I mumbled under my breath as I left the immigration area. When I exited through the main door of the arrivals area into the August heat, I found Leo parked right out front. Summer in Ottawa was the only time the weather was in league with the temperatures in South Florida. Dragging my carry-on bag, I dashed over and opened the back door to the SUV. "Thanks for coming to get me," I said, tossing my bag in the backseat before climbing into the front. "Thank goodness for air-conditioning," I added, shutting the door and the heat out.

"Safer this way," Leo said, hitting the gas the minute I had my seatbelt secured. Surprisingly, the safety ended there as he drove us to North Haven at a speed that far exceeded the speed limit, getting us there in record time. "You training to be a racecar driver?" I questioned as we pulled into the driveway.

"Sorry," Leo said, exiting the vehicle. "We're all anxious to have you here."

I got out, grabbed my bag from the back and promptly followed Leo to the front door and was thankful again for the cool interior that had central air.

"Lynn, finally you're here," Julian's shaky voice greeted me as I came through the front door. His shoulder-length salt and pepper hair was uncharacteristically loose and messy, like he'd run his hands through it too many times.

Max was there too, but he captured me up in a hug in greeting first before uttering, "Good to see you."

Normally, the pair were well groomed and smartly dressed, but not today. Today, they were both unshaven, and their mussed clothes appeared to have been slept in, though their faces were haggard and showed the worry shadows of parents who hadn't gotten any sleep. Who could blame them? I wouldn't have been able to keep my shit together if it had been one of my daughters that had gone missing.

"Nic should be here soon," Leo informed me. "He was just finalizing his report with the Dartmouth police."

"Where is everyone else?" I glanced past them to the kitchen.

"Kris is with Jana at the restaurant," Leo stated. "And Natalie and Shea are with Mason over at his place."

I nodded, glancing around the open space, unsure what to do with myself. I hadn't met Shea yet, but Lane had sent me some recent photos of her. She was a stunner for sure and built like a female bodybuilder. From the knees down, she had high-performance lower-leg prosthetics. Lane had told me they were advanced artificial limbs designed to restore mobility and enable a person in a wide range of activities, including sports and high-impact activities. However, she rarely exposed her legs in public to avoid unwanted sympathy or the expectation of vulnerability, of which there were none. The prosthetics featured specialized components like carbon fiber feet and advanced knee and ankle joints that incorporated microprocessors for enhanced control and responsiveness, and were perfect for the training and the bodyguard role she performed, making her a great asset. I, on the other hand, still wasn't sure how I could help.

"We've got you set up in Den's room," Julian said, wringing his hands like a worried mother.

"Thank you, I really appreciate it." I already knew Den rarely used his rooms at North Haven, having South Haven set up as his main residence now when he wasn't in Amsterdam watching the facility there. Leo had told me they would have given me Zach's suite, but since he's been coming and going from South Haven to North Haven as part of the pursuit to find Lane, he had been occupying his space.

"And we heard from your friends Mac and Alison. They're on their way over," Max added, taking Julian's hand, curbing the wringing.

"Okay, great—let me go put my things away, and I'll be right back."

"We'll meet you in the kitchen," Julian said. "I'll fix something nice for lunch."

After dropping my suitcase off in Den's bedroom, I swapped out my blue jeans for loose cut-offs and then returned downstairs. I had expected to find Julian rushing around the kitchen making lunch for everyone as he readily did, but instead I found Max alone in front of a big pot on the stove.

"Hungry?" he asked as I approached, moving to set out a lone bowl of what looked like chili atop the long island counter. Next to it, he placed a basket of fresh bread rolls and a dish of butter.

"I could eat," I said, climbing up on the stool in front of the place setting of food. "Is this another one of Julian's masterpieces?"

"No—Ben made it. Vegan chili, his specialty." He gave me a tired smile.

"It smells wonderful." I remembered hearing Ben made a mean chili.

"Julian went to lie down," Max added, his expression grim.

"The two of you must be going out of your minds with worry." I was struggling over the fact Lane was missing, so how could they not be?

"As parents, you always worry about your children." Max handed me a spoon for the chili and a knife for the butter. "But…."

"You could never imagine something like this happening," I finished for him.

He nodded.

"Where's Leo?" I asked, breaking open one of the soft warm rolls.

"He's down in the tactical area with Nic and Lyndon."

"Right," I said, but I figured Lyndon would be out scouring the earth for Lane.

"Can I get you a beverage to go with your meal?" Max freed a tall glass from the cupboard and then filled it with water from the fridge dispenser.

"Water is perfect," I said, not wanting the exhausted fella to fuss over me.

"Okay then, I'm going to go check on Julian."

"Of course. And don't worry about me."

Max gave me another tired smile and then went off up the hall to their private quarters.

As I finished rinsing out my dish in the sink, a soft rapping came from the front door. When no one came to answer it, I put my dish in the rack and went over to see who was there. Upon opening it, I was relieved to find both Mac and Alison standing there. "I was told you two were on your way over—come on in," I said, waving them in.

"Hey, Lynnie," Mac said, giving me a big hug. Her hair was up in a messy bun, and she was wearing a rust-coloured t-shirt knotted at the hip over a peasant skirt in the same colour, and flat strappy sandals.

Alison hugged me next. "Hi ya, Spook." She was dressed in calf-length faded jeans and a t-shirt, hers a simple black in contrast to my white one. Like mine, her hair too was pulled back in a long loose ponytail. "How is everyone holding up?" she asked, scooching past me and over to the sofa in the living room.

Mac followed after her and rested down on the long sofa, settling her big tote purse next to her feet.

"I wish I could say *okay*, but Max and Julian are barely holding it together." I slumped down into one of the soft, comfortable armchairs across from them. "Got any witchy stuff in there?" I pointed at Mac's bag.

"As a matter of fact, I do." She patted her purse affectionately.

Alison pulled a notepad and pen from her own purse. "Tell us about the dream." She flipped pages in her notepad in search of a blank one.

"Nightmare," I corrected, before leading them through the bizarre and shadowy ordeal. "I only wish I knew why the twins had to share in my horrible dreams."

"Holy shit," Mac said, rubbing her arms like she'd just felt a chill.

Alison's mouth gaped, then she closed it and began frantically writing it all out in her notebook. "I can see it, Spook. The girls—all of it."

"I don't understand the abandoned hotel and indoor pool. It's not a place I know." I fidgeted with the hair tie holding my ponytail.

"Who do you think the two people were?" Mac asked, kicking off her sandals and tucking her feet under her butt.

"No idea." I shook my head.

"And what's with all the flowers?" Alison questioned, looking up from her note-taking.

Mac wrapped her arms around herself. "What about the girls and the mirror?" She visibly shivered, then said, "Nearly every culture in the world attributes some superstition or myth to mirrors. Modern Wicca practitioners use mirrors for introspection, glamour spells, repelling negativity, scrying, and sometimes as a gateway to alternate dimensions, but I still haven't found any spells to make a mirror a conduit."

"Any chance you could do a locator spell?" I stared down at her huge purse.

"I've already tried using a pendulum," Mac said. "The silver and amethyst one I made when trying to find Kris."

"It's supposed to help open the crown chakra for clearer thought, connect you to your higher guides," I recalled, glancing up at her.

"It's better for finding lost things. Not so great for people." She pushed out her lower lip in a mock pout. "I thought to try a *Beason*

Spell, tap into local spirits around this house, help Lane find her way back, but…."

"But Lane's not lost, she's missing." I blew out a breath.

Mac nodded.

"Any other options?" I asked, glancing at both of them.

Mac chewed the corner of her lower lip, then said, "Journeying."

Alison cut a glance at Mac.

"What?" I glared at Alison and then back at Mac.

"She'd have to visit the spirit world to interact with nature spirits," Alison stated, flipping her notepad to another blank page.

I scowled. "And?"

Mac stared down at her purse. "For a lost person, I'd need to journey to the *Middle World*." She glanced up at me then. "The shadow side of the physical world—the invisible facet of the mundane."

"Ya, no—that's the super risky spell—I remember now. You are *not* doing that one." I crossed my arms over my midsection.

"What about the stinky spell?" Alison suggested.

Mac grabbed her purse from the floor and set it between her and Alison on the sofa. "It was only stinky because of the sulfur linked to Iceland—it wasn't the spell." From her purse, she pulled free her cellphone and clicked on an app. "It's a full moon, and since it's Friday—just like the last time I did this spell, the planetary influence is Venus once again."

I glanced at Alison and shrugged.

She grinned back at me. "I'd tell you what was next, but I don't have that notebook with me, of course."

"No need—I have everything," Mac informed us. "I brought the pink and aqua green candles, and I have all the herbs associated with Venus." Retrieving each item from her purse, Mac set the mortar and pestle and her wand to the side on the coffee table between us. Then she placed the coloured candles for the spell-making out in front of her. Next from her bag, she rescued a large plastic pill box divided into several rows and columns, each with individual labels affixed to the lids of the compartments. "I have… elder, foxglove, iris, orris root, periwinkle, thyme, and this time I have the catnip needed." Digging into her purse once more, she produced a small black notebook. "If you recall, I need to write out the incantation—the spoken part of the spell." She cracked open the book and flipped to a fresh page. "*Intention*," she said, then wrote out what the spell needed to accomplish. "*Grounding and centering*." Mac took several moments with her eyes closed, murmuring meditative words of affirmation to herself. Opening her eyes, she said, "Lynn, I'm going to need something of Lane's."

"Oh right! I'll check her room," I said, then dashed off to Lane's room up the hall. I returned with a deep raspberry colour hair scrunchy, a few strands of Lane's long wavy black hair still snagged around the fabric. "Here—is this good?" I handed Mac the hair tie.

"It's perfect." Mac laid the scrunchy in front of the candles and began the spell. "Everyone, close your eyes."

Like before, the incantation took about 20 minutes to perform, but unlike the last time, where the spell had created the odor that reeked of sulfur, this time Mac's spell gave off the scent of… *dirt*, like potting or garden soil, along with the fragrance of flowers… that faded with a soft fuchsia pink sparkle of mist just as I opened my eyes.

"I smell flowers," Alison said, leaning forward. "Mac, did you see anything?"

"A pool," Mac and I said at the same time.

"You saw it too?" Mac questioned.

"Yes, but it wasn't like the pool in my nightmare." I rubbed my eyes. "It was an in-ground pool, but this one was empty of water. And there was soil and flowers…," I pointed at Alison. "…on the bottom, but the room, the walls and windows around the pool, based on the condition, the place did look abandoned. Like in my dream."

Mac's eyes were wide. "I saw it too—just as you described, Lynnie."

"It's the same place," Alison stated with conviction, adding an annotation in her notebook. "The one in your dream, Spook, and the place you both just saw—they're the same."

I wasn't sure how that bit of information helped, and we all just sat there staring at one another as though hoping for clarity.

Voices echoed up the hall, breaking the silence as Leo and Zach came into the living room followed by Lyndon. The three of them, all dressed in black training gear, looked like triplets.

"Oh, hey ladies," Zach said when he noticed us.

"Ladies," Leo said, nodding at Mac and Alison. "Good to see you both again."

Alison gave them a sweet smile. "We're here to help wherever we can."

"At your service," Mac added, tucking the remaining spell-casting items back into her purse.

"Hi," I said, standing and embracing Zach.

Zach lifted me off the ground. "I'm so glad you're here," he said before releasing me.

"I'm not sure how I can help—but I felt I needed to be here," I said to no one in particular.

Then, to my surprise, Lyndon stepped up, arms open for a hug. "Lynn, thank you. I am grateful you are here," he said mid-hug.

"We're gonna find our girl." I looked up at him to see his expression portrayed the same worry I'd seen in the faces of Max and Julian. "Mac just did a spell that corroborated my dream." It was clear to me that we all needed some semblance of hope.

"And it may have something to do with where Lane might be," Alison said, bringing in another hint of joy.

"Lyndon feels we need to go to Norway," Leo said. "He thinks that maybe Addison took Lane."

"Why Addison—and why Norway?" I questioned, scrunching up my face at the idea.

"Addison because he's been sniffing around asking after Lane," Lyndon growled out. "And Norway because I found out that the facility there was never sold—it's been sitting abandoned all this time."

"And what—you thought it would make a great place to take Lane?" I shook my head and shrugged. To me, it seemed quite a distance to take someone.

"Maybe—I don't know," Lyndon said gruffly.

I shook my head again. "Look, I can't explain it, but you need to trust me. My intuition says we need to search abandoned places near Ottawa, ones with indoor pools."

Lyndon scowled, shooting a look at Leo.

I understood that my spidey-sense skill was new to Lyndon, and I said, "Lyndon, my dreams are never wrong—I know what I saw." I turned my attention to Leo. "Can you do your eidetic-memory-recall thing for any abandoned buildings around the area, ones that may have or had a pool at one time?" I glanced over my shoulder at Mac and Alison.

Leo closed his eyes as though searching his memories. Opening his eyes, he said, "Nothing. My personal memory banks are drawing a blank, but I can check my electronic files."

"Go ahead," I said, but I had another idea.

Without another word, Leo headed for the lower level with Lyndon and Zach trailing after him.

In the meantime, I sent a quick text to my realtor friend, the one who had helped sell Vicki's place. I wrote,

> *Hey there, it's Lynn Westlake. I have a bit of an odd question for you. Do you know of any abandoned buildings in the Ottawa area, ones that might have had an indoor pool?*

Being the professional that she was, she sent back a message immediately,

> *Hi, Lynn. As a matter of fact, there's an old YMCA off Bank Street that's scheduled for demolition in the coming months.*

She followed up with another text, specifying the proper address.

Then, like a well-coordinated team, Zach, Leo and Lyndon returned to the living room *just* as Nic came through the front door.

"Lyyyynn. Leo told me you'd be here when I got back! But it's certainly an unexpected pleasure to see you both," Nic said, waving at Mac and Alison.

"Nice to see you, too," Alison tossed out.

Mac waved back. "Always a pleasure to see you, Nic." She grinned at Alison. He *was* a handsome devil.

"All hands on deck," he said then, leaning down to embrace me.

"Hey, Nic." I squeezed him back. He let me go, and I turned to Leo and said, "I have a place for you to check out."

"That's good, because I found nothing," Leo confessed. "But I'll keep checking just in case."

While Nic returned with Leo to the lower level to continue his search, I handed off the information to Zach along with a description of the images I'd witnessed from Mac's spell. Then, he and Lyndon left to check out the place. Following their departure, Mac and Alison stated they needed to go and get dinner ready for their families, but said they'd come back if I needed them. I told them I always need them, but that I understood they had to attend to their regular lives right now.

Less than 40 minutes later, the two returned, and unfortunately, they were empty-handed.

"There's nothing there resembling what you described, Lynn," Zach reported. "And there was no sign that anyone had been there other than to put up *no-entry* signs and demolition notices."

"I still think we need to go to Norway—search the facility there," Lyndon proposed again. "And we're going to need you with us, Lynn."

I shook my head, frustrated. "You know I can't sense Lane—wish I could."

Zach rested his big hand on my shoulder. "But you're the only one who can tell if there are any other Earthbound in the vicinity."

"Since the facility closed, we don't have any intel on what's been going on there," Zach added.

"Well, one of you is going to have to speak to Redmond about this, because I'm not going to be on the other end of that conversation." I tightened my lips and raised my eyebrows.

"Already done," Leo said as he came back into the room. "I spoke to Redmond, told him I'd been counting on Purah popping in so I could ask her if *she* recalled any locations or facilities that fit the description."

"That would be valuable," I said, hopeful.

"Unfortunately, she's not expected back for a few days, and I fear we can't wait any longer—and that's when I told Redmond you needed to go to Norway."

"What did he say?"

"He said to go ahead."

"*Go ahead*—that's all he said?"

"And to keep you safe."

Chapter 24 

It's been almost 13 hours now since Lane went missing, and despite us leaving on the 7:00 p.m. charter Leo had arranged for us, it was still a 10-hour overnight flight before we reached our destination of Bergen, Norway.

Once we were in the air, Lyndon explained to me that this trip was a bit of a longshot, but he felt that Addison had shown a little too much interest in Lane. "Nothing came of it at the time," Lyndon said, moving to the seat beside me. "But then just days after Thaddeus announces he's coming back to Ottawa, Lane goes missing?"

"You think Thaddeus might have her?" I leaned my seat back.

"No—I don't know, but if Addison told him his assumption of who he thinks she is…." Lyndon paused, drawing in a heavy breath. "He tracked me down again, asking who Natalie was."

"Does Leo know about this?" Zach asked, sorting through the clothing he'd packed for the mission.

"Yes, I spoke with him about it. I didn't think it was relevant at the time because he mistook Lane for Anael's daughter, and I thought I'd convinced him she wasn't. I hadn't known about Natalie back then. But I wouldn't put it past Addison to use Lane somehow against me."

I frowned. "Why?"

"He'd questioned my watching Lane back then. Found me at the university watching her and Julianna."

I watched as Lyndon scrolled through a few photos of Lane on his phone.

"How did he know about Natalie?" Zach handed Lyndon a pile of tactical gear.

"He must have overheard Julianna. Leo told me she'd been on a call with Ben that day." Lyndon assessed the pile he'd been given.

I leaned my seat forward again. "Feels like a bad coincidence."

"I don't like coincidences," Lyndon grumbled.

"Maybe he thought you knew something back then, or you were up to no good," Zach suggested, checking size tags on another set of gear.

"Either way, his asking about Lane's whereabouts is enough for us to make sure we cover all our hunches," I assured him.

Zach and Lyndon had opted to fly with me in the plane since neither of them had any tactical gear local to the facility we were traveling to. "Why do we need this type of gear?"

"The place is abandoned—we don't know what we'll find there, or who we might encounter. Better safe than sorry." Zach gave me a tight smile.

While Zach continued going over the clothing and gear needed for the mission, Lyndon sat quietly staring at more photos of Lane on his cellphone.

"Here," Zach said, handing me a pair of black tactical combat pants, a long-sleeved shirt with padded elbow patches, and a pair of what he'd called *squad* boots.

Leo had been the one to gather the gear for us, but to save time we'd opted to change on the plane since it was such a long flight. The inside of the 8-passenger private jet featured face-to-face seating, a galley for food service, fold-out tables, luggage storage, and a private lavatory, to which I promptly got up and used to change into my new gear.

Shortly after midnight, I'd fallen asleep, but apparently my companions had continued to go over the building's blueprints that

Lyndon had been able to scrounge up. Thankfully, they'd let me sleep right up until we landed at 5 a.m. Ottawa time, 11 a.m. Norway time. And upon arrival at the Flesland airport, there was a nondescript midsize SUV waiting for us that Leo had also arranged, and to my amazement the temperature outside the airport was an agreeable 19 degrees Celsius or 66 Fahrenheit.

At approximately 11:30 a.m., we pulled up to the one-story *closed* Sterope Facility, just outside the village of Flesland.

Before exiting the SUV, Zach handed me a lightweight soft body armor vest. "It's rated the highest protection, thinnest IIIA, and all for your safeguard."

"Oookaaay," I said, confused over what IIIA was but grateful for the protection. They had promised Redmond they'd keep me safe after all.

As their weapon of choice, both Zach and Lyndon had donned Glock 45s with slide-on tactical lights, being that the inside of the facility would be in total darkness since it was no longer in use. I was the only one of us unarmed, and now I was seriously wishing I had made the time to learn how to use the gun gifted to me by Kris. I'd never been scared on a mission before, but for some reason my nerves were raw, and it wasn't my spidey sense; it was *fear*. It was unfortunate that I was the only one who could sense the Earthbound, because had Gabriel bothered to come when I'd called out for him, he could have easily gone inside to let us know what we were up against.

At the moment, I couldn't sense any celestial signatures other than Zach and Lyndon's. "The place looks pretty shut down," I said, standing near the main doors.

"I brought my security key fob for the place, but there doesn't seem to be any power," Lyndon noted, scanning the building and then the grounds.

"I'm going to check around for a way in," Zach said before taking off at a jog, disappearing around the right side of the building.

Lyndon came to stand near me, taking a protective stance. "You okay?"

I shrugged. "The place kind of gives me the creeps." I stared into one of the darkened floor-to-ceiling windows.

"All the facilities have a *creepy* element to them," he said. "That's what happens when you have a psychopathic monster running the enterprise." Heavy footfalls sounded from the left, and Lyndon drew his gun, aiming it in the direction of the far corner.

"I found an emergency exit," Zack announced, then halted, raising his hands at seeing Lyndon's Glock aimed at him. "Whoa— hey now—easy."

Lyndon immediately lowered his gun. "Sorry," he said, grimacing. "Place has me on edge too," he directed at me.

"The far emergency exit door's ajar," Zack clarified, waving for us to follow him.

Once inside, I found myself grateful for the thick canvas pants and heavy long-sleeved pullover I'd been given to wear because the interior temperature was significantly colder than the exterior.

Lyndon led the way with Zach at our rear as we started working through the dark offices along the main hall, which in the glow of the tactical flashlights showed evidence of water damage. Having been unoccupied for over 2 years, the scattered furniture displayed dust-covered surfaces. Some of the desks had forgotten personal items like keyboards and office supplies. The place was unnervingly quiet, and there was an emptiness that palpated the senses.

Past the offices, we moved stealthily on to the central lab area, which contained a substantial main treatment space and a single surgical room. There we found remnants of outdated medical equipment, clipboards that would have held medical records and patient charts, along with several old pairs of discarded hospital scrubs, and a few broken wheelchairs. The shadowy lab space held a more unsettling, almost horrifying atmosphere than that of the offices. A musty, stagnant smell permeated the air, and I counted us lucky that there wasn't a morgue in the building we had to search, since it wasn't a regular hospital.

As I watched Zach and Lyndon silently check the perimeter of the room, I was reminded of the young girl who had been here the day I'd been given the tour. She had been having blood drawn, and though I couldn't tell if she was a halfling or not, I could see by the pallor of her skin and frailness of her body that she was not well. I blew out a slow breath and considered what awful things might have gone on here. Now, all the spaces were empty. "Did Thaddeus have a private lab here as well, like in Ottawa?" I directed at Lyndon.

"He did—on the lower level. We can take the stairs," he said, pointing a hand and indicating the direction to take.

In the lower lab we found *nothing*. It was empty, like the other spaces, stripped of most of its furniture and equipment.

We exited the darkened stairwell back into an equally dark hallway on the far side of the treatment area. When Zach's flashlight skimmed the wall across from the entrance, I noticed the same framed photo of a Norwegian landscape I'd seen last time. "Shine your light here again," I directed him. I stared at the image, recalling how a butterfly had landed on the frame, a white one with dark grey outer edges, virtually identical to the ones I'd witnessed in the Celaeno building's greenhouse. Then I remembered something else and shot a glance up the pitch-black hall.

"What is it?" Lyndon asked, lifting his gun, turning to face up the hall.

"Isn't there an elevator here?" I squinted into the now dimly lit hallway.

Zach lifted his gun, aiding in lighting the hall.

"Yes, but there's no power. Besides, it just takes you to the lab we were just in," Lyndon stated.

Ignoring him, I pivoted and strode in the direction where I'd seen the elevator the last time I was here. Stopping in front of it, I found that the elevator door was wide open. "Why is there a door on both sides?" I pointed to the opposite side.

"That leads to Thaddeus's private suite." The light was too bright as it reflected off the steel door, and Lyndon lowered his gun.

"Do you have access?" Zach asked, coming to stand behind us.

"I did, but...."

"We need to get in there," I interrupted. "Try your key fob." I crossed my fingers and held my breath.

Stepping into the elevator, Lyndon pulled the fob from his front pants pocket. Then he swiped the fob over the pad and pressed the button marked 'X'. The keypad instantly lit up, and then the elevator door rumbled and slid open.

At the door opening, Zach grabbed hold of my arm and yanked me back, placing himself between me and the now open door. "Stay behind me," he ordered.

"Looks like someone's been living in Thaddeus's suite," Lyndon said, stepping through into the living space.

The open-concept room was lit up by wall sconces and contained a small kitchenette, a king-size bed, and a view into an overly-large closet, and was considerably warmer than the rest of the building. On the kitchen counter, dishes were stacked precisely with cutlery laid out in neat lines on a cloth dishtowel. I opened the fridge and found rows of kid-size drink boxes, water bottles, and several bottles of whole milk. I pulled open the freezer and spied small containers of ice-cream, popsicles, as well as chicken nuggets and mini pizzas. Next to the fridge in the cupboard were boxes of children's cereal, Kraft Dinner, individual packages of Goldfish crackers, along with plain saltine crackers. "Was a kid living here?" I suggested, surveying the rest of the room.

"Not likely," Zach said, exiting from the closet into the main space. "There are seven tailored suits, with paired shirts, ties, socks and shoes, all in double XL adult sizes in there." He pointed a thumb over his shoulder.

"And based on the OCPD perfectionism and rigidity of things, I'm *positive* it's not Thaddeus," Lyndon said.

I knew what OCPD was only because when talking to Grier about Thaddeus, I'd asked her about the different types of personality disorders. She'd told me about Obsessive-Compulsive Personality Disorder, explaining it was characterized by an intense preoccupation with orderliness, perfectionism, and control, often at the expense of flexibility, openness, and efficiency. Most individuals with OCPD are excessively devoted to work, detail-oriented, and inflexible in their beliefs and behaviors. She also said that they may also struggle with emotional intimacy and forming close relationships due to their rigidity and need for control. "Who do you know like that?" I asked Lyndon, walking over to the bed. The sheets on the bed were pulled tight, the surface smooth and wrinkle-free with sharp hospital corners at the foot of the bed. A single blanket was spread over the top sheet, aligned with the head of the bed. The lone pillow was set lengthwise; the open ends of the pillowcase tucked back into the double edge of the case. *Definitely OCPD*, I considered. On the nightstand was a neat stack of five journal-style notebooks. Examining them, I found that two of the notebooks were full of repetitive nonsense in stiff handwriting, one was half-full, one was empty, and the last one resembled the same style of notebook that Thaddeus used. Flipping it open to the first page, I found more writing but in a different hand. "Check this out," I said, waving the last notebook in the air.

"What do you got there?" Lyndon asked, taking up space on my right.

"This is Thaddaeus's handwriting—he must have left it here." I flipped through the pages to show him. "The others are in a completely different handwriting."

Lyndon leaned in. "How do you know it's his?"

"Because it's exactly like what I saw in Thaddeus's private lab in Ottawa. And like those, I can't read this one because it's in that stupid code language he likes to use."

Zach leaned over my shoulder. "That's a week before this facility was shut down," he said, tapping a big finger on the top of the page next to the date.

I snapped the notebook shut. "Clearly, there's power in this section of the building. What else is on this circuit?" Not waiting for an answer, I was out of the living space and back through the elevator door in search of more. I tucked the notebook under my bulletproof vest and focused the other way down the hall. It was too dark to see anything, but the last time I'd been here, something hadn't been right about the dimensions of this place and the areas we'd been shown. On my previous visit, I had seen a set of double doors at the far end of this hall.

Lyndon and Zach came through the elevator door and stood on either side of me, both aiming their guns and flashlights in the direction I was facing.

"What's through there?" I asked when the double doors were illuminated.

Zach lowered his Glock, but Lyndon kept his gun aimed up the hall. "Past the doors used to be a patient play area."

I started for the doors, but Lyndon hustled in front of me, leading the way, while Zack covered our backs once again.

Lyndon swiped his fob over the security panel, and the double doors opened with a sound like they'd previously been suctioned closed. But before we could take one step through the doors, we were ambushed by an odor that assaulted the senses, the overly warm room giving off a putrid stench of advanced decay that resembled rotten meat, vomit, and a sickly sweet undertone like sour milk.

"The smell of death," Zach uttered, stepping forward, checking the four corners of the room.

Covering my nose with my sleeve, I followed Zach and Lyndon into the room. On the far wall of the partially lit room, the children's video game *Super Mario Brothers* was paused on the big TV. A long sofa had been dragged over and set in front of the wall-mounted TV. Seated on the sofa, head back, was the motionless frame of a large Earthbound male. *Kendrick.*

Covering both my mouth and nose, I held back a gag when I saw that the front of his throat had been slit so deep the cut went clear through the anterior muscle structure of his neck, his trachea and esophagus, right to the cervical vertebrae and spinal cord, leaving his head barely attached to his body. No one, not even a Seraph, could heal from that type of wound. In contrast to the gore at his neck, the rest of his body was clothed in old-fashioned, two-piece, dark-green plaid flannel pajamas. Next to the body on the armrest of the sofa sat the paused game controller. Next to it was a blue recycle bin filled with empty drink boxes, crumpled goldfish packages, and crushed water bottles.

Zach tapped the bin with the toe of his boot. "Seems he's the one who has been living here."

"The poor bastard had no direction since Thaddeus left," Lyndon suggested.

I pulled the neck of my shirt up over my nose. "Do you think Thaddeus killed him?" I muffled through the fabric of my shirt.

"He wouldn't have left the body." Lyndon circled around the sofa, his back to the TV as he faced Kendrick's decaying corpse. "Last thing he would want is a dead body linked back to him, even if he was an employee," he said, doing finger quotes on the word *employee*.

"What do we do now?" I asked through a wave of nausea.

Lyndon removed the small flashlight from his gun. "I'm going to remove any signs that Kendrick was even here, should Thaddeus come here for any reason," he said, continuing to hold the light while holstering his weapon.

"I'll get rid of the body," Zach offered. "The stench will dissipate if I get rid of the sofa too. "

"How are you going to do that?" I moved back towards the entrance and away from the gruesome scene, needing to separate the signs of death in a room designed for children.

"Pyrotechnics and explosives expert," Zach said, holstering his gun. "I'm a firefighter, remember." He cracked his knuckles and grinned. "I know what elements are needed to disintegrate a body. And the sofa will be easy."

"Great," I said, trying not to inhale through my nose. "Don't tell me—I don't wanna know."

While Zach remained to take care of *things*, Lyndon drove us back to the airport. And since Taylor had remained distraught over Lane's disappearance like we all were, Lyndon chose to fly back to Ottawa under his own power and check in on Taylor at the group home.

We hadn't found any signs of Addison, nor that he or Lane had even been there. We did, however, find where Kendrick had been holding up all this time. Unfortunately for him, someone else had found him first, and now he was dead. Zach would be reporting back on what we'd found, but Lyndon would *not* be reporting back to Thaddeus's people, because no one needed to know he had been to Norway snooping around the abandoned facility.

Who had killed Kendrick? We didn't know.

What I did know was that I had to take the slow boat—or plane, as it were, back to Ottawa alone, *and* that Lane was still missing.

Chapter 25

Lyndon sat next to Taylor at a table in the large playroom, seeking to assure his son that they would find Lane.

Taylor made a 'B' handshape with both hands, fingers extended, thumb tucked in, bringing them near the sides of his head with palms facing him, moving both hands down, forward, up and back, signing the word, "*worry*," over and over.

"Please don't worry, my sweet angel," Lyndon told Taylor in a soft voice.

"Thought I'd find you here," bellowed a startling and unwelcome voice from behind them.

Lyndon turned to find Thaddeus standing several feet away from where he and Taylor sat.

Taylor immediately began rocking and signing, making the '8' handshape with his fingers extended and middle finger and thumb touching, forcefully flicking his fingers at Thaddeus, shifting between the signs for "*hate*" and "*awful*".

"What the hell is he doing?" Thaddeus scrutinized.

Lyndon stood and waved over a staff member. "Could you take Taylor to his room, please?"

The staff member nodded and quickly wheeled Taylor out of the room.

"I should have disposed of that useless cripple a long time ago." Thaddeus's hair was a tad unkempt, and his clothing looked like he'd just gotten back from some fancy safari expedition.

Lyndon never expected to see him here of all places, but he was prepared with the narrative that he and The Guards had come up with.

"Why do we even keep this place running again?"

"It's good for your reputation," Lyndon reminded him, extending an arm to direct the disruptor out of the playroom.

"Right." Thaddeus scowled. "Whatever."

"What brings you here?" Lyndon wanted to ask where he'd been, but he didn't want any trouble. Plus, he needed to get back to North Haven and work with the others to find Lane.

"I just flew in—on a private jet." Thaddeus glanced around the playroom as they exited, his expression full of disgust. "It was quite decadent—I plan to fly using this method more often."

"Flew in—from where?" Lyndon walked calmly in the direction of the main door.

"I'll get to that later."

Lyndon continued skillfully guiding Thaddeus to the hall that would lead him out. "Did you drive straight here from the airport?"

"Me drive? Don't be absurd." Thaddeus barked out a laugh. "I had a chauffeur waiting out front when I arrived." He turned to face Lyndon. "I have so much to tell you, but first I need to get cleaned up and brief Amahle and the others that I'm back." Thaddeus headed for the entrance as if it had been his idea to leave. "Meet me at my condo in two hours," he said, taking his leave, not waiting for Lyndon to respond.

And Lyndon had nothing to say on the matter other than *go to hell,* but he did need to call Leo and let him know that the asshole was back. Lyndon pulled his phone out and hit the contact number for *Handyman.*

"Lyndon, what's up?" Leo answered.

"Guess who's back in town," he gritted out.

Lyndon could hear Leo sigh through the phone. "We've accomplished a lot in his absence—we don't want to mess up now. Do what you need to do, and we'll keep working to find Lane."

"I won't mess up," Lyndon grumbled.

"Lane is precious to us, too. If he has Lane…." Leo paused. "You have to do this, Lyndon, for Lane's sake, for all our sakes."

Lyndon stared at the shut door Thaddeus had left through. "I'm not going to let any of you down—especially not Lane."

"Keep us posted as best you can," Leo said.

"Will do." Lyndon ended the call. Then he went to check on Taylor before heading out.

Lyndon stood in the open space near the small kitchen in the condo as Thaddeus flitted in and out of his oversized closet. The open-concept condo looked much like Lyndon had left it after his review of the place. The only difference now was the two empty open suitcases tossed near the door into the condo. Those and the short stack of *notebooks* on the bedside table Lyndon had noticed that were exactly like the one Lynn had shown him.

The entry door behind Lyndon opened, and in walked Amahle *and* Marcus.

"I've closed the Tokyo location," Thaddeus announced before any of them could speak. He exited the closet barefoot, wearing only a pair of jeans. "Amahle report."

Amahle glanced at Marcus and then back at Thaddeus before resting her hands behind her back. "Business as usual, and the new lab you requested on the sixth floor is complete. The aviary has been converted into a new state-of-the-art lab with all the necessary equipment."

"Good. I will review the changes myself shortly." Thaddeus went into the closet again and then returned wearing a pale yellow golf shirt. "Right now I need you for a special assignment."

When Amahle nodded, Thaddeus returned to the closet.

"Both Sabastian and Lazarus will be in Ottawa for now. Sabastian will fill Amahle's spot while she is working with me." Thaddeus paused in the entryway of the closet, socks on this time but no shoes. "Any questions?"

No one said a thing, but Lyndon had plenty of questions. The first one being, why was he bringing in another tracker here, when Marcus was down a tracker?

"I've already spoken with Nathaniel and Atticus at the Electra facility in Rome." He turned, retreating back into the closet. "And Soriel and Malcolm at Alcyone in Amsterdam," he called out from the closet's confines. "All have reported to me on what they have been doing while I've been away."

Again, no one spoke.

"Marcus," he called before returning, loafers on this time. "How have you spent your time while I've been busy?"

Marcus stepped forward from their small line of three. "Business as usual, while also keeping an eye on that rogue female, Francesca, and her mate, *and* that restaurant she runs." Marcus stepped back into line. "Which I'm pretty sure is a front for something. I just haven't discovered for what yet."

"Marcus, Amahle, you are dismissed." Thaddeus waved a hand for them to go.

Marcus gave Lyndon a quick sideways glance before turning to leave.

When the door shut, Thaddeus asked, "And you?"

"I've kept myself busy with learning a variety of new hand-to-hand combat styles, martial arts, and weaponry training." Lyndon felt the need to stand at attention, but he held his casual stance. He wasn't the same obedient Seraph he'd been before Thaddeus had left. And he was even fitter and more muscular after all his training with The Guards.

"Really?" Thaddeus began to walk a slow circle around Lyndon.

"Yes. I reached out to several masters in the field, one in the Netherlands and one in Japan. Plus, I've improved my computer security and hacking skills. Tested new surveillance software, face recognition software, the ins and outs of travel, visas, and establishing residency for various countries." Lyndon stared straight ahead as Thaddeus came back around to stand at his left side.

"Why?" Thaddeus squinted as though studying Lyndon's profile.

Lyndon knew his skin now had a healthy golden glow from spending time outdoors with Lane versus the sickly pallor he'd had before with so much time in the basement, and he boldly turned his face to stare back at Thaddeus. "I wanted to be ready… for anything."

"What about your tracking skills?"

Lyndon followed Thaddeus's movement as he came to stand directly in front of him. "That's part of it. Computer hacking is the modern way to find just about anything and anybody." In reality, he had learned these skills from Leo and the others.

"So you've located Ms. Westlake then, have you?" Thaddeus questioned.

He'd known that question was coming. "No."

"No?" Thaddeus crossed his arms, causing his golf shirt to bunch.

Lyndon felt his jaw tighten. "Every lead had me running into a brick wall."

"So even after all that… *training*… you are still useless." Thaddeus dropped his arms.

Stick to the plan, Lyndon told himself. "After the dead end on the target, I thought it wise to expand my techniques. I went as far as to speak with the women the target was seen with at the group home. That was a dead end." Lyndon paused briefly, then continued with the fake narrative he'd practiced. "They were just colleagues and not personally connected. I originally kept surveillance on them all as well, but found it was a waste of resources. With deeper digging, going way back, I found out that she has only one remaining sibling left. I even looked into the ex-husband in Japan—did a thorough background check on him—nothing there. Seems he hasn't been in touch with her since their divorce. He even thought she was still living in Miami in their old home. I've been trying to find her, but she seems to have gone completely off the grid."

"What does that mean?" Thaddeus frowned down at his now wrinkled shirt.

"There was no trace of her after she and her husband split."

"No trace?" Thaddeus questioned, disappearing into the closet.

"Nothing physically nor digitally."

"How is that possible?"

"Possibly she realized someone was looking for her—perhaps her ex-husband told her someone had been to see him, that they asked about her. She must have gone into hiding."

Thaddeus returned this time wearing a dark navy three-button t-shirt. "Tell me you're still looking for her."

"I am—I have a computer program that runs 24/7 pushing all kinds of search protocols that keep watch for any kind of digital signature or facial recognition. If anyone can find her, it's me."

"Did you speak to Sebastian or Lazarus while you were in Japan?" Thaddeus strode past Lyndon into the kitchen space.

"No." Lyndon turned to watch Thaddeus rummage around. "When I got back from Japan, I retraced Zuriel's steps, going to the home under hers and her now ex-husband's name but found the same as Zuriel, that she had sold the house quite some time ago and the new owners didn't know where she had moved."

"Where is the traitor?" Thaddeus opened the fridge and grabbed a bottle of the fancy water.

"I don't know."

"What do you mean you *don't know*?" Thaddeus opened the bottle and took a swig. "I instructed you to drop him on the doorstep of that female."

Lyndon's shoulders bunched and clenched his fists. "Obviously, I didn't know where she was or lived. So I dropped him back in the town where I found him, at the hospital where he said she worked. I went back to see what happened to him but was told he'd checked out once they had tended to his wounds." When his knuckles almost cracked from the pressure, he loosened his fists. "So, no, I don't know where he is."

"Hiding, I would imagine." Thaddeus took another sip of water then left the bottle unopened on the counter.

"I would guess so. No one has mentioned seeing him, so…."

"Fine." Thaddeus opened the cupboard next to the fridge and took out a box of pricey truffle crackers. "I have other matters that require my focus right now, anyway."

Lyndon's shoulders relaxed.

But then Thaddeus raised a hand and flicked the collar of the dark-green short-sleeved polo shirt Lyndon was wearing. "Who are you trying to impress?"

Lyndon worked his jaw. "Just felt the need to clean myself up." He fought the urge to look down at his clothes. "Have you heard from Kendrick?" he asked, redirecting the conversation.

Thaddeus rested back against the counter and popped open the cracker box. "Should I have?"

"He's been unreachable since after he went with you to Brazil."

"I have no clue where he is—nor do I care." Thaddeus sniffed the contents of the box, grimaced and then tossed the box on the counter next to the water.

"I was under the impression he was supposed to secure new test subjects for you?" Lyndon knew the full story on that now.

"He failed." Thaddeus drew another box from the cupboard.

Lyndon said nothing and only nodded, knowing it had been Lynn who had posed as the woman, and that Kendrick was dead.

Thaddeus sniffed the contents of the second cracker box. Seemingly pleased, he took the box and the bottle of water with him to sit on his bed. "Let me tell you about what I've been doing."

Lyndon gritted his teeth but took a tentative stride towards the bedroom space. The last thing he wanted to do was listen to Thaddeus prattle on about his latest gruesome endeavors. But Leo was right; if Thaddeus had anything to do with Lane's disappearance, it was best he stuck around. Lyndon knew the others were doing everything in their power to find Lane, so he could stand here and suffer Thaddeus's existence.

Thaddeus set the water bottle on the nightstand next to the stack of notebooks. "I've spent the last two years experimenting with epigenetics and reproductive endocrinology, as well as cellular regeneration."

Lyndon stared, speechless.

"Thought you'd find that last one thought-provoking." He popped a cracker into his mouth.

"Who have been your test subjects?" Lyndon asked, worried to know the answer.

"Human females." He grinned devilishly up at Lyndon.

Lyndon's hands clenched into fists again. "Who?" If this bastard has done anything to hurt my female, he was going to pay.

"Just prostitutes, nobodies—you know the ones nobody sees, nobody would miss—nobody cares about." He crunched down on another lavish cracker.

The memory of the Brazilian news Leo had informed him of surfaced at the mention of *prostitutes*. Was Thaddeus the one murdering those women in Brazil, Lyndon wondered? The authorities had referred to the killer as the Brazilian Jack the Ripper. Knowing Thaddeus's thirst for depravity, it wouldn't be a huge leap for him.

"My new focus is on human males breeding with Earthbound females," he said, pulling Lyndon from his reflections.

"Why females of our kind?"

"I want to see what sort of offspring I can produce from this type of pairing."

"I see." Lyndon counted his lucky stars that Thaddeus was not aware of Julianna's son, Mason, nor was he privy to Natalie's existence, having only experimented with human females.

"I've been going about this all wrong, focusing on the results of the human-angel coupling. Spending too much time on the weakest beings when I should be focusing on the strongest, my kind." Thaddeus tossed back another cracker and chewed. "It's a shame I don't have contact with that Steward, Purah," he said through the mouthful. "She would have been an excellent candidate for my testing." He took a gulp of water. "But my deceptions burned that bridge, as they say." Thaddeus paused as though taking a moment to think about it.

Lyndon found it interesting that Thaddeus had dropped the idea of finding Lynn. She would have been crucial to Thaddeus's plan now that he needed to locate the females of his kind, but Lyndon would take the win.

"Is Julianna still here in Ottawa?" Thaddeus turned the box to the side as though reading the ingredients. "Maybe she's an option."

"I don't know," he lied. "When she proved not to be a threat, I discontinued trailing her." Lyndon blew out a slow steady breath. "Why?"

"Do we know the whereabouts of any other Earthbound females?" Thaddeus asked, ignoring Lyndon's *why*.

"I'll have to check." They had all been on high alert waiting for Thaddeus's return.

"I need to get my hands on a few for my new experiments." He dug another cracker from the box and tossed into his mouth. "What about Francesca and the other, Inanna?" he asked, chomping.

"They've not been part of my regular surveillance." Lyndon was growing impatient with all this talking. Thaddeus had never chatted with him this much before. "Marcus reported he'd been keeping an eye on them."

"Right." Thaddeus swapped the box of crackers for the water on the nightstand. "In the meantime, you can use your new *skills* to locate other Earthbound females. I've already texted you a list. You can start with them.

Lyndon checked his phone and found a text message from an unknown number. Thaddeus's new one, apparently. Lyndon ran down the list of names in his head,

> *Anastasia*
> *Tuyet*
> *Michaela*
> *Khalilah*
> *Noella*
> *Maricela*
> *Laurinda*
> *Verena*

"I'm going to need to find some exceptional human *males* as well."

Lyndon glanced up from his cellphone. "Exceptional?"

"Like those from professional human sports teams. We have four local male groups here in Ottawa you can pick from." Thaddeus took the notebook from the top of the stack. Flipping it open, he read, "Senators hockey, Redbacks football, BlackJacks basketball and the Atlético soccer team. Think *big*. The bigger the better."

Lyndon nodded. With regard to the female Earthbound, he was going to have to engage Marq to go over the list and make sure the others and the list of females were aware Thaddeus was searching for them.

"I'm assuming that business with Addison was *your* doing?" He snapped the notebook closed and set it back atop the short stack.

"What business?" Lyndon slid his phone back into his pocket.

"Didn't Marcus tell you? He found him dead in the alleyway outside the New York City facility."

Dead? "When was that?"

"He found him this morning."

"And you assumed I offed him?"

"He left me a message after I'd announced my return, stating he had some *interesting* news to tell me. I had him watching *you*, so I presumed you were the subject of this *news*."

"News about me?" It had to be about Lane and Addison's assumption that she was Anael's daughter, Lyndon suspected. "Not sure what it could be about," he lied again.

"His throat was slit, by the way—sliced his head nearly clean off." Thaddeus drew his index finger across his own throat.

"Knives aren't my thing," Lyndon deflected, though he'd welcome the chance to slit Thaddeus's gullet.

"But we know whose *thing* it is." Thaddeus's perfectly groomed eyebrows rose up his forehead.

Lyndon said nothing.

"Has anyone seen that pathetic turncoat, Ariadne?" He ran a finger over one brown.

"Not to my knowledge." Lyndon glowered. "Besides—why would she kill Addison?"

"Because she's demented." Thaddeus tapped the side of his head. "Frankley it was the only thing I valued about her."

"Deranged is more like it," Lyndon falsely sympathized. He actually respected Ariadne, thought she was the most courageous of them all. She'd been a little unhinged perhaps, but you almost had to be in order to survive and escape the clutches of Thaddeus. She'd done it wisely, getting out right away and before Thaddeus could hold something over her. Lyndon was envious of her fearlessness and wished he'd left with her in the beginning. But he'd been naïve in believing Thaddeus would create a comfortable world for them here.

"Yes, but unfortunately it made her much less easy to control."

"Maybe he saw her, and she didn't want him to talk…," Lyndon began to say.

"Talk—ha! Probably because she hasn't been able to. Not since I sliced her throat." He did the finger across the throat thing again.

"That was you?" Lyndon assumed it had been one of Thaddeus's henchmen.

"Yes, it was a warning, but I should have sliced her through."

Mayhap she did kill Addison, Lyndon mused. "You know he has a way of getting on your nerves. It wouldn't have taken much for him to piss her off, if she was the one who killed him." Lyndon held back a grin.

"If that's the case, it could also mean she's in NYC."

"Who will be covering for Addison now?" Lyndon asked, considering if Ariadne was here in Ottawa or had been. If she were here, who was her next target? Had she killed Kendrick? Was she coming after Thaddeus next? Or was she taking us all out, one by one?

"No one *yet*," Thaddeus said, jarring Lyndon from his musings.

Chapter 26 

When I arrived at North Haven from the airport, it was close to 6:00 p.m. local time and felt like the longest day ever. I'd tried to sleep on the flight, but the contrasting images of Kendrick in the kids' play area wearing flannel PJs, dead in front of that paused children's video game with his throat slashed, was more than an enemy to my ability to sleep. The question of who had killed him and *why* only increased my sleep deprivation.

Leo hadn't been at the airport this time; instead, there was a female Uber driver holding up a sign with my name on it waiting for me as I exited the arrivals area. It was just as well; I wasn't in the mood, nor did I have the energy to talk. I carried the canvas tote that held my mission gear over to the waiting car and got in. Then we rode in silence the whole way to North Haven.

Through the front door, I found… no one. There was not a soul around in the main living space, so I went straight to my room to clean up. Post-shower, I towel-dried my hair, then scooped it up in a loose ponytail. Afterwards, I changed into the navy yoga pants and tank top I'd packed, then slipped on a lightweight long-sleeved t-shirt in the same colour. Next to my discarded clothing, on the lid of my open suitcase rested the notebook I'd confiscated from that condo-style room. I planned to show it to Leo when I finally saw him. I didn't know if it held anything vital, but found it strange that it had been carelessly left behind in the condo. Or maybe Kendrick had stolen it at some point, who knew. But I was confident that he hadn't been able to read it either because I think he would have added his own comments about it in one of *his* notebooks, versus the repetitive affirmations he'd painstakingly written, *I believe in myself and my abilities; I am capable of doing hard things; I trust myself to make the right decisions,* and *I am strong and courageous,* on page after page. However, once we got it to Dereck to decipher, then we'd know what was in it.

Leaving the notebook where it was, I grabbed my phone from where I'd left it to charge and sent Redmond a text. I let him know I was back safe and sound, and ended it with a green heart, our code emoji for *I'm okay*. He wrote back that he'd been brought up to speed on how things had gone down, meaning that we'd found Kendrick deceased, and that our undertaking to locate Lane had failed. I was just about to text him a response when my phone rang in my hand. It was Redmond calling. "Everything okay?" I said, answering.

"Sorry, yes—I just wanted to hear your voice."

I smiled at that. "How are you doing?"

"Better now that you've finished roaming around some abandoned torture facility."

"Me too." There hadn't been any torture equipment thank gawd, but we *had* found someone expired. "How are the girls?"

"They seem okay—they don't really talk to me like they used to, though." I heard him sigh.

"*Tweens*," I groaned, resting down on the corner of the big bed.

"I'm just about to make them dinner."

My stomach rumbled. "Lucky them. I haven't eaten since before the flight to Norway, so I better go see what food scraps are left for me in the kitchen. Food goes fast around here with so many staying in the house now."

"Better get to it then," Redmond said, his tone light.

"Okay. Hey—thanks for being so understanding about my going to Norway." I was still surprised he had let me go.

"Anything to find Lane," he said. "Plus, I knew you were in good hands."

"I was." It had been impressive to watch Zach and Lyndon work together as a team.

"Go eat. And I'll get the girls fed."

"Text me before bed," I said, wishing I was home with them.

"Will do. Love you."

"Love you too," I said, ending the call.

Pushing up from the bed, I followed the amazing aroma of what I recognized as fresh pasta and tomato sauce that was now wafting its way up to my room. On the lower level, I spotted Max *and* Julian in the kitchen preparing the evening's nourishment for the home's current occupants. However, this meal seemed to have a frantic approach to its preparation. "What's going on?" I asked, sidling up to the kitchen island.

"Thaddeus is back!" Max shot out as he plated bowls of pasta.

"Oh crap! Where is everyone?" I cut a glance towards the hall that led to the entrance to the basement level.

"Den and Marq are at their target locations," Julian said, cutting into a second loaf of fresh bread.

Max began ladling out red sauce onto each mound of pasta. "Kris, Leo, Nick, and Zach are downstairs brainstorming, working on another plan to find Lane." He paused after the sixth bowl and looked over at me. "Natalie, Shea and Mason are with Jana at the restaurant. They needed the distraction of keeping busy." He gave me a weary smile.

"And Jules is with your friend Derek," Julian added, beginning to spread butter on the soft bread slices.

"What about Ben?" I questioned, wondering how I might help them with the task of meal service.

"He went to check his target location in Japan, but just sent word that it looks like it's been shut down." Max spread sauce over two more bowls of pasta. "He's going to keep watch and let us know if he learns anything more."

I watched as Julian paired each well-filled bowl of pasta with two slices of buttered bread, and my stomach grumbled again. "And Lyndon?"

"Where else?" Max said, retrieving a stack of large plastic cups from the cupboard.

"With Thaddeus," I grumbled, realizing he would have to suffer firsthand with that asshole's arrival. "Can I help with anything?"

"We have it all under control—but thank you, Lynn," Max said, setting one of the bowls of pasta he'd prepped in front of me on the island.

"Oh, thank you—you don't know how bad I needed this." I pulled out the barstool and climbed up. Setting my cellphone next to the bowl, I stared down at the beautiful pasta in front of me.

"Here you go, dear." Julian leaned a thick slice of buttered bread against the bowl. Then, with bowls and bread organized on two large trays, Julian and Max took the food out of the kitchen, up the hall, and down to our dedicated guardians.

In an effort to stay out of everyone's way, I sat quietly at the kitchen island enjoying the fabulous dinner they'd prepared for me. Rigatoni and a light, fresh, and simple tomato-based marinara sauce with garlic, basil, and oregano. I sniffed and then bit into the butter-slathered freshly baked sourdough bread, relishing the crisp, deep golden-brown crust and its light and chewy, airy interior.

As I finished the last bite of the comforting meal, my cellphone pinged with another message from my realtor friend. She'd stated there was an old inn scheduled to be torn down next month that was just an hour outside of Ottawa in Smiths Falls, and I sent a quick text to Leo downstairs, asking if he could come up.

A moment later he came through from the hallway into the kitchen and I said, "I have another location I feel we should check out."

Without question, Leo called for and gathered Kris, Nic, and Zach in the living room to go over the new information and location of the soon-to-be demolished small-town inn together on Leo's laptop.

"I messaged Lyndon, but he's unresponsive," Zach said, holding his cellphone up.

"He's likely stuck with Thaddeus," I said, knowing that more than anything he wanted to be here with us working to find Lane. I shook my head, feeling for the poor guy. "I don't think we can wait for him though." It was nearly 8 p.m. and darkness would be rolling in soon.

"I'm going to go to the restaurant, check on the others," Kris announced. "Text me if… you find anything." He forced a smile as if trying not to think the worst.

While Nic, Leo, and Zach went to get what they needed for exploring the new location, I went and retrieved the body armor I'd used in Norway. I didn't know if it was needed or not, but it was bad enough I'd be traipsing around some abandoned hotel unarmed; the least I could do was protect myself.

When the guys returned to the living room, I was waiting for them at the front door. "I'm going with you," I announced.

"We got this, Lynn," Leo said, checking his gun before holstering it.

"You just sent me all the way to Norway to hunt around some creepy deserted office/medical facility, so don't think for one minute you're keeping me from checking out this old hotel with you." I pounded my fist on the front of my body armor.

"She's got you there," Zach agreed, knocking his knuckles on the back of my protective gear.

"I'll have to drive then," Leo said. "Let's go!"

We drove the 417 highway that took us through Carleton Place and on into Smiths Falls, while Nic and Zach took the faster way through the air. Once again, Leo drove at a speed well above the limit, making what should have been an hour car ride into a less than 30-min drive.

Nic and Zach were waiting for us out on the driveway of the old inn when we pulled up.

"We did an area survey of the property," Nic said, "and a quick check of the grounds."

That was a lot to survey, I thought. Considering it was 43 acres of prime lakefront property as indicated in the writeup link Leo had found. It also stated that it had been a long-established luxury resort that operated from 1903 until its closure around 2011. The property was purchased in 2016 but was never revitalized and has since been largely abandoned. Demolition was to begin next month due to severe disrepair and property standard violations.

"Anything suspicious?" Leo asked, removing his gun from his holster.

"The property near the hotel is pretty overgrown—no way in but through the front," Zach answered, heading for the steps that led to the main door.

Zach went first through the doors, then Nic, and then me with Leo at my back. Immediately through the entrance was the reception area, which contained a front desk, a lounge with a large fireplace, and a back office that was mostly empty except for a small rolling office chair. To the right was a large decorative staircase that, based on the layout Leo found, led to the guest rooms and suites above, but we wouldn't be taking the stairs to the upper level. That was due to the fact that, like a severed spine, there was a huge gaping break in the middle of the staircase separating access from the lower to the upper floor.

"Clear," Zach announced, moving forward and onto the next space on this level.

The reception room had been easy to navigate with the light coming through the windows, though dark was coming in fast, so we followed behind Zach into a restaurant bar area. Like the first room, it held barely anything but a few broken tables and chairs. Off this space was what looked like a banquet hall for bigger events. The air was dry and smelled of dust and rotting wood; however, it too was empty, and we moved quietly across the floor to the double doors on the far side of the event space.

"There's a staff passage through here that will take us to the recreation area." Zach pointed at the doors, then gave me a sideways glance before turning back to Nic and Leo.

"Lynn, are you feeling anything?" Leo asked when Zach stayed put.

"No." I shook my head. "But it's hard to pick up on any other sensations with your three signatures humming around me."

Just then, all remaining light in the banquet hall suddenly dissipated, the sun finally setting and leaving us in utter darkness. As fast as the sun left, three tactical lights clicked on, with guns aimed at the double doors.

"Ready?" Zach asked.

"Ready," I whispered, my nerve endings suddenly raw.

In the same formation as before, we emerged into a long dark hall. The dry, dusty air of the banquet space transformed drastically into a strong, thick, unpleasant odor of mold, mildew, and decay, indicative of a closed, humid environment. Much like the other spaces, the hall had an eerie quality. The combination of decay, disuse, and lingering remnants of what was once a vibrant place was replaced with something chilling and unsettling. It didn't help that the only light we had now was from the small gun flashlights.

At the end of the hall, we stopped at another set of double doors, the glass surfaces of which were fogged over.

"Guys," I said, causing the three of them to halt.

"What is it, Lynn?" Leo questioned, coming up from behind to stand next to me.

"In my dream… I was in a hall with two large double doors, just like these, cloudy windows and all." I glanced back over my shoulder to the way we'd come, into the shadows, into the darkness. I turned back and stepped up past Nic and Zach. "In my dream… I pushed open the doors."

"Lynn!" Zach shouted, grabbing for my arm to hold me back.

But it was too late.

Immediately we were assaulted by a nasty stink of mold and mildew. The expansive long-ago fancy space with its high ceilings and impressive architecture was now a mess of decay, showing serious water damage with black mold on all the surfaces. The far wall had large windows, but the view out of them was mostly obscure, and if there was a garden beyond them like in my dream, I couldn't tell. Although, like my dream, moonlight did sneak in through the windows with broken panes.

"Place looks rough," Zach stated, gun still out, tactical light hitting all the walls and surfaces as he moved through the large space.

Similar to my dream, the once-appealing space was filled with trash, fallen tiles, and pieces of patio furniture, offering proof of neglect. But the unnerving silence did not hold the sound of dripping water as it did in my dream. Saying nothing in response to Zach, I strode forward to the pool. In the dream, the surface of the pool held stagnant, murky water, which evoked a sense of unease and discomfort, but.... "Someone shine a light over here, please." I gasped. Where I expected to find dirty water, in its place the pool was filled with… *dirt*. Dark earth filled the inner shell of the in-ground pool just shy of 2 feet from the top edge. And in the middle, where a large rectangular raft-like object had floated in the water, at its center was now a platform raised to a height level with the perimeter deck. I jumped down into the now shallow depths of the pool onto the level ground, following the beams of light set on the platform. As I walked slowly towards it, it was then that the mildew in the air shifted to a sweet fragrant scent. There, resting in the center, was a bed draped in white satin. Surrounding the bed were dozens of white flowers with thick dark green leaves. My heart sank then as the realization hit me, because unlike in my dream vision, there was no one lying on the bed; only the impression remained that someone had lain there.

I felt Zach, Nic and Leo at my back as I stared down at the empty bed. "This is the place. She was here," I said, my voice catching in my throat.

"Are you sure?" Leo asked.

I nodded and picked up a grouping of flowers. "What was Addison's skill before he was stranded on Earth?"

While Leo and Nic roamed the perimeter of the pool, Zach circled to stand in front of me. "Addison… his specialty was soil, compost and scat," he tossed out. "Lyndon told us that he even bragged about that coffee… you know, the one where the cat eats the beans and shits them out—how people pay a fortune for the stuff."

Normally I would have laughed at that little tidbit, but right now, humor eluded me. I sniffed the flowers. "These smell so fresh."

"I believe those are Shasta daisies," Zach said, shining his light on similar clusters around the bed.

"My vision… in the dream, the pool was filled with water, not dirt. This is his doing." I stared down at the ground.

"How can you be certain?"

My brain went to the vision of the tall dark male figure standing on the far side of the pool. "I just know." I glanced up at him. "There was someone else here, too."

"And you know this because?"

"Because there was another person in my dream."

"Were they together?"

My memory flooded with the vision of the second figure appearing behind the first. "I'm not sure." The lighting in my dream had marred my ability to see if they were male or female, but their presence exuded a sense of calm and dignity. I sniffed the bundle of flowers again, their subtle light scent was green and herbaceous, reminiscent of fresh-cut grass. "What about Ariadne—what was her expertise?"

Zach's brows rose. "Well, she and Amahle were paired for their skills with phytotoxins."

"Sorry, what?" I frowned.

"Deadly animals… and plants—the poisonous ones."

I dropped the flowers. "Oops-a-daisy," I quipped, wiping the palm of my hand on my jeans.

"Don't worry—those aren't poisonous," Leo stated, sidling up next to me. "But those over there…," he shone his light on a grouping of flowers with trumpet-shaped snow-white blossoms with dark green lance-shaped green leaves. "Those are oleander blooms. They're toxic. The poisoning can even cause a human to pass out."

"Really?" I took a cautious step towards the nearest grouping. "But they're so pretty."

Leo snatched up a blossom. "They contain potent cardiac glycosides that are toxic to humans and animals. It can disrupt the heart's normal function and affect the nervous system, leading to various cardiac abnormalities, like a slow or irregular heartbeat. It can reduce blood pressure and lead to weakness, confusion, dizziness and even seizure or coma in severe cases."

"Can it kill a person?"

"Humans, yes, but it depends on the amount of oleander ingested, and a person's health status, really."

"Why would someone mix a poisonous flower with daisies?" *For the aesthetic*, I wondered?

Leo tossed the lone flower, then grabbed up the bundle of daisies I'd dropped. "Strange indeed," he said, breathing in the bouquet's aroma. "White daisies are meant to represent purity, innocence, and new beginnings, like with a wedding or a pregnancy, symbolizing hope and fresh starts."

"Can you remember anything else from your dream, Lynn?" Zach asked.

"A floor-length mirror near the right side of the pool...," I said, my words trailing off as I recalled seeing the reflection of Hayley and Ryley standing together holding hands....

Zach swept the flashlight beam over the earth near the far edge of the pool, and something shiny glinted. "What's that?" I pointed to the area.

"Where?" Zach swept the light over the area again.

"There!" The light reflected on it, and I jogged over. All three Guards were at my side as I bent down to retrieve a tiny gold object.

"What is it?" Nic asked.

"It's Lane's earring," I announced. It was one of the pair Lyndon had gotten her. "That proves she was here."

"They must have moved her," Nic said. "But where?"

Chapter 27 

Leo and Zach opted to do a thorough search of the surrounding area and the roads leading to the old inn, while Nic swapped with Leo to do the task of driving me back to North Haven.

"I'm going to change for work at the hospital," Nic said as we entered through the main doors. "But I don't need to leave for another few hours." A buzzing sounded, and he yanked his cellphone from his back pocket. "Leo and Zach are on their way back," he called out to Max and Julian.

I nodded and then dragged my sorry ass over to the kitchen, where Max and Julian were at it again with the meal prep. When Julian glanced up from dressing a wooden board with sliced meats and cheese wedges, I gave him a weak smile. "I'm sorry," I said, climbing onto the barstool at the end of the long island.

"Sorry for what, my friend?" Max asked, adding woven crackers to the board.

"That I didn't find Lane—that I couldn't bring her home." I rested my elbows on top of the island's counter and leaned my chin against my closed fists. "I feel like I've failed you all."

Julian set a large, frosty glass of water in front of me. "Lynn, that's the closest we've gotten so far." Julian drew one of my hands away from my chin and held it. "We're going to bring our girl home, I know it." He patted my hand and gave me a hopeful smile. Then he turned away and continued loading up a tray with a large water jug and a stack of glasses.

The sound of the front door opening had me turning in my seat just as a model-tall woman with jet-black wavy hair to her waist came through the door. "Hey, Jules. I thought you were visiting Derek?" I called out, sliding down off the bar stool to go to her.

"I was," she said, arms wide for a hug. "But considering you-know-who is back—thought it was best I was here."

"It's good to see your beautiful face in person," I said, releasing her from the embrace.

"You're the one who's a sight for sore eyes," she said, giving my ponytail a toss. "Derek's on call if we need him, by the way." Her amber-coloured eyes brightened at speaking his name.

"That reminds me," I said, pulling my cell phone from the side pocket of my yoga pants. "I've got some mystery writings for him to solve."

I typed out,

Shortcut, I hear you're on call.

He wrote back instantly

Like the good ol' times

What I wouldn't give for the stress of those days. I responded with,

I have something new for you to decipher, but for now, can you check on a few things for me?

Then I texted him the location we'd been at and the information about Addison and Ariadne's skill sets, along with the facts about the flowers and the dirt.

He sent a simple message back,

I'm on it!

But I knew what he'd uncover wouldn't be simple information.

"Hungry?" Max asked Jules and me.

"What do you got?" Jules strode over and around the long island into the kitchen work area.

"Nothing fancy—just cheese, meat, and crackers."

"Looks perfect to me, fellas. Need help to bring it down to the guys?" Jules grabbed the tray that contained the water and glasses.

"That would be lovely," Julian said to her, taking one of the two charcuterie boards off the counter and heading for the lower level.

Jules followed him.

"Help yourself, Lynn," Max said, taking the second board. "There's plenty." He smiled and then hurried off after the other two.

Strangely, I wasn't hungry.

My phone binged with another text message from Derek,

> *Check your email.*

Bringing up my email on my cellphone, I saw that he'd sent me a long message titled, *A Comprehensive Study of Soil.*

I groaned at the uninteresting subject line, then began reading the lack-luster study of soil as a natural resource on Earth's surface.

The use and management is called Soil Science, which has several branches and related areas of study, some of which are directly related to compost and the breakdown of organic matter like poop and manure. "I was wrong—this isn't boring—it is painfully boring," I muttered to myself before reading on. The first details were about its formation, classification, and properties like physical, chemical, biological, and.... *"Fertility?"* I questioned aloud, which wasn't what I thought it was, the understanding of it becoming clearer as I continued reading the oh so riveting data. Soil fertility was the soil's capacity to support plant growth by providing essential nutrients and creating a suitable environment for roots, water, air, and microbial activity, *blah, blah, blah.* "Sorry, Derek," I said, skipping ahead. I was more interested in the information about poisonous flowers.

Derek had written,

> *Yes, according to Mount Sinai, oleander poisoning can cause you to pass out. More specifically, the study of plant poisons is known as phytotoxicology.*
>
> *Phytotoxicologists specialize in the chemical composition and properties of plant toxins. How toxins are absorbed, distributed,*

metabolized, and excreted by living organisms, and developing methods for diagnosing and treating plant poisoning.

I have more on the treatment part for the most common toxic plants.

"That last part will be important," I mumbled. Knowledge of the treatments would be crucial if we find Lane has been exposed to anything more harmful than oleander toxin. I closed the email app on my cellphone and sighed. Then, a strange yet familiar tingle ran across the back of my neck, and I glanced over my shoulder but found no one. I rolled my shoulders. With so many Earthbound in one place, my nervous system was in overdrive.

Then a single firm "*Knock*" sounded from the front door.

"Guyyyys!" I called out to nobody, apparently. Everyone was downstairs in the tactical area of the soundproof lower level. I moved closer to the front door. "Aaanyyyybooodyyyy!" I screamed at the top of my lungs this time, the sensation across my skin heightening with every second.

The door to one of the suites opened, and Nic rushed out. "What happened—are you okay?"

"I feel them—the unknown earthbound."

Nic's eyes bulged, and he moved to stand by my side. "Where are they?"

Before I could say anything, a double "*Knock knock*" sounded this time, and I shot a look back at the door.

"Let me get it!" I demanded, throwing an arm out like a protective mother of a professional linebacker. I stepped forward and grabbed the doorknob, then twisted it, yanking the door wide.

My jaw dropped. I was instantly dumbstruck by the tall, pale-skinned, stern-faced beauty standing before me on the front step, a large bundle weighed in her arms. She wore gender-neutral beige cargo pants and a long-sleeved fitted pullover, which stretched over an athletic build. Her hair was snow white and cut short, and her beautiful, white-lashed eyes were a pale violet like the other I'd seen in my dream, but her features were so akin to Amahle's it was indisputable who she was.

"Ariadne?" Nic said, addressing the long-lost Seraph.

Ariadne's focus transferred from me to Nic, her expression softening. The top covering of the bundle slid down to reveal the unconscious face of our missing family member, *Lane*.

"What the hell?" came from behind us, and I turned to see Max and Julian standing in the opening from the hallway.

"Nobody move!" I warned. Ariadne's attention swung back to me, and I sucked in a breath. Den told me she'd killed one of Thaddeus's human henchmen, slit his throat with the tip of an arrow when he'd tried to touch her one too many times. Marq had called her a *killer*, but right now, standing here looking at her, all I saw was a breathtaking Angel, who currently had my niece, my friend, in her muscular arms. Her stern expression was now gone, replaced by a friendly smile, as though she were trying to convey she was not a threat, although her pale eyes glistened with sorrow. My focus dropped from her stunning eyes down to the brutal scar that ran across her throat. "It was you—at the hospital that day when Lyndon brought Zuriel there, outside SNOW in New York, and… at the Christmas music gala."

Ariadne nodded and then extended her arms out to me.

"Nic," I said softly, seeking assistance. Ariadne gazed at him, her expression filled with what I could only translate as *admiration*.

Nic stepped forward into the doorway and retrieved Lane's unconscious body from Ariadne's arms. "Thank you," he said, then he turned and retreated towards Lane's room with Max and Julian on his heels.

"Somebody call Lyndon," I called out, watching them retreat. When I turned back… she was gone.

Chapter 28 

The Celaeno Building, Sunday P.M. August 10th, Ottawa, Canada

Thaddeus set Brutus's bowl on the custom eye-level stand in front of the floor to ceiling window in his massive walk-in closet. "There you go, my handsome friend. Enjoy the view." Thaddeus knew the life expectancy of a Siamese fighting fish was short and, based on the behavioral changes his finned companion was exhibiting, he also knew his friend might be dying. "Now, Brutus, let's put a little pep in your step," he said to the lethargic betta.

The Rosetail fighting fish's vibrant, rare, deep purple colour had begun to fade several weeks ago, and it had been part of the reason Thaddeus had returned. He'd researched and consulted experts about Brutus's condition, but they'd not given him much help. All he'd been told was that he might be able to save him by ensuring his environment was clean and properly aerated, which it always was. He'd even gotten him a specialized 10-gallon hospital tank with a heater and sponge filter ideal for treatment, along with providing him stress reducers and meds for any infections he might be fighting off. Unfortunately, Brutus had been showing more advanced symptoms in the last few days, like bottom-sitting and hiding, and if things continued like this for a prolonged period or beyond a certain point, he realized he might be beyond saving. Thaddeus had been watching him closely for the next stages, and thankfully Brutus had not advanced to the lack of appetite or breathing problems he'd read about, nor had he shown any other physical issues like lesions or patches of fungus that would indicate a serious infection, or dropsy which was a serious condition where the fish's body swells and scales protrude, the results of which was a quick death.

"It's a good thing we are back home now. Seems things have gone awry in our absence." Thaddeus pressed his index finger to the bowl and Brutus tapped his tiny head gently at the spot. "You already know about that traitorous Zuriel—he's gone into hiding. Addison, well, someone ended his existence. More than likely, it was that turncoat Ariadne—useless female. And Kendrick—he's another failure. Who knows where he is these days. But… my ever-faithful Amahle will be assisting me in the next stage of my research. Not that she's got anything of value to contribute, but she will serve to further my testing." The sinister smile that spread across Thaddeus's face reflected off the surface of the glass fishbowl. "Would you like to hear about my research?"

Brutus tapped the glass again.

"Great! Let me get something to drink first and then I'll tell you all about it," Thaddeus said excitedly, before leaving the closet.

Wearing nothing but his expensive boxers, Thaddeus strode quickly over to the kitchen and liberated one of the pricey bottles of water from the fridge. He removed a canister of high-protein floating fish pellets from the cabinet over the fridge. The formula he'd gotten Brutus included a special blend of algae, probiotics, and vitamins for immune system support developed around a betta fish's natural diet. Rushing back into the closet, he said, "Fertility!" Popping the lid on the canister, he sprinkled a few pellets on the water's surface.

But Brutus did not swim up to eat them.

"Don't wait to eat on my account." Thaddeus opened the water bottle again and took a long drink, watching for his little friend to eat. "No need to rush either," he said, capping the water and setting it aside. "In the meantime, let me tell you all about the tests for fertility. There is a lot of testing for the females, mainly because they are so inferior, but I'll get to that last. More important are the tests that need to be done for the males. There's semen analysis, which evaluates sperm count, motility, and morphology to assess the quality. Hormone testing—that's no big deal, and transrectal ultrasound of the testes. This involves a probe and lubrication gel—nasty business." Thaddeus shook his head and gave an exaggerated shiver as though it were frightful. "The worst part of the testing procedures is having to do the lengthy list needed for the females," he huffed out. "The lesser beings of the genus make things difficult. It's a shame females are needed at all." He paused to observe his friend.

Brutus had changed his position from staring out at him to hovering just below the food on the surface.

"Don't let me interrupt you. Go ahead and eat."

For a few seconds, Brutus did nothing, then he tilted his body, head up, and snagged a tiny fragment of food.

Pleased with his companion's efforts, Thaddeus went on with listing the bothersome tests needed for the females. "Hormone testing is required for them as well. Ovulation testing and tracking menstrual cycles—disgusting if you ask me. There's the hysteroscopy and a laparoscopy, both minimally invasive in my opinion." Thaddeus began sliding the hangers of his dress shirts one at a time as he hunted for just the right one to wear. "Last on the list is the hysterosalpingogram X-ray done with a dye to assess the fallopian tubes and uterus. I'm told it's the most painful fertility test, but I think it's just melodramatic complaints from weak females. Oh, and they have to have a transvaginal ultrasound to check for structural abnormalities, but males have to have an ultrasound too, as I mentioned." Thaddeus moved a crisp white Oxford button-down shirt to the retractable brass valet rod for further examination. "What do you think of this shirt, Brutus?"

Brutus was once again staring out at Thaddeus, though most of the food pellets were still floating above him on the water's surface.

"It can be worn for both smart-casual and professional settings." He focused back on the hanging shirt. "I think it offers the polished appearance I'm looking for." He slid the shirt to the far end of the rod to make room for his next item of clothing. Moving to the selection of trousers, he said, "Have I ever told you about Dire Wolfe cloning?"

His unwell friend was still facing him, but now he was lower in the tank, closer to the bottom.

"I know talk of trivial females bores you—it does me too, so you'll enjoy this next part." He went back to his selection of pants. "Scientists believe they have resurrected the dire wolf." He glanced at Brutus for his reaction. He knew that betta fish could recognize their guardians, and if treated well, they usually swam about excitedly in the presence of their protector.

But Brutus showed no change in his enthusiasm over what Thaddeus was saying and only stared straight ahead at him.

Hoping for more zeal from Brutus, Thaddeus went on. "This species of wolf died out some 12,500 years ago, and now it lives again due to the world's first successfully *de-extincted* animal, according to a Dallas-based biotech company that is. They created three dire wolf pups using ancient DNA, cloning, and gene-editing technology to alter the genes of a grey wolf, the prehistoric wolf's closest living relative. The pups are essentially a hybrid but comparable in appearance to the larger original." Thaddeus chose a pair of navy slim-fit dress pants from the selection and then hung them in front of the shirt on the valet rod. "Do you remember that TV show *Game of Thrones*? We watched it together." He glanced over his shoulder at Brutus.

He hadn't moved; nevertheless, his attention appeared to still be on him.

"The dire wolf was the inspiration for the fearsome canine featured in the series. But the best episode was the *Red Wedding*. It was touted as the most brutal massacre and slaughter of the whole series, hence the use of the word 'red'. Although, to me it just showed you that *nice guys finish last*, as they say," he added, ending the sentiment with a snort of laughter.

As though energized by his laughter, Brutus had left the bottom of the tank and was heading for the food at the surface.

"I thought you'd appreciate that," he said, encouraged by Brutus's energy spurt. "However, apparently human cloning is a felony." Thaddeus shrugged. "Although I've read that some universities are doing some research on organs. But there's a difference between reproductive cloning—creating a genetically identical individual, and therapeutic cloning, which is the creation of embryonic stem cells for research and potential medical therapies. The latter remains widely opposed and… *unattempted*." He winked at Brutus and then passed a hand over the soft leather of one of his beloved Gucci Horsebit loafers on a nearby shelf. Then, he moved to stand in front of a chest-high column of drawers, where he bent and retrieved a pair of navy designer socks from the bottom drawer. The rest of the tower was dedicated to a variety of his undergarments, but he was already wearing one of his favorites.

"I'm sure this has you wondering about cloning versus IVF now, doesn't it?" He returned to the extended valet rod and rested the silk socks over the hanger that held his trousers, then glanced over at his buddy.

Brutus was back, floating midway up the tank and focused on Thaddeus.

"Let me summarize it for you," he said, leading into the comparison. "While both IVF and cloning involve manipulating cells in a laboratory setting, they are fundamentally different in their purposes and ethical considerations." He went on to explain the fertilization process. "Ethically, it raises some concerns, particularly with religious groups." Thaddeus rolled his eyes. "Frankly, I was more interested in the unused embryos. The ones I had got my hands on were helpful in my research." He nodded once. "Cloning, on the other hand, aims to create a complete, living organism—which is largely banned or subject to strict limitations worldwide. Something to do with ethical concerns about *human dignity* and whether a clone would have a soul—yada yada yada. It's banned here and in Brazil, unfortunately, but in the U.S. its only restriction has to do with federal funding. Note there was nothing about *private* funding." Thaddeus waggled his eyebrows.

His apathetic friend was once again resting at the bottom of the tank.

"Why so glum, chum?" Thaddeus shot a glance at his arrangement of well-selected clothes. "How about I stay in with you today? We can play video games—Amahle bought me some new selections. What do you say?" He pressed the knuckles of his right hand against the glass of the tank.

Brutus ignored him at first, then he floated up in front of his fist and bumped the glass lightly.

"Okay then!" he said, rushing out of the closet and over to the kitchen again.

He pulled a plain white dish from the cupboard before retrieving two cloth napkins, then a fork and knife from the cutlery drawer. From the fridge he took out one of his treasured mini icebox cakes, the chocolate wafer whipped cream sweet treats that Marcus had procured for him, and set it on the plate. Not that he was going to thank the ungrateful bastard or anything. Lastly, he fetched a pinch of brine shrimp from the fridge and placed it on a second napkin for Brutus. The nutritious treat was a supplemental food that provided protein and vitamins that could improve his health and colour. Then he arranged everything on a portable tray, further transferring it onto his king-size bed alongside his pillow.

"*Attendant*, call Amahle," he said aloud to engage the automated personal assistant connected to his cellphone app.

"*Call going to voicemail*," a soft-spoken artificial male voice announced through a hidden overhead speaker.

Thaddeus checked the clock next to his bed and saw it was past midnight.

A single "*ding*" sound followed the voicemail notice indicating for him to record his message.

"Amahle… review the list of fertility exams I left in my lab, indicated for female test subjects, then commence with having them prepared and performed on yourself." Then he said, "*Attendant*, end call."

With that done, he went and fetched Brutus from off his stand and brought him over to rest on the nightstand next to his stack of notebooks. "You know, Brutus, I'm missing one of my notebooks," he announced, getting comfortable on the bed. He had all but one, a single notebook from his lab in Norway that he swore he had brought with him, but wondered now if he had left it behind in Brazil. "No worries," he said, not wanting to spoil his evening with Brutus. He had stored most of it to memory and had extra findings in his current notes. "What should we play?" he asked, sorting through the bundle of new video games. "*Killing Floor three*?" Thaddeus shook his head. "No, it's a multiplayer game. *The Dark Pictures Anthology: Directive 8020*? It's a horror one. Or *The Sinking City two*? That's a survival horror game."

There was no feedback from Brutus.

"How about this one, *Indika?*" He held up the case for Brutus to see the artwork on the cover. "It's set in an alternate nineteenth century Russia, has an ostracized nun with the devil's voice in her head, aaaand a frozen hellscape."

Brutus bumped the glass and then sank to the bottom as though resting down to watch Thaddeus play the game.

"Indika it is," he said, removing the disc and sliding it into the game console next to the bed. Then he typed in his leetspeak username, 3astard5on, *bastard son*, and said, "Here we go!"

Chapter 29 

"Time is free, but it's priceless. You can't own it, but you can use it. You can't keep it, but you can spend it. Once you've lost it you can never get it back."
~ Harvey MacKay.

Lyndon had come to North Haven immediately after Leo had got ahold of him, and he had stayed by Lane's bedside throughout the night.

Lane's eyelids felt heavy as her body awakened from a state she could only describe as relaxed paralysis, her brain bleary yet waking, vision clearing, and her muscles transitioning from inactivity to alertness. A weighted restriction in the movement of her legs had her momentarily panicked until she realized the heaviness was from Lyndon. He was kneeling on the floor next to the bed, his head face down on the covers, and his big arms were outstretched and draped over her legs as if for protection. His position reminded her of the Angel of Grief sculpture that she'd seen at the Protestant cemetery while in Rome. Its full title by the creator was *The Angel of Grief Weeping Over the Dismantled Altar of Life.* As her mind cleared further, she recalled reading that the death of the artist's wife had devastated him so badly that he lost interest in sculpting, but had been inspired by his children to create the monument to memorialize their mother. It was his last major work prior to his death a year after his wife's passing. The life-size winged angel collapsed and weeping, draped over the tomb, spoke more of the pain of those left behind. Lane reached out to brush Lyndon's hair then when her movement was restricted, she realized her wrist was tethered to an IV line attached to a bag of some kind of liquid hanging off a pole next to the bed. Using her other hand, she brushed her palm over Lyndon's dark hair, and his head lifted. "Hi," she said in a groggy voice when he turned his head to look at her. "I didn't mean to wake you."

"Hi, yourself," he said, teary-eyed yet smiling. "And I wasn't sleeping."

"You look like the *angel of grief* resting there." She caressed his cheek.

"Like the one in Rome," he said, as though recalling their time there.

She nodded. "I had the strangest dream." She paused. "I was floating in a dark pool of water, surrounded by dozens of white flowers. There was a woman there, and she had pale skin and white hair, and… she had the most incredible eyes. She looked… like an *angel*."

"She was," he said, withdrawing his draped arms from over her legs.

Lane's memory rushed with visions of a dark space lit by moonlight, and an earthy scent that mingled with that of fresh flowers. "My memory… is a mess," she confessed. "What happened? How did I get here?"

"You were kidnapped."

"What—by whom?" Her eyebrows pinched together.

"Addison." Lyndon looked away. "And it's all my fault."

Her eyebrows tightened. "Why would it be your fault?"

"Because if I hadn't put my attention on you—brought you into my world, Addison would never even have known you existed." He turned back to her with tears welling in his eyes.

"Hold up. I've been a part of your world my whole life—it's my world too, you dumbass. Besides, you found me."

"No," he said guiltily. "Ariadne found you."

"Ariadne? But isn't she…"

"She saved your life," he interrupted. Then he went on to explain that it wasn't until after Ariadne left that they'd realized there'd been a handwritten note tucked into her jean's front pocket that explained how she had been following Addison. Unbeknownst to him, she intended to kill him. But before she did, Addison told her that he planned to take you to Thaddeus. "Once he revealed where he'd stashed you, it was then that she'd killed him and went to recover you. Apparently, the others had just missed you both at the last location they'd searched."

She shook her head, confused. "Why did Addison kidnap me?"

"He believed that you were Anael's daughter, and he planned on handing you over to Thaddeus." Lyndon's breath caught in his throat. "Never in my whole existence have I ever been so afraid. I couldn't let myself believe you might be dead," he confessed. "I know how the angel in that statue must have felt… I love you, Lane." He took up one of her hands and kissed it.

Lane's chin quivered, and she began to cry. "I love you, too—and I'm so sorry I put you through this," she choked out.

"Don't you think for a second that any of this is *your* fault," he rushed out before brushing a tear from her cheek. Still on his knees, he moved closer to the head of the bed, eyes locked on her face. His gaze dropped to her mouth, and then he leaned forward and kissed her.

The kiss was soft at first but then intensified as they shared breath like neither had been able to breathe before. "I am so grateful for you—do you know that?" Lane said, breaking the kiss.

"And I, you, my beauty," he whispered against her lips.

Lyndon dropped his head to Lane's chest, and she ran her hand through his hair again. "I'm home."

Glancing up, he said, "I don't think I would have survived, had you…." Lyndon pulled in a ragged breath but didn't finish the sentence.

"I'm safe," she assured him. "You said the others were searching for me—how did you even know where to look?" Her mind was fuzzy about so much.

Lyndon cleared his throat. "Lynn had a dream the night before you went missing. In fact, it's eerily similar to the one you said you had. And she helped us find you."

"My Aunt Lynn is here?" Lane lifted her head and then thought better of it as her temples instantly began to throb. She closed her eyes briefly and then focused back on Lyndon.

"Lynn came as soon as she heard you were missing. I had assumed Addison had taken you to the Norway facility—because it was deserted, but she knew better." He gave her a weak smile and then scowled.

"What is it?" Lane gripped Lyndon's hand.

Lyndon patted her hand and gave her a thin smile. "Lane, you need to rest."

"Tell me," she demanded.

Lyndon dropped his focus to their clasped hands. Looking back up at her, he said, "Thaddeus is back. And… he's got big plans." Lyndon led her through the series of events that followed Thaddeus's arrival at the group home, what had transpired prior in Norway and after outside of Ottawa with their searching for her, and then how Ariadne had shown up at the door with Lane unconscious in her arms. "After reading her note, we considered she must have killed Kendrick too."

"Wow, and I was asleep through all of it," she said, her tone sardonic.

"Nic has been checking on you every hour and reporting back to the others. And your parents sat by your bedside most of the night with me."

A soft "*knock-knock*" pulled their attention to the door to Lane's room.

"Come in," Lane called out, her hand promptly going to her aching head.

I pushed open the door, relieved to hear Lane was awake now.

"Aunt Lynn," Lane said warmly, her voice a tad raspy.

"Hey, sleepy-head," I said with a wave, smiling and leaning against the doorframe.

Lyndon stood. "I'll go let the others know you are finally awake," he said to Lane. "And I'll get you some water and something for you to eat."

He went to leave, but Lane held tight to his hand. "Thank you," she said, then mouthed the words, *I love you*.

He bent and kissed Lane's hand, and then he said something in a whisper I couldn't hear. Lane nodded and released his hand, and then he strode my way. Pausing in front of me, he said, "I want to apologize for not trusting you. And for wasting time going to Norway."

"It's all good. Lane is home, Lyndon," I said, giving his big arm a few pats. "That's all that matters. Besides, Norway wasn't a complete bust. We found Kendrick. And we now know what happened to him *and* Addison," I reminded. "I also found another one of Thaddeus's notebooks for Derek to decipher." I gave him a reassuring grin.

Lyndon drew in a reassured breath and nodded. "I noticed when I was at the condo that Thaddeus has a bunch of those notebooks stacked on his nightstand."

"You need to find a way to get a look at them—get copies for Derek," I said eagerly.

"I agree. And Lynn… I promise to trust your… *intuition* next time."

"Let's hope there is no *next time*." I patted his arm again.

He nodded. "Back in a bit," he called over to Lane. "I'll let you two ladies chat."

I walked over to the bed and took up residence in the small chair next to it, turning it to face Lane. "Here," I said, opening my closed fist in front of her.

Lane's hands went to her ears, touching each lobe. "I hadn't even realized I was missing one." She took the earring from my palm and brought it to her naked earlobe. Then she went to sit up in the bed. "Oh boy," she moaned, clutching her head.

"Easy now. Waking up after being drugged can be severely disorienting." I leaned forward and eased her into a sitting position.

"Thought I was poisoned." She gently readjusted herself against the pillows.

I sat back again. "You were—but same deal."

"Must be what a blackout feels like—or an intense hangover," she groaned, rubbing her temples.

I leaned on the arm of the chair. "Besides the hangover, how are you feeling?"

"Well, when I woke up I knew I was in my room but I had no memory of how I got here." She massaged her forehead and eyebrows. "And my head hurts, and I feel a bit weak and shaky."

"Nic said your heart rate has returned to normal—so that's good. How's your breathing?"

She took a few long breaths in and out. "Seems okay."

"And your vision?" I leaned in again.

She let out a soft chuckle. "I'm good, Doctor Westlake." She grinned at me.

"Worried Auntie here," I reminded her. "What's the last thing you remember?"

"It's all a bit foggy, but I can recall leaving the cottage and heading to get into the Uber waiting for me.

"Ya, that *was* the Uber car, but that *wasn't* your Uber driver."

She nodded slowly.

"Addison must have attacked the guy and stolen his car. The guy is okay, just a little worse for wear, I'm told. They found the abandoned Uber in the overgrown brush near the inn that Addison had taken you to."

Lane shook her head slowly back and forth. "I feel so stupid. I was in such a hurry to get home."

"What? You're stupid because you were in such a hurry you didn't realize the driver was an imposter? Seriously?" I crossed my arms.

"I just can't believe I let this happen to me. That I worried everyone so much, and you had to come all this way."

"Lane, this is absolutely not your fault."

"Lyndon said the same thing—he thinks it's his fault."

"His fault?" I uncrossed my arms and leaned forward again.

"For bringing me into his world—but I reminded him I've been in it my whole life." Lane put the palms of her hands over her eyes.

"Look, I'm not a therapist, but Grier told me that something like this can take an emotional and psychological toll on a person. She said to watch you for increased anxiety, or an overwhelming sense of fear or panic, especially since you'd lost control and have gaps in your memory."

Lane dropped her hands to her lap. "I'm sure everyone will be watching me for PTSD symptoms now."

"Yes, it's rough having so many people care about." I smirked, then reached for my necklace.

"Tell me about it," Lane said, reaching out, tapping a finger on my hand. "The sentiment, I mean."

I leaned in further. Then, using both hands, I separated the charms and lifted up the tiny butterfly. "This one is in honor of my mom—she loved butterflies." I moved on to the next. "The XO kiss and hug symbol signifies *good friendship*." I slid to the next.

"Is that the number four?" She squinted.

"This fancy-looking number four is the atomic symbol for the number *fifty*, which is also the symbol for *tin*, and a traditional gift for a tenth anniversary."

"How cool!" She took the tiny charm between her fingers. "Wait, haven't you been married thirteen years?" she questioned, dropping her fingers from the charm.

"We have—although, as you know, I wasn't sure we were even going to make it to eleven." I gave her a half-smile. "But we did. And he gifted me this tiny *citrine* stone charm for our thirteenth anniversary last December. It represents the sentiment of *embracing all the joys of life*."

"Oh, I love that—but I love even more that you guys worked things out."

"Me too." I kissed the group of charms before releasing them.

"Especially for the twins—they must have been wondering what the heck was going on with you two." She raised an eyebrow. "It wasn't often, but I always knew when my parents weren't getting along."

I leaned back in the chair. "Do you and Lyndon ever talk about having your own kids? I know you're only twenty-seven, but we've never talked about that kind of stuff."

"Lyndon doesn't like to discuss anything too far in the future, for obvious reasons. And honestly, the idea of my getting pregnant terrifies him. Besides, kids were never really on my radar. I love Taylor very much, still he has so many challenges. And knowing what I know about halflings, I'm not sure if I could put a child through those perils, or myself for that matter." She gave me a sad smile. "And there are no guarantees that a child of ours would turn out healthy like Natalie or Mason."

"Your feelings are completely understandable." I knew Seraph females produced almost perfect children. It was the human women who gave birth to the ones with issues, and often life-threatening for both. "You know, Lane, having kids is not something you simply check off your life list. It's a big decision, and there is no rush to make any resolutions. Just enjoy each other for now."

"You're right. And I'm not in any rush." She smiled.

"Hey, this is my second marriage, and I didn't have kids until I was forty-five. There is no timetable other than *reproductive*, of course. And if you wanted to just expand your little family with Lyndon, there's always adoption."

Her smile brightened. "That's true," she said, nodding.

"I'm adopted—and you could only be so lucky to adopt a prize like me," I boasted.

Lane chuckled. "If I could be guaranteed that—or have kids like your girls, that would make for an easier decision."

"Aaah yes, you say that now, but you have to realize that twelve-year-old girls with all those puberty chemicals kicking in are basically fierce emerging monsters that only revert back to tame humans near their eighteenth year." I gave her my best serious face.

"Com'on, they can't be that bad."

"Oooh, you have no idea. I'll enlighten you another time." I sighed. "Right now I'm missing their first day of junior high."

"Oh no."

"Not to worry, I'm heading home. Since I missed their official send-off, I want to be there when they get home. And they were so thrilled that we found you—they didn't care about my not being there." I drew in a shaky breath, letting the magnitude of having her back safely wash over me. "Everyone is so relieved to have you home, Lane."

"Lyndon told me Thaddeus is back," she said then, her smile turning down.

"Yup." I lifted a hand and rubbed the back of my neck, blowing out a breath. "Remember when I told you that you weren't the only female born into this?"

"Yes."

"That was the same conversation we had when you said that you thought you should move out on your own," I noted.

"And you reminded me that I wasn't a child, but I still needed protection."

I nodded. "Now you fully understand who you needed protection from."

Chapter 30 

I'd only been home long enough to embrace Summer and Snow with kisses and ear-scratches, toss my suitcase in the bedroom, and change out of my running shoes into flip-flops and a pair of shorts, when Redmond had arrived home with groceries. I was starving, but my hunger could wait. Right now, Redmond and I were seated on the couch together, awaiting the arrival of the girls after their first day of junior high.

"I was surprised when Leo told me you'd given the go-ahead for me to travel to Norway."

"Of course I did. You were with *them*. Now, had he said you were going on your own—that would be another thing."

"Yup." I wasn't going to argue with him. Going out on my own in the past *had* brought success, but it hadn't been a smart move safety-wise. The last time I'd ventured out on impulse had brought me face to face with Lyndon, the tracker Seraph who had been hunting for me. Although that unforeseen meeting had been a win in our *and* Lyndon's favor. On the flip side, my actions had brutally impacted my relationship with Redmond and his trust. I never wanted to hurt him, but I had, and would never let that happen again.

"Leo told me what you found in Norway. But you haven't said anything about it."

"*Who* we found in Norway, you mean," I said before diving into the adrenaline and *fear* I'd felt. I'd been elated with finding another of Thaddeus's notebooks, then utterly shocked and sickened at finding Kendrick's dead body.

"Not what you hoped to find, obviously."

Changing the subject, I asked, "How upset were the girls that I wasn't here to see them off?"

"Not as upset as you'd think. *'Not cool, Da,'* Ryley said when I told them I'd be dropping them off. They wanted to take their bicycles to school, and they reminded me that I had said they could do so when school started."

"They've always been smart. Now they are getting to that saucy smarty-pants stage," I said. They had gotten new bikes from their Nana and Poppy for their 12th birthday back in May. They hadn't had bikes since we lived in Palmetto Bay, but those had been small bikes with training wheels. Ryley had outgrown hers first, but they both had abandoned interest once we'd moved to the beach house and had started learning to surf. Since the reintroduction of the bikes in the spring, they had started cycling with Redmond on weekends, the rides morphing into daily morning ones during the summer. They had become quite good and had asked if they could ride to school once the new year started. It wasn't far at all to their new school, but it did mean they would need to have their own bike locks and would be responsible for securing them at school. After several trial rides with Redmond instructing them to get off their bikes at the school crosswalk, and how to use the combination locks, he'd informed them that come the start of school, they would be allowed to go on their own. "Maybe you could ride over with them tomorrow," I suggested, knowing he was just being a protective father and his nerves were high considering what had happened to Lane.

"Maybe," he said with a sigh. "Their knapsacks were pretty heavy with everything they needed to bring with them now. Not sure they'll want to carry them on their backs and ride over."

"Even if their packs are heavy, they won't tell us—you know that." I'd been surprised at the school supply list that had stated each child had to submit a ream of copy paper and two packs of college-ruled loose leaf filler paper to their homeroom teachers. There'd been a list of items needed for all classes that the student had to have with them each day like pens and pencils, a pink eraser, colored pencils and a sharpener, highlighters, a glue stick for what I didn't know, and their own computer mouse for all the classes. But they'd also needed specific items in addition for each individual class. Math required a 2-inch (3-ring) binder with dividers with tabs, a ruler, a 100-page composition book, wide-ruled, and an EOC compliant calculator. English Language Arts called for a ½ inch binder with filler paper and 5 dividers labeled *Greek/Latin Roots, Grammar, Notes, Poetry*, and *Reference*. Science involved both a ½-inch (3-ring) binder for daily use and a 2-inch (3-ring) binder that stayed in class. Social Studies too needed another 3-ring binder with dividers and filler paper, so all together that was a lot to carry in one backpack. We'd gotten them new heavier-duty ones for the load, and my only hope was that they didn't break their little backs.

"They are stubborn that way," Redmond tossed out. "Wonder where they get that?" He gave me a wry smile.

"You, of course," I tossed back, giving him a toothy grin. "I know you are worried—and we should be cautious. I'm unsettled too, but Lyndon assured us that Thaddeus had softened his interest in locating me. He told him about the high-tech software surveillance he was using for location and facial recognition." He wasn't, of course, but he was using it to keep tabs on any suspicious movements at the remaining facilities. He and Marq had set up several avenues to watch the comings and goings from the facilities, plus any of the known whereabouts Thaddeus's crew lived or frequented.

"I know. But we're still not letting our guard down where the twins are concerned, especially with Thaddeus and his henchmen still roaming free."

"Agreed." Protecting my loved ones was at the forefront of my priorities, but I still hadn't learned to use my gun. I had taken it out of its secure hiding place a few times just to look at it. Redmond had said he understood if I didn't *want* to use a gun, but stressed that it would be worthwhile for me to at least learn *how* to use it. I was warming to the idea of the learning part, but *using* one, I was still cold on that. He'd said that once I learned how, the comfort of using it might come easier to me. My hesitation was more about *having* to use a gun. Still though, I'd start with learning how first. Redmond had offered to teach me, but I'd told him I'd be too nervous to do it in front of him. "On a normal note," I said, changing up the tone of the conversation. "I spoke with Alison about raising a teen in this day and age." I asked Mac as well, but her boys were basically grown now.

"What did she have to say?"

"She said that obviously, boys are different," I laughed out. "But she mentioned that she dealt with a lot of teen girls in her work, and that for girls the twins age, talking is an important tool for navigating social life, that they often tell long, detailed stories about their day, friends, *and* feelings."

"Oh, really," he guffawed. "When is that supposed to start?"

"Any minute now." I grinned. "There's lots of weightiness and drama brewing underneath, apparently. "

"They've already started testing boundaries and expressing independence," Redmond pointed out.

"Alison said this is a period of messy yet *natural* separation from parents when girls assert their autonomy."

"When they begin to question authority and want more independent decision-making, you mean?"

"Exactly. Oh, and it's supposed to be when sarcasm starts to appear in their vocabulary—but I think we've witnessed that already." I rolled my eyes.

"Did Alison share any tips?"

"A lot we already do. Like showing interest in what they care about. Listen more than you solve—don't rush to fix their problems, just listen with empathy. It builds a trusting relationship and helps them feel supported in solving their own challenges."

"Makes sense, and we do that for the most part."

"What time is it anyway?" I glanced around for my phone but then remembered I'd left it in the bedroom to charge.

Redmond retrieved his cellphone from the pocket of his cargo shorts and checked the time. "Just after four—they should be home soon."

Their school hours were different this year, 9:30 a.m. to 4:00 p.m. instead of the elementary school hours of 8:30 a.m. and 3:15 p.m. which meant they had more time in the morning but would be home later.

Less than 10 minutes had passed when the front door opened and Ryley came strolling through accompanied by Hayley. Without so much as a *hello*, they both dumped their overly-heavy backpacks on the floor near the entry table.

They were both dressed in the new white sneakers and knee-length jean shorts I'd gotten. Hayley had paired hers with the vintage long-sleeved Led Zeppelin concert t-shirt that Lily had given her for her birthday in May. Hayley was vaguely familiar with their music because of Redmond, but she'd liked the shirt because of the depiction of the Swan Song Records logo of the winged man that was on it. And Ryley had matched her jean shorts with a white long-sleeved Florida Oceanographic Society t-shirt that Zuriel had picked up for her.

"I feel like I'm training for the military, climbing those stairs with this backpack on," Ryley announced with a groan and a huff. "Hey, Mum."

"*Hey, mum*—that's all I get?"

"Sorry," she said, coming over to the couch for a hug. "I'm glad you're home." She had her wavy, sun-kissed russet hair back in a smooth French braid clearly done by her sister. Redmond had only just mastered a basic braid.

"Me too." I gave her an extra squeeze before releasing her. I focused on Hayley. "You're awfully quiet. No greeting for your mum?"

Hayley frowned and dragged herself over as if she were still wearing the backpack. "Hi, Mum," she said exhaustedly, collapsing into me for a hug. Her hairstyle of choice hadn't been a French braid.

Instead, her pale blonde hair was up in a high ponytail that hung silkily to her shoulders, and her newly trimmed bangs were pushed to one side.

"You okay?" I put the back of my hand against her forehead. "You're not running a fever."

"She's just worn out because she had to keep up with the grade-eighters today," Ryley answered for her, sticking out her tongue.

"Shut up, Ryley," Hayley berated her sister, throwing out a clenched fist to hit her.

"Hey now. Enough of that," Redmond cut in. "I think we can give your mother a better homecoming than that. Both of you go get cleaned up for dinner—and take your bags with you."

Without another word, they shuffled over and got their bags, then took off to their rooms.

"Niiiice," I praised him. "No backtalk. Well done."

Redmond did a double bicep flex as though he'd won a battle. He had in a way, but we had many more ahead of us.

"What's for dinner?"

"I'm making welcome home homemade pizza," he said, flexing one bicep and then the other.

"My hero," I swooned, giving his right bicep a squeeze. I grinned in appreciation of the way his plain navy t-shirt was snug over his shoulders and arms yet draped loosely over his muscular torso.

A mere 40 minutes following the brief battle, we were gathered around the table, happily eating Redmond's fresh-made ooey-gooey cheesy, crunchy crust pizza made with his special tomato sauces.

"So tell us, how was your first day?" I asked before chomping down on my second piece of pizza.

"I signed up for volleyball," Ryley said, jumping in. "I saw a few of my friends from last year, and we ate lunch together." Ryley mirrored me, taking a big bite of her pizza slice. She grinned as sauce escaped the corners of her mouth.

I held back a laugh to avoid encouraging her and addressed Hayley. "How was your day?"

"It was okay," she said, picking at the pepperoni on her slice.

"Just okay?" I glanced up at Redmond, then back at Hayley.

"She had to find her classes on her own," Ryley interjected, mouth half-full.

"You didn't even offer to help me—not once," she countered, shaking her head, ponytail swinging.

Redmond tapped a finger on the edge of Hayley's plate. "You and I talked about this. You knew you would be on your own most of the day."

"She can barely carry her own backpack," Ryley teased, shoving the last of her pizza crust in her mouth.

"You're just jealous that I'm in mostly grade eight classes and you're stuck behind in grade seven." Hayley gave her sister a smug smile.

"At least I'm the same height as the grade eights—you're smaller than most of the seventh graders," she taunted, flipping the end of her braid at her sister.

I scowled at Ryley. "No more of that kind of talk, young lady." *Oh, my goodness, I just turned into my mother*, I immediately recognized. "Apologize to your sister."

Ryley stared at me for a moment like she was calculating how well she was going to fare if she didn't, but then she turned to Hayley. "I'm sorry," she said with a pout, guilt setting in. Then she reached out a hand to her sister, and they did some kind of finger-tapping secret handshake thingy.

"Okay then," Redmond said, as though he understood what had just transpired between them.

"Did you know that starfish can grow their arms back?" Hayley tossed out.

"What?" I questioned, still trying to grapple with the compact that had just been exchanged between my daughters.

"Is it arms or legs?" she added, scratching her head like it would help her remember. "We were talking about ocean creatures in science today. But it was Lyndon who told me they can grow back."

"Really?" Redmond inquired, holding up the crust end of his last piece of pizza.

I wasn't sure if the *really* was for the starfish fact or that it had been Lyndon who told her.

"Yup, how cool is that?" Hayley nodded proudly, like she'd just delivered some earth-shattering news.

"Well, speaking of ocean creatures. How about you two go finish your homework, and then you can go with me for a quick surf before it gets too dark—sound good?" Redmond suggested.

"I did mine in class," Ryley announced, dropping her napkin on her empty plate.

"Righto. Then Hayley, you get your homework done and then we'll all get in some surfing time," he restated.

"You guys go," Hayley said, pushing her plate aside with the unfinished pizza slice still on it. "I have too much homework—I won't be done in time."

"Are you sure?" Redmond asked as Hayley got up from the table with her plate.

"I'm sure," she said. "Besides, I need to find out how starfish grow their legs back. Or is it arms?" She shrugged.

"I'd like to hear about that," Redmond said. Then, before she could leave the table, he snatched the half-eaten slice from her plate, making her giggle.

"Suit yourself," Ryley added, pushing up from her chair and heading to the kitchen sink with her plate.

"Did you want to come watch?" Redmond asked me, chomping on the cold crust.

"I would, but I have a video call scheduled with Mac and Alison."

"Oh right. Say hi for me, would you?" Redmond got up then and took both our plates to the sink.

"Will do. Have fun," I said, getting up from the table. "I'll be in my bedroom, Hayley, if you need anything."

She smiled and nodded, then turned back to finish cleaning her plate off.

Summer and Snow followed me into the bedroom and slumped down on the floor next to my side of the bed. Then I shut the door and climbed up onto the bed next to my waiting laptop. Piling the pillows behind me, I got ready for the video call.

"Hey, you two," I said when Mac and Alison's faces appeared on screen together. They were on Mac's big couch in her living room.

"I bet you're happy to be home," Alison said, leaning to one side and draping her arm over the back of the couch.

"I am—but I wish I'd had more time with you guys. And doing something other than hunting for lost people." I raised my eyebrows.

Mac maneuvered herself to sit cross-legged and then snatched up a couch pillow to hug. "How are the girls?"

"Unfazed by my absence, it seems," I scoffed. "They're growing up too fast."

"What about Lane? How is she faring?" Mac asked, squeezing the pillow.

"She was still a bit shaky when I left, but she's in good hands. Lyndon is waiting on her hand and foot."

"It's going to be a rough road for those two," Alison pointed out. "But they are clearly in love, so that helps."

"I guess."

"You guess?" Alison questioned.

"Don't get me wrong, I'm grateful they have each other, love each other, but their relationship comes with unique challenges."

"Lynnie's right," Mac agreed. "How do you navigate a relationship with someone who doesn't age?"

"Lyndon ages," Alison said, giving Mac an annoyed expression.

"Yes, but he's still going to have to watch the love of his life grow old and die," Mac said harshly, rocking and clutching the pillow this time.

"I asked her about having kids," I confided.

"What did she say?" Alison asked, turning to sit forward, hands in her lap.

"She said, Lyndon doesn't like to discuss anything too far in the future, and the idea of her getting pregnant terrifies him."

"I can understand that," Mac said, fiddling with the corner of the pillow.

"I told her that having kids wasn't something you rushed into and that they should just enjoy each other for now. And I reminded her they could always adopt."

"Did Lyndon give you guys any updates about you-know-who?" Alison asked, reaching for her purse. She pulled her usual notebook out along with one of her favorite pens.

"He did." I adjusted the pillows behind me again and leaned back. "The asshole showed up at the group home."

"No way?" Mac smacked her hand on the front of the pillow.

"And of course Lyndon was with Taylor—and you know he freaked out."

"That poor sweet boy," Alison said, her expression sorrowful.

"Thaddeus made some sick comment about how he should have gotten rid of the cripple long ago. I don't know how Lyndon kept his cool." I shook my head. "Thaddeus told him to meet at his condo in two hours—like drop everything, the emperor has returned."

"I expect as much from Thaddeus," Alison said, jotting down the details. "What happened at the condo?"

"Lyndon wasn't the only one there with him. Amahle and Marcus were there too." I paused for a second, then said, "He told them he had closed the Tokyo location."

"That makes two facilities shut down now," Alison stated. "What else?"

"Apparently, Amahle set up a new lab on the sixth floor—and she'll be working on some special assignment with Thaddeus."

Alison glanced up from her note-taking. "What kind of lab and what assignment?"

"No idea." I shifted my laptop off my lap, crossed my legs and set the laptop on the bed in front of me. "But he also found out that Sabastian, the manager from Tokyo, and Lazarus, the tracker, will be set up at the Ottawa location now."

"For what purpose?" Mac asked this time.

"Sebastian is supposed to be covering for Amahle while she works with Thaddeus, apparently. Not sure what they are going to do with a second tracker. Lyndon said with Addison gone, Marcus was down a tracker in New York."

"It would make more sense to send him to New York," Mac suggested. She and Alison already knew about Addison and Kendrick being dead and that it had more than likely been Ariadne who had taken them both out.

"I think so too. Lyndon also said that Marcus has been watching Frank and her mate—thinks something fishy is going on at the restaurant." I rolled my eyes. "Thaddeus asked Lyndon about Zuriel."

"Shit!" Mac hugged the pillow harder.

"Oh, it gets worse," I said with a grimace. "Thaddeus told Lyndon that he'd spent the last two plus years experimenting with reproduction and cellular regeneration…on humans, female test subjects."

Mac said nothing, waiting for more, as Alison feverishly made notes.

"Thaddeus said he'd used nobodies—prostitutes, people that wouldn't be missed. In other words, he killed them in the process of his research."

"What a fucking bastard," Mac stated, her jaw clenching.

"Ya, well, his new focus is on breeding human males with Earthbound females. And he wants Lyndon to track down this list of Seraph females he gave him, even asked him about Jules or Frank as an option. And he wants him to find some prize human men."

"Prize human men?" Mac questioned.

"Lyndon is having Marq track down the list of females—not to hand them over, obviously, but just to warn them."

Mac nodded and began rocking again. "And these men he requested?" she asked.

"Professional athletes—the bigger the better." I rolled my shoulders and rubbed the back of my neck. "I'm giving up my volunteering at the hospital," I tossed out, needing to change the subject.

"What—why?" Alison asked, setting her notebook and pen to the side.

"Because there haven't been any opportunities for me to be more involved, and one can only chase so many wheelchairs without losing their mind."

"Financially, you don't have to work, so do something you love," Mac suggested, halting her rocking and releasing her grip on the pillow.

Clearly she was in need of a subject change. "Other than my family and friends, I don't know what I love."

"Is there anything safe you can do locally—maybe with or for Zach?"

"Maybe." I shrugged. "I'm training with him next Tuesday, so I'll ask."

Mac leaned back in her seat, still holding the pillow. "Something that could keep you busy and out of trouble?"

"Speaking of trouble. Where do you think Ariadne went?" Alison inquired.

"Hopefully, she's gone to kill Thaddeus," Mac proposed.

I nodded agreeably. "We could only be so lucky."

Chapter 31 

The twins had been at their new school for a week now and seemed to be thriving, and Lane was safe and sound at home recovering from her ordeal, but I still couldn't shake this unease that had been with me since that dream about Lane and the twins in the mirror. I'd mentioned my restlessness to Redmond, and he'd suggested I go have a training session with Zach, use exercise to reduce whatever stress or anxiety was haunting me.

"How about we try a three-three-three circuit workout?" Zach suggested when I stepped out onto the training mat. "That way we can target various muscle groups."

"Will it exhaust my brain, or at least my nervous system?"

"Well, a varied circuit routine triggers dopamine release, and the combination of physical activity and the mental challenge from learning new patterns will contribute to positive brain changes…" He paused and grinned at me. "…Which can enhance your mood."

"Good enough," I said, exhausted already, putting my hands on my hips and twisting my torso in an attempt to limber up.

"Great," Zach said, clapping his hands enthusiastically.

I groaned, knowing this routine was going to be brutal and completely kick my ass. "How does this work?"

"First, we divide your workout into three distinct circuits, with three different exercises per circuit. I've got those workouts already. You have to complete three sets of each exercise within each circuit."

"Got it," I said. But I didn't have it.

"First circuit will be squats, push-ups and plank—I'll do it without."

"Sure, kill me and humiliate me," I tossed out, leaning over with my hands on my thighs, already full of regret. "You know those are my least favorite exercises."

"That's why we're doing them first—to get them out of the way." Zach assumed a body squat position. "Set yourself up."

"Okay-okay." I adjusted my feet shoulder-width apart, toes pointing slightly outward, chest up and my core braced to maintain a neutral spine. I knew all the exercises I'd been taught by heart, but that didn't mean I hated them any less.

"Three sets of twenty," he said, and then he hinged at the hips, pushing them back like he was about to sit. "One."

I followed, bending my knees, continuing to lower my hips down, back straight and chest tall, descending until my thighs were parallel to the ground before pressing my feet firmly into the ground and driving my hips and legs back to a standing position.

"Two," he said, and I repeated the movement nineteen more times.

"Two more sets," Zach announced, not even winded.

Between each set, we took a 30-second pause, then after a 60-second break, we moved on to exercise number 2, push-ups, and I dropped to the mat and assumed the position. After three sets of that, we did plank, which I dreaded more than any other core exercise. After a 1-minute rest, we moved on to the next 3-exercise circuit of dumbbell rows, lunges, and crunches. Last of the 3 circuits was overhead press, bicep curls, which I loved, and lastly, wall squats.

"How long?" I asked, going over to the side wall to start my *devil's chair*, as I called it.

"Sixty seconds," he said, coming to stand next to me, his back against the wall.

I nodded, knowing there was no point in complaining. Plus, I was actually feeling better despite my shaky limbs. "Remember when I could barely do ten seconds?" I chuckled, leaning against the wall, walking my feet forward out two feet, and then slid down until my thighs were parallel to the floor, knees at a 90-degree angle. Keeping my back flat against the wall, I engaged my core.

"How are the twins doing?" Zach asked as if we were having a casual sit-down. Though he was probably trying to distract me from the agony of this exercise.

"One week down at their new school," I said, pushing through my heels to maintain the position.

"And how did it go?"

"You know how smart they both are. But they are different when it comes to their *love* of school. They both get straight As, but Hayley is the one who always goes the extra mile, does the extra homework questions, the bonus question on tests, and asks for more independent reading assignments. Ryley just does what is expected of her. Not that it's bad or anything. Hayley just loves school."

"Up," Zach announced when the timer buzzed 60 seconds. "And you're worried about it?"

I pushed up into a standing position, shaking out my legs. "I'm worried about them, but for different reasons."

"Like what?"

Zach resumed the chair position, and I copied him. "Like with Ryley, she's always been the bigger—taller of the two, so she's had that advantage, but now her sister is doing schoolwork ahead of her."

"So the dynamic has shifted."

"Yes. But on the same note, she has always been very protective of her sister." I explained the dialog they'd exchanged my first night home, then pushed up to standing at the 60-second mark.

"Sounds like a conflict of emotions. Between feeling bad for her sister's challenges with grade eight classes and a *serves you right* kind of thing.

"Exactly." I shook out my legs, thankful we only had one set left. "Grier assured me it would be good for them to have some independence of each other for self-growth, but I don't want them to become rivals."

"Down," Zach said, lowering for our last torture minute. "The dynamic between sisters must be very unique, especially with twins."

"I've only had brothers, so I don't know firsthand. But in my extensive reading about twins, there is often a lifelong bond marked by intense emotions and deep intimacy. And a complex mix of rivalry and loyalty that evolves over time."

"That makes sense. I mean, they did spend nine months in the womb together. Now they have to navigate two identities."

"Two identities?" I questioned. The timer indicated the torture was over, and I pushed to standing.

Zach pushed up and away from the wall. "Their unique selves and their identities as twins. It's hard enough to establish one's own identity."

"I never thought about it that way. They've been best friends since birth, and now with school separating them into both different grades and classes, they are also having to navigate their world alone—so to speak. Grier told me that sibling relationships are crucial for developing a sense of identity and learning how to form attachments, as well as manage conflict and relating to others—so the separation now is supposed to be a good thing." I shrugged.

"What is their school schedule like now that they are in junior high? I've never been to school other than university, so I'm not familiar with how it all works. Do they have any classes together?"

"They do, but for some of the core classes, like mathematics, science, and language studies, Hayley attends grade eight classes. Their schedules alternate between 'A' days and 'B' days, so students attend different classes every other day. It allows them to take a wider variety of elective courses plus have longer class blocks, allowing for more focused learning."

"You're a mother, you are programmed to worry," Zach said, giving me a pat on the back. "How do you feel now after that workout?"

"Good, actually." I smiled up at him. I really did feel much better. But my body would hate me later.

"Hey, you two," Marq's deep voice bellowed from the far side of the training space. Then he jogged over *barefoot* to meet us where we stood. He was in his usual white t-shirt and worn-out faded jeans, the hems of which were frayed.

"Hello, handsome," I said, giving him a sweaty hug. I often wondered if he ever had a bad day, because he was always smiling brightly. Or maybe his smile only seemed brighter against his beautiful, lush midnight skin.

"How come you don't greet me like that?" Zach asked, pushing out his lower lip in a mock pout.

"Because Marq never abuses me like you do," I said, jutting out my tongue in added rebuttal.

"In that case, we'll do a six-six-six circuit next time." He gave me a playful shove.

"See," I countered, attempting to shove him back only to fail greatly. "What's the latest?" I said then, focusing on Marq.

"I'll show you what I've been working on." Marq turned and jogged over to the elaborate computer station setup.

I turned to follow, but I was not jogging.

Marq slid into the seat in front of the monitor displays. "Only Rome and Amsterdam are still up and running, so Ben doesn't need to watch the Alcyone facility in Tokyo now. But Den just reported that there's something going on at the Amsterdam facility, similar to Norway, with staff leaving, etc."

"Have you spoken with Lyndon about this?" Zach asked.

"Not yet, but Leo was going to speak to him today."

Marq spun in his chair to face Zach and me. "He did, however, inform Leo that Amahle had left."

"Really—why?" I'd never heard of one of Thaddeus's people leaving, not voluntarily, that is.

"No idea."

"Lyndon said that she and Thaddeus had been putting in long hours the past few weeks on something in the new lab," Zach stated. "Lyndon said he set up additional surveillance after she left, so he could see into the lab from his home system and from Marcus's system."

I scowled. "Why set up more surveillance for Marcus?"

"He needed to make it look like that's what he was establishing to explain the cameras in the lab."

"Makes sense," I agreed. "No word of where Amahle went?"

"Nope." Marq shook his head.

"Maybe she was with Ariadne?" It was a far stretch, but there'd been no sign of Ariadne since, nor had I or the twins sensed her.

"Obviously, we are going to keep an eye on what Thaddeus is doing." Marq spun back to the computer monitors.

"Lyndon says he can only do so much, and he already set up surveillance in Thaddeus's condo, private lab, *and* monitoring for every floor in the Ottawa facility, which can be accessed from his home office and Marcus's office."

"Tricky." I was good with computers, but I was grateful I hadn't had to attempt any of that.

"He'd had to show Marcus the Ottawa monitoring because he'd had to do it with him there," Zach explained. "He told him it was just added security for Thaddeus when he travelled, or went to New York and wanted to monitor things."

"Every little bit helps, I guess." I knew monitoring had already been set up at the other locations during Thaddeus's time away.

"Marcus didn't give a shit," Zach added, "so it hadn't been as problematic as Lyndon had anticipated."

"With that other tracker, Lazarus here, Lyndon is going to have to be extra careful," Marq pointed out. "Amahle let him do whatever he thought was needed during their break from Thaddeus, but now with the change in managers, he doesn't know what he'd be able to get away with. But after Thaddeus's sudden appearance, he does plan to upgrade the security system at the group home."

"Smart. Doesn't it seem suspicious to you how Amahle left without a word?"

"It does," Zach agreed.

"I'd love to know what she and Thaddeus were doing in that new lab of his. Lyndon said they spent a lot of time there," Marq said, bringing up the list he used to keep track of all the Earthbound. He changed Amahle's location status to *unknown*.

"Keep me posted if you get any more intel," I said before wandering back over to the training mat.

"We're done," Zach said, walking with me. "Unless you want to go another round?"

"Thanks—but no thanks." I plunked down on the long bench next to the mat.

He sat down next to me. "Something on your mind?"

"Ya lots," I laughed out.

"Like?"

I glanced over at the entrance to the shooting range. "I'm considering learning how to shoot a gun."

"Really—you feel ready now?"

"Ya, maybe, I don't know." I stared down at my running shoes. "Could you teach me?" I asked, glancing up at him.

"I could, but I think Kris called dibs on teaching you when you were ready."

"I just hate to make him come all the way down here, you know." Kris had been the one who had gotten me the gun and offered to show me how to shoot way back.

"With Lane safely back home, maybe he'd be down for a visit to go over things with you," he affirmed.

"Redmond and the twins would love a visit from him. I'll ask. Maybe both he and Jana could come for a visit," I proposed.

Zach bumped my shoulder with his elbow. "What else is on your mind?"

I blew out a breath then asked, "Do you know why Seraphim can't conceive babies together?"

"Wow, I wasn't expecting that."

"Sorry," I said, slumping.

"Don't say sorry," he said, his tone softening. "We don't know, actually. The essential elements are there, but… they don't communicate, it seems." Zach turned, straddling the bench to face me. "In fact, as the Earthbound began to age, they found that the females began to have menstrual cycles, followed by follicle production and ovulation."

"I never thought about them having cycles like humans." They only started aging once they were stranded here, so it made sense they would develop more human traits the longer they were on Earth.

"Their cycles are very infrequent, like once every ten to twelve months. And it's very difficult to monitor the other phases, I'm told."

"It can be hard for humans," I said. "What about the guys?"

"It's the same with spermatogenesis—the maturing of sperm cells."

I thought about what Lane had said about having kids with Lyndon. "Do you know why some halflings are healthier than others?"

"We believe it has something to do with our evolution here on Earth and our mutable genetics."

I frowned.

"Meaning the sperm are often damaged, specifically concerning the genetic material. For humans, it's referred to as having sperm DNA fragmentation."

"Fragmentation?" I questioned.

"It involves breaks or lesions in the DNA strands within the sperm cells, which can significantly impair fertility and the ability to conceive a healthy pregnancy."

"Has there ever been an instance where a female Earthbound gave birth to a baby with major issues or perhaps died young?" I didn't like the question, but I wanted to know.

"Come to think of it, the only offspring born with any major issues were to human females. Mason can't speak, but other than that, he's golden."

"I don't know if you can answer my next question. But how did Anael and Thanael make you exactly?" I stared down at my shoes again, suddenly feeling bad for asking about such a surreptitious topic. "I know there were special rings involved, but what happened to create you? Is it some kind of magic?"

Zach took a long moment as though gathering what to say, and I wondered if maybe he wasn't allowed to share this information, but then he said, "No, it's creation, like with all living things, then they evolve."

"Did you start out… *primitive*?" I hadn't thought about the Guards as something that would evolve.

"No-no, we adapted, is all. If we'd been created in the stars, we would have adapted to living there."

"I get it." I nodded slowly. "Do you ever get lonely?" I knew that was a personal one, but we'd wandered into deeper questions.

"Lonely?"

"For a different kind of connection?"

"Sometimes."

"Do you have someone in your life?" I asked, braving an even more private question.

"No, not for some time." He paused as though remembering. "Emotional attachments are difficult, as you can imagine. Kris and Jana, Lane and Lyndon, and Zuriel and your friend Grier, they all have a tough road ahead of them."

I nodded, feeling a wave of sadness wash over me.

"For me, trusting Lyndon was one thing, but watching Lane— seeing how her affections for him have grown… has been an emotional rollercoaster to witness. We know… I know the heartache they will all face one day."

I couldn't imagine what life on Earth had been like for Earthbound. It pained me even to think about it. "Do you know what slows your aging? You'd think you'd start to age even faster as you evolve, especially you and your brothers, since you were created here," I rushed out.

"We figure for the Earthbound, it has to do with the concept of their immortality and now *not* being immortal while on Earth. A change in their basic chemistry."

"What about your chemistry?"

"Not exactly sure, but we were meant to be created on Pleiades, and immortality comes from the stars." Zach rolled his shoulders. "In comparison, humans have a very short life expectancy, so we may be affected by that since we were made on earth."

"I guess that's what they call unprecedented." I smirked. "Do you know any other Earthbound who have had their wings cut off?"

Zach winced, and I regretted the inquiry immediately.

"Sorry."

"No, it's fine. And *yes*, but none who survived it."

That was enough deep talk, I figured and went with something more scientific. "What do you know about regeneration?"

Zach's expression lightened. "A little, but that's something you should ask Lyndon about. It's his—was, his expertise." Zach checked the military clock on the wall. "He should be dialing in any minute, as a matter of fact."

"Lyndon's on the line," Marq called then from across the room

"Speak of the angel," I said, pushing up from the bench.

The two of us rushed over and stood at the monitoring station behind Marq. Lyndon, it appeared, was at the group home in his apartment.

"Don't you need to be at Thaddeus's beck and call?" I threw at him.

"Hey Lynn, great to see you. Zach told me you were coming to train today. You'll be pleased to know that I got copies of those journals—the ones from Thaddeus's condo. And I already gave Nic a copy, and he and Derek are working on them as we speak."

"Wow, excellent! How did you do that?"

Lyndon laughed as though he were about to tell a funny story. "Thaddeus summoned me to his condo—stating he had a task for me." He laughed again. It was good to see him laugh. "When I got there, he told me to take out his trash."

"Yer kidding?"

Lyndon shrugged his shoulders like it didn't faze him. "It was his leftover food—normally the chef picks it up, but Thaddeus was being his usual intolerant-self. He likes to treat *me* like I'm trash." Lyndon shrugged again. "But then he left. Leaving me alone in the condo with the notebooks." He raised his eyebrows.

"Niiice!" I cheered. "Was the trash removal your task?"

"Oh no. He wanted me to track down Earthbound females from a list. That's where Thaddeus thinks I am right now." He gave me a playful grin. "Marq shared their whereabouts with me last week, but I've been avoiding telling Thaddeus what I've *discovered*, for obvious reasons."

"But what are you going to tell him—you have to say something?"

"We'll come up with something plausible for Lyndon to tell Thaddeus," Zach cut in.

"Naturally." I grinned. "Can I see the list?"

Marq handed me a printout, and I scanned the list. Then I read aloud the first *two* names, which were highlighted in blue on the list,

> *Anastasia*
> *Tuyet*

"They were paired at the time of the cast-down, and are still together," Marq shared.

I continued with the next three highlighted in green,

> *Michaela*
> *Khalilah*
> *Noella*

"They are all hiding out in remote locations."

"What about these two in yellow?,"

> *Maricela*
> *Laurinda*

"Unfortunately, we have not been able to locate them," Marq said dejectedly.

"But if we can't find them, neither can Thaddeus," Lyndon presented, adding hope.

"What about this last one with the star beside her name? *Verena*."

Lyndon's levity shifted. "She was originally first on the list. Her last known location was in the *Cook Islands*. Beautiful place—I can see why she went there."

"So you found her?"

Lyndon's face turned mournful, and he glanced away.

"What?" I turned to Marq to see his expression was grief stricken. "Tell me," I demanded.

"We didn't exactly *find* her." Cracking knuckles sounded through the monitor's speaker.

"What did you find?"

"Her last known location was Palmerston Island, a coral atoll in the Cook Islands. And I went there looking for her." Lyndon went on to explain how instead of finding the Earthbound female, he'd found an elderly Polynesian man named Keola, tending to flowers out front of a small cottage. "When I asked him if he'd ever heard of someone named *Verena*, the old guy just smiled and pointed to a grave marker with a single name on it, no dates, just *Verena*, surrounded by white, star-like flowers, their national flower. Next to the first gravestone was a second with a caduceus etched into it next to another single name, *Lani*. He said it meant heavenly or sky."

"So, Verena died? Who was the old man?"

"He said he was Verena's husband."

"Husband?"

"He said he was 101 years old, but that they met when he was nineteen and they married two years later."

"Who was Lani?"

"Their daughter—she was a nurse. But apparently she died of dengue fever during an outbreak this past May. She was seventy-eight." Lyndon let out a heavy sigh. "Verena took her life days after."

I brought my hands up, covering my mouth. "Oh my gawd," I breathed out through my fingers.

"I felt the same, Lynn. Then he said, '*I know what she was.*'" Lyndon brushed his hand across his scar. "He said she didn't age and had to cover her face when they were around others because they told a story about how she had burned her face from oil on the stove. Their daughter knew the truth. Keola explained that dengue fever isn't always fatal, but since Lani was born with CF cystic fibrosis, contracting it had been deadly for her."

"The median age for people with CF is fifty-three, so she lived considerably longer than most," Marq stated.

"She may have lived even longer if it hadn't been for the viral infection," Zach offered up. "As for her parents, not too many couples can say they've had 80 years together."

"That's true." I turned back to the video screen. "Speaking of living longer, I've been wondering about a few things. Lyndon, when you have time, do you think could give me a brief education on starfish, and your specialty, *regeneration?*"

Chapter 32 

The Beach House, Wednesday A.M., August 20ᵗʰ, South Florida

After the girls left for school, and Redmond had headed out over to South Haven for his own punishing training session with Zach, I set my laptop up on the coffee table in the living room for my video call with Lyndon. He'd offered to circle back this morning to go over the basics of starfish and their regenerative capacities, and I had one of the girls' spare notebooks next to me and a pen at the ready should I need to take notes. I had considered having Alison dial in for the note-taking part but felt it best I wait before bringing anyone else in on the discussion, not until I understood things more and could make clearer the idea I was forming.

I sat cross-legged on the couch in front of my laptop and hit the video icon to connect with Lyndon. "Hey," I said when his face came into view. Once again, he was in his apartment at the group home.

"Hey, yourself," he responded, smiling. "I like the option of video calls. Lane and I used this all the time when she was away for work."

"I have to agree—I use it with my friends and family up there all the time. I prefer actual face-to-face visits, but I'll take it."

"I feel the same," he tossed out. "You said you wanted to learn about starfish?" He chuckled.

"I know it sounds silly—but what I'm really curious about is the regeneration part. How their arms grow back—or is it legs?"

"Arms," he corrected, amused, laughing again. "Starfish can regenerate lost limbs through a process involving cell de-differentiation, epimorphosis, and morphallaxis."

"Oh, gosh—you sound like Derek." It was my turn to laugh. "He likes to give me the scientific terms for things too."

"Well, that Derek is an intelligent fellow."

"Don't I know it. He knows it too, but don't let him know you think so."

"Ha! *Don't feed the monster*, you mean."

"Exactly."

"Okay. Let me take an easier approach here. If a starfish loses an arm, the wound seals off, and specialized cells migrate to the area to regrow the limb.

"How is that even possible?"

"You want the easy answer, or the scientific one?"

"How about... somewhere in the middle?" I reached for my notebook and pen.

"Biologically, it starts with wound sealing and the initial repair. When a starfish loses an arm, there is a fluid-filled cavity within the arm that seals off to prevent fluid loss and infection."

"Okay," I said, jotting down my own notes. "Then what?"

"Then the arm wall contracts, and special cells called coelomocytes assemble to form a clot and remove any debris." He paused as though letting me get my notes down, and then said, "The epithelial cells then stretch inwards from the wound edges, forming a continuous layer of new tissue."

"Got it. That seems basic enough."

"Now, the regeneration mechanism is where things get complicated." He paused again.

"I'm ready—go ahead."

"Epimorphosis," he said, grinning. Before I could say anything, he held up a hand. "Stem cells at the injury site multiply and form a blastema, which is a mass of undifferentiated cells that will develop into the new limb."

"Like a tumor?"

"No, these are embryo-like cells that have the capacity to grow and regenerate into organs or body parts."

"Wow, really?"

"Yes, some starfish can even regenerate an entire new starfish from a single arm with a portion of the central disk."

"That's wild." I put two stars beside that note. "Then what happens?"

"Morphallaxis. This is where the existing tissue remodels itself to create the replacement limb. Followed by cellular differentiation."

"Wait, let me guess this one. The cells separate into different cell *types*, like muscle, nerves, etc."

"Correct!"

"Derek would be so proud," I laughed out, raising my arms in the air like I was cheering. "Okay, so I get the arm thing—what about a whole other starfish?"

"That's a form of asexual reproduction where the individual produces offspring that are genetically identical to the parent."

"Like natural cloning."

"Sort of, yes."

"Why can't humans grow back limbs?" This was what I was really interested in, if my idea was going to come to fruition.

"That's due to a combination of evolutionary factors and biological mechanisms." He went on to explain the reasons for scar tissue formation, the evolutionary factors that favor traits for enhanced survival, and the fact that humans don't form blastema cells at the injury site. "Not to mention the complexity of the human limb with its intricate bone, muscle, nerve and blood vessel structure."

"So it's impossible?"

"There is research, like with bioelectricity and stem cells, where the understanding of these mechanisms could potentially lead to therapies that encourage limb regeneration." Lyndon went on to explain the successes and challenges in regenerative medicine. "New research is happening all the time."

"But regrowing limbs is way off in the future."

"Yes, but look at the human liver. When part of the liver is damaged or removed, the remaining portion will grow back to the original size and allow the liver to function like it did before."

"I've heard about that." I nodded. "So all hope is not lost." My cellphone beeped, and I grabbed it. "I just got a text from Derek. Says he's got some interesting news."

"Nic just texted the same. They must have found something intriguing in Thaddeus's journals."

"Let's hope it's helpful. I'll let you go and hit up Derek." I set my cellphone down. "Thanks, by the way—for all this."

"Anytime, Lynn. I don't often get to share my knowledge from my *old* life."

"I really appreciate it. Chat later."

"Later," he said, logging off.

I grabbed my phone and texted Derek back,

Video call?

Derek video dialed me without responding to my text.

"You've got news?" I asked when he appeared on screen.

"I do!" He wriggled his eyebrows. "The notebook you found in Norway has some fascinating stuff in it."

"Tell me what you deciphered?"

"Did you know that the blood from the feathers of an Earthbound has regenerative healing properties for humans?"

"Shut up!"

"Seriously. Nic confirmed it. That's how the Earthbound heal so fast."

"Has Nic ever tested the healing properties of their wing blood?"

"Not until now."

"He tried it?"

"He tested some of his blood on a small burn Julian got working in the kitchen. It healed the burn immediately, but then several hours later the wound was back, although it *was* partially healed."

"What about halflings?"

"Nic contacted Mason to come by North Haven later today, so I guess we'll find out. I suppose he could have just asked Natalie."

"Maybe he can test both, see if there is any difference between males and females."

"Good point. I'll text him your suggestion."

I grinned. I was feeling smarter after my session with Lyndon.

"Speaking of testing, you should see my latest computer setup."

"Your geek console?" I teased.

"Hey now, my gaming and computer setup is a meticulously chosen, high-performance, and personalized command center optimized for both immersive gaming and computing tasks. I built it for maximum speed, efficiency, and comfort during long hours of use, and don't forget my distinct, custom aesthetic." He reached his hands out to the sides and patted his side monitors. "Powerful CPU and GPU. Ample RAM, superior cooling, multi-monitor display, mechanical keyboard for superior responsiveness and durability, and a high-DPI mouse." He rested his hand on the mouse. "And don't forget my ergonomic chair." He spun in his office chair.

"I get it—you have new toys. Now let me tell you what I learned from Lyndon this morning." Interestingly enough, Derek sat quietly listening while I went through different regenerative treatments involved in stimulating the body's natural healing abilities to repair or replace damaged tissues, like *Stem Cell Therapy* where the treatment utilizes the body's stem cells often harvested from bone marrow or adipose tissue, and that possess the unique ability to differentiate into various cell types and promote tissue regeneration. There was also *Prolotherapy* which involved injecting a dextrose solution into injured ligaments or tendons to trigger an inflammatory response that encourages tissue repair. As well as *Adipose Tissue Therapy*, which utilizes fat cells by injecting them into the injured area to promote healing. "And PRP, *Platelet-Rich Plasma Therapy* which involves concentrating platelets from a patient's own blood and injecting them into the injured area."

"Sounds similar to the method Thaddeus mentions in his notes," Derek shared.

"Lyndon said that platelets contain growth factors that can accelerate tissue repair and reduce inflammation. PRP therapy has shown promise in treating musculoskeletal injuries. How crazy is that?"

"You think that's crazy? I should send you some of the bizarre stuff I've read," Derek countered.

"Like what?" Normally I wasn't interested in the details of what Derek typically shared; my interest was in quick facts, but this time I wanted to know what else was out there regarding regeneration.

"Vampire Facials," he announced.

"Seriously?"

"Evidently, it's done using a patient's own blood and micro-needling. Modern medicine is exploring various approaches right now to extend human lifespans and health spans," he said, before leading me through a series of research articles he found about extending the human lifespan, starting with beauty treatments. *Bird Poo Facials* was an ancient Japanese treatment using nightingale droppings. *Snail Facials* involve snails crawling on the face to deliver beneficial mucin. "And my personal favorite, Penis Facials, using progenitor cells from newborn baby foreskin."

"Oh my gaaawd!"

"Throughout history, people have pursued various methods to slow or reverse the aging process. Obviously, some of these are considered unusual or bizarre by today's standards."

"Ya think?"

"Want to hear more?"

"Sure, why not."

"You'll love these." Derek clacked away on his keyboard, then said, "Cleopatra was rumored to have bathed daily in donkey milk, believing it had anti-aging properties that softened and rejuvenated her skin."

"Why would she ever think that?"

"Not that she would have known this, but sour donkey milk contains lactic acid, a natural AHA alpha-hydroxy acid which you find in many modern-day exfoliants."

"I saw a documentary about her recently; she was a clever and powerful woman."

"This one aligns with what we were discussing about using blood. Countess Elizabeth Báthory, a 16th-century Hungarian noblewoman, is infamous for allegedly bathing in the blood of young women, believing it would preserve her youth and beauty."

"What would provoke people to think that? Insanity?"

"Madness for sure. The rejuvenating power of young blood also appears in myths *and* popular culture, like that episode of *The Simpsons* where Mr. Burns is revitalized by a blood transfusion from Bart."

"Don't think I caught that one." I don't think I've watched that show since I was in college.

"Oh, this one's the best. John R. Brinkley, a self-proclaimed doctor, gained fame in the early 20th century for transplanting goat testicles into men and goat ovaries into women, promising restored virility and youth."

"Shows you the lengths people will go to in their pursuit of longevity."

"I wonder if Thaddeus ever tried any of these experimental treatments."

"Yeesh! I don't want to think about it."

"We're still going through the copies of the other notebooks Lyndon sent Nic and me. I've set up a new algorithm to decipher them quicker. Had to change it some from the last one because it appears Thaddeus is using a different code for his notes now."

"It can never be easy, it seems, can it? Let me know what you find out and keep me posted on what Nic discovers with the halfling blood."

"As soon as I know—you'll know." He waved. "Shortcut out!"

"Later," I said, giving him the peace sign as I logged out.

"Vampire facials," I chuckled to myself, picturing someone micro-needling their face with blood. "But what if...," I brought up a new browser window on my laptop and typed *Platelet-Rich Plasma Therapy* into the search field. When the results came back, I reviewed how it worked, the procedures involved with drawing blood and injecting it into the injured area, *and* the recovery phase. Then I grabbed my cellphone and typed a text to Grier,

> *Hey girlfriend. What's your schedule look like today?*

Grier texted back with,

> *Wide open. Wanna come over?*

I texted Grier back,

> *On my way!*

and then I did the quick 20-minute walk up the beach to her cottage.

Grier had a lemon-cranberry loaf fresh out of the oven, sliced and plated when I arrived. "Your home always smells so delicious."

"Lynn, you know I like to bake. And I've been doing a ton of cooking and baking since Zuriel came into my life."

"What's the saying? *The way to a man's heart is through his stomach?*"

"It's not just about satisfying hunger. A home-cooked meal represents a deep sense of being nurtured and cared for."

"Well, you can care for me any day," I said, taking a big bite from the generous slice she'd given me.

"How's your day been so far?"

"Funny you should ask," I said, running through the educational discussions I'd had with Lyndon and then Derek.

"I've heard of PRP and its ability to improve blood flow to treated areas, and the treatment shows promise for brain injuries."

"Have you treated many people with brain injuries?"

"Some. Most people don't realize that psychiatry plays a crucial role in the treatment of brain injuries, through evaluating and treating the resulting psychological and emotional issues, like depression or anxiety, and behavioral changes."

"I figured you may have had a few patients."

"It's extraordinary what you told me about the wing blood and the regenerative properties." Grier tapped her chin with her index finger. "I wonder if it would work on Zuriel's scars?"

"Zuriel's shoulder snowflakes—what do they look like now?"

"They still look like snowflakes, sort of, but distorted and rough where, like a tattoo, it would be smooth. Somewhere between the delicate, symmetrical shape of a snowflake and a permanent, imperfect mark of a scar."

"I was worried about that. The scarring may have pulled at the skin, changing the once-sharp, defined edges. Like a real snowflake that has endured a difficult journey."

"My sentiment exactly. I told him that a scarred snowflake is a visual symbol of survival and the strength found in embracing one's past."

"That's a good way to look at it instead of focusing on the trauma. Not that it wasn't horrific, but now it's a permanent yet altered record of what was, now existing alongside the reality of what is."

"Oh, I'm going to tell him that one."

"I'm guessing he's at work?"

"Yes. Work—his job — has been great for him. He is in heaven, I guess you could say."

"Anything is better than the hell he was in under Thaddeus."

"He says the same thing."

"I'm guessing you've seen his wings?"

"I have."

"Does he ever look at them?"

"He did at first, when Lyndon brought them to him. But not so much now. He keeps them in a controlled microclimate container similar to a museum-grade archive storage for biological artifacts."

"I never considered the need to preserve them."

"For the feathers and bones to remain intact, the container needs to prevent natural decay and mold growth. They're in an oak box, cushioned with acid-free and lignin-free foam and a cover that blocks all light. We have it set up in the guestroom closet."

"His are black-tipped. Leo and the others have white with grey tips."

"That's right, I forgot they were different."

"Halflings have grey wings with white tips."

"Zuriel's reminds me of swan wings. Bigger obviously, and so powerful. They are remarkably structured to support such a heavy body. Extended, they showcase a broad, curved shape covered in thousands of soft, thick feathers." Grier reached out her arms as if she were performing a ballet move.

"Does he ever talk about flying?"

"Just that he wishes he could have taken me up in the sky with him." She gave me a somber smile. "I know this is nothing new to you, but even after all this time, I still find the fact that he had wings—that the others have wings — overwhelmingly fascinating. And they are beautiful, clearly, but you seem overly interested in Zuriel's wings."

"Trust me—it still blows my mind. And Zuriel's loss of his is tragically heartbreaking. The thing is… I have an idea—a theory, really."

"An idea about Zuriel and his wings?

"Yes. But it's a long shot."

"Lynn, what's going on?"

"Look, I don't want to get Zuriel's hopes up. And I know it will be hard, but I need you to promise me that you'll keep what I'm about to tell you between us."

Chapter 33 

The Beach House, Sunday early A.M., August 24th, South Florida

This time of day is my favorite.

Everyone is still asleep in their beds, even Redmond, and I get this rare time alone to watch the sun come up. People say they love a sunset, but our expansive beach house deck faces east to the ocean and gifts us with the best possible views and the most amazing sunrises, creating a space for relaxation and connecting with nature. It has been a lively place for parties, and a peaceful spot for quiet contemplation. Several years ago we invested in comfortable, resilient outdoor furniture, and my choice piece for mornings like these is the big armchair with the flat armrest to set my coffee on, and the matching cushioned ottoman to rest my legs upon. It's the early morning moment of twilight, deep purples and blues, just before that first line of orange sun peeks above the horizon that I find so magical.

A soft warm breeze brushed over my bare arms and feet, and swept gently across my cheek. "Where have you been?" I said aloud even before Gabriel showed himself. I turned away from my view out to the sunrise to see him sitting on the patio couch at the end next to me staring forward at the view.

Without turning my way, he said. "Performing my other duties."

I turned back to the lazily rising sun. "So what? I'm just one of your duties now?"

"Like the others… Michael, Vretil, Raphael, and Uriel, who watch over your friends, I have…."

"Why didn't you come when I called out to you?" I interrupted, continuing to face forward. I could see in my periphery he had turned his head and was looking my way.

"I can't always come when you call."

I turned and set my focus on him. "What if I were in danger?"

"You were not."

"We could have used your help to find Lane."

Gabriel frowned. "She is safe now, is she not?"

"Yes—no thanks to you," I said, crossing my arms, facing forward again. "You're the one who connected me with Leo and the others to find Kris."

"I did." Gabriel remained facing me.

"So you can involve me to help find another celestial, but you can't help me find a human?"

"That's not fair."

"Or is it that you don't care anymore? Now that the big gathering is done and over." I knew that was harsh, but I hated how things were now. I wanted everything back the way it had been.

"It is the exact opposite, in fact."

I turned my head and glared at him. "What, you care too much?"

Gabriel nodded.

"How is that a problem?" I asked, uncrossing my arms to hold my hands in the air in question.

"The others don't engage in the lives of their Charges."

"But I'm not just your Charge."

"No, but neither were the *first* daughters, yet still, other than teaching them what they needed to know, they stood back, only watching over them, with no unnecessary involvement."

I crossed my arms again. "Well, you've been involved in my life since the gathering *and* with my family. You've even met and spent time with Redmond's parents."

"I know," Gabriel said, facing the emerging sunrise again.

"So what's changed?" Tears welled in my eyes, obscuring my vision, the blue, pink and orange sky blurring.

"My behavior… my involvement these past several years has…."

"What—pissed off your boss?" I cut in, my tone bitter.

Gabriel glared at me.

"Sorry," I said, sniffing back tears. "I just don't understand."

"It's also the reason Diniel has been hanging around," he huffed out.

"What do you mean?"

Gabriel turned away again. "She has been observing my interactions, learning about my time with you and the twins."

"Your family, you mean."

Gabriel's jaw clenched. "She doesn't see it that way."

"So she snitched on you?"

"No… not exactly."

"She was what—just curious?" I asked, incredulous.

"Concerned is more like it?"

"About what?"

"About my continued relationship… my *over-involvement* with you." He blew out a frustrated breath.

"Over-involvement?"

Gabriel turned fully in his seat to face me, his arm stretched out on the backrest, knee bent up and resting on the couch cushion. "Please never doubt my love and devotion to you—to you and your family."

Tears blurred my vision again, and I turned back to the orange and pink sky. "Don't you mean *your* family?"

"I care deeply about Redmond, and I cherish the twins wholeheartedly—you know that," he declared emphatically.

"They love you." I twisted in my seat to face him. "I love you."

"I wish…." Gabriel dropped his hands to his lap, his head lowering. "I want to be here with you, and the others, but…."

"But you have other duties. I get it." I crossed my arms again but didn't look away.

He lifted his head. "Do you?" he questioned, his expression mournful.

"No, but I do understand you would be here with us if you could." I dropped my arms and sighed. "So I won't push."

"I know you are mad at me."

I shook my head. "I'm not mad, just confused." I pulled my knee up onto the chair to fully face him. "You can't tell me if there is a heaven or hell, or what happens after you die. And I just sit here, in my little bubble, watching the world on fire around me... it's a mess. I don't know who created this universe, but it's clear that Mother Nature is struggling to keep it clean." I put my elbow on my knee, resting my cheek against my closed fist.

"Lynn...."

"I know, I know." I wiped away a determined tear.

Gabriel leaned forward and took my hand from my cheek. "How I feel about you... and the way I must conduct my duties, do not run in parallel. Remember, I have been performing my role for several millennia."

The reality of his words weighed down on me. "And my existence in your life is infinitesimal."

"I didn't say that," he growled. Holding my hand tighter, he said, "You are *my* daughter... it is a rare thing to be granted such an honor, the privilege of witnessing one's own progeny."

I glanced down at his hands holding mine. "What's the big deal? Humans do it all the time."

He tugged on my hand, causing me to look up. "Is that how you feel about your own children, that they are *no big deal*?"

"That's different."

"How so?" Gabriel released my hand. "I don't have a job that requires me to abandon them," I stated, resting my cheek against my hand again.

Gabriel's mouth gaped. "I have not abandoned you."

"Sometimes it feels like you have," I said, feeling tears sneak into my vision again.

"I apologize for that." He gave me a loving smile. "But then you are not a child... and you do not need me."

"I never said I *needed* you in my life," I said, sitting up and dropping my leg down. "I just… *want* you in it." I turned forward in my seat.

"And I want to be in it, but…."

"Your duties keep you away," I said, cutting him off again, nodding. "I get it." I swallowed back tears.

Gabriel scooted right up to the end of the couch next to my chair. He took my hand again and then turned to watch the remaining sunrise. "How are the girls?" he asked then, releasing a calming breath as the sun rose above the horizon.

"They are good for the most part," I said, before delving in deeper about their conflicts of late. "I worry about both of them." I shifted my focus away from the brilliant sky to gaze at him.

"Lynn, if you are ever in danger, I promise to come when you call."

I forced a smile and nodded. "I'm going to ask you a question that you may *not* want to answer."

"How unlike you," Gabriel chuckled out, still holding my hand.

I rolled my eyes. "How old are you?"

He laughed again. "Older than dirt," he replied, making me laugh this time.

"Are archangels the oldest?"

"Yes." He nodded once.

"What about the Seraphim from Pleiades?"

He glanced up at the sky above us. "They are as old as the earth."

I glanced up too, but the stars were no longer visible in the morning sun. "I keep forgetting that Lyndon and Zuriel and the other Earthbound are older than Leo and The Guards."

"That's true."

I glanced at him. "I asked Zach if he knew of any other Earthbound who'd had their wings cut off, and he said '*yes*', but none who survived."

Gabriel's grip on my hand tightened briefly, and he bowed his head.

I swallowed hard at witnessing the grief he must be feeling. "Have you ever known a Seraph to grow back their wings once they'd been severed?" I asked, hopeful.

Gabriel drew in a long breath and then raised his head. "I know of no Pleiadean Seraph. But like Zach told you, there have been Earthbound Seraphim destructively impacted by their time on Earth, who have… lost their wings. I, too, have never known of any who lived." He squeezed my hand gently. "Zuriel is very lucky in that regard."

"That's the thing… I'm not sure it was luck."

"Why do you say that?" His brows pinched.

"I don't think Thaddeus just wanted to punish him… I think he wanted to see if he could do it—remove them without killing him."

Gabriel turned in his seat again, still holding my hand. "What do you mean?"

I shifted to face him. "He could have just killed Zuriel, but he chose to keep him alive." I sat up straighter. "I think he removed Zuriel's wings, testing a method—his method, to see if he would survive."

"You mean, like one of his experiments? For what purpose?" he questioned, tilting his head like an inquisitive dog.

"Absolutely like one of his sick experiments. The *why* part I haven't figured out yet. But with that psycho, anything is possible." I placed my free hand over our joined ones. "Can't you and the other Archangels just take him out or something?"

He gave me a thin-lipped smile. "I wish it were that simple."

"I guess if it were, you'd do the same with all the monsters of the world, eh?"

Gabriel gave me a weak, yet understanding smile. "It is not our role to pass judgement, even if one's actions go against everything we believe."

I glanced down at our held hands. "What about the Watchers?"

"What about them?"

"How old are they?"

"The original Watchers, like Shamsiel, are almost as old as the Archangels." Gazing past me, he swept his free hand across his jaw. "However, the Watchers who reside in Sanctuary…,"

"Are different?" I interjected again.

Gabriel released a chuckle of amusement. "In a way. The Watchers—the ones you know as the *Fallen*, those who supported them and their decision to breach their duties as observers…," he began to say.

"Wait, there were angels who *supported* the Fallen?" I hadn't heard this part of the story. I let go of his hand and turned fully again in my seat, bending my legs up and wrapping my arms around them.

"They supported the idea of… *choice*," he corrected.

"The choice to what… *mingle* with humans?" I finger-quoted the word mingle, already knowing there was much more involved.

"It wasn't so much the *mingling*," Gabriel said, copying my finger quotes. "The support came when it produced progeny."

"Yer telling me there was a group of angels who were all for the idea of making Nephilim?"

"Offspring, yes."

"Back up. You told me that there were Watchers who resided in a place known as Sanctuary, and that they were granted by Archangel Zadkiel with the ability to have children. And now you're saying they were supporters of the Fallen who stepped out of bounds in their duties?" My mind whirled as if it were witnessing pigs fly.

"More or less."

"How was any of that possible?"

Gabriel's gaze dropped to the open space near his feet. "War," he said on an exhale.

"War?" I gasped out.

He nodded slowly. "When war broke out, the *for* and *against* factions were sequestered into a slice of time to fight it out." Without my even asking, he dove into the story. Those who were *for*, were granted the ability to have offspring, but they would also suffer like humans did, the casualties of wartimes, including the potential death of their children. Over time, despite those *against* being strong, their numbers dwindled. Those *for*, lost many, but their numbers grew, with their offspring reaching maturity at the equivalent of 25 human years. At such a point, the leader from each side was granted passage to the human world via a portal, to bear witness to the human advancements. Upon returning, the leader from the *against* side asked to join with the other side, stating that he felt they were no longer fighting for their beliefs and that too many had died from anger and pride, and that the *supporting* side now only fought to protect their own and not their original cause. Then he called on Archangel Zadkiel to bring an end to their war. "But there were very few left who fought in the original war."

"What about their children? Was the Watcher I met an original or one of their offspring?"

"He was in fact the son of an original, the leader for the supporting side."

"And I'm guessing the war was stopped?"

"Archangel Zadkiel came to Sanctuary and granted them all two options. They could either return to their original posts or remain here and live out their lives in Sanctuary. The remaining members on the *against* side returned to where they'd been before, and only their leader remained. There were just under a thousand left on the *for* side, and none chose to leave."

"I'm feeling like that wasn't the end of things."

"For those who remained, it meant they would begin to age, similar to what the Earthbound experience, one year for every ten human years, but they would be able to continue to have these lives without war."

"Well, that was good—wasn't it?"

"For a time. About a hundred years into their new lives, which obviously involved mates and children, Archangel Z came down again, this time to confront one of the leaders because he had been found to have been with a human woman, and she had gotten pregnant."

"Which leader?" I asked, not that it mattered really.

"The one who had originally been against *mingling* with humans. The other leader, the father of the Watcher you met, asked for forgiveness for his friend, stating that the other leader had once been in a position to end his life, but instead he chose to come to their side. Had he struck him down, he would not have had the joy of his family."

"I'm sure Zadkiel wasn't impressed."

Gabriel raised his eyebrows. "That's an understatement. He told them they had not learned anything from what had happened to humans regarding the offspring of the Fallen. They had not only created *great* men, but evil men as well. They had enjoyed the results of having children and family, but they had not learned the price humans paid for the choices of the Fallen. That even with the gift of family, one of them had chosen to involve himself with a human. But he did grant them redemption, along with two choices."

I said nothing, waiting patiently for the rest.

"The first option, the leaders would be taken from their families, both celestial and human. Or the remaining originals could all leave Sanctuary, as the others had done long ago, but their children and grandchildren would then be destroyed along with the existence of Sanctuary."

"Obviously they chose to leave their families behind?"

"Yes. But their children and their children's children and so on, would have to carry the burden of their leaders' choices."

"What burden?"

"A quest was set out for them… but that is a story for another time," he said as though he were closing a children's book at bedtime.

"Aaahhhhh, yer kill'in me," I groaned.

Gabriel laughed, then tilted his head inquisitively again. "Why did you ask me about the Seraphim and their wings?"

I tightened my lips, giving him a half smile. "Because… I have a theory."

Chapter 34 

The group home, Monday morning, August 25th, Ottawa, Canada

Lane had come to the group home to assist Lyndon with setting up the home's new upgraded security system. She hadn't been much help, to be honest, but she had cheered him on. And as her reward for all her encouragement this morning, he'd offered to make her favorite breakfast of buttermilk waffles with fresh blueberries.

"You know, we are lucky I was able to find blueberries. The season is almost over," Lyndon said, topping off Lane's coffee as she ate her meal at the small table in his apartment. He was still wearing the work pants and the old t-shirt he'd donned to work on the security system.

Lane popped a blueberry into her mouth. "I think you'll find the season runs to the end of September. But you could always fly to Surrey, BC to get some if we run out," she ribbed, popping two more berries into her mouth. Lane hadn't needed any protective clothes, but she still wore faded jeans and a worn-out old t-shirt of his. Lane was tall, but the shirt was so big it hung down to her upper thighs.

"I would fly anywhere for you," he countered, leaning down to kiss her smiling lips.

"What else do you have planned this morning?" Lane asked, sipping her coffee.

"For once I have nothing to attend to." Lyndon picked up their now empty breakfast dishes and took them to rinse off in the kitchen sink. "How about you?" he asked, hopeful she had no commitments for the day.

"I'm as free as a bird," she said, getting up from the table, taking her coffee with her to the lounge space. "You're stuck with me." She lowered herself down onto the new leather sofa he'd gotten. He'd done away with the armchairs so they could cuddle together when she visited his home.

"Good thing I have a book to keep me entertained then," he quipped. But he did have a book he wanted to read to her. "If you're good, I'll read it to you."

"How good—is good?" she said playfully, wriggling her eyebrows up and down.

"You have to keep your hands to yourself while I'm reading," he teased, plucking the book from the shelf.

"Can I… snuggle against your chest and put my arm over you?"

Lyndon responded with a doubtful expression, but then said, "Okay, but no tickling." He crossed to where Lane sat, then slid over the two old ottomans that had previously been paired with the armchairs.

"Oh, good idea," Lane said, lifting her legs as the ottoman met up with the sofa. "What book did you pick?"

Lyndon pulled the book to his chest, hiding the cover. "I want to hear about your plans for your PhD first," he said. "Or are you planning on taking another work contract?" He dreaded her taking a job in another city.

"I'd rather work on my PhD now that I've had some time in the field." She smiled at him, and he blew out a sigh of relief. "Unless you'd like me to take a job in Timbuctoo?"

"Not a chance," he said, pulling her closer. "Tell me about the program you're looking into."

"If I get accepted for the program, I'll be doing a PhD in *Marine, Estuarine, and Environmental Sciences* focused on complex environmental issues."

"How long will it take you to complete?"
"Typically, 3-6 years. It requires a significant commitment to specialized research in areas like marine biology or physical oceanography. The core of it is a substantial research project, which will form the basis of my dissertation."

"I'm exhausted just hearing about it," he confessed, holding back a grin.

Lane smacked his arm. "Okay, back to the book." She lifted his arm over his shoulder and snuggled in.

"Have you ever read anything by Diana Gabaldon?" Lyndon asked, assuming a reclined position next to her. "You may have seen the TV series."

"I haven't had a chance to watch TV in years," she laughed out. "Let alone read a book for fun."

"Well, that's good because this book — which is part of a series, was first published in 1991."

"I would have been six years old," she laughed again.

"Yes, I know — I'm an old man," he tossed back.

"Says the guy who doesn't look a day over thirty-five." Lane tapped the book he held against his chest. "Book — tell me," she urged.

"Right." He pulled the book away from his chest. "Outlander," he said, glancing at Lane.

"I've heard of it — keep going." She draped her arm over his torso and rested her head against his chest.

"It's a historical fiction involving time-travel." Lyndon paused to look down at her. When she said nothing, he went on. "The main characters are Claire Randall, a twentieth-century former combat medic, and Jamie Fraser, who's a Highlander."

"Is it a romance?" Lane tilted her head to look up at him.

"Yes… and no. It's a love story with adventure… suspense… and wonderful historical details. It starts out when Claire is accidentally transported back to eighteenth-century Scotland after she falls through a ring of standing stones at Craigh na Dun in the highlands while inspecting a plant."

Lane frowned up at him.

"What?"

"You read it already," she chided. "When did you start reading books like this?"

"I've read the whole series. You've been gone a lot these past few years. I had to fill my nights with something," he confessed. "But I swear you're going to love it."

"Okay," Lane said, stretching up to plant a single kiss on his lips. "Read away."

Lyndon brought the well-worn novel up and turned to the first page, then he began to read, *"It was a relief to feel the hard ground beneath my feet, but the relief was short-lived."*

Lyndon had scarcely begun reading about the annual gathering of the *Clan MacKenzie* in Chapter 10 when his cellphone chimed.

"Nooo," Lane whined, as Lyndon shifted out from under her hold to reach for his phone from the side table.

Lyndon ran a hand down his face and then pushed up from the sofa.

Lane sat up. "What is it?"

"Who else?" he grumbled, marking his spot in the book with an old leather bookmark. "I'll be back as soon as I can—I promise."

"And I'll read to *you* when you get back." She gifted him one of her amazing smiles.

"Sounds like a plan," he said, leaning down and planting a kiss on her beautiful lips.

Lyndon stood outside Thaddeus's new lab on the 6th floor, waiting for his infuriating boss to arrive. Normally, Lyndon wouldn't have rushed so fast over to the Celaeno building, but he was eager to get back to Lane. And the sooner he dealt with whatever it was the asshole wanted from him, the sooner he could get back to what he loved most, time with Lane.

The lab door next to where Lyndon stood made a distinct whooshing sound, followed by a slight vacuum sound, revealing a smug-faced Thaddeus. "Good—you're here," he announced, waving Lyndon into the lab.

The deceitful douchebag was actually wearing a lab coat over his dress shirt and navy pants, with *Dr. Thaddeus Smyth* embroidered over the left breast pocket and the name of his bogus organization, *The Celaeno Foundation*, under it.

Lyndon held his tongue and strode in, hoping what came next would be quick and painless. Thaddeus was certainly no doctor, he had no ethics, and any foundation he thought he had would soon be crumbling under his feet, Lyndon considered.

"The lab is finally ready—let me show you all the equipment I've procured for my latest endeavor." Thaddeus extended an arm towards the first piece of medical equipment like one of those models from that price-matching game show Lane's father Julian liked to watch when he was sick. Not that Lyndon had watched the show, but he had helped Max make his husband homemade soup last winter.

"Time-lapse incubator," Thaddeus said, pulling Lyndon from his musing. "Unlike traditional incubators that require embryos to be removed for observation, time-lapse incubators provide continuous, uninterrupted monitoring." Thaddeus stepped to the side of the machine but then paused, scowling down at Lyndon's shirt.

Lyndon glanced down to swiftly realize his shirt was overly wrinkled, the result of which had come from Lane's snuggling up to him. He drew a hand down the front of his shirt, making a fruitless attempt to smooth out his shirt.

Thaddeus scowled again and then shook his head before continuing with his explanation of the equipment next to him. "It features a high-resolution camera system that captures images every ten minutes, generating a complete video history of each embryo's development," he added.

Lyndon realized this was not going to be quick. If he were lucky, he might escape pain-free, though the jury was still out on that.

Continuing, Thaddeus said, "This is the Micromanipulation station. It's for procedures like *Intracytoplasmic Sperm Injection*. These workstations are equipped with powerful microscopes and laser technology for delicate and precise handling of gametes and embryos." He pointed at two more similar work spaces.

Lyndon had a sudden need to protect nether region, but he held himself still. So much for the not painful part.

"Here we have automated storage. Sperm, eggs, and embryos are preserved in these large, high-capacity cryobanks. Automated tracking technology tracks and verifies every specimen, creating a secure, digital chain of custody that prevents any mix-ups. With continuous monitoring, these storage systems are constantly monitored by alarm systems that alert staff — me, if conditions, such as the liquid nitrogen level, are anything other than optimal."

Lyndon nodded, wishing for this to be over soon.

"You know, Lyndon. A modern medical fertility lab has to be a pristine, high-tech environment dominated by advanced technology, extreme automation, and a meticulously controlled atmosphere. Air quality for one. I've installed powerful HEPA, carbon, and Purafil filters to continuously scrub the air and remove harmful particles, gases, even odors and viruses. The system maintains a positive air pressure — meaning air flows out of the lab rather than allowing contaminants in."

Lyndon knew what positive pressure was, but he avoided showing any feeling towards Thaddeus's condescension.

"The lab has separate areas divided into sections with restricted access. The sterile area is for handling sensitive genetic material, while the non-sterile areas are for tasks like administrative work."

Lyndon held back a groan.

"A modern lab like this requires a robust backup power system, guaranteeing that critical equipment like incubators and cryo-tanks will continue to function without any interruption," Thaddeus added, oozing with hubris. "This is a list of all the laboratory equipment in the lab, should it need any support or maintenance." He handed Lyndon a binder filled with sheets of paper.

Lyndon tucked it under his arm, sensing that his time here was coming to an end.

"Now that Amahle is... *gone*, I'm going to need an actual assistant. Oh, by the way, I've shut down the Netherlands facility in

Amsterdam. And I'm having Malcolm take Addison's open spot in New York City."

"What about Soriel?" If he wasn't managing a facility anymore, he could take Amahle's spot as Thaddeus's assistant.

"What about him?" Thaddeus crossed his arms over his chest.

"For your assistant," he suggested, hoping not to get pulled into the role himself.

"I need someone who knows how to use this equipment. Although, I do need someone who wouldn't be opposed to my methods," he added, tapping his chin with his index finger.

"I'll find you someone," Lyndon redirected, needing to get out of here.

"You think you can find me someone, really?"

"Yes."

Thaddeus straightened his stance. "How are you going to do that?"

"I have my ways—I've gotten good at sourcing the type of discrete staff we need." Lyndon mirrored Thaddeus's posture.

"Fine—but don't keep me waiting."

On the drive back to the group home, Lyndon called Leo to inform him of what Thaddeus's new lab was for, *and* that he had a plan to get someone on the *inside*.

"Zach could pretend to be a specialist in human genetics," Leo suggested.

"Wouldn't it be better if Nic did that, considering he specializes in genetics and diseases? He'd be able to talk the talk. The inside person needs to be convincing, or Thaddeus won't go for it."

"Even better," Leo agreed.

"Let me call you back. I just pulled in at the group home."

"I'll reach out to Nic in the meantime."

"Perfect," Lyndon said before ending the call.

When Lyndon entered his apartment, he found Lane asleep on the sofa. Not wanting to wake her, he went over to his desk and woke up his computer. Finding what he needed, he dialed Leo back.

"I'm sending you over the list of equipment for Nic to review and create the perfect resume. You'll need to do your magic by providing me with the contact numbers for the fake references. I'll present Thaddeus with four candidates, three women and one man. That way he'll be sure to pick Nic. I'll tell him I already investigated him, that he's accomplished, but his former employers say his methods were questionable and labeled him as morally grey. And that he's been let go for unethical practices and it was in our best interest to steer clear of him."

"Sad to think that's what Thaddeus will be looking for in an assistant. But your plan to have an inside man is brilliant, Lyndon."

"We've been waiting for a break like this," Lyndon said, elated at the potential opportunity to take Thaddeus down. "Oh, I'm also sending you over a description of what Nic should wear to impress Thaddeus. Experience is key, but Thaddeus will scrutinize his attire just as much."

Chapter 35 

Thaddeus hadn't wasted time in choosing Nic as the ideal candidate to interview, of course, and had made false excuses as to why the other applicants had not been ideal. The CV that Nic and Leo had provided Lyndon to submit to Thaddeus had been excellently composed, having lengthy experience in both the fertility arena *and* cloning, which Lyndon hadn't realized was part of the equipment list he'd been given. Fortunately, Nic had caught the items on the list and had added extensive research within that field to his resume. To impress Thaddeus, Nic's phony resume as a physician needed to be an in-depth document detailing his extensive academic, clinical, and research history, while demonstrating the highest level of specialized training, including his medical degree, residency, and a competitive fellowship. Lyndon was confident Thaddeus had found a kinship in *Dr. Nicolas North* because Lyndon had portrayed his character as morally grey, someone willing to bend or break the law and societal norms to achieve Thaddeus's objectives. Thaddeus has always considered his choices to be neither purely heroic nor villainous, but driven by ambiguous motivations, driven by his unique personal agenda, and what he referred to as *difficult circumstances*, thinking he was someone who operated outside the simple good vs. evil dichotomy. In some warped way, Thaddeus believed he was somehow saving the world.

Lyndon had been told to meet Thaddeus's *potential new assistant* at the main doors and personally escort him to the new lab on the 6th floor, which worked out perfectly for both Nic and Lyndon for obvious reasons. "Dr. North," Lyndon said, greeting Nic in the front lobby, extending a hand. "I'm Lyndon. I'll be escorting you up to meet with the founder of our organization for your interview."

Nic shook Lyndon's outstretched hand. "Nice to meet you, Lyndon," he said, responding as though they'd never met before.

"Right this way," Lyndon said, extending a hand towards the security desk. "You'll need to sign in and leave your cell phone with security," Lyndon pointed towards the sign-in blotter.

"It's… very spa-like in here," Nic stated, handing over his nondescript, dated cellphone.

"It's meant to feel relaxing," Lyndon said. "To put clients at ease, but we have cameras everywhere, visible and hidden." Lyndon raised his eyebrows as if to say, be careful; we are being watched and recorded. Through the door, past the security desk, Lyndon removed his key fob. He'd upgraded the security system, doing away with the multitude of rectangular plastic cards in their array of colours and card readers, and setting the key fobs to have the exact access needed based on who you were, not where you were going. Lyndon brought the fob up to the security pad right next to the door. When the green light lit up on the security pad, the door made a sound as if releasing a suction, and then with a soft hiss it glided open. Then Lyndon led the way through the door and into the small antechamber with another door opposite. "You look sharp, by the way."

Nic's attire, consisting of an expensive suit made of high-quality, luxurious fabric combined with meticulous craftsmanship construction for superior fit and drape, an Egyptian cotton mother-of-pearl button dress shirt, a hand-sewn slip stitch, 100% silk tie, and a Gucci Horsebit belt and complementing loafers, which were not the most expensive shoes but they were Thaddeus's favorite, had been devised with Thaddeus in mind, as per Lyndon.

"Thank you," Nic said, checking his tie.

There had been some concern about Nic's long hair, but Lyndon assured him that he should let it hang loose, and that doing so would give the effect of both confidence and rule breaking. Nic was the rule-breaker that was needed.

"Hope you're not claustrophobic," Lyndon kidded. The area was tight, the ceiling low, and there was barely enough room for the two of them to stand comfortably in the space.

"I'm good," Nic answered, just as the door they had come through shut. The bright overhead lighting went out, replaced by blackness, succeeded then by bursts of colour, the flashing running through a series of varying intensities of magenta, cyan, teal green, then abruptly returned to basic white again. "Are we being sanitized or disinfected or something?"

Lyndon held back a smile, lifting his key fob this time to a sensor on the door in front of them.

When the sensor displayed another green light, the door suctioned open like the one before. Through the open door, they stepped into a wide-open space similar in size to the high-ceiling open area of the front lobby.

"Everything is so… *white*. And stark in contrast with the soft warm woodgrain of the front lobby." Nic glanced around the large space. "The air is different, too. Dryer and much colder. And no windows."

"Clean and sterile," Lyndon stated, proceeding to the opposite wall that displayed three sizeable elevator doors.

"These are like the elevators in hospitals, for transferring patients on gurneys."

Stopping at the door on the right, Lyndon smiled and nodded, knowing it was more than likely they were being watched. Then he used his key fob again on the pad next to the door. The elevator door opened then, and Lyndon extended an arm, allowing Nic to step in ahead of him.

"I'm unsure which way to face," Nic said, noting the elevator had another door on the opposite side.

Without a word, Lyndon faced the door on the far side, and using his key fob on the sensor pad inside the elevator, he then pressed the button for the sixth floor.

"Exceptionally smooth elevator," Nic remarked as the elevator emanated a soft hum. "You can barely feel it move."

Lyndon smiled graciously again, then said, "The second floor is where we have and use our advanced diagnostic capabilities for patients. The third floor is dedicated to studying and testing cystic fibrosis and a condition called *primary ciliary dyskinesia*."

"I see," was all Nic had to say, understanding Lyndon's subtle way of saying this was not a safe place to speak.

"The fourth floor," Lyndon continued, "is where we address aerodigestive disorders."

"Congenital abnormalities of airway and lung development," Nic said, recognizing the terminology used at the hospital where he actually worked.

"Yes. The team focuses on rare lung diseases, including interstitial lung disease and bronchiolitis obliterans, such as TBM, tracheobronchomalacia. The fifth floor supports both the short and long-term medical needs of our patients. When we have patients, we have pediatric pulmonary staff on site who care for the children."

"I'm sure you prefer it when there are *no* patients in for treatments," Nic said. "Do you have a specialized pediatric social work team, too?"

"We do. We also coordinate with audiology and speech-language pathology teams to provide integrated support for children with speech, language, and swallowing/feeding disorders," Lyndon added.

"*Sounds like a sales pitch,*" Nic mumbled, loud enough for Lyndon to hear.

Lyndon tightened his jaw for fear of laughing, and he glanced down at his feet. "The next floor contains the new lab, and it's our destination," he said, lifting his head, his expression stoic.

"New lab?" Nic queried, despite having all the details from Lyndon already.

"The sixth floor used to be used for research on birds. Studying their respiratory diseases for lung and airway disorders. It was *alternative* research, like the greenhouse," Lyndon explained. "I can show you that later."

"And the seventh," Nic asked, like any normal person would after hearing about the other floors.

"That floor has the boardrooms and Thaddeus's private office," Lyndon shared, knowing Nic already knew what was on that floor.

When the elevator finally stopped on the sixth floor, the door opened automatically. Waiting across from the open elevator stood Thaddeus, and standing with him was Lazarus.

He wore a simple black dress shirt and black trousers. The Seraph's strong, well-defined jawline, prominent cheekbones, and a straight prominent nose resembled that of a handsome Arab prince, with large dark deep-set eyes framed by thick black eyelashes that matched his black hair and well-groomed beard. Although those dark-colored eyes of his were red-rimmed and his olive-tanned skin now appeared sallow and grey, all due to a nasty drug habit he had picked up while living in Amsterdam, the toll of it showing in his now gaunt appearance. Thaddeus, of course, had on his fake doctor's lab coat again.

Saying nothing, Lyndon extended an arm for Nic to exit the elevator as he followed behind him.

"Dr. North, welcome," Thaddeus greeted from across the hall, where he had anticipated his potential assistant's arrival. "Lyndon, you may go—you're no longer needed," he added dismissively.

"It was a pleasure to meet you, Doctor," Lyndon said with a quick bow before retreating into the elevator.

"Same. And thank you," Nic said before the elevator door closed.

When the elevator door shut, Thaddeus said, "Lazarus, please see to Lyndon's needs." Thaddeus gave him a mock smile.

Lazarus knew '*needs*' was code for him to follow Lyndon. "Sir, could I have a quick word?" he requested, stepping away from the doctor and closer to the elevator.

Thaddeus stepped up close to him. "*What?*" he said through clenched teeth.

"*Again, sir?*" Lazarus questioned in a quieter voice.

"Is that a problem?"

Continuing in a low voice, he said, *"It's just that he's pretty routine. He just went to the group home the last time you asked me to follow him."*

"I don't care—just do as you're told." Thaddeus hissed before cutting a glance over his shoulder at the visitor. Then turned back to Lazarus. "And please report in after," Thaddeus added in a neutral voice before turning his attention back fully to Dr. North.

Without another word, Lazarus took his leave and was off in quick pursuit of his fellow tracker.

On a hunch, he drove to the group home first and found Lyndon precisely where he expected to find him. Lazarus took out his cell phone and texted Thaddeus,

Boring as usual. Back at the group home.

A text from Thaddeus came back right away,

Stay on him.

Assuming he was here for the long haul, Lazarus pulled his car into a parking lot across the way and got comfortable. But to his surprise, only a few minutes later, Lyndon was on the move again.

Lazarus pulled out onto the road, keeping a good distance from Lyndon's truck as he followed him onto the Queensway highway in the direction of downtown Ottawa.

When Lyndon pulled into a street parking spot in the Byward Market, Lazarus turned up the next street and into the parking garage adjacent. Getting out of his car, he stalked towards the pedestrian exit and used a parallel street to where Lyndon had parked. He knew better than to follow directly behind someone, especially Lyndon, whose tracking and trailing ability was exceptional. Hiding while pursuing his target was much easier here in the vibrant historic district with its array of bars and restaurants, the entertainment of street performers, and because of its lively atmosphere filled with both locals and tourists, he could blend in. Pausing near the corner of York Street and the Byward Market Square, he observed as Lyndon crossed the street to a building with a distinctive rustic brick façade. Then he entered through the main doors of an establishment with the name Après SNOW set over the door and imprinted on the large front window.

"You meeting your little girlfriend, Lyndon?" he muttered under his breath, crossing the street to situate himself in the alleyway between the recessed entrance of the tobacco shop and the Après Snow restaurant next door. He waited patiently to see if he would exit again, but then a tall, muscular brunette with a Wolf Cut layered hairdo with a feral look seized his attention. *"Shea?"* he murmured, glaring at the female in black cargo pants and a matching black tank top. *"I thought you were dead."* He'd seen her before, tracked her down years ago. Even after months of trying to locate her, Thaddeus hadn't wanted her in the end, for two reasons. She was *female,* and she was deformed, crippled, missing the lower half of her legs. Plus, she had been a teen at the time, and Thaddeus had stated that she would have been difficult to handle due to all that human puberty crap, which would also get in the way of his testing. She'd disappeared soon after. But whatever.

Lyndon exited the restaurant then, stopping to talk with the elusive halfling. Hugs were exchanged. *"What the hell?"* What was Shea doing hanging out with Lyndon, Lazarus wondered. He tuned in his preternatural hearing in an attempt to listen in on their conversation, but then a young blonde human female wearing tan shorts and a light blue blouse exited the restaurant and sparked up more conversation with Lyndon and Shea. The word *sister* was tossed around, and though Shea and the other female looked nothing alike, the blonde too looked *familiar* to him. No, not familiar, that wasn't it. What he found remarkable was the female's uncanny resemblance to one of the Earthbound females, *Anael.* He listened in again. However, conversation had broken off as they'd all turned and headed up the street towards where Lyndon had parked his truck. Not wanting to lose their tail, Lazarus went back up the side street to the parking garage to get his vehicle. He exited the parking area just in time to catch Lyndon's truck speed by.

Following Lyndon back onto the highway, Lazarus kept several cars between him and the truck, adjusting his speed and distance based on the traffic flow. He assumed Lyndon was heading back to the group home, but when he took the exit two ramps before the one that normally brought him there, he changed lanes and stealthily shadowed his maneuvers. Keeping a lengthy distance back, he drove the long stretch of road. Then the brake lights of the truck illuminated, and the speed of the vehicle slowed as it approached a turn onto what appeared to be a hidden roadway. Lazarus continued past the turn and then circled back once the truck was clearly out of sight. Then slowly he turned onto the road and inched up the unfamiliar route. Ahead, he spotted the truck turn again, and as he rolled up and came to a stop hidden from view, he noticed it wasn't another road, but a driveway up to a very unusual building. At first he thought it was a two-story motel, but with further observation it appeared to be someone's residence. Exiting the car, he then maneuvered through the trees that hid his car from any onlookers at the house. *"What the blazes is this place?"* he mumbled to himself as he peered through the thick brush.

A twig *"snapped"* behind him, and he whirled.

"Arriadnee?" he stammered. "What the fuck are you doing here?"

She grinned but said nothing in response. Then her gentle smile lazily morphed into a cruel twist of her lips. Her remarkable lavender eyes, now cold and cunning, glinted as her expression manifested into something wicked, something that voiced he was not long for this world.

Chapter 36 

Thaddeus had held back his exuberance when leading Dr. North down the hall to the entrance of his magnificent new lab and research area. But now as he stood inside amongst all his shiny new state-of-the-art medical equipment, he could barely contain his excitement. He followed eagerly beside his potential new assistant as he wandered through and examined each of the different apparatuses and unique work stations. Thaddeus had been impressed with the candidate's curriculum vitae, which was not a standard resume, no. Of course it had his name and his board certifications, his credentials, as it were.

His professional synopsis had been a concise, three-sentence summary that highlighted his key qualifications, career achievements, and potential contributions that targeted Thaddeus's goal of unprejudiced experimentation. The doctor's advanced educational background listed a Reproductive Endocrinology and Infertility Fellowship, Residency in Obstetrics and Gynecology, Medical School, Undergraduate Studies, followed by his Board Certifications and Medical Licensure. Which led into his Post-graduate training, clinical skills, and clinical and practice experience. He also had several research publications.

"Are you familiar with EMR systems, Doctor?"

"Yes, I'm proficient with several electronic medical record systems."

"I recently returned from South America, where I was doing… comprehensive work with several endocrinologists. And I saw on your resume that you completed a *Reproductive Endocrinology & Infertility* fellowship recently."

"I did. At the University Hospitals in Cleveland, Ohio."

"This lab is specific to IVF procedures, so please have a look around."

"You have incubators, microscopes, centrifuges, sperm analysis equipment including sperm counting chambers, a semen analyzer, and devices for sperm preparation," Dr. North stated with fascination. "And you have a micromanipulation system."

"A micromanipulator and a micro-injector, used for intracytoplasmic sperm injection, to be precise."

"For ICSI. Very nice." Nic continued forward. "You also have cryopreservation equipment. Liquid nitrogen tanks, cryogenic vials, and devices for vitrification," he said as though impressed.

"We have various types of pipettes, including serological and micropipettes, that are used for transferring fluids and samples," Thaddeus boasted. "Your fellowship was in what specific research area?"

Dr. North paused in his perusing. "Predictors of IVF success in patients with PCOS, *Polycystic Ovary Syndrome*."

"Where did you do your residency again?"

"Parkland Health System in Dallas."

Thaddeus nodded. "I remember seeing you have a Bachelor of Science."

"Yes, in biology." Nic moved to the next area. "Warming plates, water baths, and devices for gas and temperature validation of incubators."

Thaddeus appreciated the doctor's enthusiasm. "We have ample equipment for sperm collection, IUI catheters, embryo transfer catheters, and oocyte collection sets." He pointed to the wall of stark white cabinets between each station.

"You have three ultrasound machines and sperm separation devices," Dr. North stated, noting the additional tools.

"There is also PGT equipment over there," Thaddeus said, directing him to the far area. "Including a laser system for embryo biopsy and specialized software for PGT analysis." Thaddeus was simply delighted by this young doctor's knowledge. "And safety equipment, of course. Cryo-gloves, face shields, and oxygen monitors for safety in the IVF lab."

"I noticed you also have a variety of cloning equipment."

"We do. For gene cloning, reproductive cloning, etc. and specialized tools for DNA manipulation."

"How exciting," Dr. North said, his expression balancing between approving and mischievous.

Thaddeus liked that. "Your CV also states you have clinical experience as a *Fertility Specialist*, if I recall. What exactly did you do there?"

"I administered IVF cycles and monitored patient progress and led a multi-disciplinary team, including embryologists and nurses, to manage complex infertility cases."

"And what was the outcome of your time there?"

"We developed new evidence-based IVF protocols that reduced cycle cancellation rates by 20%."

Remarkable, Thaddeus thought, but he didn't voice how impressed he was out loud. Instead, he took a moment to admire his formal business attire, which projected competence, professionalism, and trustworthiness, and despite the long waist-length loose hair, he had a well-groomed appearance that complemented his qualifications without being a distraction. "Your suit—is it a Brioni?"

"This one, no. *Tom Ford*. Although I do have a navy blue pinstriped Super 210's wool *Brunico* suit from the *Brioni Vanquish II* collection, but I don't wear it for work."

The Brioni Vanquish II collection included the *most* expensive Brioni suit ever sold at a fresh $43,000 apiece, if Thaddeus recalled correctly. "Dr. North," Thaddeus began again.

"Please, call me Nicholas. Or *Nic*—my friends call me Nic."

Right. "As I was saying, I just returned from Brazil where I was involved in reproductive and regenerative analysis."

"Brazil? I hear it's a fascinating place," Dr. *Nic* said. "I'd love to visit someday."

"I had a research lab and clinic there, but I'm focusing my resources here going forward." Thaddeus's cellphone beeped in his lab coat pocket, but he ignored it.

"It must have been wonderful to work there, surrounded by such diverse and stunning natural beauty."

His phone beeped again, and he retrieved it from his pocket. The lock screen showed an urgent text message from Marcus. When he went to put it back in his pocket, his cellphone beeped with a third and fourth urgent message popping up on the screen. Instead of reading them, he shut the sound off and slid it back into his pocket. "I suppose," Thaddeus said, focusing back on the doctor. "Although I didn't venture out much." He forced a smile. "Let me show you my latest research lab," he said, but then his phone began ringing in his pocket. He ignored it, but then it started ringing again. "Excuse me. I'll be right back." Thaddeus pulled the phone free and went out through the open door of the lab and into the hallway, cellphone to his ear. "I'm in the middle of something extremely important," Thaddeus spat. "What is it?"

"Who is with you?" Marcus questioned.

"What do you mean?"

"The guy in your new lab?"

Thaddeus glanced up the hall. "How do you know there is someone in my lab?" he demanded.

"I'm looking at him right now on the revised surveillance Lyndon set up," Marcus declared. "He set up monitoring for all the labs so you can keep an eye on things. Told me it was to cut down on travel, being able to watch from afar. Were you not aware?"

"No, I was not." *I'll have to have that shut down,* Thaddeus considered. "That guy, as you call him, is Dr. North, the geneticist I told you about—he's here for an interview." *Although he'd make an excellent human specimen,* Thaddeus pondered.

"Well, for your information, that's the same guy I met in Brazil— said he was a conservationist. And we gave him a tour of the facility."

"What are you talking about?" Thaddeus checked over his shoulder to see that the man was still inside the lab.

"Back when we were shutting things down. I personally showed him around. He'd been especially interested in the lab space. Said he wanted to make sure we weren't leaving behind any hazardous materials or chemicals and such."

"You're sure it's him?"

"Yup. Same face. Same long, black, shiny hair."

"I'll call you back."

"So, Dr. North, what do you think?" Thaddeus asked, stepping back into the lab.

The good doctor turned away from the incubator he was exploring to look at Thaddeus.

Thaddeus remained where he was, standing just outside of the reinforced steel door.

"State-of-the art," he said, glancing around the room. The imposter returned his attention back to Thaddeus only to see the door suddenly shut, the security bolts thudding into place.

From outside the lab, Thaddeus glowered at him through the thick plate glass viewing window in the door.

The man's attention shifted to the green light next to a speaker near the entry door as it lit up, just before Thaddeus's voice echoed through it. "How would you say it compares to my lab you saw in… *Brazil?*"

* * *

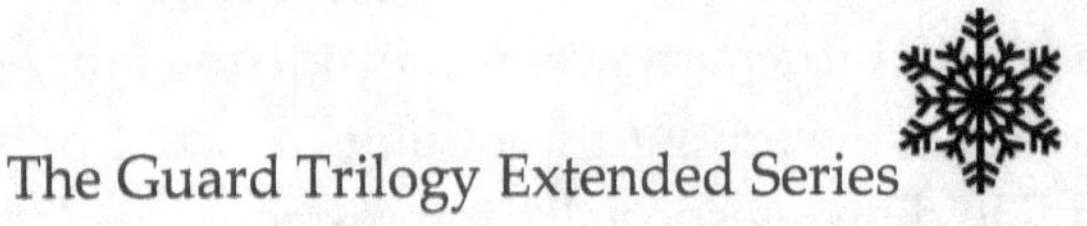

The Guard Trilogy Extended Series

Book 7 – Haven Sent
More books coming…

Learn more about author N. L. Westaway at
www.NLWestaway.com

The following is a list of the main characters and their roles from the original trilogy, as a refresher, should you need it.

Lynn Westlake – MC, The Seer/Oracle, Halfling Daughter of Gabriel
Redmond Credente – Lynn's husband, The Believer, descendant of Azazel

Vicki Quinn —The Linguist, descendant of Michael
Olivia White —The Healer, descendent of Raphael
Mackenzie (Mac) Miller – The Sorceress, descendent of Uriel
Alison Kiely — The Scribe, descendent of Vretil
Luc Marin — The Theologian, descendent of Baraqel
Derek (Shortcut) Jones — The Cipher, descendent of Kokabiel
Darius Stori — The Guardian, descendent of Shamsiel
Dunya — Lynn's neighbor, eventual love interest of Luc Marin
Lily Shade – Redmond's studio manager, Darius's girlfriend

The Archangels
Gabriel — Lynn's birthfather
Michael — Celestial Warden of Vicki
Raphael — Celestial Warden of Olivia
Uriel — Celestial Warden of Mac
Vretil — Celestial Warden of Alison

The Leaders of the 200 Fallen (There are 20 Leaders in total.)
Shamsiel – The Celestial Warden of Mitra, Dunya, and Darius
Zaqiel – The Horseman Death, the Celestial Warden of Lynn's Birthmother, Mother, Aunt, and friend Louise
Azazel — The Horseman War, the Celestial Warden of Redmond
Kokabiel — The Horseman Conquest, the Celestial Warden of Derek
Baraqel — The Horseman Famine, and the Celestial Warden of Luc
Armaros — Lynn's original Nemesis. The 11th leader of the 20 who led the original 200, also known as the 'accused one'.

* * *